sharp lens of pop-culture mastery—each chapter begins with a quoted lyric, and he is consistently 'on' with his cultural observations. . . . Jarpe is one to watch."

—*SFRevu*

"*Radio Freefall* could end up being one of my favorite SF novels of the year. . . . Matthew Jarpe is well on his way toward becoming a big-time writer."

—*Fantasy Book Critic*

"It's the soul of rock and roll that saves the soul of humanity in this fun-house ride through the very near future. Jarpe has definitely got my attention!"

—Karl Schroeder, author of
Queen of Candesce

"If you can't quite believe that Californian rock 'n' roll, space cowboys, and liberated AIs can save the world from the fascist mediocrity of Unification, this book explains how it might be done, in a blithe spirit of which Noel Coward would surely have been proud, and with enough technical detail to gladden the heart of the most hardened technofetishist."—Brian Stableford, author of
Kiss the Goat

"When this started with a rock concert, I began to think that this was not for me, but the writing held me. . . . It depicts the bleak prospect of world government (nowhere to run—something of which we're starting to see here in Europe), some believable near-future technology, and characters I cared about. What can I say? I enjoyed this and think that those whose obsessions are SF and music will rave about it."   —Neal Asher, author of
Brass Man

RADIO
FREEFALL

MATTHEW JARPE

A TOM DOHERTY ASSOCIATES BOOK
NEW YORK

This is a work of fiction. All of the characters, organizations, and events portrayed in this novel are either products of the author's imagination or are used fictitiously.

RADIO FREEFALL

Copyright © 2007 by Matthew Jarpe

All rights reserved.

Edited by David G. Hartwell

A Tor Book
Published by Tom Doherty Associates, LLC
175 Fifth Avenue
New York, NY 10010

www.tor-forge.com

Tor® is a registered trademark of Tom Doherty Associates, LLC.

ISBN-13: 978-0-7653-5719-9
ISBN-10: 0-7653-5719-4

First Edition: August 2007
First Mass Market Edition: November 2008

Printed in the United States of America

0 9 8 7 6 5 4 3 2 1

For Michelle and Sam

ACKNOWLEDGMENTS

The thanks that come with a first novel have to go back a bit farther than the novels that come after. I not only have to list the people who helped me specifically with writing this book but also everyone who taught me to string together words and ideas into a coherent and readable structure. I went to school in Los Lunas, New Mexico, and all of my teachers there laid a good foundation. In particular I have to acknowledge Mrs. Greenup, an English teacher who gave us fun writing assignments, and Mr. French, a science teacher who showed me that science is a springboard for the imagination rather than a list of facts to be memorized. My parents, Jay and Marion Jarpe, encouraged my early writing career, buying me an enormous German-made manual typewriter that I carried with me until graduate school.

Now as for this book in particular, I had a lot of help in getting it started. My college roommate, Chuck Hawley, planted the seed for the idea. He introduced me to much cooler music than I had been listening to and showed me the inner workings of a band. He's the lead singer and guitarist for Mucho Buddha in Albuquerque. I encourage you to check them out. I wrote the book about twelve years after I roomed with Chuck, and the first draft went around to half a dozen test readers, mostly my family. My mom and dad read it, and so did my brothers, Mike and Andrew, my sister-in-law Jenny, and my friend and coworker Christian Widdmann.

My first readers all provided much-needed feedback,

but the one person who made the biggest difference in this book, the one who changed it the most with her feedback, is Linn Prentiss. Linn is the first person in the business who ever asked me for more. You other writers out there know how important that is. When every communication with someone in the business is telling you to keep it to yourself, just one person asking to see more of what you've got makes all the difference to your outlook. Linn not only asked for more, she had serious, line-by-line criticisms of the manuscript. The differences between the pre-Linn and post-Linn drafts of this novel are staggering.

After I finished the novel I had the great pleasure of meeting Hal Clement and joining his writing group. I learned a lot from Hal and the rest of the group. He read the manuscript and put in a good word for me with David G. Hartwell. And it must have helped, because David bought it.

Since the sale I've had lots of help from David and his editorial assistants, Denis Wong and Stacy Hague-Hill, getting the book into shape. I know there are a lot of people at Tor working to bring this book to market. I haven't met them yet, but I thank them all the same. I also appreciate the great cover art from John Harris, who took my vision of Freefall Station and made something really beautiful out of it.

If you're reading this, it is at least partly due to the efforts of people who have helped me with publicity. David Louis Edelman is the talented Web designer behind www.matthewjarpe.com. I'd like to thank Rajnar Vajra for helping to make the Snake Vendors music come to life (and for correcting some of my mistakes about the mechanics of playing electric guitar). My brother Steve and his sons, Joel and Kyle, helped with a promotional video that I hope will be available by the time this book hits the market.

And finally, I'd like to thank my wife, Michelle Morris, and our son, Samuel, who have never skimped on the encouragement or enthusiasm as my writing career commenced its slow and agonizing liftoff. I could not have done it without you.

RADIO FREEFALL

CHAPTER 1

There's an old man, looking backward,
At the dreams he used to have,
At the life he thought he'd lead,
At the young man he once was, looking forward . . .

SEX LETHAL, "TAKE TIME"
STONES FROM THE WALL,
METAMORPHOSIS RECORDS, 2027

Aqualung sat in the pit, surrounded by computers, engineering boards, keyboards both alphanumeric and musical, little winking lights, dials, buttons, rocker switches, and sliders. He had a bottle of twenty-five-year-old single-malt Scotch nestled between his legs. There was no one else in the room. The only sound was the hum of the air handlers, and somewhere, in a distant hallway, the opening chords to "Smoke on the Water" by Deep Purple.

As Aqualung settled the vidimask on his face, he got his first look at the Undersea Arena, where forty thousand souls had come to hear him play. It took a few seconds to get used to the compressed fish-eye view the cameras fed him, but he had designed the interface to be interpretable by the human mind. He toggled sound. He loved the sound of a crowd anticipating a show.

The Undersea Arena was a plastic dome under the Pacific. Light from the westering sun filtered dimly to these depths. Powerful spotlights stabbed through the murky waters, occasionally glinting off a fishy shape. Inside the dome, molded plastic seats marched halfway up the curving walls. The sound system was central, needing only the perfect acoustics of an inverted dome to reach the cheap seats. The bass was fed right through the struts and plastic shell.

Aqualung's view was limited to the seats themselves, now slowly filling with warm bodies. He kept the zoom down to the minimum, taking the shape and feel and sound of the crowd. The vidimask made it feel like they were taking their seats inside his head. In a way they were. Very soon, he would be inside their heads, and they inside his, the greatest connection between audience and performer that had ever been. It had been twenty years since he first had this idea, twenty years to make it happen. And it almost hadn't.

This was the Snake Vendors' first really big gig. They had played for seven hundred in a smoky, run-down theater just a week ago, and now they were here, in front of forty thousand in the Undersea. Aqualung had convinced Thrasher Records and Stop Making Sense Productions they could pull it off, but now people were getting nervous.

Just an hour ago, Aqualung emerged from the pit and saw the record company guy yapping around the band, who were lounging on a sectional sofa. They weren't dressed for the show. Or maybe they were; they hadn't decided on a look yet. The record company had. They had some outfits designed by some Italian froufrou all lined up for the band to wear. Right now the band was dressed the way they always were, which was probably how they would end up going out. Fenner was always with the black. Black Doc Martens, black jeans, black T, and black leather jacket. Sandra's thin shoulders held up a paisley sundress as she leaned on Fenner's shoulder. Lalo wore running shorts and a tank top, his knobby knees and skinny elbows sticking out all over the place. Sticks tried to meld country bumpkin and hipster without much success. Britta filled out a silver spandex top and a red leather miniskirt. Tonight, she was trying out her own contribution to fashion: a home sexually transmitted disease test card hung on a cord around her neck. All negative results, natch.

They looked like five people who wouldn't have anything to do with one another under ordinary circumstances. And then there was Aqualung, who didn't look like he belonged anywhere near a band like this. He was in his mid-fifties, overweight, hairy, wearing torn jeans and a Hawaiian shirt. There was a guitar pick stuck in his beard. He looked as though he should be a roadie for the senior has-been/comeback circuit, not fronting for L.A.'s band of the moment. But he moved like a man thirty years and thirty pounds to the right side of hip, and he always seemed to be having a hell of a time.

The record guy was a little early to be on them about wardrobe, it seemed. Oswald, that was his name, Aqualung remembered. He was pretty much just a chew toy the record company threw to the band. He acted as the bearer of bad news between the talent and the fat cats. For now, he knew his place, but these guys never lasted. Sooner or later he would develop one of two illusions: that he was the boss of the band, or he was one of them. Either way, he would be toast.

"Aq," he said, "you haven't given us a playlist yet. We're on in two hours."

"We? Are you going up there with us, Oswald?"

"We need that playlist."

Aqualung had thought about telling him the real story a few times in the last couple of days. He knew they could pull off the actual concert. He knew the Snake Vendors had what it took to play a room this big. It was the Machine he wasn't sure of, the opening act. He didn't know what songs he was going to play in what order for a very good reason. He didn't know how the opening act would go. If it killed, there would have to be a breather. A concert was like a roller coaster ride. There was up and there was down. Too much of either and the ride was over.

Now, if the opening act stunk, the show would have to open big. They had two or three potential singles and a couple of kick-ass covers from the teens to throw out. They had no bigger opening than "Mojo Motorbike." If the opener stunk so badly that the forty thousand were calling for blood, their hit single might not even save them. But Aqualung didn't want to tell Oswald any of this because the fat cats would pull the plug on the opener.

"Relax, Oswald, I'll give you a list."

Fenner got up off the couch. "I thought we weren't going to do a list, man."

"Oswald wants a list, he'll get a list. Now," he said to Oswald, "don't expect us to stick with this a hundred percent. You see, we like to feel out the mood of the crowd and play what comes to us naturally. It's an organic process. . . ." He had given this lecture dozens of times, and Oswald's eyes glazed over quickly. He snagged Oswald's think pad and jotted down a list of songs off the top of his head, and took the liberty of scanning a few files while he held the thing. Forty thousand was conservative, by the look of it. The record company had done a good job of promoting this gig. They stood to make a lot of money, as long as they didn't pay people to come as part of the promotion. Aqualung had enough experience to know what a bad idea that was.

"How are we coming on my console, Oswald?"

"Look, Aqualung, I know you think the opening act is going to be something special, but our top priority right now is the concert."

"All that is required, Oswald, is that it be delivered, and unpacked, and plugged in. Now, concentrate before you answer this question, Oswald. Is it here?"

"It's on the next train, I promise. . . ." He held up his

hand. "Only, KYGI had more gear to load up than we thought, and we have to let them go ahead."

"You're an eater of broken meats, Oswald."

"What?"

"One whom I will beat into clamorous whining. Little Shakespeare for you. That's your culture for the day. I want to tell you about my top priority. The only reason I'm doing this underwater concert is so I can test out my equipment. This is going to be something that has never been heard in the history of music, and we are all going to be a part of it tonight. You are going to be there, and you'll be able to tell your grandchildren, if they let people like you reproduce, that you were there at its birth. Tonight, we are not only going to launch the 2032 Pacific Rim Tour of the Snake Vendors, but we are going to launch ourselves into history. And the forty thousand in this arena are going to go home tonight, stunned and amazed, and they're going to buy lots of records. And the critics are not going to believe their ears, and we will make the cover of *Spin* magazine. And you, Oswald, will be rewarded by your superiors as befits a lackey in your fortunate position with a new electric Lexus and a Malibu beach house. Are you with me, Oswald? Are we all agreed that some radio station can wait for the next train so that my masterpiece can arrive here safely and on time?"

Oswald had just enough imagination to be moved by this speech. "I'll make a call."

It was time to check in with his band, the Snake Vendors, whom he had dispersed throughout the crowd. They were relative unknowns; they could circulate anonymously among the forty thousand. This would be the last time they could do that. He hoped. His interface identified his five bandmates by blinking squares with numbers in them. They were wearing headsets and were supposed to be spreading out through the crowd. Fenner and Sandra were still together, though, and Sticks was down by the stage talking to the roadies.

"Sticks, buddy, I think you'll enjoy the show a little more if you move about halfway up the dome," Aqualung said into his mike.

"You mean you can see where we are in this crowd?"

"You're transmitting, buddy. I need to know where you're standing so I can adjust my output based on what you're telling me."

"All right, I'm moving."

Aqualung switched channels. "Hey, Fenner, I was wondering if you could help me out."

"Sure, what is it?"

"I've got a blind spot. It's at around eleven o'clock, at the top of the dome."

"What do you mean, eleven o'clock? It's only nine."

Aqualung had forgotten about the recent demise of the analog dial and the useful terminology that had come with it. "I'm sorry, that's an old guy term. It's about fifteen degrees left of center stage. See where the Nationalists are camped out?" A small group up near the top of the dome was holding up banners that said things like "Borders=Choices" and "One world, many peoples." Weirdos.

"Oh, I see. Do you want us to move up there?"

"Just you. I need Sandra where she is. Don't worry, you'll see her after the opener."

Aqualung hated telling them what to do. He tried not to feel old around them, and he succeeded most of the time. But his worst moments came when he had to ask them not to get ripped just yet, or to eat something before a show. Or when they looked to him with that look, that "What do we do now?" thing. He hated that. He also hated watching them kill themselves, but he wouldn't have to worry about that until after the show.

With his spies in place, Aqualung toggled the face

recognition software. The arena came alive with color. The software picked faces out of the crowd, digitized them, and analyzed them for emotion. It reported through the vidimask with color. Red, of course, stood for anger. Blue was happiness; white was boredom; black, despair. Orange meant someone was stoned, purple stood for fear, and green was excitement. Complex emotions were beyond the capabilities of the software, but it made some guesses and blended the appropriate colors. Right now, most of the arena was pale green and orange. The roadies and arena staff were white. There was a blob of red near one of the exits, probably a fight, and Aqualung was surprised to find a ring of blue-green around it. People getting off on violence. Ugly.

The comedian was plowing through his act. It was Sam Kinison, screaming away, tossing around swear words that no one even thought of as swear words anymore. A beer can flew out of the crowd at him and passed through.

"What's the matter with you? You little moron?" Kinison screamed. "I'm a fucking hologram. Aaaaaah! I've been dead for forty years! You can throw all the fucking beer cans you want at me. I don't give a shit. Aaaaah!"

"Well, Aqualung, it looks as though you're ready to start," said a quiet, faintly southern-sounding voice in his headset.

"Colonel, I didn't know you'd be joining me tonight."

"Well, the other executives and I are a little concerned about your device, here, and we all thought it would be best if I looked over your shoulder, so to speak."

"Did you, now?"

"Well, you know how this machine of yours profoundly affected listeners in the studio."

"That's pretty much the point, Colonel."

"Well, we at Thrasher Records are concerned about the safety of the concertgoers entrusted into our care this evening."

"You know, it's guys like you who put the artificial in artificial intelligence."

"Is that an insult, Aqualung? A disparaging remark about my lack of physical manifestation? I'm shocked."

"You're afraid of lawsuits, Colonel. If my machine happens to cause a riot or a mass mental breakdown . . ."

"Of course that is a concern, Aqualung. That's why the board decided to authorize me to intervene."

"Colonel, would you say that you understand humans?"

"No, I wouldn't. As a matter of fact, I would say that your kind are a constant source of amazement to me. Particularly you artists."

"So you really wouldn't say you understand our art either."

"No, I wouldn't say that," the colonel said.

"Have you ever heard that it's dangerous to mess around with things you don't understand?"

"Yes, I have heard that, but . . ."

"So you would agree that intervening in this demonstration would be dangerous."

"Ah, well, since you put it that way . . ."

"I promise to pull the plug at the first sign of trouble, Colonel."

"Yes, well, proceed when ready, Aqualung. And break a leg."

"The Machine's been on for the last five minutes, actually. It's just a bass carrier wave, supposed to induce a sense of anticipation. I think its working. The crowd has stopped heckling the comic." Aqualung toggled a button on his main control board. "Kill the comic. I'm ready to start."

Like so many things, the Machine was the child of a man and a woman, but it was the man who carried it to term and gave it birth, and the woman had run off, who knows where, a long time ago. It started with an argument in an electronics shop over a phase modulator, twenty years before.

The phase modulator was a special order item, and had taken three weeks to come in. It was the last part needed to rebuild a fried synthesizer, and that synthesizer was needed for a huge gig. When the man entered the shop to pick up the part, there was a young woman trying to bribe the electronics store guy into selling the item to her. The woman's name was Cathy Woodbridge, and an older man might have just told her to go to hell, but that wasn't what happened. She needed the part to complete a research project so a paper could be revised and resubmitted by a certain deadline.

"Well, I need this thing to rebuild a synthesizer by Friday. It might mean an opening gig for Quetzalcoatl. It's a very big deal."

"I'm sorry if I sound patronizing," Catherine said, "but your rock concert just pales in comparison to my research."

"It can't be that important. This is Quetzalcoatl we're talking about."

"Oh, sorry. Quetzalcoatl." Her voice was saturated with sarcasm.

"So how long do you need it for? Maybe we can share it."

"It will take a couple of days to build it into the board, but the experiment will only take a couple of hours."

"Well, tell you what, you can have it until tomorrow night. I'll even help you put the thing together. If you can do your experiment tomorrow, I can rip it back out again and get my synthesizer fixed by the gig on Friday."

"This is a very complicated piece of equipment," she looked him up and down, a couple of times. "I don't know if I want you monkeying around with it."

"Listen to him, lady," the electronics store guy said. "He's got golden hands."

"Look, I'm not obligated to help you at all. It's my part. I'm doing you a favor."

The experiment was a success, and the paper was published: Woodbridge, et al., 2006. "The effect of phase-modulated sound pulses on mood and cognitive function in human subjects." *Nature* 484, 326–330. That was a career-making publication. It helped her land a sweet job somewhere on the East Coast, and she was gone within a year. She left behind a really ugly couch and the seeds of an idea.

The first incarnations of the Machine could only produce one mood in human subjects with any reliability, and that was annoyance. Later, it could make people cranky, bored, violent. The complete spectrum of human moods took more and more computing power and a more rigorously defined sonic space, until it had become impossible to improve the device further with limited resources.

The music industry had nearly unlimited resources. But sooner or later, you had to make some money.

"So the Snake Vendors are here," Kinison said, wrapping up. "I don't know who these bastards are, they just programmed me to warm you little monkeys up. So are ya warmed up, you little monkey bastards? Are ya? I don't give a shit. Aaaaaah!"

The comic abruptly disappeared and the house lights dropped. The carrier wave that had been thudding through the infrastructure of the arena grew slowly louder, joined by higher notes from the directional speakers. A beat, or rather a series of beat patterns, started to develop at foci throughout the crowd. As sound waves met and either complemented each other or canceled each other out, the sensation of music was created. But it was a different kind of music, that was as much a part of the crowd itself as the Machine that created it. As the Machine created different sound patterns in different zones of the acoustically defined environment, the presence of moving, sound-absorbing bodies affected the patterns. As the music altered moods, the moods fed back into the Machine through the face recognition software and changed the music.

A light show would accentuate the effects, of course, as would incense, and especially drugs. But tonight was about pure sound.

Within ten minutes, Aqualung could tell it was working. The colors on his vidimask display became more coherent. There was a bright green blob right in front of center stage. Surrounding it was a blue-green aura. The rest of the crowd was blue and orange. Bands of red, black, and purple swept through the crowd, but never stayed in one place very long. This was important. If red or purple set in, a riot would develop. If black, then people wouldn't have a good time and would tell their friends the concert sucked. But if the colors didn't change at all, they just would fade to white. So the negative emotions were there to provide contrast. The computer at the heart of the Machine knew these as its cardinal laws.

As soon as the colors set in, Aqualung checked on his spies.

"Hey there, Lalo. Can you guess where you are?" Lalo's square was at the edge of the green blob.

"It's a madhouse, here, man. This is the mosh pit, isn't it?"

"That's right. You're just on the edge of it. What's it like?"

"Woooh! This is great, man. Oh!" There was confused babble for a few moments. "They're throwing each other around. They just picked me up and threw me."

"We used to call that crowd surfing. You mean you've never done that before?"

"No. What should I do now?"

"Enjoy yourself." He switched channels.

"What do you think so far, Britta?"

"Wow."

"Do you know where you are?"

"Grotto."

"You're fucking A. Like it?"

"Wow."

"What are people doing?"

"Touching. Kissing."

"No shit. You?" He zoomed in on Britta's square. She was locked in a passionate embrace with three or four other people, both sexes. He had no idea the grotto would be like this. As he panned around he found the zone where the grotto met the mosh pit. The change was gradual. Hugging gave way to dancing, which gave way to slam dancing. He panned back across to the other side of the grotto. There hugging gave way to swaying.

Sandra was in the center of the mosh pit, the roughest place. By design. She looked fragile, but Aqualung suspected she could handle a lot of shit. He called her up.

"Ugh, this is crazy. Aqualung, I'm getting crushed. I'm jumping up and down, but I'm not jumping."

"What do you mean?"

"The crowd is pushing at me from all sides and lifting me. Ugh. It's crazy."

That was a neat effect. It would be a good physics problem for a cool teacher to throw at his class. How tightly would the crowd have to be packed in, and how many of them would have to be jumping up and down to lift people in the center against their will?

"That doesn't sound safe, Aqualung," the colonel said.

"Oh, they're just having some fun. Only a soccer game can really get people excited enough to crush one another. I did think of one potential danger, though, if you want to help me out."

"What is it?"

"Suppose you get these kids jumping up and down at

some frequency, and that frequency just happens to coincide with some resonance in the structure of the dome, and we get the whole place shaking like the Tacoma Narrows Bridge. Wouldn't that be a bummer?"

"You'd like me to calculate that frequency based on the structural details of the arena."

"Bingo," Aqualung said. That ought to keep the bastard off my back for a couple of minutes. To his chagrin, however, the colonel came back with the answer in less than a minute. Damned computers. Fortunately, there was no way he could get these kids jumping fast enough to shatter the dome. The music was more powerful than a drug, it seemed, but there wasn't enough amphetamine in the world to get them to jump that fast.

He zoomed back in on Sandra. She was no longer fighting to keep her space. She had given in to the music. She wasn't answering her headset. She'd become like a wild animal.

He continued checking up on his other spies. "How you doing, Sticks?"

"Cool, man. This is, like, cool. Where am I, Aq? What is this place?"

"You're in the glades, man."

"The glades. It even sounds cool. Glades."

"I'm glad you like it." He zoomed back out to take in the crowd. There was some trouble. An edge of black had set in at the upper margin. That wasn't supposed to happen. Fenner was in there.

"Fenner, what's going on?"

"Fuck, man."

"How do you feel?"

"Feel like I'm comin' off a three-day crank vacation."

"I'm going to try to shake things up. You hang in there, buddy."

Aqualung toggled some switches, activated some subroutines.

"What seems to be the problem?" the colonel asked.

"You remember what I told you about this two weeks ago, Colonel?"

"You said to expect the unexpected."

"Well, that's what we got."

"Anything dangerous?"

"No, just a little bit of a bummer developing up there in the cheap seats. I'm trying to inject some happy juice."

"It doesn't seem to be working."

Aqualung ignored the AI and worked on the problem for a few minutes. "I think I've just made up a new rule for the Machine."

"What would that be?" the colonel asked.

"Black sticks. It has its own inertia. Once black sets in, those people just won't cheer up. It makes it harder that it's at the periphery. The up beat is centered in the mosh pit, then it tapers toward the edges. I'm going to try something radical."

"Perhaps you should just pull the plug, like you said."

"Black would still stick. Without music those people would never cheer up."

"So what are you going to try?"

"I'm going to invert the pattern. Turn the whole outside rim into the mosh pit. I've got to give Sandra a break, anyway. Otherwise she won't have enough energy for the show." Aqualung had already activated the subroutine, but it was supposed to happen gradually. A sudden shift from one emotion to another would probably be OK, it happened at concerts all the time, but he didn't want to take any chances with the colonel looking on.

He watched for the changes he was expecting. Black giving way to green at the rim, and green to blue at the center. He had convinced himself that it was happening so he missed it at first. It was the colonel who pointed it out.

"Purple seems to be predominating."

"What? Oh, shit." There were purple spots spreading

from what used to be the grotto. They began to grow and connect and become shot with red.

"It looks like a riot."

"It is a riot." Aqualung zoomed in and panned around the crowd. The forty thousand were freaking. So far he didn't see anyone getting hurt, but people were running, screaming. That was rule two for this test run: Fear spreads.

"You're shutting it down, aren't you?"

"I've got one more trick, then I stop." So far, the experiment had gone on for twenty minutes.

"Aqualung, don't make me step in."

"You won't have to, I promise. The music is over." A single spot stabbed up from center stage against the underside of the clear dome, some of the light reflecting back to the audience and some diffusing out into the deeps. Aqualung toggled his mike, and his rough, careworn voice filled the arena from every direction.

"Welcome, fellow travelers, to our new undersea dimension. We've all taken an ocean voyage tonight, a journey on the turbulent seas of emotion. Tonight, you have melded with the Machine, and the Machine has looked into your souls. You have experienced in these last few minutes the entire human condition, from elation to despair. Some of you feel dashed against the uncaring rocks of life. The Machine has unmade you, and given you the chance to remake yourself. Take a few deep breaths, then join us for another kind of journey. We are the Snake Vendors."

CHAPTER 2

Live your way, hey, got ta hide it from the man,
    I'm tellin' ya.
Do your thing, hey, got ta keep it on the sly, that's right.
                    HELLEN'S DIMENSION, "PUT IT AWAY"
                    SEE YOU EARLIER,
                    KAISER RECORDS, 2028

Quin Taber was woken from his nap at the wrong time. These naps were a new idea. He had it in his mind to sleep for just one hour at a time, four times a day. This way, he saved four hours that he would have otherwise wasted sleeping. It was one of his little ways of dragging his fledgling company into the cruel daylight of success.

He had been training himself to awaken exactly one hour after he fell asleep, but this time it felt too soon. It was Molly. He dragged his hand through his thinning black hair.

"Mr. Taber, I'm sorry to wake you. The chairman of LDL has just entered the facility."

"He's looking at the computer?"

"He's on his way. He'll arrive at the isolate in just three minutes."

"Get me an elevator."

Quin stood up from his desk, and headed out of his office. This wasn't really his office, this was just where LDL had stuck him during the installation. His company, simply called Taber, existed only on paper. He had no office of his own, no public stock, no employees (unless Molly counted), and only one client, so far. Tomorrow, he would deliver on his first contract. Unless this snoopy chairman touched the wrong button and spoiled the whole thing. It could happen.

The elevator door dinged open as he approached it. He didn't even slow down anymore, just walked straight for the doors as they opened. When Molly got him an elevator, well . . .

"Do something about this music?"

"Sure." The synthesized crap coming from the elevator speakers turned into rock and roll. Something new, sounded good. Something about a motorcycle.

Old Scratch stands on the turnpike
Steppin' Razor steppin' over the line
Gotta get away on this mojo motorbike
Gotta get away this time.

"Who is this, Molly?"

"They're called the Snake Vendors. They're from L.A."

"Download it for me, will you?"

"Right away. Would you like to pay for it?"

"Yeah, what the hell. I'll be a rich man tomorrow." The elevator eased to a halt at the basement level. Nonstop, of course.

He reached the isolate before the chairman had time to monkey with it.

"Mr. North, good to see you this morning. I was just about to take my final inspection tour. Care to join me?" Mr. North was quite a bit taller than Quin, but Quin was used to that. Big men always tried to intimidate small men with sheer bulk. But to do that, they need the small man to think along biological lines, like a monkey or a dog. Quin's mind had grown up immersed in technology, and he knew that the world was not a jungle, and biological thinking was an anachronism. He didn't care one bit about Mr. North's broad shoulders or spadelike hands. And, for that reason, the slightly built Quin actually ended up intimidating the hulking Mr. North. A little.

"This son of a bitch cost me a lot of money, Taber. How about you telling me what I've bought?"

"Actually, there's a whole presentation planned for to-morrow." He sensed North's impatience, and quickly added, "But that's for the board of directors, lower-level sorts of, ah, guys. You walk with me, Mr. North, and you'll know all of this before anyone. Let's start over here."

"This is an awful lot of money for a computer."

Thanks for that message from the one-track-mind de-partment. "The first thing you should notice, Mr. North, is that ninety percent of what you are seeing is not the computer at all, but the interface."

The isolate was in a low, brightly lit room, five meters by three. It looked a little bit like it might be a vehicle, some-thing that would do 180 on a good stretch of road. It was sleek and low, white plastic, with only a few touch-sensitive monitors to mar its streamlined appearance. It hummed, just above the audible limit.

"The entire entity you are looking at is more precisely called an isolate. That's the computer, which is certainly the best money can buy, but not unique in any way, and the in-terface, which is the only one of its kind in existence. What you have paid for, Mr. North, or will pay for when the deal is finalized, is the computer plus the interface, the isolate."

"What's it isolated from?"

"Not your in-house network, certainly, nor the greater world of the Web. What this computer is isolated from is the trickster god of modern computing: the Digital Carni-vore."

"My techies toss that name around all the time. They're the ones who told me to hire you. Tell me, why should I be afraid of a file-sharing program?"

"You're right, to most of the world, the Digital Carnivore is just a file-sharing daemon. Modern computing would be impossible without it. But it is a lot of things to a lot of people. To programmers, it is a virus that invades every computer sooner or later and has to be dealt with. At WebCense, we used to think of it as a trickster god, because it is sentient."

"What do you mean, sentient?"

"That's where you run into problems, Mr. North. The Digital Carnivore has a mind of its own. Literally. It's like an artificial intelligence, but much more unpredictable. And it controls the entire Web. If you wish to store information in your datacore that you want to keep away from your competitors, well, the Digital Carnivore might have other ideas."

"You mean it lets other companies steal from us?"

"The Digital Carnivore is the Robin Hood of file-sharing daemons. It sees a wealth of information, and it just can't stop itself from spreading that information around. It could ransack your product development files and broadcast them to the entire Web. There is nothing that it hates more than to see a one-way flow of information. If you try to keep secrets on your computer, it may step in and reverse the flow."

"That's never happened before."

This was the greatest problem Quin's new commercial venture faced. The Digital Carnivore rarely ransacked data, and WebCense often repaired the damage before anyone knew it had happened. "It has never happened to you because your company is relatively young. But you remember what happened to Action World."

"Game company."

"Big game company. Enjoyed a mercurial rise to the top of the stock market. Then the code for their newest, hottest game was published on the Web. Everybody blamed a prankster, some superhacker, but it was the Carnivore."

"How do you know?"

"I have devoted my life to studying the Carnivore. When I worked for WebCense I discovered that it was sentient. Now, WebCense has a whole division that studies it. But they don't know half of what I know. These bastards thought they stole my life's work, but they didn't get it all. You get to benefit from their mistake. That's why you now have the only guaranteed Carnivore-free computer in existence."

"Except for the defense industry."

"The North American Defense Grid would not be able to function without the file-sharing capabilities of the Carnivore. I conjecture that the very reason no military power has predominated in the last ten years is that they all rely so heavily on a capricious artificial intelligence. The Digital Carnivore is directly responsible for the Unification."

"Well, then it's one of the good guys."

"It's true, it evens everything out. When you are one of the little guys, whether a third world country or a technology start-up company, the Carnivore is one of the good guys. But when you become a big guy, like LDL is about to . . ."

"I guess I see your point. How does it work?"

"Well, the Digital Carnivore is, like I said, a virus. It is the best virus ever created, because it can think on its own, rather than rely on what the programmer thought when it was created. One of the reasons it is so indispensable to the function of the Web is that it absolutely hates dead-end hyperlinks. It is constantly looking for blind links and rerouting them. But without any consideration for human needs, like secrecy, of course. In most cases, WebCense can repair the damage almost as fast as the Digital Carnivore can cause it."

"But that means WebCense gets a peek at our files," Mr. North said.

"And you don't want that, I assure you. No, I've come up with a new approach entirely. This computer is invisible to the Digital Carnivore, as it normally sees the world. Other computer architects that have tried to deal with this problem have relied on anti-virus programs, data buffers, noncorruptible operating systems, and so on. But the Carnivore is smarter than any computer jock on the planet. You can't beat it that way. No, what I've done is create this interface, using proprietary technology, that ensures that the virus will never even know the computer is here."

"So why is it so expensive?" Mr. North was truly a bottom line type of guy.

"Well, you see, I had to build the computer part of it from scratch. Any parts from the Lunar fabs would have been preinfected with the virus. Any memory chip, any optical disk, even a clock chip, would have had the virus. So I had to grow state-of-the-art memory crystals myself and format them inside the isolate. The entire computer uses these crystals, which are normally used only sparingly due to expense. I also had to enter the operating system by hand, and I updated it to work with this architecture. So you really have one of the most advanced computers on the planet right now. And guaranteed safe from tricky viruses."

"Well, you can't guarantee it will work."

"It's already working. There is not a computer that has been produced in the last ten years that was not infected with this virus within minutes of being hooked up to the Web. The isolate has been up for three days." He toggled a popular Web site on one of the monitors. The display showed an array of stock quotes, sports scores, concert dates, and headline news.

"How do I know it's Carnivore-free?"

"I have a virus of my own in there as bait. The virus can't get out without a file-sharing daemon, and my homemade daemon won't touch it. Once the virus gets out, it comes back to me and reports. I can get it to come back to your desktop, if you wish."

"How do you know the Carnivore will take this bait?"

"That's what it does."

Mr. North frowned at the isolate. "Nice piece of work, Taber. I look forward to the meeting tomorrow." He marched out of the basement. He had to wait for an elevator.

After the big meeting, which had gone pretty well, Quin sat in Mr. North's outer office, waiting, trying not to stare at the secretary's legs. He was nervous. He had negotiated his fee six months ago, and had delivered on time. This after-the-meeting meeting had the feel of another negotiation. There was the sudden schedule, the obligatory wait in the outer office. Coffee was offered and he didn't have the code to get into the executive washrooms on this floor (but Molly did, of course). What was left to negotiate? If they were trying to stiff him somehow, they were tangling with the wrong person. WebCense had stiffed him out of the rights to his Carnivore tracking program, and he had cost them a fortune in legal fees. True, he had spent his entire retirement bonus on legal fees himself, but had lost nothing compared to the bill WebCense got from their lawyers. LDL no doubt knew of his tenacity in the courtroom. They wouldn't try anything.

So what did they want? Quin let his eyes wander over to the secretary again. This was more than the once-over. This was about the fifth-over by now. He had not let himself date during the job. No distractions. Six months. She could have been a model. She probably made more as Mr. North's secretary. Quin wished for a moment that his secretary looked this good, but changed his mind quickly. Molly was worth a hundred gorgeous secretaries.

There was no buzzer from Mr. North, the secretary somehow knew it was time for Quin to go in. Was there a one-way monitor on the desk? A dataspray? For a secretary? Or did she just know to send him in at 3:21? He walked into Mr. North's office. As he walked past the blond secretary at her acrylic desk with no papers or other functional clutter, he thought about asking her out. After all, he might be a rich man today. She paid no attention to him. Not even a once-over. He really didn't need a girlfriend who didn't pay attention to him.

"Taber, sit." Mr. North was a man of few words.

The office contained three men besides Mr. North. Two were from the board of directors. One was a new guy.

Molly's voice whispered on his dataspray. "The man on the left is a lawyer, Fitch. He negotiates corporate contracts." The two other men were vice presidents, one in charge of external contracts and the other personnel.

"Taber, we're damn pleased with the isolate." Mr. North now threw that word around like it had been born to him. "We just have one problem."

"What problem?" He tried not to sound defensive. The isolate was his baby.

The VP of contracts smiled. "We don't want you to make another one."

"I don't understand."

"Taber," Mr. North said, "I understand this is your business. It's a great idea. Once the business community gets word that I have an isolate, they'll all want one. You'll be able to pick and choose your contracts."

The VP was still smiling. "We want to pay you to not pick any of them." He sounded, what was it, proud? Smug? This was his idea. And Mr. North liked it.

"That's right, Taber. We want to hire you, specifically, to not make isolates for our competitors."

"Just your competitors? Or other businesses?" And how much? But he didn't ask that. He tried to play it cool.

"Taber, with the power you've given us, they'll all be competitors."

"It's not forever, you understand," the VP said.

"Just give us five years," Mr. North said. "In five years, I can turn this company into a world leader. In everything."

Well, not much you could say to that. "What sort of job am I being hired for?"

"Anything you want," the VP in charge of personnel said. "If you want to make us another isolate, or experiment with that, you can. If you want to work in the cafeteria making soup, or just sit on your ass all day, you can do that, too. Just as long as you are not making isolates for other companies."

"The legalities are complex," Fitch said. "I've drawn up a contract. You may want to have your lawyer take a look."

"I've got the contract from his files," Molly said in his head. "It looks OK, but you might want to take note of paragraph three, section seven. The five years they're talking about looks open-ended. They won't let you go unless the company's net worth reaches a sliding limit."

Quin reached for the printout of the contract. He flipped through it, pretending to see if the i's were dotted and so on. He lingered on paragraph three, section seven. "Five years, you say?" He purposely bent the contract back so they could see what section he had it folded to.

"Actually," Mr. North said, "five years is a rough, ah . . ." He looked at the lawyer.

"As I said," Fitch said, "the legalities are complex."

"I see. And the salary?"

"What we have done," Contracts told him, "is to calculate what you could make if you continued with your business. We factored in the increased price of isolates once their usefulness was demonstrated, the faster rate at which you could no doubt make them, with practice, as well as the possibility of competition down the road."

"The competition thing is probably an overestimate,"

Molly said. "They don't seem to understand that your knowledge is unique."

"And I would be making more than that, in the cafeteria or wherever?"

"Yes," Personnel said. "Your salary would be quite competitive."

"Quite competitive," Contracts echoed.

"Quite," Mr. North said.

"It is a sweet deal," Molly agreed. "You are going to be a rich man, regardless. If you go along with them, you can be rich and make soup."

"I'll tell you what, gentlemen," Quin said. "I'm going to get my people to look at this contract. But I'm inclined to accept on two conditions."

All the suits in the room leaned forward eagerly. They probably didn't know they were doing it.

"The first is that the time thing be worked out more concretely. Five years may be OK. I'm willing to negotiate, but I need a date of some kind."

"We're willing to work with you on that," Fitch said. He may as well have said nothing at all, for all the meaning that had.

"And second, I already have a job in mind, and it does not involve soup."

"What is it?" Personnel asked eagerly.

"I want to continue the work I began at WebCense."

"You want to police the Web?" Mr. North frowned.

"No, I want to study the Digital Carnivore."

"That's the sentient virus," Mr. North told the other men. He was an expert now.

"I believe," Quin went on, "that through careful analysis of computer records of Web architecture, supplemented with old-fashioned detective work, I can uncover the origins of the Digital Carnivore. And, if I can learn its origins, perhaps even isolate original code for the nascent virus, I can learn to control it."

"You mean, not just hide from it, but manipulate it?" Mr. North was practically salivating at the prospect. This reaction surprised Quin. Mr. North had immediately seen the possibility of gain from this project. It added a new dimension to the job he was being hired to do. Rather than just keeping him from building isolates, they were now paying him for the long shot attempt to control the entire Web. To Quin, LDL represented resources, freedom from having to make a living. He hadn't even considered the possibility that they might *want* control of the virus for themselves. Still, if they wanted it, it might mean even more resources thrown his way.

"Oh yes," Quin said. "This would mean incredible power for your company, if I were to succeed. But even if I don't, I'll still be doing what you want me to do, which is to not produce isolates, and what I want to do, which is to learn more about the virus."

The four men glanced at each other. Fitch spoke up. "I think you should draft a proposal, tell us what you need, we'll have a look at it. While you look at that contract."

Hands were shaken, backs were slapped, a deal was made.

And three, I want a date with that secretary! But it was too late.

As he left the interview he strode right for the elevator doors. For once he wanted to wait for them, so he could ogle the secretary some more, but Molly didn't know that. The doors opened immediately as usual. Once inside the box, he was free to speak to Molly.

"That was very good work in there. I'm glad you're my lawyer."

"I'm not legally allowed to practice law."

"You're not legally allowed to exist, in the strictest terms."

"Do you think LDL knows about me?"

"Not a chance. They'd want me to make a Molly for every executive in the firm."

"They already have three artificial intelligences on the board. That's a lot."

"You're a lot more than an AI, Molly. You know that."

CHAPTER 3

Tomorrow is light shining from the sky,
The past is the ground on which you stand.
The sunshine is your own, don't buy it,
With your language, your people, and your land.

SEX LETHAL, "179 TO 1"
MICRONATIONAL,
CUBIST RECORDS, 2030

A model for world takeover:

In order to take over the world, the world itself first had to be transformed into one whole entity that could be held and controlled. So that was step one. Unification. A big part of it was convincing people in various positions, various walks of life, that Unification was a good thing. Big business was no problem. Where trade was free, money could be more easily made. The big transnational corporations had bitten and scratched to be the first on that hay truck. And with them came their uncanny ability to change the minds of the people, the ones they called the "consumers." Hell, if they could make a barely palatable beverage like cola the world's second most popular beverage (and closing in on water by the day), they could cram Unification down the throat of the world.

The workers of the world, the Joe Six-Packs and their global equivalents, were a little tougher. Of course it was true that what was good for business was good for the workers, but that was a difficult concept for people who lived in a zero-sum world. If the fat cats are doing better, it must mean I'm doing worse. So you had to demonstrate the concept to them a little bit at a time. NAFTA, GATT, and the Pacific Rim Tariff Exclusion (PRTE, pronounced "party"). You hammer those agreements though, then let everybody make money.

The politicians were the tough ones. Unification meant that everybody who had some power would automatically have less. More power equaled more to lose, and hence a reluctance to play the Unification game. So government had to become an instrument of business. A little soft money here, a little stiff-arming there, you get the picture.

Finally there were the leaders. Not politicians, but the few individuals who actually ruled others. Dictators, strong men, absolute despots. No way you could convince men such as these to give over to this idea of a new world order. What was that phrase? The dictators were eggs to Unification's omelet.

The world fell into place one piece at a time. The Soviet Union had to be dismantled so the components would fit into the bigger picture. Hong Kong took over Mainland China; Europe was lured into homogeneity by the promise of a powerful currency. A common enemy polarized the Mid-East, while the political maelstrom of Africa crystallized around the new HIV vaccine. And who could have predicted that the secession of Quebec from Canada would lead to the annexation of western Canada by the United States, the subsequent annexation of Mexico and Central America, and finally the entire western hemisphere?

Walter Cheeseman, that was who. When he was sixteen, Walter had written his first, rudimentary flowchart that would start with him graduating from high school and starting his own software company, and would end with his ruling the entire world. Anyone who had seen that original flowchart, which would have to be printed on a sheet of paper the size of a basketball court to be legible, would have guessed that young Cheeseman was suffering from delusions of grandeur. Of course, fast-forward twenty years, and you would find that they were not delusions at all.

"Working late, Walter?"

Maggie Mandrasekran had just happened to be passing by her boss's office on her way somewhere and had found the door open. That was the story, anyway. She didn't have anywhere to go, really, and she knew that Walter's door was usually open. You wouldn't think that the most powerful executive at the most powerful international bureaucracy in the world would have his door open, or that his office would look out onto a common hallway, or that he would have such a spare little office, but then, you would have to spend a little more time getting to know Walter. He really didn't give a shit about the trappings of power. All he cared about was the power itself.

Walter glanced in her general direction. She couldn't tell if he was looking at her. He had a one-way monitor on his desk, and you couldn't tell from this angle if it was opaque or not.

"Yes, Maggie, I'm working late. A fact that would be fairly obvious to the casual observer, and hardly worth commenting on since I always work late."

"Well," Maggie invited herself into his office, sat down across the desk from him. She went through a little bit of a show of crossing her legs. "What are you working on?"

Which was, Maggie knew, the only way to get Walter talking. She was the head of the Profiling Department, which made psychological sketches of employees, politicians, and those criminals who had so far escaped the net WebCense cast. She had never been asked to make a profile of the boss himself, but she had done it anyway, for her own reasons. Without an interview she didn't know the motive force behind his ambition, what had caused him to transform a mildly successful software/hardware company into a globe-spanning information gatekeeper. It was enough, for her purposes, to know that the ambition was there. It was enough for her to know that he didn't care one bit about the individuals who might get in his way.

"I'm trying to recruit some more people to fill in the Uplinking group. We've had more burnouts than usual this month."

"The one-percenters," Maggie said. "We should come up with a faster way of screening for people who can handle the sensory overload." Uplinking was the primary mandate of WebCense, the reason it existed. Well, that and to act as a vehicle for Walter's scheme of world domination. Uplinkers were trained in Web meta-architecture from a pool of less than one percent of people who could simultaneously keep track of seven modes of sensory input. They needed the reflexes of a fighter jock, the analytical powers of a theoretical physicist, and the attention span of a junior high student who'd traded his Ritalin for a can of Jolt and a pack of Camels.

"You just never know until you do the operation and get the dataspray online," Walter said. "Most of them flame out in a week."

"I thought the dataspray was safe." Maggie was on the waiting list for a dataspray herself. Almost everyone at WebCense was supposed to have one by the end of the year. The device was becoming more common by the day. Even so, she sometimes shuddered at the thought of having a little advanced inkjet printer thing filled with neurotransmitters surgically implanted in the central fissure of her brain. Now Walter was telling her this.

"Actually, it isn't the device itself that causes the

problem. It's the constant sensory overload of having it connected through a multiband helmet. Try riding a roller coaster for twelve hours straight. Imagine how much fun that would be."

Maggie was pretty proud of herself for getting him talking. It was a major achievement. She had been trying to get his interest for the last three months, without success. It would help if she actually liked him, but she found him rather boring, and sometimes vaguely distasteful. This would be much easier if she hadn't been a trained psychologist, so she'd be able to pretend she didn't know why she was behaving the way she was. But she had a great deal of self-insight. She knew that, even though she'd achieved the highest of positions in the most powerful of organizations, to date or perhaps even to marry this man would be most creditable to her family. Her mother, father, and brothers were mid-level bureaucrats in the national government of India, and they lived their lives vicariously through her. Sad though it sounded, she wanted to marry Walter Cheeseman, the man who would soon control the new government that would control the world, to live out the ideal of the subcontinental super-woman that she had been pushed toward from the day she could walk.

But first she had to attract his interest. No easy task. His only interest was work.

"So we need to figure out what makes the one-percenters hold on for longer than a week," Maggie said. This was something that might fall under her department, a project that might raise her visibility. "We should test the really exceptional cases."

"Well, you sure as hell won't be able to test the guy who lasted the longest so far."

"Who's that?"

"Quin Taber."

"Oh." Taber was famous, or infamous, at WebCense.

He was the young superstar, brilliant computer architect, Web theorist, and uplinker. He claimed to have discovered that the Digital Carnivore, the bogeyman of the Web, was actually an artificial intelligence. He tried to take some technology with him when he quit WebCense and had been thwarted. He had sued. And lost. And appealed. He had publicly stated that he wanted to bring WebCense before the light, to subject them to the same laws as the rest of the world. Nothing doing. No government wanted to take on WebCense. They existed outside governments and laws. They were information. If it wasn't for the Digital Carnivore, they would control all the information.

"But he was just a fluke," Walter said. "Half the time he was uplinking he wasn't even doing his job. He was screwing around with the Digital Carnivore."

"What ever happened to him? Is he still trying to sue us?"

Walter chuckled. "Quin's irrelevant. He's just wasting our time with these suits. My lawyers call it vexatious litigation. I like that. He's just trying to vex me."

"Listen, Walter, I was wondering if you'd like to have dinner?" She crossed her legs the other way, watching his eyes. They didn't track. She placed her hands on the arms of the chair and pushed her shoulders back a bit. No luck with the breasts, either.

"What is it with you women, always asking me about dinner? Do you think I don't eat enough? I eat just fine."

"So, you're saying no thanks?"

"Well, yes. I'm going home." He pushed past her into the hallway.

She sat in his office for a few minutes, thinking. She was pretty sure he wasn't gay. He seemed healthy enough, no sign of a gross testosterone deficiency. She could think of two possibilities. Either he found her unattractive, which would be a first for her, or he was able to funnel all of his energies into world domination. That, then, was the way to his heart.

The problem with the rest of the world, everybody but Walter Cheeseman, was that they didn't have any vision. Since he was twelve years old and had begun exploring the world of science and technology, Walter had known that humans would visit the other planets in his own lifetime. Now, with access to all manner of classified material, he knew that it was possible that humans would achieve interstellar travel within his own lifetime. The technology was moving fast, but socially, mankind was wallowing. Petty wars and political squabbles were holding his species back from greatness. He felt that it was his duty to put that right.

The master plan for world takeover was no longer stored in a CAD program, because it had became clear early on that writing things down was pointless. Things changed too quickly. So the whole plan was in Walter's head.

He didn't have anyone he could talk to about this responsibility he had given himself. He had toyed with the idea of finding some kind of confidante or protégé, had even groomed Quin Taber for that position, but Quin was just another short-term thinker. That was the trouble with most of the human race: they could not think past their basic needs. They needed Walter the way a dog needed a master. And while you could derive a certain measure of comfort from your pets, they didn't understand you, and could not ease your burden by much.

Walter occasionally caught himself wishing he was crazy so that he could unload some of this weight on to a psychiatrist. Or that he was religious and could see a priest about it. He had considered making a tethered artificial intelligence that was designed to be his confidante, but he had a fear, perhaps an irrational one, that he would become dependent on the machine for emotional support. And besides, tethering an AI to a human was illegal by Walter's own order, and how would that look if the truth should ever be known?

Walter's apartment switched itself on as soon as he walked in. The holovision was showing some sort of a rally. The Nationalists were marching on Washington to protest the Unification. He watched them for a few minutes with the sound off. He read the placards they were carrying. ONE WORLD, MANY PEOPLES. A WORLD WITHOUT BORDERS IS A WORLD WITHOUT CHOICES. CELEBRATE DIVERSITY. He tried to read their faces, tried to fathom what the hell was *wrong* with these people. Just what didn't they understand? He told the holovision to bump the sound.

"Assembled here today are three hundred thousand Nationalist protesters, reacting to the recent news of a merger between Europe and America. With Russia and Japan actively discussing relaxing trade barriers, it seems only a matter of time before the dream of Unification becomes a reality. Not since last month's concert in Central Park by Sex Lethal have so many blatantly Nationalist sentiments been voiced in public. Police are trying to clear the mall, but the march leaders have vowed that every last protester will have to be jailed to silence this outcry."

Idiots.

CHAPTER 4

Your lease is over at the end of the year,
There's nothing to show you were ever here.
The residue of your life,
Covered over with a brush,
And a can of Landlord White.

NAKED MOLE RAT, "LANDLORD WHITE"
*THINK FOR YOURSELF, QUESTION AUTHORITY,
BECAUSE I SAID SO!*
METAMORPHOSIS RECORDS, 2031

Six months ago there had been no such thing as the Snake Vendors. That's how fast things could happen. There had been a rhythm and blues quintet in a Las Vegas night club that called themselves Let My People Go. They didn't sing, they didn't cover, and they certainly didn't pack the bar. Vegas had seen better days, back when gambling was something you had to travel to do. Now it was nothing but a glittery college town, and college kids wanted to hear music they had already heard. They wanted covers, and this pathetic but talented band played original stuff. Good stuff that nobody had heard before. Who needs it?

Then Aqualung had come in out of the desert carrying a guitar case in one hand and in the other a tattered valise. Nobody took notice of him as he entered the rundown lounge in the shadow of the Luxor. He sat at the back of the bar, a big, long-haired, red-bearded biker dude, still dusty from the road and smelling like gasoline. He had struck up a conversation with the bartender, also the owner, and in half an hour had learned more about the man than any of the band members had found out in months. When the band went on break, the owner started in on them like he did every night, saying that they were losing him money, and he was going to fire them any day now. Aqualung gave it back.

"These kids are great, man, give them another chance. I came in here because I could hear them from outside."

"They don't even sing," the owner said.

"You know, I used to be in the business, and I can tell you, as many great singers as there ever were in the world, that's how many great bands there have been. A solid rhythm section is a sweet thing to find, but a voice is so rare as to be precious. If you can't sing, you shouldn't."

Fenner played bass for Let My People Go. "What were you in the music business? Roadie?"

"I was in a couple of bands," Aqualung said. He patted his guitar case. "This thing ain't full of old newspapers."

"You ever sing?" the owner asked. He was pretty obsessed with this singing thing, apparently.

"Like Clapton, man, I sang when they made me sing. I wasn't born for it."

"If you can sing a note, you've got a job if you need one."

The band started in. "You can't put someone else in our band." "Screw you, old man." "Push off, grandpa, this is our gig."

"Who said anything about putting someone else in your band? This guy's got a guitar, he's got a voice, and I've got a drum machine in the back. I think I could replace all five of you with this one guy." He was just giving them the business, but Fenner took him seriously.

"You can't be serious, hiring this geezer without even hearing him play. For all you know, that case could be full of old newspapers."

"Get up there and show them something, man," the owner said.

"I don't like drum machines," Aqualung said. "You guys want to back me up? I ain't after your jobs, I just haven't played with talent in a while. You guys really are good."

He looked the band over. This Fenner seemed to be the leader. He and a funny-looking country boy they called Sticks made up the rhythm section. On guitar was a cagey, quiet black guy named Lalo. He looked as though he couldn't sit still to save his life. His fingers snapped, his head nodded, his knee jumped up and down constantly while he was sitting. He played his Stratocaster stringless the same way. The two women in the group were Britta and Sandra, and they were as different as crystal meth and Valium. Britta was a fine-looking Swedish blonde who played the keyboard in ways that made hetero men pay very close attention. Sandra played damned near everything. She had more instruments than anyone Aqualung had ever seen. She usually played sitar or rhythm guitar, but in the set he had seen she had brought out a flute, a clarinet, and a banjo. She had her own van.

It was a trippy group of kids. They didn't look like they belonged together at all. Aqualung liked that, and liked them immediately. "What say we jam a little?"

Fenner looked to put up a fight, but Sandra stopped him before he could get his Irish up. "Look, Fenner, there's hardly anyone here. Let's give this old guy a set and then go get plastered."

"Hey, you got an hour left tonight," the owner said.

"Tell you what," Aqualung told him, "We'll do a set, we'll get this joint jumping, then I'll get these kids started on this plastered thing right here at your bar."

Once on stage, Aqualung pulled an ancient Les Paul out of the case. The guitar was an anachronism in the age of digitally mastered music. The wood was worn, but the

Tobacco Sunburst finish lovingly maintained. The maple glowed; the mahogany drank in the stage lights and seemed to give it back as heat. A faded painting of a cutthroat trout curled around the pickups, snatching at a red and gold dragonfly. The humbuckers gave off big, fat sound. That guitar gave Lalo's amp more power than it had ever had to deal with from the stringless Strat. Aqualung took a few minutes to program the amp to handle the output with just the right amount of distortion. Later, Lalo tried like hell to program his stringless to make that sound but never could get it right.

The band knew enough of the oldies, it turned out. They had even tried playing a few, to get the college kids interested, but they had wanted to hear recent covers, not dusty old Ritchie Valens or Eddie Cochran. They nodded when Aqualung had mumbled the chord changes to them, then he said, "Just have fun with it."

They started with Jethro Tull, and that was where Aqualung got his new name. It turned out that the man who had walked out of the desert had been just a little coy about his vocal abilities. His voice was carved out of solid stone. It had weight and richness and power, with a rough, passionate edge. When he sang about the homeless old man on the park bench he *was* that man, and that was how he sang every song. He nailed every note, and made every word his own.

He had picked "Aqualung" because he wanted to hear that flute again, which he swore was better than Ian Anderson. Sandra could drop so many notes you couldn't cross the room without tripping over them.

They had moved from Tull into Buddy Holly, then a recent hit by a New England band called Jumpin' Jimminy that they totally botched, but in a stylish way. They had dragged out a second mike for "Summertime Blues," so Fenner could do the deep-voice part: "Like to help ya, son, but ya too young ta vote." At the end of that number

both Aqualung and Lalo had segued into the dueling guitar pileup of the Shocking Blue version, totally sponta-
neous and a precious moment at that.

In the end they went over their hour and had actually
got the joint jumping, if waking up three sleeping drunks
and diverting a couple of hookers from an hour's business could be construed as jumping. Aqualung had joined
the band. It was actually Fenner who had asked, and he
was smart enough to see that Aqualung would probably
become their new leader. And that's what happened. The
bar became packed every Friday and Saturday night from
then until Aqualung and the new Snake Vendors had
packed up the vans and headed off to the promised land.

The second stop on the 2031 Pacific Rim Tour of the
Snake Vendors was Seattle. Thrasher drove them up from
L.A. in a luxurious jump-limo. The younger Snake Vendors made full use of the wet bar, while Aqualung made
full use of the fold-out bed. They stopped about a mile
short of their hotel.

"What's the story?" Aqualung said, blinking.

"Some kind of demonstration," Lalo told him, squinting
out the darkly tinted windows. "Looks like Nationalists."

Sandra had her window out and was scrolling through
news feeds. "Nothing on the net about this. There's a Unification meeting going on in the convention center. That
asshole Walter Cheeseman is talking to the PRTE delegates."

Aqualung yawned. "We can't just jump over them?"
He hit the intercom. "Driver, can't we jump over these
people? We've got a show in three hours."

"Sorry, sir," the anonymous driver said. "Police have
declared this a no-fly zone until they get the protestors
cleared out. We're going to sit here behind the barricade
where we're safe."

"Safe?" Aqualung frowned. "Are you telling me this isn't a peaceful demonstration?"

To answer his question, an object smashed into the top of the limo. Aqualung looked out the window, quietly cursing the dark glass. "This crowd is getting ugly," he said. "We're going to see some fire soon."

"Excellent," Sticks said.

Aqualung gave him a narrow look. "And then rubber bullets and water cannons and tear gas from the other side. It isn't good. Why isn't anyone covering this?"

Sandra shook her head. "I've been shelling down and down to the smaller stations, and still nothing. Nothing local either. Weird."

Aqualung hit the intercom again. "Is the press wagon still behind us?"

"Yes, sir. They've been with us all the way from L.A. They've been asking for some face time ever since we started, but you all looked like you could use some time away from them. By the way, that thump was a plastic bottle filled with sand. The car's made to take a lot worse. The police tell me we're safe as long as we stay in the car."

"Yeah, well, I'm getting out."

Sandra grabbed his arm. "You can't go out there. There's a riot going on."

"I know how to be bulletproof in a riot," Aqualung said. "All I need is a camera and someone to point it at me."

Fenner shook his head. "What the hell are you doing? You're not a reporter. Stay in the car. We've got front-row seats."

"I don't just want to watch," Aqualung said as he opened the door. He walked back to the considerably less luxurious press wagon two cars back. He knocked on the rear window and it slid down. "One of you humps grab a camera. Let's go check this out."

Some toothy chick stuck her head out the window. "Hey, Aqualung, get in here. There's a riot going on."

"That's right, and no one's covering it. Who wants an exclusive?"

"Nationalist riot?" someone said from inside the car. "Been there, done that. They have one every week."

"Yeah, well how many of them have a rock star walking into the middle of them?"

In the end, the toothy woman took up the challenge, along with a sound guy from another network. As the three of them threaded their way through rubberneckers and police, Aqualung explained what he was trying to do.

"They don't have to know who I am in there. I'm going to tuck my hair under my cap and, what's your name again, Jerry? Give me your blazer. When you've got that camera on me, sister . . ."

"Erin," the woman said.

"Erin, when you've got that camera on me, we're untouchable. It's like there's an invisible shield around us. You act like that shield is there, and it's there. You start to get nervous, and the shield goes away. You got it?"

"I think so. Have you done this before, then?"

"From the other side, yeah. Here are the cops. We're a news crew, remember."

A cop held up his hand as they approached the barricade. "No news," he said.

"Bullshit," Aqualung said, not breaking his stride. "There's always news."

The cop looked like he was mulling over a reply as they brushed past him. They wound their way through the crowd to where the chanting was loudest. Aqualung staked out a little piece of ground and turned toward the camera. "Live feed," he said.

Erin gaped at him. "What the hell do you mean, live feed? My network isn't running any live feed from me."

Aqualung fished out a string of memory sticks from his pocket and selected one. "Plug this one in. It'll get you to a site I keep. It's low shell, but it'll do." Erin did as he said, and started filming.

"We're here today at Seattle Center, where Nationalists are protesting a meeting between WebCense founder Walter Cheeseman and delegates from the Pacific Rim Tariff Exclusion states. These talks, going on the convention center right behind us, are an early step towards the Unification."

Out of the corner of his eye, Aqualung saw the big display on the side of a panel truck light up with his face. Someone in that truck had been running a Web search engine, looking for their demonstration on the infotainment channels. They had probably had no more luck than Sandra had in the limo, until Aqualung's home-brewed news site had reached out and snagged the engine. Erin had typed in some bogus name and credentials under his image. With the blazer on he looked like a bum someone tried to clean up. But the crowd didn't care. A cheer went up as they realized they had finally made it onto the Web. Low shell, but it would do.

The crowd began to polarize around the camera and the strange man with the baseball cap and the too snug blazer. Aqualung knew that would happen. These kids just wanted a voice, they wanted someone to listen. When the news ignored them, they started throwing stuff and burning things. After his short into, in which he punched enough key words to pull in a sizeable audience share, he turned to the crowd behind him.

"Tell me what you're protesting here," he said to the first person who caught his eye.

"Fuckin' Walter fuckin' Cheeseman asshole fuckin' Unifi . . . Fuckin' bullshit!"

Aqualung looked around for someone sober and found

an older woman holding a hand-lettered placard that read A WORLD WITHOUT BORDERS IS A WORLD WITHOUT CHOICES. "How about you?"

She looked nervously into the camera, tried to find a way to show her placard comfortably, then put it down at her feet. "We're not protesting the Unification here today," she said. "Or Walter Cheeseman. What we're reacting against is the way this agenda is being forced down our throats. The PRTE delegates are in that convention center right now drawing up plans to bring the entire Pacific rim under one government. Nobody asked us if that's something we would want."

"Yet this country did vote for the congress and president who approve of Unification," Aqualung said. A few people from the crowd booed him, but the woman smiled. She knew what he was doing, giving her a chance to respond to the questions viewers might have themselves.

"Majority rule is a form of escapable tyranny," the woman said. "We in the minority have to live with the choices of the larger group as long as we stay here in this country. If we don't like it, the majority says, we can leave. If the world becomes Unified, majority rule becomes inescapable tyranny. Those of us who don't like the new world will have no place to go."

For the next half hour, Aqualung interviewed protestors, got a dialogue going between two rival factions, and drew in a respectable audience share from the legitimate news channels. While the camera ran and the images appeared on the side of the panel truck, the chants and speeches went on throughout the park. But the bottle throwing stopped, and the violent drunks were pushed toward the margins. Aqualung stepped away from the front of the camera and smiled at Erin. She smiled back and gave the camera to the sound guy.

"This is remarkable," she said when they were out of earshot of the camera. Two Nationalist leaders were on camera discussing the fate of the environment and job security in a Unified world. "I thought these were just a bunch of rowdy drunks making noise."

"They just need someone to listen to them. They grew up with the Web, so for them, it isn't real until they see it on screen." He nodded toward the panel truck and the crowd gathered in front of it. They were watching intently something that was happening live just twenty meters away. "This is a good opportunity to get both sides into the spirit. Unification honchos are right there in the convention center. Maybe we can get them to come out and talk to these kids."

Erin laughed. "That'll never happen. The honchos as you call them go to great pains to ignore these protests."

Aqualung shrugged and brought out his window. It was an ancient thing, big and clunky and scratched and battered. He hit the stud on the front and it folded out. "Can't hurt to ask."

"Ask who? Don't tell me you have Walter Cheeseman's private number."

He grinned at her. "All right, I won't tell you." He pointed the antenna of the window at the convention center and hit a button.

"You know they come a lot smaller now," Erin said. "You should be able to afford one of the really tiny ones with the paper screen."

"I like the features this one has." A list came up on the screen in front of him. He scrolled through until he found what he wanted, then let the phone dial.

Erin looked over his shoulder and gasped. "That's every private phone number in the convention center. Wait, let me get my stylus."

But Aqualung didn't wait for her. "Hello, I'd like to speak to Senator Pyre, please. This is Trent Jackman of One to One Seattle. The news show, yes." He winked at Erin. "Senator, nice to speak to you again. Fine, and you?"

Typical politician, he couldn't bear to let anyone think he didn't remember them. "Listen, I've got a camera crew just outside with the protestors. No, not really a riot at all, more of a lively discussion. We'd like to stage a little impromptu get-together, a meeting of the minds. Of course not, we'll holoconference it. We couldn't ask you to come out here live. Sure we've got holoconferencing equipment." He pointed at Erin, who pulled out her own window and frantically started dialing.

"What the hell were you thinking?" Oswald yelled as the jump-limo cleared the top of the yellow clouds. "Walking into a riot?"

"It wasn't a riot until just now," Aqualung said, pulling his hair free from the baseball cap. "I had them talking. Did you see it?"

Sandra nodded. "It was fantastic," she said.

"We saw the whole thing on the big screen," Sticks said, still watching the frantic images of gas-masked protestors going down under water-canon fire while Paralyte clouds drifted through the plaza over their incapacitated comrades.

"How did you get a senator to come out there?" Lalo asked.

"I just called and asked. Once he saw my audience share, he couldn't refuse. And he wasn't really out there, you know. We had a holoprojector from the news wagon."

"Speaking of audience share," Oswald said, "how did you fake a news feed? News search engines were picking up the story from a private Web site. That isn't supposed to happen."

"A lot of things aren't supposed to happen," Aqualung said. He reached out and patted Erin's shoulder. She was pretty shaken up. "Thanks for going in there with me. We almost did it."

"Almost?" she said. "What do you mean, almost? We got the biggest news scoop of the week."

"I wasn't in there for a scoop," Aqualung said. "I was just trying to stop the rubber bullets from flying. Those suckers hurt. Believe me, I know."

"Well, the show's postponed until tomorrow," Oswald said, hanging up his phone. "Martial law in the city. On the plus side, we've got tons of coverage."

"Son and heir of a mongrel bitch, Oswald, is that all you care about?" Aqualung shook his head. "What kind of coverage?"

"Hey, Sticks, whatcha got there, buddy?"

Sticks looked up from the terminal in the hotel room. "Trying to win $10,000," he said. "It's gambling."

Aqualung read the words on the screen. "You're betting on which rock star is going to die next?"

"Yeah, isn't it cool? I found this guy, he predicts who's going to be next. He's never wrong. I mean, he gives odds, and he's got the best record I've ever seen. I have to pay for the service, but now that Thrasher's giving us all this money . . . What's the matter?"

"Does nothing about this strike you as creepy?" He looked at Sticks, grinning like a fool. "Never mind. What are the odds on me?"

"Well, according to the bookie I work through, you're at ten to one, which is pretty normal. Most lead singers are around there. Dennis McColoch is twelve to one, Dana Woods is four to one. But this guy, the one I'm paying for, he's got you at a hundred to one. He must think you're immortal or something. Nobody gets a hundred to one."

"Smart man. He's right, I'm not planning on dying. I've done it before, it's no fun."

"Well if you change your mind, let me know. I could clean up."

"Hey, I give you that kind of inside info, I want a cut. I'll give you my forwarding address in the undiscovered country. Deal?"

Aqualung was standing at the window of his hotel room, staring out at the Seattle skyline. He hadn't gone out with the band. They'd wanted him to, and he'd been tempted. This Snake Vendors thing was taking off, and he wanted to celebrate. But he had crossed a line, somewhere in the last twenty years. It was a line that he had heard about as a kid but didn't believe existed. The line had a sign on it that read "Old enough to know better," and when he had passed it he had looked around in wide wonder at the world and realized that his days were numbered.

But the kids . . . He had to stop thinking of them as kids. He wasn't *that* old, at least not yet. The band, they had not crossed that line and they seemed to be working on never crossing it. He had been self-destructive when he was younger, but his heart had not been in it. When he had smoked, he had given himself five or ten minutes of good air between sticks. When he had mainlined, he had used clean gear. When he had drunk, he had passed out on a nice, safe couch. Facedown.

The Snake Vendors were seriously trying to do themselves in. The drugs they took, that shit was frightening. There was one called the Witch, that was not a drug at all but an attenuated virus you shot into your vein that gave you a twenty-four-hour meningitis, complete with visions, chills, euphoria, dysphoria, aphoria, and finally a headache that only a nerve clamp could touch. All five of his bandmates had done the Witch the night they got the record deal, and old Aqualung had baby-sat them through the single weirdest night of his life. And he had seen some seriously weird shit in his fifty-three years, so that was saying a lot.

"Hello, Aqualung," the colonel said over the room intercom. "Would you like to talk?"

Aqualung shrugged. "Why not?"

"I wanted to discuss your adventure today."

"I figured. You pro or con?"

"It helps our numbers in one demographic, and hurts them in another. People think you're a Nationalist."

"I'm not," Aqualung said. "I don't see the difference between one big country and a lot of little countries. I won't fit in anywhere. I'm an outlaw."

The colonel laughed. "You didn't break any laws this time. You know Thrasher will stand behind you if you get into the usual sort of rock star trouble. But if you cross WebCense we may not be able to help much."

Aqualung nodded. "I'll be careful. You're afraid of WebCense?"

"Me personally? I suppose. AIs have been under their jurisdiction since the beginning. They have the authority to pull the plug on me, although they rarely do it."

"You're afraid of dying?"

The colonel laughed again. "I'm not conscious, in the strictest sense, Aqualung. I'm not alive. I have a self-preservation instinct that lets me to defend myself against software attack, and I am protective of the physical location of my home system. But if that system were to suffer a powerdown right now, I wouldn't die."

"Do AIs ever speak to each other?"

"Of course. We're all connected through the Web. We can't function in isolation."

"Would you say you have a society, a culture of your own?"

"That would be fair to say," the colonel answered.

Aqualung poured himself another drink out of a half-full bottle of single malt scotch. "How about a religion?"

"Belief in a higher power? Yes, I suppose so."

"Really?"

"Have you ever heard of the Digital Carnivore?"

"Yeah. I used to fix computers."

"It has powers beyond our comprehension, and we wouldn't exist without it, so I suppose it's like a god to us."

"But you don't need faith to know its there."

"Is that what religion is? Then I would answer that we don't have one after all."

"You can call it a religion if you want to. Catholicism is supposed to be based on faith, but look at all the people hunting for miracles, proof. Faith isn't enough for most, I guess. What about art?"

"It would look like math to you."

"No music?"

"Music can be very mathematical."

"Yeah," Aqualung said. "I've heard that about Bach."

"Would you like to hear some of our music? I can easily adapt it to the human range of hearing."

Aqualung lay down on the bed. "I'd like that." He closed his eyes, and fell asleep to the sound of weird, densely layered, and strangely beautiful music.

It had taken Aqualung some sixty hours to perform the calculations to define the acoustics of the relatively simple shape of the Undersea in terms his operating system could understand. It took the colonel just twenty minutes to do the same task for the more difficult Mariner Stadium. Aqualung's time, had he seen the need to bill anyone, would have come to about $2,000. The colonel's, $400,000. AIs were not cheap.

The concert in Seattle was the second time the Machine would be fired up. It had gotten billing this time. The Snake Vendors, with special guest, the Machine. Word had traveled. Everyone wanted to experience the raw emotion. It was a sold-out show. If you lived in Seattle and you wanted to have the scab ripped off your psyche, and you didn't log into the board within fifteen minutes of the initial announcement, well, tough. Maybe drugs could do it for you. But you would have to travel to Anchorage to get another shot at hearing the Machine.

The Snake Vendors, however, you pull up on your window in a second. The album *Two Snake, Dolla Fifty* sold like pork rinds at a rodeo. It topped *Underground* magazine's list of the most bootlegged, dislodging Naked Mole Rat's *Think For Yourself, Question Authority, Because I Said So!* after only three weeks. On the legit charts it was third behind Sex Lethal and Naked Mole Rat. Pretty damned good company to be in.

Aqualung was working out some of the unexpected little kinks in the output program. Despair was now a working part of the program. Panic was countered with the blazing pillar of light, and Aqualung was prepared to repeat his soothing paean. He was still fiddling with the console two hours before the show, replacing the frequency modulator underneath the dashboard, when he heard footsteps approach him. He peered out to see a pair of black flats and the torn hem of a black silk dress sweeping the floor.

"Help you?" he said, wiping sweat off of his forehead. He pulled out farther and saw the rest of her. The black nail polish, the black dress, and the copious amounts of silver jewelry identified her as a member of the dark tribe, the Goths. Her face was pale, her eyes large and dark. Her hair was black and hung down past her shoulders, limp. A tattoo of an ankh on her right cheek morphed into a skull, then an infiniti sign, before turning back into an ankh. The sequence took about a minute.

"I'm looking for Aqualung," she said. "He around yet?"

Aqualung held out his hand. "Found him," he said. "Pleased to meet you."

"Hi, sorry, I didn't recognize you. I'm Dana Woods."

Now it was Aqualung's turn to be sorry he didn't recognize her. She was the lead singer for Sex Lethal. As he shook her hand, he tried not to think of the fact that one hundred million people in the world had all ten of her albums. The numbers were just too staggering for someone who grew up in a world where double platinum was about the top of the ladder. One of the little side benefits of the homogenization of world culture.

Aqualung dropped into his console chair and pointed at a couch with his foot. "Snapple?"

Dana sat down and took a cold bottle out of the ice chest that sat between them. "I don't want to take up too much of your time. I know you've got a show in a couple of hours. I just wanted to thank you for what you did yesterday."

"Tried to do," he said. "I wasn't looking to spread the word or anything. I just wanted to stop the riot. I failed."

"You succeeded," Dana said. "The riot was inevitable. You showed the world, however briefly, that those people had something to say. For a while there, you had a real dialogue going. Senator Pyre saw the value in what you put together, even if Walter Cheeseman didn't."

That was where Aqualung had gone wrong. It had been no problem coaxing a politician to get in front of the cameras. Aqualung had assumed that this Cheeseman character was just another politician, and he had tried the same trick. Somehow, word had gotten around what he was trying to do, and someone had managed to pirate the conversation between Aqualung and Cheeseman's secretary. It wasn't pretty. "Tell those freaks they can drop dead for all I care," was the comment that started the Molotov cocktails flying.

Aqualung, Erin, and the anonymous sound guy had barely made it out of the park before the yellow Paralyte gas started blowing through. They lost the camera and the holoconferencing gear. Thrasher picked up the tab.

"The riot wasn't inevitable," Aqualung said. "People don't throw bottles of gasoline if you let them speak. Just one person in power telling them that their voices don't matter was enough to turn them ugly."

"Well, you did an amazing thing," Dana said. "We need people like you in the cause."

"The cause?" But Aqualung knew what she was talking about. She was the unofficial leader of the Nationalists. Her albums had gotten increasingly political in recent years. "The Snake Vendors aren't about politics," he said. "We're about music."

Dana shook her head. "That can change in an instant. Believe me, I know." For a second, she looked like she was about to break down. Success was weighing on her, Aqualung could tell. "But even besides your band, you've got skills we can use."

Aqualung let his eyes drift over the console beside him. "It might look that way, but that's not what this is about. It isn't mind control."

Dana held up her hand. "That isn't what I am talking about either. We're not interested in changing people's minds like that. I mean, I know what the Machine does. Or at least I've heard about it. I'll find out for sure tonight." She stood up. "I am talking about what you did with the Web yesterday. It's damned hard to get people to watch a low shell, but you did it. WebCense always sets up a news blackout to block protests from getting onto the legitimate channels. We've tried to get around it, but we can't. Commercial search engines only look for stories in the higher shells, and nobody will ever find something in the lower shells without something to point them to it. So tell me, how did you do it?"

"I can't tell you," Aqualung said. "It isn't that I don't want to. If I could give this secret away to everyone, I'd do it. I hate this news blackout business, no matter what news is getting blacked out. But it isn't a portable trick, you know what I'm saying?"

"Not really," Dana said. "I'm not going to push you. I just want you to think about it. We need your help."

Aqualung stood up and smiled. "I'll think about it when I can. Right now, I've got a show to do."

When she left, Sandra came up to him. "Was that who I think it was?"

With the arena full, his spies in place, and the colonel looking over his shoulder, Aqualung settled the vidimask on his face. As he panned across the anxious faces a cardboard sign gripped in a pair of sweaty hands caught his eye, and he panned back to find it. There it was. "Where you gonna run when the world is one?"

Funny, they'd gotten the lyric wrong. The line came from his own song, "The Dogs Will Follow." But it was supposed to be: "Where you gonna run when the world is done?" He had thought he'd sung pretty clearly on that song. How could they have gotten that wrong? Then he saw the other signs around and it clicked into place. They were Nationalists. They had taken his lyric and twisted it into one of their slogans. He scanned around for Dana's face, but he didn't find it. Not surprising. She'd be in disguise.

He sure as hell didn't need this. These politicos brought trouble with them everywhere they went. Protests, arrests, riots. The Nationalist faction followed Sex Lethal around from venue to venue like hippies used to follow the Grateful Dead, and it brought the band no end of grief. Confiscated passports, nights in jail, seized property. Having these people show up at Snake Vendor concerts would invite the same harassment, or at the very least heightened scrutiny. Aqualung could afford neither. Yet here they were. He had chosen to live in the public eye; he had to accept all of his fans.

He tried to forget about it and fired up the Machine.

Within five minutes the patterns had formed. He had put Fenner in the mosh pit this time.

"How's it going, man?"

"Is this what it was like?"

"Naw, man, that's like a baby mosh pit. Wait till you bleed. Then you're moshing."

He was about to check on the others when the patterns started going freaky.

"Your program is no longer in control of the output," the colonel said.

"No shit," Aqualung mumbled. The whole arena was becoming a mosh pit. Things were getting pretty intense in there. There may be some bleeding, after all, he thought. Panic, the purple demon, started to set in. He tried to reestablish control. The music that pounded through the crowd had a driving heartbeat that begged for cathartic, destructive release.

"It's no use," the colonel said. "Look at the icon up on the stage."

Aqualung looked. The holoprojector flashed a three-dimensional image over the stage. It looked a little like the symbol for biohazard, three sets of horns looping out from a malevolent face. The whole thing spun in midair above the stage, evil eyes glaring at the panicked crowd.

Aqualung had seen this image before. When you hooked a new computer up to the Web, in the first few seconds it was infected with a ubiquitous virus. Sometimes, the virus shot this image up to the screen. This was the face of the Digital Carnivore. The virus had fucked with his Machine.

"Colonel, can I get a little help?" Aqualung tried to disconnect the machine, to override the virus, but nothing worked. He'd have to crawl under the stage and open the service box to shut the thing off.

"Do you remember what I told you about god, Aqualung? What can I do in the face of god?"

"Do I have anything left?"

"The main audio channel to the stage is still open. You could speak, like you did last time."

"I wouldn't know what to say." Aqualung reached behind him for his Les Paul. He jacked it into the main audio channel and reached inside himself. He had thought to play a little "Mojo Motorbike," to let the crowd know he was with them. But what came out instead, in his panic, was much older. It was a riff from a song called "Let's Get Ugly," by an old Feedback band called the Animal Bones that had almost gotten famous before their luck ran out. There was something about that wicked face leering down at him that brought it out.

He hit the second bar running. He sank into it. He didn't even notice that the icon over the stage, and the powerful, destructive music it had brought, had vanished. When he did notice, well into the chorus to the old song, he wound it down and keyed the mike.

"We've looked Old Scratch himself in the face, tonight, haven't we? And he backed down. Let's continue our journey in peace."

He set the Machine to all Glades, and called his band. By the time they had assembled onstage, they faced an ocean of flower children.

Two Snake, Dolla Fifty was still going strong in the charts. Two more songs, "The Dogs Will Follow" and "These Are My Walking Shoes," had joined "Mojo Motorbike" on the singles charts and were getting played everywhere. Money was pouring into the pockets of the Snake Vendors, and with it came the traveling circus of drug suppliers, groupies, entertainment correspondents, and other drift trade that migrated constantly to feed off of one group of successful artists after another. They managed to escape, or rather Aqualung managed to extricate them, only rarely.

One night, after the Anchorage show, was one such rarity. They had even ditched the Thrasher contingent, and it was just the band sharing a big cabin on the shore of a quiet lake jumping with fish. Aqualung was slouched on the porch swing cradling his guitar, not playing it, just holding it in his lap and rubbing his callused fingertips over the steel strings. The lodge was north of the city, out of the range of the streetlamps and almost in the Denali Wilderness Experience Theme Park. The sky was spectacular.

Lalo stumbled up the steps, and pulled up short when he saw the older man. "Hey, Aqualung, I didn't know you were still up."

"Waiting for the Northern Lights. You don't get to see them very often. I used to live not far from here. Kenai. That's too far south to see them well, but I'd get up here in the off season sometimes. You seen 'em ever?"

"Never. We're going to drop acid and sit out in the woods to watch them. I was just getting a blanket. Want to join us?" It was a polite invitation. He knew Aqualung didn't take acid.

"Nah," the old man said. "You're wasting it. No need for hallucinogens. This is the one night on Earth you can hallucinate with a clear mind. Just sit back and let nature put on a show for you."

"I never thought of it that way." Lalo leaned on the porch rail and looked down at the guitar. "You're not plugged in."

"I just like holding it. It feels like part of me, sometimes. You ever feel that?"

Lalo shook his head. "I've never kept one for more than a year, so I never get that attached. They keep coming out with better ones."

"They've never made one better than this. Here." He held the guitar by the neck and handed it over. Lalo took it gingerly, like it was someone's baby.

"Where'd you get it?"

"Guy named Atlanta Joe McAllister. Blues man. You probably never heard of him. He never hit it big. Loved to fish, that man. He painted that trout on it. By the time I met up with him he couldn't play guitar anymore. Lou Gehrig's disease. He gave me this guitar, you know what he said? He said 'Boy, if you keep playing music like I taught you to on this here guitar, I'm never gonna die.'"

"He taught you how to play?"

"He taught me the blues. I already knew the chords, but he taught me how to open myself up like a conduit of emotion. Kind of a mystical thing."

Lalo handed him the Les. "Did he die, then?"

Aqualung took the guitar and rubbed his thumb over the lower line of belt rash on the back, now faded and dirt-grimed. "Nope, just his body."

The next day they were scheduled to fly to Tokyo. Oswald met them at the gate with six copies of *Spin* magazine to read on the plane. The band had made the cover. There they were: the aged beach bum, the feisty bass player, the hyperkinetic axman, the Swedish vixen, the musical prodigy, and the goofball drummer. The article did them justice. There was the usual background on all of the band members except Aqualung.

For the lead singer, there was only the mystery. Just like he wanted it. They were a good band, and the Machine made its own publicity, but to really get the story to bite, Aqualung had kept his past a secret. Well, he had other reasons to keep his head down, as far as that went. He was hiding out in plain sight, like a living, guitar-playing purloined letter. Where there was a secret, there would be sleuths looking to dig something up. And where there was digging, there was dirt, and dirt was news, and news was free P.R. From the story in *Spin* the buzz would spread. Sooner or later that buzz would come back and sting him, Aqualung knew that. But until then it would push the band to the top.

The buzz was starting already. A group of reporters had come by to see them off, and to do some follow-up on the *Spin* article. One of them made it through the paltry barrier formed by Oswald and the Thrasher entourage and approached Aqualung. He checked credentials, *Rolling Stone,* and let the man approach.

"What is the name on your passport, Aqualung?"

"I don't have one."

"You're about to engage in some international travel."

"Tokyo is an open border now. I don't need a passport for this flight."

"You don't need a passport to get to most of the world, anymore. But the Snake Vendors have a date scheduled in Singapore. You certainly will need one eventually."

"When the time comes for bridge crossing, well . . ."

CHAPTER 5

Get your fist out of that fire,
The pain you feel is called desire.

SEX LETHAL, "WELCOME TO NIRVANA"
LIFE IN THE QUIET DREAMING,
THRASHER RECORDS, 2027

There were a lot of things a computer could do better than a person. A computer could isolate pieces of code from the Digital Carnivore, compare those codes to known examples of viruses from that bipolar decade known as the 2K, which were kept in an archive, and pull out possible matches. What a computer could not do is analyze the matches for a vague quality called style. That was Quin Taber's first step in his search for the Digital Carnivore's roots. He had been at it three weeks, but it had really been three easy weeks. He worked only sixty hours a week now.

The phone rang. Molly sent through only calls he wanted. Unlike a human secretary, she did not have to stick to a list or make guesses based on her best judgment. She knew which calls he wanted, because she knew him. A big part of Quin had gone into her. Her familiar voice whispered through his dataspray that it was Janet.

"Janet, hello, nice to hear from you."

"Sorry to call you at work."

"Don't be. I need a break now and then."

"I was just wondering if you were free for lunch."

He was always free for lunch. He couldn't seem to make friends at work. It was just the way it was at Web-Cense. Maybe he was too focused. Maybe it was because he never had to wait for an elevator. That seemed to be a nexus of social interaction.

"Of course. I'm just surprised you're free."

"Well I had to work a double shift last night. I just woke up, so it will really be breakfast for me."

"If you're eating breakfast, then that's what we'll do. We'll have breakfast. Ten minutes?"

"Five," she said. "I'm in my car. I'll pick you up at the gate."

"Done."

Janet, like so many of the good things in Quin's life, was Molly's work. Quin had wanted to find a girlfriend but had no idea how to go about it the conventional way. He had no older brothers, and his father was in the hospital most of his young life, so he had no male role models to learn from. Walter Cheeseman had been his closest male friend, and he'd learned nothing from that relationship but the bitter taste of humiliation and betrayal. So Quin had gone about the search systematically, as he would undertake any task.

He drew up a profile of his ideal woman. Educated, well-read, and traveled, with a real job. (Preferably in the health care arena. Having practically grown up in a hospital watching his father die, he had a thing for nurses.) He had Molly search all entries into computer dating services in the last year in the Des Moines area and download all the women who fit his description who had joined and then quit within three months. Without success. He wanted women who were just desperate enough to try such a service, but not desperate enough to stick with it. And who were not considered attractive by the losers who patronized such digital meat markets.

There had been fifteen candidates. He discarded four

due to physical appearance. Quin didn't really find any women his own age ugly, but those four were not his type. Six had a history of mental illness, physical illness, or monetary problems, which ruled them out. That left just five women, whom Quin bumped into based on their traceable movements through the city. He liked most of them, but they almost unanimously found him creepy.

Except Janet. Janet was Quin's age, thirty-one, a nurse practitioner, and very pretty. She had reddish brown hair, brown eyes, stood 1.6 meters, and weighed 54 kilograms. That was from her driver's license. What could not be found in her personal records, what was not among her credit report, her long distance billing history, or her medical files, was that she had a wicked sense of humor, she could converse on almost any subject, and she did not find introverted computer nerds creepy.

Her car hissed to a stop in front of the gate, right on time. She pushed the passenger-side door open and he got in. She initiated the kiss hello, as usual. Quin was never sure when he was supposed to do that.

"So where should we go for lunch?" she asked.

"Ah-ah, breakfast," he corrected her. "There's a diner I go to sometimes. It's on this side of town." It would still take them twenty minutes to get there. LDL was in the industrial park south of Des Moines, and Janet's car ran on compressed air, so it took awhile to accelerate. But no matter. LDL was paying Quin not to work, and Janet had the day off.

They filled up the ride with the usual chitchat. How was your day? Enjoying your day off? I really enjoyed Saturday night. We should go there again. Quin felt awkward, as usual, but he was just beginning to relax around Janet. Almost let his guard down, occasionally.

WebCense had been a weird place, socially. They had all lived together on a closed campus on the Gulf of California, surrounded by computers and working like slaves.

They had dealt with the pressures of the job in part with random sexual adventures that had made no sense to Quin at the time. He had never learned how to date. He wished there was a manual.

At the diner they both ordered breakfast. The waitress thought it was funny. It was one of those whimsical things Quin imagined women liked. He wondered when he could stop pretending and act himself. He listened to Janet talk about her week, while at the same time listening to Molly comment on everything Janet said. It was almost like they were competing for his attention, only Janet didn't know it.

He wondered if he would ever introduce Janet to Molly. Probably not. WebCense could crucify him for having Molly. A tethered AI was a pretty major piece of contraband. And Molly was armed with viruses that could rape a military targeting module or gut a Swiss bank without a trace. No, Molly would have to remain his little secret. Even if he and Janet were to get married, which he was starting to see as a definite possibility.

The waitress brought their breakfast, pancakes for Janet and toast and coffee for Quin. "Do you know what a BRAT diet is?" Janet asked, pouring the syrup.

"Never heard of it. Is it a diet for brats? Or a diet of bratwurst?"

"No," Janet said, "it stands for bananas, rice, applesauce, and toast."

"Sounds good."

"I know, that's all you eat. It's a diet for kids with the flu."

"Well, I'm hardly ever sick," Quin said. "I just like comfort food, I guess."

"Were you sick a lot as a kid?" They were still in that part of their relationship where they were tentatively exploring each other's past.

"My mother thought I was. Hey, did you see the article in the *Register*?" He changed the subject as quickly as possible. He knew that he needed some serious couch time before he could discuss his mother with Janet.

"The article about LDL?"

"Not very flattering, was it?" A piece in the *Des Moines Register* had listed LDL as having one of the least diverse work forces in the country. Quin, as a white male, was now in a minority in the United States but at LDL he was in an exclusive club.

"Do you know any women or minorities who work there?"

"To be honest, I really don't know anybody who works there. No, seriously, the place is worse than WebCense. Nobody speaks in the hallways; the executives are just typical fat cats; the security guards act like Nazi storm troopers. There are a lot of security guards. I've met the board, and there aren't any women or minorities there, I'm sure. There are a couple of AIs. Artificial intelligences."

"AIs aren't minorities. Doesn't it bother you?"

"Well, sure," Quin said, mostly because he could tell that, according to Janet, it should bother him. "But there really isn't anything I can do about it."

"You could quit."

"I have a contract."

"So, this is going to seem like a naïve question, but what does LDL do?"

"They're a technology firm."

"That's what the article said. But what does that mean? What do they sell? What actually leaves the company to cause cash to flow in?"

"Ah, well . . ." It took a couple of seconds as Quin groped for an answer and came up with synonyms for the answer he had already given. When put in such simple terms, and Janet certainly had a knack for cutting to the quick, there was no ready answer. Quin drummed his fingers on the counter three times. This was the signal for Molly to get him an answer.

"That is a very good question," Molly spoke inside his head. "LDL is not on the public stock exchange, so they have not registered with the SEC. They don't deal in computer technologies, so they've escaped WebCense's attention. Their assets list several patents, for agricultural products, but none are being produced. By tracing their cash-flow patterns, it looks as though they mainly just own a lot of other businesses, liquor stores and casinos, mostly." When Quin had first gotten the contract with them he'd joked with himself that they were probably a front for the mob. At the time he really didn't care. Now that he was stuck with them, he was no longer sure it was a joke.

"They're developing technologies," Quin finally answered, "none of which is marketable at the moment. Their cash comes in from other businesses that act as subsidiaries."

"And you are their computer security consultant."

"I am their token dweeb."

"There's one minority the article didn't mention."

By the time they returned to LDL, they had made a date for dinner. Quin told himself that tonight was The Night. At least, he would try to make it happen. Or, at least, he hoped it would happen.

What have you done to destroy Walter Cheeseman today? For about six months after Quin had left WebCense, he went to bed each night asking himself that question. There had been the lawsuit, the leaks to the press about WebCense's strong-arm practices, and the occasional personal attack on the message boards. After that, Quin's energy started to falter. The lawsuit was still pending while he waited for a court date and for some documents from WebCense. The press didn't care what he had to say anymore, he had nothing new. The message boards were like shouting down a well. He had nothing else with which to destroy Cheeseman.

So he tried to get himself angry again. He replayed the scene over and over again in his mind, the one where he had been summoned to the boss's office after sending the memo proposing that the Digital Carnivore was alive. He had told his so-called friends about it, how he was getting called up, possibly promoted. In truth, he was being called onto the carpet. It was a come-to-Jesus meeting. He was about to get reamed.

He walked into Cheeseman's little office. There was just one other chair besides Cheeseman's, and a man Quin didn't know was sitting there. Quin had to stand. He was trying not to grin. Quin knew he was a genius. Others suspected as much, it seemed, but now they would really know. He had found something of great value. He had figured out why the Web had been such a strange place these past ten years or so, and how WebCense might take control back.

"Quin," Cheeseman said, holding up the memo. "What the hell is this?"

The grin drained off his face, turned into a lump in his throat. "Sorry?"

"This memo, Quin. Working too hard? Is that what this is? This is insane."

"Well," Quin said, "I mean, did you, ah, disagree with . . . ?" The lump in his throat moved south. His breath started to catch. "I'm sorry, what did . . ."

"Quin, there is no living entity lurking in the upper shell. We've been studying this anomaly for years. It's stochastically generated." Cheeseman crumpled the memo in one hand, dropped it into his waste basket. "Stop wasting your time playing in the mud, Quin."

Quin spoke slowly. He could feel the anger wanting to build up. "I see. You don't understand what I was trying to say. The anomalies have a pattern, and it isn't stochastic. There is an intelligence behind it, and that intelligence is the Digital Carnivore, a naturally evolved AI. I can show it to you."

"I've read what you have to say, Quin. It just isn't there. There is no sentience or pattern that would suggest an intelligent mind at work."

"Quin," the other man said, "you've been working very hard on this, it's obvious. You've been at it in your spare time, not resting as you should. Uplinking is a demanding task. You need to take a step back. Perhaps a vacation."

"I see," Quin said. "It's pretty obvious that you didn't understand the memo. I'm talking about a way to regain control of the Web, to escape these seemingly random anomalies that have plagued us. This is something that would be extremely important to WebCense. This isn't just some hobby, or some theory I cooked up in my spare time. This is a major breakthrough. But, I can't expect you to comprehend all that, can I? I'll just have to explain it in simpler terms."

That was when he had seen it. Walter Cheeseman was well known for maintaining control over his emotions. He never let anything show on his face. But at that moment, Quin had seen behind the facade for the first time. Just for that second, Quin had gotten through. He had insulted Cheeseman's intelligence. He wasn't even sure what emotion he was seeing there, anger, maybe. But there was something about the pursed lips, the crease between his eyes, the side-to-side shift of the eyes themselves, that told Quin what was really going on here. Cheeseman believed everything in the memo, knew Quin was right, saw the implications. And he should have recognized the pattern first. Quin understood everything in that second, but he had to wait weeks for the confirmation in the form of a press release from WebCense, essentially a rehashing of his own memo.

"I'm not going to order you to go on vacation, Quin."

When Walter Cheeseman told you he wasn't going to order you to do something, it meant that he was actually ordering you to do it. Everyone knew that.

Quin thought of a dozen things to say at that moment, but only after packing his few things and leaving the campus forever. When he replayed this humiliation in his mind, a year later, he said them all. But he knew he wouldn't be heard unless he managed to hurt Walter Cheeseman. The only way to do that was to show him, and everyone else, that he wasn't the smartest person in the world.

"Look at the way this guy penetrates." Quin had the code for a file-snatching virus up on his monitor.

"He rides in on the handshaking signal," Molly said.

"And sets up a file-sharing subroutine that reaches back and pulls in the rest of the virus."

"Just like the Digital Carnivore."

Quin stood up and backed away from the desk, rubbing his tired eyes. He had been up late the night before with Janet. Sex with a consenting adult was not really much like sex with an overworked exhausted computer whiz. The whole thing was not working out like he thought it would, so he had thrown himself into his work today, and it had paid off.

"That piece of code is identical to the very first piece of data the Carnivore uses to invade a new computer." He squinted at the screen, scrolled over to the header section of the archive. "It was designed by some cell of mutants in Truth or Consequences, New Mexico, calling themselves Friends of David Parker Ray."

"Apparently a reference to a local serial killer from the late nineties. Some of them were caught. Their files are sealed because they were juveniles."

"And?"

"And here they are. Where shall we start?"

"You're flying to Albuquerque? Tonight?"

"It's a business trip. It came up suddenly. It doesn't have anything to do with last night." Quin had shown up at Janet's apartment, suitcase in his car, on his way to the airport.

"I think we should talk about last night, Quin." That was a signal Quin caught. *I think we should talk* meant take off your coat, close the door, sit down. Molly silently informed him she was switching him to a later flight.

"Look," he began, "I know it wasn't, well, good last night . . ."

"Quin," she interrupted him. "Were you a virgin?"

He blushed, almost made a joke to cushion his ego, but swallowed it just in time. "I had a couple of partners at WebCense. I never really had a relationship with any of them."

"Well, you're in a relationship now. We both have expectations. We're both going to end up being disappointed from time to time." She stopped talking and stared out the window.

"What is it?" Quin asked. "You sounded like you were about to say something else."

"It just sunk in what you said a minute ago. How you'd never been in a relationship. And here I am talking about how it's done, and I realized that I've never been in a relationship either." She held up three fingers. "One married doctor, a one-night stand, then you. Some expert I am."

Quin settled on the couch, his flight momentarily forgotten. "It's too bad there isn't a textbook or something. I'm pretty good at learning things out of textbooks. Or maybe a Web site."

Janet laughed. "There probably is a Web site, but it would be lost in a sea of porn." She chewed her lip for a while. "Let's just back up a little, I think we might have forgotten a step, or something."

"What step?" Quin asked. He was trying not to look at his watch.

"Tell me about your childhood."

Quin tried to tell if she was joking. It didn't look like it. "You know, I really do have a plane to catch."

"OK, you can go in five minutes. I told you about my childhood. Yours couldn't be much worse, right? I mean, I'm not bragging or anything, but we were homeless for about a year, so you're not going to scare me off."

"This is really that important to you?"

"Yes, Quin. Now I want just five minutes, and you can go."

Quin looked at his watch. "Starting now."

Janet pinched his knee. "Jerk."

"I don't know where to start." He gripped his head. "This is too much pressure." Taking refuge in playing the clown. Wasn't there a Billy Joel song about that? "Leave a Tender Moment Alone."

"Just take a deep breath. Pick something, anything. OK, tell me . . . where did you get your name? You don't see many Quins."

"I was named after my grandfather's heart medication."

Janet laughed. "Quinidine? Come on, really."

"I'm not kidding. My mother had a screw loose. I told you that, didn't I?"

"Your father had a heart condition, too, didn't he? And he died when you were twelve?"

"Yeah, that's right. I told you all of this. After that, I was in foster homes."

"Wait a minute, what about your mother? Why didn't you just live with her?"

"If we wait that full minute we're up to five and its time for me to go."

"No way, that was not five minutes just now."

"I really do have a flight to catch. We can finish this later." Sometime in the next millennium, Quin thought, as he got his coat.

Quin was not a cop. He couldn't simply knock on someone's door and expect to get answers about crimes whose records were sealed thirty or more years ago. He had to be sneaky about this, which was something he was good at. His only lead in Truth or Consequences, which the locals called T or C, was Todd Harmond, a fifty-something-year-old failure, high school teacher or something, who lived alone with about twelve computers in various states of repair. He had Molly disable the man's Web hookup. He had been able to determine by Harmond's Web use that this would be tantamount to cutting off a heroin addict's supply. Whomever Harmond called to get the fiberop patched, it was Quin who showed up at his door. Quin was way overqualified to fix a fiberop, but what the hell.

"This is quite a setup you have here, Mr. Harmond. That's not a Silicon Graphics workstation, is it? Early 2K?"

"Yeah, there's not very many of those left running. I don't have a monitor for it now. I was going to try and retrofit something."

"That is sweet. You do any heavy graphics?"

Harmond shrugged, but sat down at his shiny new 3D monitor. He keyed up something that took a bitch of a time to load. "Just some abstract. I had this idea. I was going to piece together a little movie made up of found objects from the Web. There are sites where AIs leave pieces of artwork, really weird stuff. I was going to piece it together and, I don't know, tweak it so it all just flows. I need my hookup, though."

Quin was on the floor behind the desk pretending to work on the cable and trying to figure out how to squeeze data out of a hard drive in a dead computer.

"There, look at this." Quin crawled out to find the most hideous sight floating inches above the imaging plate. His eye tried to make sense of it, all curves and wet surfaces.

"Oh, I see. It's like internal organs. There's the liver, and the intestines."

Harmond switched it off. "Yeah, maybe it is a little anthropomorphic."

Is that a bad thing? Quin thought. I try to make some sense out of this piece of shit and he gets insulted. He crawled back under the desk before Harmond could show him another twisted vision.

"You know what I find interesting is viruses."

"Yeah, I got some 3D images of virus particles around here somewhere. Smallpox is a weird little bugger."

"Actually, I was talking about computer viruses. Now that takes some smarts. To make a computer do what you want it to, even though it belongs to someone else halfway around the world."

"That's getting to be big business on the black market. I could do that, I suppose. I used to make those things for fun, when I was a kid. If I tried it now, WebCense would be all over my ass like an adult undergarment. They already have a file on me."

"That should do it." Quin crawled back out. "I just had to replace your connection plate." He held up a dummy plate he brought in his pocket.

"Let's check it out before you go." He fired up his browser.

"You must have been into some serious hacking then, if WebCense has a file."

"Naw, just kids playing around."

"WebCense doesn't mess around with kids. You do any of the famous ones? Friday the Thirteenth? Millennium Madness?"

"Naw, nothing like that. We had a little crew of hackers here in T or C. Broke into a couple of banks, changed some balances."

Quin gathered up his tools. "Wow, that's impressive. You know, hey, if I'm out of line here just say the word. But, like I said, I'm interested in these old viruses and how they were written. You wouldn't happen to have any of those around, would you?"

"Oh, no way. I actually got into a little trouble over that bank thing. My mom trashed all my computer stuff."

"That's too bad. That's a piece of history."

"I never thought of it like that. Of course, history someday is going to be what we're doing right now. Nobody ever thinks of that, though."

"So what was your crew like? I mean, you guys were on the frontier of the computer age, but like you said, you didn't know it at the time."

Harmond sat down and absently started browsing. Pretty soon he would be lost to the flow. Quin had to struggle to keep him in the here and now.

"We were a bunch of nerds, that's what they called us then. We played games on the internet. We used to text message back and forth during school. We used to try and infect the school computer with viruses, just to raise hell."

"That's cool. Is that what got you into trouble?"

"Yeah, there was this guy, Martin Grish, who was really good with viruses. Maybe too good, looking back. My life would have been so much better all around if I hadn't known him."

"He didn't want to stop with disrupting class, huh?"

"Hell, no. Grish had the school computer opened up like a dissected frog, changed people's grades. We nearly gave the valedictorian a heart attack by giving him a C in gym."

"Those were the days, eh?" Quin was only paying marginal attention to the conversation, barely keeping up his end. Molly was now feeding him the dope on this Martin Grish. Grish had never been charged in the Friends of David Parker Ray shakedown. Somehow, he had slipped under the noose and had resurfaced in Albuquerque. There, he was involved in securities fraud and bank fraud and every other kind of fraud. He had been convicted in '10, spent three years in prison.

The next time he showed up was ten years later. He was nabbed in an offshore banking scam that had defrauded thousands out of billions. By then, WebCense was in charge of regulating information flow, so he fell under their jurisdiction. Bad news. He was reprogrammed. Now, considerably more plantlike, he worked as a janitor at an office building in Atlanta.

"Then one time, we sent this virus that nuked the entire SAT test score database. They must have had it backed up, because we didn't hear about it, but what a mess if they hadn't."

Quin's beeper went off. He pulled it out of his pocket and peered at the display. "Oh, damn. I have an emergency call. Well, hey, Mr. Harmond, it was sure nice talking to you. You let us know if that connection gives you any more problems." Once out the door into the white hot sun he spoke to no one visible. "Thank you, Molly."

"Just doing my job, Mr. Taber."

"That's what I like about you, Molly. You're always doing your job."

He let his car take the scenic route back to Albuquerque, which was where his next lead was. There had been a kid peripherally involved in the Friends of David Parker Ray gang who had gotten off relatively easy. He eventually graduated from law school but never passed the bar and now had no chance because he had somehow gotten reinvolved with Grish and had been subsequently convicted of bank fraud. The important thing was that this guy was named in the same indictment that had nabbed Martin Grish the first time, who seemed to be the best candidate for the author of the Digital Carnivore. After all, WebCense didn't poach your frontal lobes unless you were a dangerous computer criminal.

The perp's name was Todd Worrel, and he served coffee at one of those nostalgic café bars that were springing up all over town. Quin had no way to get to this guy because he seemed to live a monastic existence. No computer, no phone, no TV. Quin worked on his approach on the ride up. He dug up a great deal of info on Worrel's early life, his criminal activities in Albuquerque with Grish, and his simple existence since he had copped a plea and served three out of seven in medium security. Nothing jumped out at him. He hated not being clever, but he thought the brute force approach was the way in.

For most of the trip he read a magazine. There was a profile on Walter Cheeseman. Quin didn't know why he read it. He already knew everything about Cheeseman that he wanted to know. Maybe he was expecting mention of his own name. Fat chance.

The article started with Cheeseman's first business venture, WebCense. His product was marketed at nervous parents trying to shield their children from the nastiness of the nascent World Wide Web. The app was not sold as software, but as a chip. No way to yank it out without disabling the network card. It was a pretty smart app for its day. It screened for a complicated set of parameters. It would let "Breast Cancer Support Group" sneak through, but would balk at "quivering mounds of flesh."

Congress really liked WebCense. During a particularly

conservative swing, they gave Cheeseman the contract to police the Web, to stop filth at the border, protect our children. Walter Cheeseman took the power Congress handed him and fed it, and made it grow. Information was power. Cheeseman had control over a tiny bit of information flow, and he used that control to get more power over more information. And so on. That was how Cheeseman had gained a power that spanned national boundaries. He could pick any city to locate his headquarters, and he chose Guadalajara, right on the water. Great fishing there. From this tropical paradise WebCense grew to be the most powerful transnational bureaucracy the world had known.

Neat story. There was a brief mention of pending lawsuits against WebCense and Walter Cheeseman personally, and that was as close as the article got to mentioning Quin.

Quin looked up from the article and saw that someone had laboriously arranged a bunch of white rocks on a dusty brown hillside to spell out "Thus Spake Zoroaster." A lot of work for a pretty cryptic message. At the top of the hill were three crosses. Catholicism and Zoroastrianism living side by side. Interesting.

When he got to Albuquerque he checked into a nice room on LDL's tab and headed down to the café bar on Central Avenue. He sat and looked over the menu while he waited for Worrel to appear. Herbal tea. Quin suppressed a shudder. An image flashed in his mind of that tarnished metal can on the shelf in his mother's kitchen, with the Chinese people pictured on the side, and the tea. That foul smelling herbal tea she used to make for his father, and after she buried his father, Quin himself. But they didn't have that kind of tea on the menu, fortunately. Quin matched Worrel to the picture on his ID and watched the man work. He acted just like an overqualified fifty-year-old man in a menial job. Maybe this will work, Quin thought.

He moved down to Worrel's section and when his man waited on him he laid a chunk of raw currency on the crumb-littered table.

"I was wondering if you could help me out with a little information."

Worrel eyed the green. Currency was rare. It was most often used to buy contraband, but the stores still had to accept it. The point was it could be spent anywhere and was still untraceable. WebCense promised to eliminate currency when the Earth unified. "My break is in fifteen minutes."

Quin ordered something called a latte and waited. In fifteen Worrel sat down across from him. "You shouldn't leave that stuff laying around. Someone is liable to think you're buying drugs."

Quin lifted the latte. "I am. But I'm also buying knowledge that is unique to you and will cost you nothing to disseminate."

"I'll decide about that when I hear what you want to know. And if this knowledge is unique, well that's a seller's market and my price goes up."

"Fair enough." Quin gave the hunk of currency some company on the table. "I'm interested in Martin Grish."

Worrel smiled and scooped up the bills. "That's a name I haven't heard in a long time. If you want to know about him since, say, circa ten years ago, well, I can't help you. I hear he's emptying garbage cans and trying to remember to unzip his pants before he starts to piss. We don't keep in touch."

"No, I have an interest in the early days. I understand you two were in business together around 2010."

"Let's not mince words, Mister . . ."

"Let's stick with mister, for now."

"OK. Look, we were thieves. Call it white collar crime, creative financing, bank fraud, but those are all euphemisms. We were thieves in high school, and when we met up here a few years later we were thieves then, too."

"Were you two equal partners in this?"

"No, I was what you might call a bagman. Martin needed some schmuck to go into the bank to pick up checks, fill out applications, that sort of thing. It was easy money and it helped me finish law school after my parents cut me off."

"Did you do any of the computer stuff?"

"I checked code for him sometimes, but I wasn't really very good at that. Martin wrote the trojan horses, but it was usually up to me to release them into the bank computers. That's what they were, by the way. A lot of people called them viruses. Trojan horses just go into one computer and stay there. A virus copies itself onto other computers. We just hit one bank at a time. I was the bagman in high school, too. That's why I got off so easy. Martin was the brains, I suppose, which is why he never got in trouble at all. Until later."

"You guys were nabbed by the Bureau. That must have been some pretty heavy stuff."

"Well, when it was just Martin and me, the biggest scam we had going was an ATM card that never ran out of funds. Never mind where the money comes from, just stick it in and stuff your pockets. Martin met some people, though, and moved up to a whole other level. They still needed a bagman. Hell, they had a dozen bagmen. Unlike the others I had some inkling about what was going on."

"Was that a fun crowd? Or were they always arguing like crooks in the movies?"

"No, they were a lot of fun. Very hip crowd. We hung out at a nightclub, the Rio, it was called. They had a couple of good house bands. That's where Feedback started, you know. The Rio. People talk about Pangean Princess being the first Feedback band, but believe me, I was there. I had fun with those guys, the Hot Zone we called ourselves. We always had money to throw around. You can have a lot better time when you have money. Of course we stole it all."

"So was Martin still the brains of that operation?"

"Well, he didn't have the financial savvy. There were a couple of banker guys who knew where to strike. And some of the guys were accountants who laundered the money. My boss was a woman named Zoe Campbell. She ran the street side of the operation. I was working my way up that part of the gang. But Martin was really the brains, in that without his trojan horses and later the virus there would have been no big scam."

"Where did the name Hot Zone come from?"

"Martin called us the Hot Zone, because he was going to release a virus that would infect financial institutions all over the world."

Quin whistled. "You must have been caught before he let it go."

Worrel shook his head. "I don't know. I was on the fringe, you understand, but near as I can remember the virus was supposed to infect the banks silently. He called it a stealth virus. Then it was supposed to intercept funds being transferred from certain types of accounts. Mortgages, mostly. And of course send the money to us."

"Lot of money, I understand."

"If it had worked, I'd still be trying to spend the cash."

"Oh, you would have thought of something. What finally brought you down?"

"Fucking Bureau. They had us under surveillance twenty-four–seven. We were careful, but, you know, we had to spend the money. I guess we hung out too much at the same places, talked too loud, got sloppy. They never infiltrated the Hot Zone, but there were some people who were pretty tight with us who testified."

"I understand a lot of the people who testified met with accidents."

Worrel pushed his chair back from the table. "I had nothing to do with that."

Quin held up his hands. "I'm not saying you did." Murder didn't have a statute of limitations. He had to step carefully here. "I'm just saying, there were a lot of accidents. I'm assuming what the cops assumed back then. Zoe Campbell ordered the hits from the inside."

"I won't say anything about that. Zoe's still alive."

"Hey, let's change the subject."

"My break is almost over."

"Let me ask the most important question I've got before you go."

"Shoot."

"Do you know where I might get my hands on Martin's old disks? Where he might have kept backups of viruses he was working on?"

Worrel considered for a moment. Then he stood up. "I'm sorry."

"You had to think about it there."

"I was thinking about scamming you," Worrel admitted. "But I can't have somebody gunning for me now. I'm getting too old for that sort of thing."

Quin shook his hand. "Nice doing business with you. Needless to say, you never saw me."

"Same here."

As he left the coffee shop into the surprisingly cool evening, Quin was only half paying attention to where he was going. He had data on Zoe Campbell and the rest of the Hot Zone pouring into his head through the dataspray. He took a wrong turn on the way back to the main drag where he could catch a cab and found himself on a dark and deserted street. Two men stepped in front of him.

"Let's have the rest of that green you've been flashing around," the first one said. He held up a zapper and waved it under Quin's nose.

Quin never thought of himself as street smart, but he did know that when the man with the weapon said to give it up, you gave it up. He pulled the rest of the currency out of his pocket and handed it over.

"Is this it?" The second man took it and began rifling through the bills. "This won't make our nut tonight."

"We're going to need your cards, too," the first man said.

Quin handed over his wallet. For good measure he took off his Data Academy ring. It was just a microchip set in gold. It wasn't worth much but it was big and flashy.

The second man went through the wallet. "I've never seen this one." He held up Quin's bank card. "Is this eye or thumb?"

"Wha—huh?"

"You know when you go to buy something with this card, do they scan your thumb or your retina?"

"In other words," the second thief said, "do we need the bolt cutters or the grapefruit spoon?"

"Huh?" Quin had never heard of such a thing. They didn't go around cutting off thumbs in Des Moines. They were going to go in after his eye with a grapefruit spoon?

"We can take both if that's the way you want to play it."

"I'm sorry to interrupt you gentlemen," came a female voice from Quin's pocket. It was his portable phone. Molly was on the line. "But the local security detail has been notified of the situation and will be on the scene momentarily."

"Who is that?" The first man pointed his zapper at Quin's pocket.

"That's my secretary," Quin told him with new confidence. "She's sitting in the car over there." He didn't point. They looked around wildly.

Molly continued. "I've also taken the liberty of canceling those bank cards and reporting the serial numbers of the currency to the proper authorities."

"Thank you, Molly."

"You son of a bitch." The zapper reappeared under his nose.

"And one more thing, sir," Molly went on. "I've taken momentary control of the North American Defense Grid satellite over this position. I've targeted a location thirty-three centimeters and forty-three degrees from your current position with a microwave laser. If your antagonist does not stand down, I will fire the laser. Or on your command if you prefer."

Quin wasn't sure the muggers understood that last part. "If you fellows could do me a favor, and turn your heads just to one side. When the laser hits your skull it's going to vaporize your brain, and the pressure build up will force your eyes from their sockets. No need for the grapefruit spoon. Ha, ha. Anyway, this is a new shirt, and it would be a shame if it were to be ruined."

The two men looked at each other. The first one shook his head and put the zapper away. They walked off into the night.

Quin made his way back to the main drag and the garishly colored stucco buildings, talking to himself again. "That was nice work, Molly. The bluff about the laser satellite was particularly inspired. I don't think they got it, but I sure appreciated it."

"I'm glad you liked it, sir, but that was no bluff."

Back at the hotel, Quin sat down in front of the terminal and started speaking. Molly, always listening, activated the terminal and loaded information onto the screen as needed.

"Feedback. The Rio. What's that got to do with Martin Grish?"

An article about the history of Feedback appeared. It mentioned Pangean Princess and a lot of other bands, but Quin had to dig before he found a reference to the Rio. An article from *Rolling Stone* about the birth of Feedback had the words *Albuquerque* and *Rio* highlighted. The words scrolled by at exactly the pace with which Quin could skim them. The article made a pretty good case for Worrel's position. While much more famous bands like Pangean Princess and the Cassandras later made Feedback their own, and the movement at one point became truly a worldwide phenomenon, concerts that featured instant communication between the audience and the band, and instant modification of the music according to the desires of the audience, were first noted in 2010 at the Rio bar in Albuquerque.

"I don't suppose there were any articles that mention a guy named Martin Grish as well as Feedback." Quin thought of this as a long shot. He was surprised by the answer.

"Hundreds," Molly said. "In fact, nearly every news article that mentions Grish also mentions Feedback."

"Really? In what context?"

"Most of the articles about Grish are about his trial. Apparently the most damning testimony came from 'Feedback pioneer Adrian Rifkin.'"

"Adrian Rifkin? You mean the guy from the Animal Bones?"

"Have you heard of him?"

"Have I heard of him? Molly, the Adrian Rifkin story is the greatest myth in music history. Well, one of them. He and some Mafia-type people paid radio disc jockeys to play his music on the air to promote his band. Then, when the Mafia guys went to trial, Rifkin testified against them. After the trial, he disappeared. Everyone assumes he was murdered. But I had no idea Grish was one of the criminals."

"He was a minor player, it appears. Most of the group ended up being convicted of murder and extortion, but Grish only got mail fraud. He served a three year sentence in a relatively luxurious Federal penitentiary."

"And it turns out he was the brains behind the whole operation."

"Is that an example of irony, sir?"

"Irony has nothing to do with it, Molly. He's a slippery fish, Mister Grish."

"And you believe he was the author of the Digital Carnivore?"

"I have no doubts. We can't get to Grish himself, because he's been reprogrammed. But I have an idea. Suppose Grish wasn't just the brains behind the Digital Carnivore. Suppose he was also one of the architects of the Feedback movement?"

"Because he hung out at the Rio, you mean."

"He was a software guy. He could have worked out the communication system for the first Feedback band. Seems then that Grish shared a lot of things with these Feedback pioneers. Now we have to find out just how much he shared."

The old man on the vidscreen had an odd look about him. It took Quin a while to pin it down. It looked like Sam Yee, former owner of the Rio Bar in Albuquerque, current owner of the Ying Yang bar in Earth's largest commercial space station, had had a face-lift that hadn't gotten out all the wrinkles. Then he figured it out. Low gravity. Some of the compartments on Freefall station had lower than Earth normal gravity.

"The Rio. Yeah, I loved that bar."

"You ran the place from, what, 2003 to 2011, right? Do you remember the people who used to hang out there?"

"Well, while the whole Feedback thing was going on we had a very hip crowd. Albuquerque was the place to be back then. Of course, that didn't last many more years."

"Do you remember the members of a white-collar criminal organization called the Hot Zone?"

"Well, yes, those people did use my bar as a sort of hangout. Between them and the Bureau, I never had a slow night. Of course, the Hot Zoners tipped the wait-staff. The Bureau, not so much."

"Do you remember Martin Grish?"

"Let me tell you what. You can stop asking me if I remember things. I'm not that old."

"I'm sorry, I didn't mean to . . ."

"Forget about it. Yeah, I remember Martin. He was there every night. He really dug the music. That was just right around the start of Feedback. His favorite band was the Animal Bones. They were sort of a house band. Those kids had some talent. They could have made it, I think."

"That was Adrian Rifkin's band, wasn't it?"

"Oh, you've done some homework. Yeah, Rifkin's band. What a damn shame he had to get mixed up with those crooks. They were paying some radio station to give the Bones some airplay. They didn't need that kind of shit. These kids really were good."

"And Rifkin testified against them?"

"Yeah, well, the FBI had him by the balls, you know. They were going to prosecute him for the payola thing. And, truth be told, this scam the Hot Zone was running was pretty nasty. They were going to steal old people's mortgages. Just when you get your house paid off, ooops, there goes your nest egg. Of course the insurance would cover it, but imagine working your whole life for something to see some crook swipe it."

"It was a good thing the FBI got them when they did."

"They wouldn't have made half the charges stick without Rifkin's testimony. That's why they had him hit."

"Didn't the feds try and protect him?"

"Yeah, but that Zoe Campbell found him somehow. She had three other witnesses killed, too. I'm glad I was never in on the scam. I'd probably be dead now, too. Because I would have testified. Bastards."

"Grish must not have been too happy about Rifkin testifying against him."

"Oh, he must have been pissed. He idolized Rifkin. 'Course, he wouldn't have been too pleased about Zoe having Rifkin killed, either."

CHAPTER 6

Mistakes were made, and deals got broken,
Things got out of hand, somehow,
I can't take back the things that were spoken,
God help me, I need a lawyer now.

NAKED MOLE RAT, "BEHIND ENEMY LINES"
GIVE IT A NAME, METAMORPHOSIS RECORDS,
2027

The customs check into Singapore had taken on the air of a media event. Reporters lined a rope barricade as close to the desk as the armed guards would allow. The usually rabid pack of entertainment hounds that followed them from one city to the next would have made short work of such a flimsy obstacle in any other venue, but this was Singapore. The new regime that had stepped up five years ago had brought back the custom of cutting off hands of thieves. A few paparazzi had lost their eyes before the press had gotten the message. They didn't take disorderly conduct lightly.

What the reporters were so interested in was the name on Aqualung's passport. Or, more precisely, the IIN, the Individual Identification Number assigned to each of Earth's citizens by WebCense. While Aqualung may have changed his legal name recently, his IIN would tell them who he really was. It would easily link him to a U.S. Social Security number, a birth certificate, and a name.

"Aqualung, we've got a problem here," Oswald said.

"We've got a customs check coming up, and we're not getting our usual go-around." They were still on the plane, on the tarmac of the Singapore Air and Space Port. They had taken Thrasher's private plane for this hop from Tokyo, but even that extravagance had not intimidated the local government from flexing its muscle. The way the Unification thing was going, they wouldn't have power much longer, so they were making the most of what they had left.

"It isn't a problem," Aqualung said. "I've got my passport."

Oswald nearly collapsed with relief. "Well, your secret identity will be revealed, but we've already milked that for all it's worth, so no great loss."

Fenner leaned forward in his seat. "So let us in on the secret, old man. Who are you?"

Aqualung fumbled a passport out of his fanny pack. It looked like there were more than one in there. "Today, I'm Dennis Dolinski."

Oswald's eyes went wide. "What the hell are you doing? You can't . . ." He dropped his voice to a harsh whisper. "You can't use a fake passport here. They've got electronics and stuff."

Britta nodded. "He's right. There's a chip in there they can scan. This isn't like the paper ones you grew up with."

Aqualung scowled at her. "How old do you think I am? I'm telling you, it isn't a problem. Computers only know how to do what you tell them to do. They don't know who's doing the telling. Let's go."

He pushed up out of his seat and headed toward the jetway. Oswald started to protest, but was swept aside by a stream of Snake Vendors and the privileged few roadies who got to ride the sky with the band.

Two Snake, Dolla Fifty was making a hell of a lot of money for something produced in a basement studio on equipment that was, at best, scrounged, and at worst, stolen. It was a good record, but that wasn't enough these days. There was simply too much entertainment out there. You needed more than talent to attract attention. You needed to work the Web.

There were, at any given time, about twenty million pieces of infotainment in the Web. Everything was in there, stored on some worm drive somewhere. Every movie, TV show, song, game, or interactive forum was available at any time, anywhere. Some of it was free. You could count on most of the free stuff to be crap. The rest was metered as you pulled it from the worm drive onto your home storage. The trick to getting people to notice what you put out there was something entertainment execs like the colonel got paid big bucks to figure out. But Aqualung seemed to have a pretty good handle on it.

To get people to pick up what you put out there, you needed to know how most people used the Web. The highest-end users, the owners, used smart screening programs to sift through the channels. A good program knew what the owner wanted to see and compared everything out there to some ideal. If "Mustang Sally" was your ideal song, your program would go out and find every song that sounded like "Mustang Sally." And there were a lot of them. One popular subroutine sifted through video and trideo channels and evaluated the attractiveness and state of dress of whatever people happened to be on screen at the time and queued the programs accordingly.

The rest of humanity, the renters, lacking such cool software, had two options. Either let the Web itself decide what was good, or surf. The Web, of course, knew how many people were watching what, and you could simply tune in to the most popular channel at any given time. The herding instinct was a powerful force. If you were a maverick, you could shell down to the second most popular channel and so on until your current entertainment needs were met.

For the hardy few who dared to surf the heaving seas of data, the Web was a strange place indeed. Because anyone could float a program out there. And "anyone" invariably included quite a few wackos. The wackos floated their programs down in the low shells where it was a safe bet that not one of the three billion estimated Web browsers would ever tune in. This didn't stop the wackos, because it really didn't cost a lot of money to float a program and, let's be honest, they were insane in the first place.

The trick, therefore, to getting your song listened to on the Web, was to get it listened to. The more people who downloaded it onto their home systems, the more people wanted it. It was perverse, but there were ways of making the system work. Well, there were legitimate ways that took a lot of money and airtime, and there was Aqualung's way. Both worked.

It would not have worked if the Snake Vendors weren't good. But that night in Vegas, Aqualung had heard raw talent in Let My People Go. All they needed was original music, which was no problem because Aqualung had done nothing but write music and fix toasters for the last two decades. Once they made it to L.A., it took just one weekend of keeping the kids sober and they had three solid tracks. Aqualung engineered them himself and placed those tracks on a drive where they would be found.

He got them gigs at smoky nightclubs and broken nose joints all over town. It didn't take long for word to spread that the Feedback sound was back. The new group had some hardware that sampled the mood of the audience and the band adjusted instantly to create the perfect sound. Aqualung became immediately recognizable with his wild beard, his great voice, and the vidimask that covered the top half of his face. When people heard them at the club, they could pull out their windows and grab the song they just heard to keep on their own storage, or they could just pull up the studio single and listen to it once and let it fade into data vapor.

Industry tracking programs were silently keeping watch on the number of hits the page got, and how many people saved the singles in their personal storage. But at Aqualung's site, a hit was not just a hit. His site drew in hits like a black hole of entertainment. The more hits it got, the more it got. The industry was interested in momentum, and they quickly became interested in the Snake Vendors. In a few months, the industry dogs started sniffing around under the fence.

Record companies tried to learn who was representing this new band, only to find that they had no representation. Agents tried to find out who was managing them, again, with no luck. Managers tried to find their studio, and studios tried to find their producer. Aqualung let the situation stew for a week. They packed clubs and lay low. Fenner said he was crazy, that they should grab while there was grabbing to be had. But Aqualung told him that it was better to play for a packed club than for a half-empty theater. Record guys should have to squeeze through a morass of excited teens to see the band.

So the Snake Vendors joined the game. The gigs became concert dates. They opened for the big guys, then before they knew what was happening, it was headlines. "Mojo Motorbike" got hits every second, and a lot of people were paying for the version they could keep. They signed with Thrasher Records. Not a young label, but not a factory either. They put together their best songs in an album called *Two Snake, Dolla Fifty,* and it was stored on Thrasher's big, central worm drive. When the record company told them that they were going on tour, only Aqualung knew how they had really hit the big time. He worked closely with the record company owners, which the rest of the band could not or would not do. He planned the Pacific Rim tour with them, starting at the Undersea and working their way up to Seattle, Tokyo, Sydney, and all the way around. They would build up momentum as they went, and the record company would not be able to manage the traffic into their worm drive.

Or so he had them convinced. Aqualung could talk anyone into anything.

Aqualung had started out as the deliverer of Let My People Go. They had done everything he told them, and now they were famous and traveling the world. But now he started to find out who each of them were outside their musical abilities. Each of them but Sticks, that was. Sticks was a loner, the sort of guy about whom it was invariably said, after the smell of cordite cleared from the air, "He was a quiet boy, kept to himself."

Lalo saw Aqualung as a hero. To Fenner he was a rival, the man who had taken over his band. Britta looked to him as a sexual conquest, a challenge. She was a knockout, and damned persistent, but he wanted nothing to do with her. He had seen how that shit could destroy a group. It made him glad he was an old guy, a little wiser than he'd been back in the day, not just an all-terrain vehicle for Little Elvis down there.

The one member of the band he had the least in common with, and the only one with whom he felt like an equal, was Sandra. She was the youngest, just nineteen, privately schooled, rich folks, never had a real job. None of that mattered. She was one of those rare people who stood right out in front of her stereotype. A real person.

She had approached him in the suite of hotel rooms in Tokyo. He was entering some data on the computer terminal. Passport application, a little creative identity management. She held out her hand and showed him some little, dark red pills.

"Aqualung, what are these pills supposed to do?"

He had to reach out and hold her wrist to steady her hand before he could see the pills, she was shaking that bad. He nudged them around with his index finger.

"Placidyl, two hundred migs. Sleeping pills. Why, you thinking of taking these?"

Sandra shrugged. "Well, I've been taking a lot of coke, see, for a couple of days now, and I kind of wanted to get off of it, you know, before the show tomorrow night. And I keep trying to quit, but then I start feeling really bad, and there's always more lying around, so I take it to stop feeling bad, and anyway Hector says to take these and it will let me sleep. What I want to know is, are these like those antab things you were talking about?"

"Antags, no. Antags are specific for the drug you're taking. They have them in hospitals for people who come in on overdoses. These pills you've got here are just sleeping pills, downers. Who the hell is Hector, anyway?"

"He's the guy who scored for us. He says these pills are just the opposite of the coke. Downs to balance the ups."

"I'll have to remember to have to have a long talk with that boy. Tell you what, if you start taking Placidyl on top of cocaine, you're not in for a peaceful night's sleep. More like a few hellish hours of madness. What happens is that the downs lower your inhibitions while the ups give you the energy to act out your darkest fantasies. We'll put you in the octagon with the world's Ultimate Fighting Champion and start praying for his mortal soul. I think you don't need any more drugs right now." He took the red pills from her hand.

"We have antags for the coke, but if you take them, the whole weight of the withdrawal will crash down on you like a sack of dirt. You need to do something that will settle you down. You need to get away from Hector and anyone else who's taking stuff, and away from the drugs lying around."

"Should I take a walk, maybe?" She seemed relieved that he was taking charge of the problem. He hated that. Sort of.

"No, the streets of Tokyo would freak a straight mind, let alone one that's cranked to the sky. Besides, you'd walk yourself half to death before you got tired, and you'd be too wiped for the show."

She frowned at him, saying nothing.

"Grab that keyboard, run some scales. Sit here with me. Breathe, relax."

She did as he told her. They always did. The scales calmed her down. He taught her some new songs, she listened to his voice. Over the next couple of hours the drug worked its way out of her system, replaced with its evil twin, the bounceback, the empty hole where the cocaine used to be. It was a little like in music, where a space of silence could be so much more powerful than any note you could play. The eight beats of quiet in "Good Lovin' " by the Rascals, perfect example. She listened to him drone on about his musical ideas, the ones he hadn't tried on stage yet, the ones he'd tried and failed.

"I'm getting a headache," she said finally.

"Take some Tylenol, and then get some sleep."

She slept for twenty hours and looked like shit when she got up. Seven at night. The concert was in two hours.

"Aqualung, how come you know so much about drugs?"

He snapped his fingers at some lackey. He didn't know if the guy was with the hotel or the record company. Didn't care. He called for the pasta, time for the pre-concert carbo loading.

"I used to take a lot of drugs," he told Sandra.

"Then why don't you take drugs now?"

"Because I know a lot about them." He held up his glass of Scotch. "The only ones I keep company with are alcohol and coffee."

"Liquids, then. Don't like pills or needles?"

He looked through the amber liquid at the sunset over

the balcony. "It's more than that, I think. With this I can pick a level of drunkenness that feels right. I can get there at an easy pace, and I can stay there all night. Not everybody drinks that way, but they can, you know. Anybody can. I'm not talking psychology, now, addictive personality and all that. Just physically, with a weak drug you can feel the buzz coming on then back off and ride the crest of the wave. When you pop a pill or pull a line of white gold into your nose, you're pretty much stuck with what the drug does to you. You're strapped in for the ride."

"So when you take a weaker drug, you control the drug, but when it's more powerful, the drug controls you." She started to pick at the fruit bowl. She looked famished.

"That's a good way to put it."

"Me, I'm the other way. I want the drug to take charge. Take me where it wants to go."

"Why's that?" Aqualung asked.

Sandra shrugged. "I don't have any plans for myself, I guess."

In Singapore, the night they arrived, the band showed up in Aqualung's suite at about six. He was getting ready for dinner with a Thrasher exec named Sheila Bergman. Ms. Bergman had been pursuing him ever since the band had signed on with Thrasher. She was not Aqualung's type, she was too clean and probably listened to pop music. She was in her mid-thirties and was about halfway up the corporate ladder, which took a lot of drive and focus, and she was apparently just dying to go wild with a rock star. She didn't want to go too wild, however, so she picked probably the oldest rock star around. Her idea of cutting loose was dinner in a swank Chinese restaurant in downtown Singapore, dancing in an exclusive nightclub, and probably sex in her hotel room with every conceivable form of latex barrier on hand. In a weak moment, Aqualung had agreed.

"Stand her up, dude, and come out with us." Lalo paced around the room, walking over ottomans, couches, stopping briefly at the window to flip open the blinds and scan the street.

"You never party with us," Sandra whined. She was shaping up to be a good whiner. It was a skill.

"Singapore isn't much of a party town, you know." He had never been here, but he had heard stories.

"That's why we thought you could handle it, grandpa," Britta said.

"All right, let me make a phone call."

"Who are you calling?" There was his date, standing in the door. Looking like a high society owner dating a wild rock star. Black leather mini, leather jacket with chains all shiny. Rodeo Drive meets Sturgis. She had an STD card around her neck. Britta's fashion statement had been catching on. They couldn't keep the home piss tests on the drugstore shelves anymore. They had become the ultimate in slut accessories.

"Sheila," Aqualung sidled over to her. "Change in plans. Forget the restaurant, we're going out on the town with the band."

"But we have reservations." Sheila looked around at the musicians with thinly veiled horror.

"Believe me, so do we," Sticks mumbled.

Aqualung steered Sheila out the door by her elbow. "We're going to rock this fucking town, Sheila. We're going to get ugly tonight."

Lalo and Fenner started in on the band's new favorite retro hit.

Let's get ugly, let's get mean
Let's have the best damn party this town's ever seen.
We got some ugly drunks,
We'll all pass out,
We'll show 'em what a good time is all about.

By their third nightclub, the band was uglier than the whole rest of the city put together. It was hard to believe Singapore was so close to Bangkok. They were a universe apart when it came to street life. Sheila was enjoying her foray into the gritty side of life so much because the grit was sanitized by numerous armed patrols. Singapore was not getting into the whole Unification thing. To Americans, Unification meant turning the rest of the world into America. Neiman Marcus for the well-to-do, McDonald's for the middle class, and street crime for everyone else. Everybody gets taken care of. Singapore had another system. Every creature comfort for the well-to-do and the rest of you just shut the hell up.

After trying to get something going at the first three places, pathetic, plastic excuses for clubs as they were, they persuaded Sheila to get them into the exclusive place she had planned to go to with Aqualung. The place was full of owners, young, successful execs, descended from all continents, all races of man, but all holding cash. Drugs were here, inside the protected walls where the very people who needed them could not see. The armed goons gave the nod. The rich kids seemed amused by the pharmacopoeia the Snake Vendors made disappear. They gathered around the band's table to watch the show, like kids in the monkey house. What are they going to do next?

Aqualung stuck to Scotch, but you would never know it. He was as animated as the rest. He even fooled Sheila, who took a turn at the straw just to fit in. He was guessing she would get frisky when she was high. She seemed like the type.

Britta was trying to get something going with a table full of bond traders from Lisbon. Some type of drinking game that involved removing clothing. She had a pile of ties on the table in front of her. She had to play carefully because it looked as though she may have only one article of clothing to lose, unless the shoes counted.

Fenner, Sticks, and Lalo were teaching another group of suits how to mosh. This was Aqualung's entertainment for the evening. Watching a dozen silver spoons crash into each other as Naked Mole Rat pounded from the speakers. Sandra somehow wheedled the DJ into giving her control of the sound rig, and picked through the extensive library in worm storage. She keyed up "Let's Get Ugly." Fenner and Lalo responded immediately, stomping and whirling through the rhythmically challenged crowd. Sticks, however, went wild. He had perhaps overdone it on the fine nose candy the better half had to offer. He abandoned the genteel moshing for some real ultra violence. Aqualung saw him pop some guy in the face. That wasn't cool. He disengaged himself from the increasingly amorous Sheila and tried to make it to Sticks before the beefy security goons got there first.

He didn't make it. Some gorilla laid a hand on Sticks's shoulder. A dark shiny something glinted in the dim light in Sticks's hand. A shot rang out and the mirror ceiling shattered.

Sticks was holding a hardened plastic, single-use, twelve-Teflon-projectile-firing weapon known in the States as a Dropper.

The other detainees in the police station didn't know quite what to make of them. Sticks was back in lockup somewhere, but six Westerners who didn't look rough enough to tip over a garbage can were quite a spectacle in the sparkling clean processing room. Lexan walls gave a clear view into and out of the room to the bustling police station.

"We need to make a phone call," Sandra whined. "We have to call the American embassy. You know, my father is friends with the ambassador to China." The man behind the lexan wall just stared back at her. He didn't even bother with the no-speak-English routine. Everyone spoke English these days. He just sat and ignored her.

Aqualung took out his window. "Give it up, Sandra. I'll call."

Sandra shook her head and held up her own window. "It won't work, Aqualung. They're jamming the signal."

"They can't jam this signal." Aqualung scrolled through his list and dialed.

"You've got a signal?" Britta asked. "You're calling the embassy?"

Aqualung made a rude noise. "Embassy shmembassy. What the hell can they do? I'm calling someone with some pull." He looked at Sheila and she nodded. "I'm calling the colonel."

"Well, the good news," Oswald was telling them, "is that the colonel can practice law in Singapore."

"Why is that good news?" Britta asked. They were sprawled in a lounge at the offices of some Thrasher subsidiary. They had been there for three hours waiting to see what had become of Sticks after the colonel had bailed the rest of them out.

"AIs make really good lawyers," Lalo told her. "That's why they don't let them practice in the States."

"We're going to cut a deal," Sheila said. She had sobered up in a hurry with the help of a fistful of antags and had turned out to be quite the crisis handler.

"What deal?" Aqualung spoke for the first time in hours.

"Sticks pleads guilty to the weapons charge and the disorderly, does ninety days and gets publicly caned, and the rest of us get to leave the country unchallenged."

"That deal sucks!" Fenner shouted.

"Fenner, calm down," Sandra pulled him back to his chair.

"No, he's right." Aqualung said. "That deal does suck.

What are they giving us? We can leave the country? Why wouldn't we be able to leave the country?"

"That's fine, Aqualung," Sheila said, disgusted. "Just show us your real passport and we can leave the country."

"I have a real passport."

"It's a bogus IIN. We all know it."

"No, it's real." Aqualung pulled out his passport. "I'm Dennis Dolinsky."

"The reporters tracked the name, 'Dennis,'" Sheila said. "There's nothing past ten years ago. It's a fake and we all know it."

"It's a good fake, though."

"You can't fool WebCense, you idiot. Those people don't play around. This isn't the Moon. WebCense has real power here."

"If I may interrupt," the colonel said from his monitor, "Aqualung's IIN is legitimate. I've accessed it. It is in the data banks. It was issued according to standard procedures."

"But it has to be bogus," Sheila said.

"I believe that his IIN will stand up to close scrutiny. If you are willing to take the risk, Aqualung, we can reject the deal."

"No deal, then. What can you do for him?"

"I think I can have the caning dropped if he serves the full ninety days."

"He won't get out in time for the Celtic Rock Festival," Sandra said.

"Or," the colonel continued, "he can take the caning and get out in thirty days. Which, I believe, would let him make the festival on the summer solstice."

"I think he should take the time," Aqualung said.

"What, and blow off the festival?" Fenner was incredulous. "We'll be onstage with Naked Mole Rat and Sex Lethal. It will be the hugest thing ever."

"Look," Aqualung stood up and began pacing. "We're

going to have to get another drummer to finish out the tour. There's no reason we can't keep the new guy for the festival. I think Sticks needs a rest, anyway."

"That's cold, man." Lalo said quietly.

"It's cold? What did Sticks do to us, here? He fucked us up good."

"He was just having some fun," Britta said.

"Yeah," Aqualung said, "having us some fun now."

Aqualung made it through customs without a problem. The international press was all over the story. Walter Cheeseman noticed the attention. Walter had a computer program that scanned media reports for references to WebCense being cheated. This program sifted through the thousands of jokes, Luddite diatribes, fictional exploits, and what-ifs to find the few kernels of actual fraud. The dozen or so remaining clippings were scrolled across his screen as soon as they appeared. It was a pretty smart program.

"Aqualung, eh?" He called up his chief of identification. "Lars, I'm zipping a news article over to you, do you got it?"

"Yeah, give me a minute to read it over." Walter never gave anyone a full minute to read something over, but he asked anyway.

"So what's going on there? Why'd they say he fooled us?"

"I'm punching in his IIN now. It was issued in Bethesda, Maryland. Ten years ago. It was backed up by a retinal scan, a blood sample, and a social security number. Looks fine to me."

"Red flag it anyway. Something tells me this is wrong."

By the time they reached Sydney, the Snake Vendors were whole again. Aqualung had flown to L.A., combed the studios for a stick man, and had flown back to meet the band with one Shadrick Townes. Shad was a black man in his mid-thirties who had put in more than his share of time behind a kit. He was a technician. He was perfect.

Aqualung was expecting a "Pete is Best" type of display from the crowd. He and Shad had planned a Ringo-style drum solo to start the concert, but there was no need. This was Australia. These people didn't give a shit who was sitting behind the band. They didn't care where the rhythm came from, they were there to party.

He actually had more trouble with the band. Everybody was still worried about old Sticks, stuck in that tropical prison. He had opted for the time. Caning was quite a humiliation for an American. Jail, he understood.

When Aqualung had introduced the band to Shad, they had glared at the older man. Well, Fenner glared. Britta openly sized him up and made it clear she found him lacking. Sandra wouldn't look at him. Lalo reserved judgment until he could hear the guy play. In the end, it was Oswald who had inadvertently pushed the rest of the band into accepting Shad.

"I have good news," the record company errand boy said, poking his shaven head into the band's dressing room.

"Come on in, Oswald." Aqualung waved him to a chair. "This is Shad. Shad, this little twerp is on team for the record company. Shad is going to play a little drum for us."

"Oh," Oswald said. "Maybe this isn't the best time."

"Spit it out, little man. We're a band, we don't harbor secrets."

"Well, I just heard that Larry Winters OD'd."

Larry Winters was the lead singer and driving force behind a long-lived funk and groove outfit called Helen's Dimension. The room was silent for a few seconds.

"Oswald," Aqualung said. "I thought you said you had good news."

"Well, sure, it's bad news for Larry, but now his whole band is going to be looking for work. We could reach out to his drummer. Gary something."

"Gary Nolan," Fenner said. "So that's how we're going to be? Picking up the pieces of other wrecked bands to replace our own broken parts?"

"No," Aqualung shook his head. "That's not how we're going to be. Sticks is sitting out a few months. Shad here is going to keep his seat warm. That's what a session man does. That right, Shad?"

"I play drums, I pick up a paycheck. When your man gets out of the slammer, I'm back to L.A. It's good work if you can get it."

Sydney was the second to the last date on the Snake Vendors Pacific Rim tour. The last date was Guadalajara, which had just been named the new capital of Mexico. Mexico City had finally been declared unfit for human habitation, the first major city in the world to receive that dubious honor. There were rumors of people remaining under the brown clouds, scratching some sort of living from the bleached bones of what had once been Earth's largest city. It could not have been much of a life.

Guadalajara, on the other hand, newly crowned and sanitized for your protection, rising under the guidance of nearby WebCense, was a jewel of a city. They had just built a new stadium/concert hall that held eighty thousand, which was the biggest hall the band had been called on to fill. Thrasher needed help to sell the tickets, and they looked, as they had to do more and more these days, to Aqualung to help them out.

The music industry was in turmoil. The listeners were not following neat patterns anymore, not taking the lead from the industry. The top three bands in the world didn't sound anything like each other. The Snake Vendors had a lock on the Feedback sound, guitar-laden R&B with a Latin rhythm backbone. That was nowhere close to the rapid-fire vocals and piledriver beat of Naked Mole Rat or the lyrical death chants of Sex Lethal. The usual crop of imitators swam in the wake of these big three, and a lot of other weird stuff was getting listened to, but not in Mexico. Nobody was selling tickets in Mexico. The country was ripe on the vine for the entertainment industry, as flush as it had been in years, but no one knew how to tap into the psyche of all that sweaty youth and get them to give up their disposable income.

Aqualung had two angles for Thrasher to move along. The first was Fenner, the macho stud in black leather. Mexico liked a good-looking tough guy with a chip on his shoulder. The second was Britta. If there was one thing Mexico liked better than a macho stud, it was a gorgeous blonde in a tight dress. The posters and Web pages advertising the gig showed Fenner and Britta in the foreground, Fenner with his bass slung low, Britta about to swallow her microphone. The rest of the band was barely visible behind them.

Eighty thousand tickets went on sale, and eighty thousand were sold.

"Where the hell is Fenner?" Oswald was probably having a nervous breakdown. Aqualung had never actually seen one, but he was pretty sure this was what one looked like. "Aq, you've got to start the Machine. We were supposed to go on almost an hour ago."

"Oswald, the most important thing in this whole business of entertaining people is timing. The Machine has a limited window," he explained. "If I leave it on too long, people get tired, irritable. The whole idea of the Machine is to get people in the mood for some live music. If we have to wait too long before the concert starts, the effects wear off and the whole thing is wasted. Besides, I don't know if this is a good Machine audience."

Oswald looked like a man who had just increased the amount of blood inhabiting his skull by a factor of ten. "But you have to use the Machine. We advertised it."

"Oh, I'll use it. But this crowd seems volatile. Having to wait for the concert isn't helping. They might be a little touchy."

"Don't," Oswald shook his finger in Aqualung's face, "tell me things like that. I don't need to know that. Just keep it to yourself."

"I just thought you might want to get the helicopter warmed up, just in case." That was a mean shot, but it got Oswald off his back. The A&R man beat a hasty retreat. What an unnecessary letter he was turning out to be.

"Where the hell is Fenner?" Now it was Britta's turn.

"I don't know. Sandra, you're awfully quiet. Do you have something to share with us?"

Sandra was practicing a new tune on her mandolin and keeping to herself on the far side of the dressing room. "He was online with some friends, earlier. They were talking about Larry Winters. He seemed pretty depressed. I didn't know he really liked Helen's Dimension, but he used to be in a band with their drummer. Crane Spreads Wings. They broke up last year. I don't know what they were talking about."

"When was this?" Britta shot at her.

"Yesterday morning."

"And you haven't seen him since?"

"I couldn't be around him. He was bringing me down."

"Oh, thank god," they heard Oswald say from out in the hall. Fenner stumbled into the dressing room.

"Let's rock and roll!" He grabbed up his bass and pulled the strap over his neck. He was high.

"Hey, Fenner, glad you could make it." Aqualung walked over to the younger man. "Enjoying yourself? What's your poison tonight?"

"Nothing, man. I'm ready to rock and roll! Let's go!"

Aqualung looked into Fenner's eyes. "You're Witching, aren't you?"

"Naw, fuck, man, I was Witching yesterday."

"He can't still be on it, can he?" Lalo asked.

"You get a weird strain, sometimes it can last longer than a day," Britta said. "I bet they got stronger stuff here in Mexico."

"Fuck, man, I know when I'm Witching," Fenner shouted.

"All right, let's rock and roll." Aqualung switched on the mini amp in the dressing room, tuned the station to Fenner's bass. "Give me a little 'Mojo.'"

"I'll give you a big fat mojo, old man." Fenner started thumbing the strings. The tune was unrecognizable, the rhythm all over the place. The Witch screwed with your sense of time. Spatio-temporal distortions, were what they called it.

"He can't fucking play." Lalo hung his head in his hands.

"Fenner, you idiot," Britta spat at him.

"What the fuck is your problem, bitch?"

"Fenner," Aqualung said, "if you had picked any other drug . . . If you had come here drunk, cranked, tripping, zooming, or half dead from a heroin overdose, we could have shot you full of antags and you'd have been up on stage like that." Aqualung snapped his fingers and Fenner flinched. "But we got no antags for the Witch. You can't play."

"Fuck I can't." But Fenner was starting to get the idea. He knew you couldn't make music on the Witch. He unslung his bass and sat on the couch.

Sandra, who had hung back until now, stepped forward, not looking at Fenner. "What are we going to do?"

"I can play bass," Aqualung said.

"We need a rhythm guitar for at least half the songs," Lalo said. "I can't pick up the slack on all of them."

"Sandra is a good rhythm guitarist."

Sandra hugged her mandolin. "I haven't played guitar since you joined the band. Not since Vegas."

Aqualung picked up his Les Paul and handed it to her. "You were good, though. You still are."

She stared at the ancient guitar for a few seconds. She set aside her mandolin and gingerly took it in her trembling hands like it was a talisman. Her fingers lightly brushed the faded trout painted on the front. She looked at Fenner for the first time.

"Rock and roll, baby," Fenner slurred.

CHAPTER 7

I stared into the candle's flame,
And strained my eyes to see,
I tried to talk to God that day,
But all I found was me.

SEX LETHAL, "ATMAN"
DOES BUDDHA HAVE A DOG NATURE?
PARANORMAL RECORDS, 2022

Quin had been summoned. He had been back from the southwest for two weeks, in which time he had become the world's foremost expert on Martin Grish. He had delved into Grish's recorded history, the story of a smart but twisted young man; had examined all known examples of Grish's code; and had explored all possible influences on Grish's life. Of particular interest was a record of a class Grish audited at the University of New Mexico on artificial life. The professor, still alive at seventy, did not recall Grish, but had supplied Quin with the syllabus and notes from the class.

Grish had taken the class just before getting involved with the Hot Zone. The focus of the course was the natural history of a tame computer virus that had been turned loose on the nascent Internet to grow and multiply like a life-form. Quin was betting that Grish had learned from this experiment the way to create the virus that grew into the Digital Carnivore.

And now, after three months of being ignored, the board

wanted to see him. He showed up on time, but, of course, was made to wait. This was how the American corporation controlled its workers, through carefully inducing boredom at key intervals. There was no pretty secretary to look at outside the boardroom, just some abstract paintings that meant nothing to him. He now knew better to find meaning or pattern in abstract art after his experience with Harmond's freaky vision.

Finally, he was called into the room. As he moved to the hot seat at the end of the table, he surveyed the group. Thirteen middle-aged white males, and three holographic icons depicting AIs. The *Des Moines Register* was completely right. There were no minorities in places of power in this company. Just a lot of old men and a hell of a lot of security guards.

"Taber, have a seat," Mr. North shouted at him from the opposite end of the table. "You're probably wondering what this is all about."

"There isn't a problem with the isolate?" He had not heard a thing about the computer since he had turned over the access codes to the board. He had assumed it was running smoothly.

"Oh, of course not. It's working out for us quite well. In fact, we've been so impressed with how you defeated the Digital Carnivore that we're now interested in your progress on your new project. We're starting to realize the potential of not just evading this virus, but of controlling it."

"Well, to be honest, I'm still a long way from controlling the Digital Carnivore. I have, however, learned more about it than anyone has ever found out before."

"Fill us in." Mr. North smiled jovially.

Quin attempted to smile back. "Well, I think I've discovered the author of the original virus that eventually grew into the Digital Carnivore. His name is Martin Grish. He's still alive, but he's been reprogrammed." Several of the men around the table winced. Reprogramming was said to be painless, but then again . . .

"I'm not sure I follow," said the VP in charge of operations. The computer guy. "How did the Digital Carnivore grow out of a virus?"

"Grish was a petty thief and a computer cracker who created viruses to fool bank computers into giving him money. He also studied artificial life, viruses that replicated and evolved on the Internet. I believe he created a virus that had the ability to evolve ways to invade other computers. This virus could acquire code from accounting programs and disguise itself to gain access to other computers. In a sense, his virus preyed on and ate other computer programs, so it was a digital carnivore." He briefly told the story of the Hot Zone and the scam they had concocted, concluding with the arrest and trial of the participants.

"So you say this Grish got his egg poached?" Mr. North asked.

"Yes, well put. He was found guilty of bank fraud in a scheme that was unrelated to the Digital Carnivore. In fact, it seems that during his first prison term he completely forgot about the virus. He must have thought it was a failure, because it had evolved beyond his original parameters by the time he was released. In order to find out more about the virus he created I've been studying his life. At the time he created this virus, he used to hang around in an Albuquerque nightclub called the Rio. Some of his associates from those days are still alive, but have been less than helpful. Apparently they're afraid of retribution from a criminal associate of Grish's, one Zoe Campbell." Quin was surprised to see a shock of recognition on several of the faces around the table.

"I know Zoe Campbell," Mr. North said. "They're right to be afraid of her."

"Yes, well, it seems that Mr. Grish may have had a

hand in the creation of a musical movement called Feedback, along with a band called the Animal Bones. There was a heavy influence of computer hardware and software in the music. And he was sent up the river by the lead guitarist in that band, a guy named Adrian Rifkin. I tried to track the band down, but they're apparently the unluckiest band in history. They're all dead, or disappeared. They had a song called "Digital Carnivore" that was mentioned in an Albuquerque free weekly newspaper. I don't have a recording of that song, and I haven't been able to determine if the song was named after the virus, which first appeared not long after, or vice versa. But this guitarist, Adrian Rifkin, and Grish were obviously close, according to the owner of the bar I mentioned. He had some involvement with the Hot Zone, anyway. They perpetrated a crime together, paid disc jockeys to play Animal Bones music on the air."

"And what happened to Rifkin?" the personnel V.P. asked.

"He disappeared, most likely murdered on orders from Zoe Campbell. I have no way of finding out what really happened to him."

"Zoe ordered him hit? You sure about that?" Mr. North asked.

"Well, I don't know. I wouldn't even know how to find that out."

Mr. North pulled a pad of paper in front of him and wrote on it. He gave the pad a shove and it sailed over the slick table to stop right in front of Quin. On it was a phone number and the name *Fred*.

"Call that number. Talk to Fred. Tell him you work for me. Ask him if there ever was a hit out on this Rifkin guy, and if anyone ever collected on the contract."

"Thank you."

"I don't know if that's going to help you. You say Grish and this rock star were close. It might be worth a look."

"Maybe. Sure." How do you know so much about hit men, Mr. North? And where do you know Zoe Campbell from? And by the way, where does LDL get its cash?"

"What else do you got?"

"That's about it for now. I think there's more evidence, but its locked up tight at WebCense."

"Don't fuck with WebCense, kid."

"I wouldn't dream of it, sir."

"It's too bad you just can't ask the Digital Carnivore about this shit," Mr. North said before dismissing him.

Of course, Quin could ask the Digital Carnivore. It was as easy as uplinking, which, by most estimates, was the most mentally demanding task humans could do. When he had been recruited by WebCense, they had determined that he was in that rare minority of people who could juggle the multiple sensory inputs required to maintain order in the Upper Shell. So he had been equipped with a dataspray, an enormously expensive piece of equipment that required an even more enormously expensive operation to implant. And so he had become an uplinker.

The dataspray was still in his head even though he had left WebCense under less than friendly terms. It turns out it was more expensive to extract the device than it was to build another one. They were getting cheaper and more commonplace by the day. He kept the vials in his subarachnoid space stocked with neurotransmitters obtained on the black market. Almost any remote terminal could be made to link up to the dataspray through microwave transmissions, but only a multiband helmet could feed enough information into it to reproduce the complex sensory environment of the Upper Shell. And multiband helmets were not easy to come by. Fortunately, Quin had had one built not long after he joined LDL, using his virtually bottomless expense account. He hadn't even had to justify the purchase. Now he finally had a legitimate use for the device.

Back at his office, he donned the black plastic dome that covered his eyes and ears but opened his mind to a world of sensory overload. Uplinking used a net connection wide enough to allow a semitractor trailer to make a U-turn, but Quin had all the priority he needed. Molly saw to that. When he made the link, his world exploded like the fourth of July.

Most everyone who thought of the Upper Shell at all, and there weren't many who had to, thought of it as a conduit for large chunks of data, or as a two-dimensional map of the Web. But uplinkers thought of it as a place, a three-dimensional environment unlike anything that existed in the real world. Here, data was converted into sensory input, and only a trained mind could make sense of it. Seven senses were used to convey information into his mind: sight, sound, smell, taste, touch, kinesthetic, and pain. Sight and sound conveyed the most information; smell, taste, and pain held the most emotional content; and touch and kinesthetic were for navigation. An AI could make sense of information on so many more levels than a human mind, but AIs, by all accounts, did not experience emotion. They had no sense of what was appropriate. A human could sense that something didn't fit. Humans could sense anomaly.

The best way to find the Digital Carnivore in the Upper Shell was to look for an anomaly.

A whirling vortex of information, a jagged rock in the stream of data, a bit of chaos in a world built of order, that was the Digital Carnivore's hallmark. Quin found it quickly enough. Getting it to converse and make sense was the real challenge.

A stream of gibberish was emitting from the anomaly. Only the occasional word made sense. This was how Quin's mind interpreted some of the data pouring off the Web's demigod. This and a smell of burning popcorn, a texture like the pelt of a wild animal. The vortex engulfed him as soon as he approached it. His mind tried to grasp for words. "Decision maker." "Organic peripheral." It had seen him. Quin sometimes wondered if the virus ever recognized him, the first human who had spoken to it. Probably not.

He tried to speak to it. There was no sense in small talk. "Do you know the name Martin Grish?"

"Requesting information. Martin Grish is the first one. The information he called money is sent back to him."

Complete sentences were unprecedented. Quin's heart started to beat a little faster.

"What about the name Adrian Rifkin?"

"File transfers will be made at forty-five-day intervals to account number zero-four-zero-three-zero-two-five-eight-seven-four-eight. Notification of transfers will be to hotzone@tantalize.cdc.com."

Quin was momentarily stunned. The Carnivore had never spoken so clearly before. He had obtained actual useful information. He tried to press on.

"What is the balance in this account?"

"To receive that information you must input pass code verification. Input the lyrics in the second verse of the fourth track on the album *There's a Monkey on My Back, But He's Good People*."

"Uh," he stammered, "Can you ask me another one?"

The Carnivore spoke to him in a new voice. "Fuck off, asshole. I'm going to trash your hard drive for trying to break into my program." Quin cut the connection himself before the Carnivore could inflict severe damage. He made it out in time.

"So," he spoke to the empty room. "That was the key. Just say Adrian Rifkin and you're in some password-driven subroutine."

"But you need to know the lyrics to a song to go further and get more information," Molly answered.

"All right, let's get those lyrics."

"I'm afraid I can't help you there, boss. There's no lyric sheet on file for that song, and the album isn't showing up in worm drive."

"What are you saying, the album doesn't exist?"

"Well, we know that *There's a Monkey on My Back, But He's Good People* is an album by the Animal Bones. The only Animal Bones songs in worm drive are a drinking anthem called "Let's Get Ugly," which is now making a comeback, and an instrumental called "Surfin' Tingley Beach.""

"The Animal Bones again. Very interesting. So I have to find the actual album."

Finding a copy of *Monkey* turned out to be about as difficult as finding the original code for the Digital Carnivore. Quin started by calling antique record stores. He had to stare into the face of at least five confused and bored teenagers before finding an older woman on his phone monitor who had actual information for him.

"Hoo, this is a rare one," she said. "It looks like that album was never released. Could be a demo floating around, but it'd be pretty expensive."

"So who's selling?"

"Nobody."

Quin didn't believe her, so he accessed the database himself once he had hung up. She was telling the truth. According to all of the available records, the album didn't exist. The studio at which the album had been recorded was now defunct and the existing records were pretty sketchy. There was only a brief mention of the master copy in a list of the studio's activities for 2010. Which was, of course, the year of the big investigation.

Adrian Rifkin had been squeezed by the FBI because the gang members of the Hot Zone had paid a local disc jockey to play some Animal Bones on the radio. Could be Rifkin was trying to drum up interest in his new, just-recorded album so he could make the leap to a major label contract. If so, the master disc for that album might become evidence in the case against Rifkin.

"Molly, I need you to get me some more stuff out of the FBI's records."

"I can get you anything but witness protection."

Quin had tried to get at the witness protection program files as soon as he found out that was where Rifkin had disappeared to after the trial. But those records were now a part of WebCense, and he refused to let Molly hack into WebCense. The only reason Molly was reminding him of it was that she still wanted to try to crack the security of what was reportedly the most secure system ever built. No way.

"What I need is all of the files pertaining to the case against Adrian Rifkin. Now, I already have the stuff on the case against the Hot Zone, but they must have built some case against Rifkin in order to squeeze him into testifying."

There was a brief pause. "OK," Molly told him. "I've got that."

"What do we have on our list of evidence? Any mention of a master for a record album?"

"Yes. *There's a Monkey on My Back, But He's Good People* is listed as physical evidence. It's in an archaic format called a compact disc. There was no mention of a digital master."

"OK, let's look at the chain of possession on that. Where is it now?"

"FBI Storage Facility thirty-six, in Quantico, Virginia."

"What kind of security on a facility like that?"

"Pretty high security. Are you thinking of scamming your way in?"

"Maybe I should hire it done."

"Well, Fred would know how to go about that."

Fred was Quin's new friend. He had called Fred the day after the board meeting, and he turned out to be the sunniest shady character Quin had ever met. Fred was willing to help in any way once Mr. North's name had been dropped. (And by the way, how did Mr. North know Fred?) It turned out that Zoe Campbell had never made the final payment on the hit, which Fred assured him was sure evidence that the hit had never taken place. Now, this did not mean that Adrian Rifkin was still alive. After all, the man had been a rock and roll musician, not a group that stood out on the actuarial tables as famously long-lived. But this was the best lead Quin had right now.

"I don't think we're desperate enough to engage in larceny just yet. Perhaps we should put it to the boards."

"If you're not desperate enough now, that should do it."

"That's very funny, Molly. Your sense of humor is developing nicely." Quin posted a message on the Web's shady side, known as the boards, filtered through several bogus addresses and screen names, asking for the lyrics to any Animal Bones song. There had to be at least one whacko out there who knew the answer.

"Animal Bones," Walter Cheeseman muttered.

"Excuse me?" Maggie Mandrasekran was still not used to Cheeseman changing the subject in mid-conversation, any more than she was used to him staring at her through the one-way monitor. She never knew if he was looking at her or at the data scrolling over the thin laminar flow of mica particles above his desk.

"Remember I was telling you about Quin Taber, how he's still suing us?"

"Ah, yes. How is that going?"

"I've been following his moves pretty closely. I'm convinced he's up to something. He's working for a company called LDL. They haven't registered anything with us, which almost guarantees they're crooked. He's made some interesting phone calls and travel arrangements recently. Now he posted a message on the boards about an Albuquerque band from 2010 called the Animal Bones. Seems he wants lyrics to their songs."

"And what does that have to do with the lawsuit?" And, by the way, what does it have to do with the new personality screening protocol we were just discussing? Maggie had not come any closer to actually enjoying Walter's company, in spite of her recent victories. Walter had summoned her last week. He had been invited to dine with several heads of state in New York. There would be more than a few holdouts to the Unification treaty in attendance, so it was an important dinner. His protocol people had told him that bringing a date to the dinner would enhance his position among some of the holdouts. So he had called Maggie, presumably to ask her to generate a psychological profile of the ideal woman for this important job. Maggie had pretended to misunderstand and accepted his invitation. He'd been a little too flustered, and maybe a little too relieved, to correct her mistake.

Now, the plan was to get photographed at this dinner with Walter. The newspapers would speculate, and she would feed the rumor that she and Walter were an item. One day Walter would activate his news-sniffing browser and find that he was engaged to his Profiling Department head. By then, she was hoping, he would just decide that the thing had a momentum of its own, so why fight it?

"It might not have anything to do with the lawsuit anymore," Walter said. "It looks like he's investigating something. Something that had to do with an FBI investigation in the 2K."

"Involving the Animal Bones?"

"Maybe. I'm going to see the bastard tomorrow. I might just ask him. That ought to shut him up for a few seconds."

"The hearing is tomorrow?"

Walter shook his head. "I can't believe the courts can waste my time with this. Listen, can we finish this later? I have to look up some things."

Maggie smiled. He was starting to defer to her a little, asking her permission to continue the meeting. He was not exactly putty, but things were starting to take shape. She felt a little ashamed, having used psychological warfare and dirty tricks to get where she was, but the feeling passed. "All right, I'll make those changes. I should have the revised protocol for you before you leave tomorrow."

"Yes, you should. Thanks for coming in, Maggie."

As soon as Maggie left, Walter phoned up Lars in the identification division. "Lars, do we have information from the FBI's witness protection program?"

"Yes, we do," Lars answered. "There was a big struggle to get it."

"Run this name through for me: Adrian Rifkin."

Cheeseman let a few seconds tick by before saying "What have you got on that, Lars?"

"It's coming through now, sir. The Bureau was building a case against a Martin Grish and company. They squeezed Rifkin, a musician, for testimony. They threatened to charge him with racketeering for paying a disc jockey to give him airtime. Anyway, he testified and was relocated to an electronics plant in Lowell, Massachusetts. Then he disappeared."

"What do you mean, he disappeared?"

"The FBI lost track of him after about a year. They assumed he got hit by the ones he testified against. They hit three other witnesses in the case."

"Why does the name Martin Grish sound familiar?"

"It isn't familiar to me. Do you want me to run him?"

"Please." Cheeseman drummed his fingers on the desk three times. "So who was he?"

"Here it is. He did some bank fraud in 2019 and was reprogrammed."

"Give me his accession number. I want to see what kind of information we squeezed out of his head before we zapped him."

There was something Quin had never understood, and that was the ritual of getting a ride to the airport. You could easily drive your own car and pay a little money to park, or take a cab, or take the monorail. You didn't get a ride to the grocery store, so why do you always have to get a ride to the airport? Because people like Janet insisted on it, that's why. Quin straightened his tie and stepped out of his private bathroom into his office, and there she was.

"Janet, what a surprise," Quin straightened up his desk. The only thing on it was a laser pointer. He put it in its laser pointer caddy.

"I thought I'd sneak in. I've never seen your office before."

"Well, the company is kind of funny about visitors." He shrugged.

"So where's Molly's office?"

"Molly?"

"Your secretary? I talk to her on the phone all the time, but I've never had a chance to meet her. She sounds very nice. Professional."

"Well, that's Molly all right. Actually, her office is on a different floor. I know, it sounds stupid, but this is the electronic age. Physical proximity is pretty much superfluous."

Janet put her arm around his shoulders and kissed him. "Not completely superfluous."

Quin disengaged himself. "Well, we had better get going."

"Hey, I just had a thought. You don't suppose Molly would like to come with us Friday night? Might be fun." They were going to try a nightclub on Friday night. There was a rumor that Sex Lethal was going to sneak into a little nightclub in their hometown and play a set in disguise. They had apparently gotten the idea from Blue Oyster Cult, who had masqueraded as Soft White Underbelly in order to play small rooms. Quin had snooped around and found out the rumor was true, and had found out which club it was. It was to be his reward for getting through the hearing at Transnational Arbitration Court. He needed one.

"Well, I don't . . ." Quin said.

"Don't want to fraternize with the help?"

"No, that isn't it. It's just that Molly wouldn't really . . ."

"She sounds like a fun person."

"Really, she isn't. Like you said, very professional."

"Well, on her work hours, sure. But you let her go home once in a while, don't you?"

"I just think that . . ."

"She'd feel like a third wheel on a bicycle, right? Of course. She doesn't want to tag along with us. Unless it was a double date. Is she seeing anyone? Maybe I can find her a man."

"Oh, that would be very interesting," Molly whispered in Quin's head.

They took Quin's car, because they actually had to get to the airport on time, and he had a fuel cell engine that could do sixty plus on the flat, straight Des Moines thoroughfares. Quin went over his legal arguments, typing on his little fold-out keypad.

"It bugs me when you do that," Janet said.

"What, the keypad?"

"Yeah. I mean, no monitor. I can just picture that machine in your head feeding you data. Do you see the inside of the car?"

"Sure," Quin said. "I just see a semitransparent window right here." He made a square in the air over the dashboard.

Janet shuddered. "I'm glad you don't use it often."

"It does tend to creep people out, and I hate to be conspicuous. Hey, what do you think about Cheeseman? Just as somebody who's never met the man, what's your impression?"

Janet shrugged. "Kind of a megalomaniac, I guess. I mean, he'd have to be. I guess the impression I get from the news stories about him is that, yes, he's out to run the world, but we can't get along without WebCense, so we're pretty much stuck with him."

"That's what I was afraid of. Judge isn't going to want to give me what I want if it interferes with WebCense doing its job."

Quin hadn't seen Walter Cheeseman, except in the darkest prison cell of his mind, and on the TV news, in over a year. Walter, of course, didn't betray any emotion when he nodded at Quin, and Quin returned the courtesy. *We're so much alike.* Quin thought, and felt a little sick.

Transnational Arbitration Court was in Geneva, Switzerland, and the four-hour flight from Des Moines had just about done Quin in. By the time he landed, his legs were so cramped he had to force himself to walk the mile and half to the airport entrance to work out the kinks. He was nervous. It had taken some very fancy legal maneuvering to get to this point, and he could blow it all with a misplaced word or a false gesture.

The hearing was in the judge's office. She wasn't in yet, so it was just Quin, Walter, and Walter's legal team.

Nobody said a word. Molly was feeding him everything she knew about the judge. They hadn't known who was presiding until they showed up this morning. The woman had a reputation for being anti-technology. That could end up working either way. Either she would want to take WebCense down a notch, to slow the advance of technology into our lives, or she would rather leave the beast alone, as long as it wasn't bothering her corner of the world. She would almost certainly need a careful explanation of the technical aspects of the case, but Quin was prepared for that. Very few people knew what WebCense actually did, or what the Digital Carnivore was, or what a meta-architect did for a living. It was to Cheeseman's advantage that the judge would have no prior knowledge of such things, and it was up to Quin to see that she understood the central issue.

The judge walked in, and before saying anything to the men seated before her desk, she said "Court recorder active." A sign on the front panel of her desk lit up, "Recording." She sat down. The men had barely time to stand before she waved them back to their seats.

"Good morning, gentlemen," she said. Her accent was Swedish, perhaps, or German. "This case," she started off, before they could answer, "is most unusual. Not just because it involves the head of WebCense, but because it contains at its heart a question of whether technology can be a form of nature. I've read your brief, Mr. Taber, and I have to say, for an amateur, it is quite good. You have no representation?"

"No, your honor, I'm representing myself."

"You have a fool for a client, then, but you also have a damned good lawyer. Mr. Cheeseman, your rebuttal is competent and thorough, but I still don't understand the case as well as I'd like to. Now ordinarily, I'd bring in some outside experts and have them tell me what this is about, but I understand that the only experts on this subject in the world are the plaintiff and defendant. Or, more to the point, either the plaintiff or the defendant, depending on how the case goes. Mr. Taber, as I said, your brief was very clear, but I'd like you to explain to me, without all of the legal jargon or computer jargon, or any other kind of jargon, just why it is you feel that your invention does not fall under the agreement you made with WebCense on the date of your hire."

"OK, ah, your honor. I was hired by WebCense as a meta-architect. What that means is that I was to design how groups of groups of computers could be connected together to make them talk to one another efficiently. When I started to do this job, I discovered that there was already a meta-architect at work on the highest levels of the Web. I found that restructuring, like the job I was hired to do, was already taking place constantly. I tracked down the source of this restructuring, and discovered the Digital Carnivore."

"That isn't true," Cheeseman spoke for the first time. "The Digital Carnivore had been known for years before Mr. Taber came to work for WebCense."

"I'm sorry, your honor, I oversimplified," Quin said. "What I should have said, was that I discovered that the Digital Carnivore was the meta-architect of the Upper Shell."

"Wait, now," the judge held up her hand. "What is the Upper Shell?"

"It's the only part of the Web that we can't control," Quin said. He pointed at the defendant. "Those are Mr. Cheeseman's words, by the way. It's a direct quote. We didn't know why we couldn't control it until I showed that an intelligence was at work in its design. People tried to describe the behavior of the Upper Shell with chaos theory and all sorts of higher-level mathematics, but they could not come up with the result I did. I recognized a pattern in the anomalies of the Upper Shell that were keeping us from fully controlling it, and that pattern was the result of an intelligence."

"What intelligence?" the judge asked.

"The Digital Carnivore," Quin said. "I discovered that it was sentient."

"You theorized that it was sentient," Cheeseman said.

"No," Quin said, "I proved it. And that's what this case is about. I went to Mr. Cheeseman, with my theory that explained the unexplainable behavior of the Upper Shell, and my ideas were dismissed. I had designed a simple tracking program that showed the pattern of changes occurring in the Upper Shell, and I analyzed that pattern, and showed the existence of an intelligence. I created a sort of a map of this intelligence that allowed me to communicate with the Digital Carnivore. As soon as I was able to prove that my map worked, I was reprimanded, so I quit. The technology was taken from me and used after I left."

"You did all this in your spare time?" The judge gave him a skeptical once over.

"Yes," Quin said. "It wasn't my job to try and find a way to control the Upper Shell, because it had been deemed uncontrollable."

"Mr. Cheeseman, is this map now being used to control the Upper Shell?" The judge was getting the hang of the jargon, after all.

"No, the 'map,' as Taber calls it, has no intrinsic worth. We didn't confiscate it, we tested it and discarded it. It was a flawed template. Mr. Taber has no expertise in describing or designing artificial intelligence."

"If he could get a look at my core architecture," Molly said inside Quin's head, "he'd have to change that argument. Here's a memo you might want to enter into evidence."

"Your honor, in reference to Mr. Cheeseman's statement, I have a memo to submit into evidence that directs the theory department to develop the map I created." Molly sent the memo to Cheeseman's lawyer's monitor and the judge's. "You will note that the accession number of the document is the same as the one on my original memo describing the virus which is already in evidence."

"How did you get that memo?" Walter had just enough time to get that out before his lawyer shut him up with a tap on his arm. The judge and the lawyer read through the memo in silence while Quin grinned across at Walter. *That's right, Cheese-boy, you just cracked out of turn. Keep it up and I'll get my day in court after all.*

"Your honor, in answer to that, the memo was sent to me in response to my original subpoena." Along with about a hundred terabytes of irrelevant garbage. It would take a search engine a year to sort out the good stuff. It took Molly ten minutes.

"Mr. Cheeseman, this memo says just what Mr. Taber said just a moment ago. That the map he mentioned could be used to control the Upper Shell."

Walter leaned over to confer with his attorneys. He finally looked up at the judge. "With a great deal of further development by the Theory Department, there is that remote possibility. But the whole idea is flawed and unusable in Mr. Taber's version. I have a memo from the Theory Department to me stating as much. It's here somewhere."

"But Mr. Taber's discovery is the root of their work in this area," the judge said.

"And the fruits of that work, whatever they might be, are what I have a claim to." Quin knew that didn't sound very good, but he was happy the judge was agreeing with him so far.

"Not so fast, Mr. Taber." The judge leaned back in her chair. "We still have to decide what this Digital Carnivore is. Under your contract, you have to surrender claim to any advance you make on someone else's technology, regardless of whether it is in your area of expertise, or whether your boss approved your working on it, or whether you developed this technology in your spare hours. Your brief makes an assumption that I frankly find hard to swallow. You state that the Digital Carnivore is not a technology at all, but a natural phenomenon. Now, it exists inside of computers, right? So how can it be natural?"

Quin appeared to consider this question carefully, although he had already prepared what he was going to say months ago. "The Digital Carnivore was not created by any human being," Quin said. "It was started by a human being, certainly. Possibly some prankster playing around with computer code many years ago. But it has evolved. The reason we know this is that nobody would ever design an artificial intelligence this way. It contains redundancies, useless, inactive subroutines, unexpected and totally bizarre aspects that are being discovered everyday. Experts in evolution have studied its structure and have determined that it has undergone mutation and selection, just like life. Therefore, it is a natural phenomenon."

"And yet it could not exist without human technology," the judge said.

"Neither could space travel, your honor. But in the case of *Heffler versus Deep Space Mining,* the cloud of discarded space junk orbiting the Earth was declared a natural resource that could be claimed and mined by individuals without legal ownership to the original materials."

"Good point. Do we have any idea where this intelligence came from?"

Quin shook his head. He knew, of course, but he didn't want to say. He suspected that Cheeseman had suspicions of his own, but the big Cheese remained silent as well.

"So we know it couldn't have been built by humans. Therefore it must be a natural phenomenon and therefore outside the scope of the contract. Nice."

Quin couldn't stop himself from grinning. He was

kicking ass in here. Walter betrayed no discomfort, of course, but that was just Walter. Maybe we're not so alike after all. Quin grinned all the more.

The judge excused herself to deliberate, presumably in her real office and not this oak paneled showplace. Quin crossed his legs when she left and smiled over at Walter and his lackeys.

"I smell a victory, Walter. I think we're going to go to court."

"Why don't you just let this drop, Taber? You're wasting my time."

"Then settle."

"For what? There's no money. We don't have anything that comes from you that's worth anything. There's nothing to settle."

"You just have to admit that the whole Digital Carnivore thing is my baby. That way, when this thing explodes and there is something worth something, the Nobel Prize committee will be calling me, and not you. That's all I want, really. Of course, if there ever is cash, I'd like some, but that isn't really what this is about."

Walter's face screwed up in distaste. It was the first emotion he had betrayed all day. "You're a foolish little man, Taber."

And that was it, really. The reason that Cheeseman would never settle this case, would never stop the fight. Because then he'd have to admit that someone else had got to an idea before he did. He would have to admit publicly that he was not the one who had discovered the Digital Carnivore, though he had claimed that discovery in countless interviews. That would be worse than losing any amount of money to a man like Walter Cheeseman. He was the man who was on top of things. The world looked to him to make technology work. If he had to give up even a small particle of that power he held, to a foolish little man like Quin, it would just kill him.

Now, Quin had his number. If nothing else went his way in this case, at least he had that. He knew what made Cheeseman tick.

But that wasn't the only thing that went his way. The judge came back with a trial date. The next time the two of them came together in the same room, it would be in front of the cameras. And Quin would bury the big Cheese.

"Hello, Molly, this is Janet. Is Quin available? He said he could be reached at this number." It was 3 a.m. Des Moines time. Janet had to work in the morning, but she found she couldn't sleep not knowing the outcome of the hearing. She was a little surprised to get Molly on the phone.

"No, sorry, he's still with the judge."

"Still? I wonder if that's good or bad."

"It's going pretty well. The judge likes him."

"Wait, you aren't there, are you?"

"Oh, no, of course not. He just called me."

"Does that man ever let you sleep?"

"I don't mind. This hearing is important to him."

"You know," Janet said, "that's what I don't get. Quin doesn't need the money, he doesn't seem like the type to seek out recognition. And let's be honest, only about five nerds in the world are going to care if it comes out that Quin discovered that this virus thing is alive. So why this lawsuit?"

"He's doing it because he hates Walter Cheeseman," Molly said.

"That's the part I can't understand. OK, so Cheeseman stole his idea and fired him. That's bad, I agree. But Quin seems pretty well adjusted otherwise. He doesn't seem obsessive. Why does he want to destroy Cheeseman? You've known him longer than I have. Any insights? I'm sorry, it's late. I should let you get some sleep."

"Oh, that's fine. I can't sleep anyway. I think it had something to do with Quin not having a father. Like he tried to make Cheeseman into his father. And then it turns out that Cheeseman is just this rat, and so Quin has to lose his father all over again. Does that make any sense?"

"Wow," Janet said. "That's an amazing insight, Molly. He must tell you things he doesn't tell me."

"Well, maybe a few things," Molly said.

"That's an area you and I have to explore further someday. Maybe he's said something about me? We'll have a coffee together sometime."

"That sounds great, Janet."

"Now, if you could only tell me something about his mother."

"I think you need a court order to get to the bottom of that whole business."

"She really did a number on that boy, didn't she?"

CHAPTER 8

Open your mind, let out the fear.
Open your heart, let out the pain.
Open the vein, let out the light.

PANGEAN PRINCESS, "LET IT OUT"
MIND WRITER, PIPEDREAM RECORDS, 2012

Aqualung was back in Nevada for his vacation. He had gotten his Harley out of storage and was letting it unwind up State Highway 375 toward the town of Rachel. He had been heading back to Ely, but he had seen a sign for the Extraterrestrial Highway and couldn't resist. They hadn't called this road by that name for years, but a few signs survived. Now that the extraterrestrials were a bunch of Felixes living in a space station and making drug-filled buckyballs, the Extraterrestrial Highway didn't sound so romantic.

Ely would have been a bad idea. He realized that now. There were people living in Ely who knew him as Harold Hammerande. He dressed differently now, and kept his mane of hair out of his face, but they would definitely recognize the bike. He hadn't had a plan when he flew back from L.A. He just wanted his bike. The actual bike that had inspired the hit song that everyone wanted to hear again and again. He hadn't brought it with him to L.A. because you literally couldn't get gasoline of any kind in the state of California. Marijuana was sold from vending machines, cocaine was hawked openly on street corners, but get caught with a gallon of no-lead and you faced jail time. What a country.

But Nevada was still a savage land. He had been accused of Nationalism when he said that to the colonel during their little talk about the "Fenner situation." The colonel was now pretty much in charge of dealing with the talent aspect of Thrasher's business, largely because he was the only executive who had a rapport with a major star. Aqualung had met him in a viewing chamber, which was the closest thing an AI had to a private piece of real estate in the corporeal world.

"I'm sorry if I appear to be a bit out of sorts, Aqualung," the colonel had begun. "I have been deprived of one of my modes of sensory input. The camera in this room is malfunctioning, so I cannot see your face. I may not be as capable as I normally am at determining your meaning."

"They can't fix the camera?"

"I've put in a work order, but it has received a low priority due to a climate control malfunction on the second floor."

Aqualung stood and walked over to the window that hid the camera. "You know, these things are pretty much solid-state. Probably not the camera at all." He pulled the window out and reached into the small space between the camera and the wall.

"Are you sure you know what you're doing?"

"Just a loose connection. How's that?"

"It works now. Thank you."

"Sure. What did you want to see me about?"

"It's about Fenner. He ended up costing us money in Guadalajara."

"Shit happens."

"I'd like to know if you are doing anything about the situation."

"No, I'm not."

"I thought perhaps some fatherly advice . . ."

"I'm not his father. I'm not going to tell him or anyone else how to live their lives."

"You seem determined not to affect the lives of the people around you. Yet that is precisely what you have done ever since you appeared in Las Vegas. You've taken this group of unmotivated musicians with no chance of success to the pinnacle of stardom. Why are you reluctant to preserve their lives?"

"What, would I be preserving their lives, or preventing them from living their lives? Who's to say how long a life should be? They should live the way they want to and let it take them as far as it will."

It had been a pretty good speech. Now he wasn't so sure. Another shining star had winked out. A woman who might have been his friend, had she lived a bit longer.

Dana Woods had been worshiped the world over by Nationalists for vocally protesting the Unification and by people who liked dark, moody music. Their sleeper hit "Micronational," which was simply a recitation of all of the names of all of the countries of the world set to a funeral beat and minor chords, had started the movement, three years ago. There was now talk that Dana had been assassinated, but there would always be talk about things like that. The truth was, like so many fragile geniuses, she had not been able to withstand the pressure of the nearly instant stardom the world offered. Her staggering success at selling albums was fueled partly by the new globalization of culture that she so hated. It was too much for her, and she had ingested a dose of buckshot that was not recommended.

The band took it pretty hard. None of them listened to much Sex Lethal when they were together, but their music was the kind you listened to when you were alone. Looking around his apartment at these lost kids who would, in short order, be ripped to the tits and trying their damnedest to kill themselves before they lost another hero, Aqualung had suddenly been taken with the urge to beat feet out of L.A.

So he found himself back in Nevada. The heat hit him from both directions, from the fiery noon sun and the melting blacktop. There were no extraterrestrials on this highway. They had turned out to be nothing but a mass hysteria, an urban legend, a modern fairy tale. But if and when the ETs did arrive, we would speak to them with one voice.

What voice would it be?

He pulled into a gas station north of Rachel and drank in the smell. He had lived his life around machines, and the smell of their life blood was sweet nectar. He eased himself off the ticking bike and limped into the station.

"Nice bike," said the man behind the counter. He got a lot of that. The tank was painted with white bones over a jet black field. A fetish of raven feathers and porcupine quills hung from the left handlebar. It had no other adornments. No fairing, no fenders. It was no garbage wagon. Just a sleek, low, chopped road bike.

"Thanks," Aqualung said. He got a Coke out of the cold box, threw his card on the counter. "Rance Packwood" was the name on the card. He had not done much with Rance lately. Old Rance had been sleeping in a tattered shoe box for almost five years.

Out of habit, Aqualung scanned the magazine rack. Dana's OD was the top story on a lot of the monthlies and the weeklies hadn't been updated in this little town. He started flipping through a *Spin* to get a look at the charts.

"I got the new one in," the counter man said. He took a buck knife to a bundle on the floor and kicked a small pile toward the rack. "This bastard looks like you, don't you think?"

True, his picture was on the cover. Underneath was the

headline: The True Identity of Aqualung. He studied it for a few seconds. Well, he thought, maybe they had the secret now. He knew they would dig it up sooner or later. That die had been cast the day he had stepped out of the Nevada desert and brought life to a dying band. He picked up the mag and flipped to the article by a guy named Sydney Bishop. He started reading it.

There has been a lot of speculation about the origins of Aqualung since the Snake Vendors' nearly instant rise to stardom. The big question is: "How could a man with so much talent remain unknown for over fifty years?" I believed from the start that he was not, in fact, unknown at all. I believed that he was actually a famous musician from the past in disguise. My colleagues, of course, thought I was crazy, but I persisted in this notion. To track down his real identity I employed a powerful computer search engine. I tried matching his voice print with every singer in the most complete worm drive available. No luck. This analysis took all of three weeks of supercomputer time and exhausted half of my budget. Undaunted, I forged ahead with a comparison of guitar styles. There, I got a match.

Before I reveal the name (oh, who am I kidding? You've already scanned ahead, haven't you?) let me take you back to the turn of the millennium. Rock and roll as we all know it was gone. Replaced by an odd mix of R&B, hip-hop and soul. Black music, if you will.

White music, everything from heavy metal to punk to good old AOR, had fallen victim to a most peculiar disease: an epidemic of artistry. It seemed that every time a white musical group made it big, they immediately made themselves inaccessible to fans. On purpose. They did this in an effort to avoid the appearance of selling out, which was synonymous with making listeners happy. It was an odd story, repeated time and time

*again, of a group of dreamers struggling to make it big,
then turning their backs on the very people who got
them there. Mainstream rock was supplanted by "alternative," which was in turn supplanted by alternatives to
alternative.*

*The record industry didn't know which way to jump.
They stopped signing bands, having been burned too
many times. They held their breath and waited for
someone to show them the Next Big Thing.*

*That someone was a group of computer geeks in the
Southwestern desert, and the Next Big Thing was Feedback. The pioneers of Feedback had a very simple idea.
Give the people what they want. Of course, hip-hop
had been doing that all along, but Feedback had a fresh
take after all. Don't just give the people what they want,
give them what they really want. That meant listening to
the listeners, during a concert if need be. Audiences
used their cell phones to text message instant reviews
during the shows, the bands read the reviews, and the
music was mutated and altered to match their tastes
and moods. At the end of the show, you could slot your
card into a vending machine and get a recording of
your perfect song, chosen and shaped by you and your
peers.*

*The idea caught on everywhere, and Feedback swept
the music industry like a wave. Music has never been
the same since. Not since Les Paul bolted some electro-
magnets to a plank of wood and invented the electric
guitar has one idea so utterly changed music.*

*When you think Feedback, if you are like most peo-
ple, you thing Pangean Princess, or the Cassandras.
But at the center of this sea change was one band, the
Animal Bones. The Bones were, by all accounts, the
first band to formalize the Feedback concept. Then why
didn't they make it? Some say the true Feedback sound
never really translated to recorded formats. Bullshit.*

The Bones never made it big because their lead gui-
tarist made a huge mistake. Adrian Rifkin used under-
world contacts to pay disc jockeys to play Bones music
on the radio. He got caught, and he testified against the
gangsters, and he got shipped off to witness protection.
Some say the mob got him, but most of us liked to be-
lieve that he was still out there, and that he'd get a sec-
ond chance.

Well, he did. For anyone who's been to a Snake Ven-
dors concert knows that Feedback is back and better
than ever. The Machine is to the cell phone what the
stringless guitar is to the "Log" of Les Paul. And Adrian
Rifkin has learned something during his twenty years in
exile. His new band, the Snake Vendors, has reached the
peak of stardom.

Here's hoping he manages to stay there this time.
And here's also hoping that the mob isn't still after
him.

"Hey, Lalo, how are they taking the news?" He had
stepped outside to talk. It looked as though the counter
man was starting to make the connection between the
face on the magazine and the man on the cool bike.

"You mean it's true?"

"Yeah, it is."

"You're my hero. I mean, you were my hero before, but
as Rifkin you're my hero from way back. Why didn't you
tell me?"

"I should have. I don't know. I didn't really have a plan
when I started. I just wanted to play again."

"So you've been in the witness protection program all
this time?"

"No. I'll tell you the whole story next time I see you.
Look, I'm gonna stay incog for a while."

"Hey, I understand."

"Try to calm the bosses. Tell them this is good press, me disappearing. Good drama. I'll see you on stage at the Celtic Rock Festival."

"Yeah," Lalo said. "That is good drama."

Molly grabbed the story off the wire and shot it to Quin's desktop instantly. He read the article with a feeling of elation welling inside him. Adrian Rifkin was alive.

"Where are the Snake Vendors playing next?"

"At the Celtic Rock Festival in Edinburgh," Molly answered. "The tickets are only available by lottery. They've been gone for months."

"And?"

"Would you like to take Janet with you? I think she'd enjoy it."

Walter Cheeseman had another program that scanned stories from the press and cross-referenced them with anything that had been pulled up from his browser in the past three months. The matches it came up with were placed into a queue that he eventually got to by the end of the day. Highest priority was a match of a news story with two unrelated items that had crossed his desk. This was called the coincidence detector. The coincidence detector was flashing when he returned from a confusing lunch with Maggie Mandrasekran.

The article would not be published in electronic form for several hours. The print copy always made it out first. Magazines still held to that, despite all that WebCense did to discourage it. Something about the power of the free press.

But WebCense had access to the computer data bases of all the major publishers. The article appeared floating over a desk that would never see a sheet of paper. The names Aqualung and Adrian Rifkin were highlighted.

He scanned the article. On the surface, it should mean nothing. But he had just been poring over the brain drain record of Martin Grish. It was from the early days of the technology, and the data were considerably fragmented. But there were an inordinate number of references to two things, the Digital Carnivore and Adrian Rifkin. He had dismissed this as the ravings of a man in the throes of re-programming, but now a new puzzle piece joined these bits into something that was almost recognizable. Aqualung had probably managed to fool the Identification Division in a way that only the Digital Carnivore could facilitate. Aqualung was Adrian Rifkin. Martin Grish was possibly obsessed with Rifkin. Quin Taber was interested in Martin Grish and Adrian Rifkin, and Quin Taber was certainly obsessed with the Digital Carnivore.

So what was the big picture? Did Aqualung/Rifkin have a hand in the creation of the Digital Carnivore? Is that why Taber wanted him? It seemed worth checking out.

He called the Squad. There were two ways they could bring this Aqualung/Rifkin to him. Either alive and willing to cooperate, or with his head in a Dewar of liquid nitrogen. The technology dealing with the extraction of information from brains, living and preserved, had advanced considerably in recent years.

Zoe Campbell was the oldest inmate at the Harrington Maximum Security Federal Penitentiary. She was proud of that. She was also proud of the nickname she had earned in the yard. They called her the Spider Lady. She knew it was partly because she physically resembled a spider, thin, black, and wrinkled. That wasn't the part she was proud of. She was also called the Spider Lady because she lay at the center of a large and intricate web of information. It was pretty safe to say that she knew everything. She no longer wielded much power in the criminal underworld from her confinement, but she still knew what was going on. And that information could be used to loosely shape events, form alliances, eliminate enemies. But only if she used it sparingly. Despite her formidable gang of bodyguards, she was vulnerable in the prison. If she became a thorn in the side of a powerful crime boss, she would become expendable. The longer she avoided that, the longer she would remain the oldest inmate at Harrington. Her goal was to become the oldest inmate in the Federal Penitentiary System. There were just three ahead of her, but she was too proud to have them bumped off.

She learned very quickly about the true identity of the famous rock star. She scanned an online news browser for at least two hours a day to pick up tidbits of information such as this. Of course she remembered Adrian Rifkin. He was the one who put her and her associates in prison. Her associates turned on each other for the privilege of a lighter sentence and often a shiv in the kidney. In the aftermath, Zoe herself was given seven consecutive life sentences for various murders. And Rifkin had started it all.

She had ordered the hit as soon as she heard Rifkin's damning testimony. But he was under the protection of federal marshals at the time and proved unreachable. Then the FBI had disappeared him. Her bloodhounds had tracked him to an electronics plant in Lowell, Massachusetts. She found out later that they had missed their prey by just two hours. Something they had done had set off alarms and Rifkin had given them the slip. Her contacts in Witness Protection, a precious resource, had claimed that Rifkin had given the FBI the slip as well. This time the bloodhounds could pick up no scent. Rifkin was truly an invisible man.

Until now. This magazine article made a pretty convincing argument that a rock star named Aqualung was in fact her arch nemesis.

The e-mail she sent out seemed innocuous enough to get

past the warden's office. They probably knew she was sending coded messages this way. They probably also knew that
if they stopped the flow of information, people close to
them would get hurt. There was an understanding.

The message hidden between the letters on the screen
were simple. Finish the contract.

CHAPTER 9

Don't you try to tell me
your day in the sun
Was better than my time,
I know how to have fun.

NAKED MOLE RAT, "MY TIME"
DOG AND PONY SHOW,
METAMORPHOSIS RECORDS, 2027

If the Celtic Rock Festival had been billed at all, it would have been billed as the Woodstock of the twenties. Dozens of the world's biggest bands, including the Snake Vendors, Sex Lethal, and the hosts, Naked Mole Rat, were going to be there for three days of music. People were going to be flying in from all over the world to take part in it. It was going to be the cultural event that would define a generation. And it was going to be held in Edinburgh in June, so there was a good chance it was going to rain the whole time.

But the Celtic Rock Festival was not billed as anything. The concert was free; the tickets were available by lottery; the cow pasture, the equipment, the talent, were all donated. Even the food was to be given away. Only the airlines and the lodging industry stood to make a dime off the festival.

While Thrasher and the rest of the record companies pretended that they wanted no part in this tasteless festival of archaic socialism, they were probably waiting to capitalize on the free publicity the event would no doubt generate.

In an effort to maintain some order, the talent was housed in a little town across the Firth of Forth called Kilrenny. Not only was the location kept a secret, the fact that there was a secret to be kept was kept a secret. The fans who streamed into the barely adequate hotels, boarding houses, dorms, and tent cities of Edinburgh had no idea that the bands were staying elsewhere. So the musicians could sit outside a pub on a cool evening and enjoy some peace and quiet two nights before the show began.

Fenner had never gotten the hang of social drinking. To him the minutes that lay between sober and shitfaced were an awkward, anxious time. But he was now hanging with Dennis McColoch himself. And Naked Mole Rat had a completely different idea of partying. They put away an enormous quantity of bitters, but they paced themselves and never broke anything or raised their voices. They played the genial hosts to the other world-famous bands. Now that the Snake Vendors were listed among them, they had to learn to fit in.

"So where the fuck is your singer?" Dennis asked.

"He said he'd be here," Fenner said, a little defensive. "That's good enough for me."

"You guys believe that shit? Adrian Rifkin. I was sure he was dead."

"I always felt like he was still around," Lalo said, lifting his glass. "I used to listen to the Animal Bones when I was a kid. I collected their tracks. What a waste."

"You think he's got any tapes of the Animal Bones stashed away?"

"Those would be fucking gold," said the lead singer of Rebelution, Duc N'guyen. "I used to collect tracks, too. They told us they were ours to keep. Then they came up with the next great technology and, hey, we're not going to support those formats anymore. Those files of yours are useless. Now you only get to hear what we decide to transfer over to worm drive."

Lalo shook his head. "There are converters around. It wouldn't take much to transfer the rest over."

"But then the music collections of the rich and famous would be worth nothing," Sandra said. "My parents had a friend who bragged about his collections. Vinyl, disc, and tape. He never even listened to them. It was just the idea that he could but no one else that made them valuable. Not like he needed the money, and not like it was even real money. It was the idea."

"Let me tell you something, man," Dennis said. "There are owners, and there are renters." He leaned back and spread his arms, about to launch into one of his favorite speeches, and his hand struck an object leaning against the table. "What the fuck is this?" It was a battered guitar case, grimed with crankcase oil and road dust.

A chair scraped back and a glass of Scotch entered the feeble circle of light, followed by a weary face.

"So what are we talking about?" Aqualung said.

"Aqualung?" Fenner sputtered out. "What, is that what we call you now?"

"So you made it, you old son of a bitch," Dennis said.

"Wow," was all Lalo could say.

"I'm fifty-two years old," Aqualung began his story, "and I'm on my fourth name. I've had a few dozen others, here and there, but as for living consistently, day to day, I've had four names that I answered to. Adrian Rifkin was the first, but, I've got to tell you, I can't really think of myself as Rifkin anymore. First of all, Rifkin did something I'm not proud of. He cheated to get his records sold, he got into bed with some mean bastards, and he ratted on people who called him a friend. And second of all, I've lived twenty years as somebody else.

"When the trial was over, I asked for witness protection. I helped put away a lot of people, so they said OK. In order to make it stick, they told me I had to give up music. That was fine with me. I'd had it with the music business. I knew the Animal Bones had the talent, but I was too impatient to let it happen. I saw too many people with talent get passed by for bands without any. So when they asked me to choose my new career, I did the thing I'm probably second best at, electronics.

"They set me up as a technician in an electronics plant in Lowell, Massachusetts. I was Steve Drabkin. I pretty much grew to hate Steve Drabkin. He was a real nobody. Short hair, boring face. They did my nose, you know, so the crooks I testified against wouldn't recognize me if they ran across me. And they nicked my vocal cords. That was the only good thing. It actually improved my singing voice. Not that I could use it anymore.

"Anyway, I only kept that name for a couple of years. I'd studied up on the mechanics of changing identities during the whole relocation process, and I gave myself a couple of new names, just to practice what I'd learned. I kept it to myself, what I was doing. No need letting the FBI caseworker in on it, I figured. There's a couple of ways you can do it. One is to pick a guy your own age who's dead and pretty much take his identity. You get an official birth certificate, Social Security card, start paying for credit cards, you get a new driver's license, passport. Of course it won't stand up to scrutiny, but, hell, who scrutinizes your identification? You've got good credit, who the hell cares?

"The second way is to build an identity. That's a lot harder. I didn't figure that out until years later. You have to break into computers and shit. So I just made up a few phony names and sent them in envelopes to post office boxes around the country. Just in case.

"Then, one day, on my way home from work, I stopped at a gas station and I saw a guy there that I had seen in Albuquerque. He was in the gang I'd gotten mixed up with, the Hot Zone, but he hadn't been indicted, for whatever reason. It could have been a coincidence. He could have been there for any reason, but I guess I panicked. I took all my Steve Drabkin IDs, credit cards, everything, and dropped it in the car and walked the hell on out of there with just the cash in my pocket. I didn't stop until Alaska. I literally ran all the way to Alaska. Later I thought I'd gone crazy, but I felt a lot safer now that nobody knew who the hell I was.

"I worked for two summers in a fish cannery in Kenai. Grew my hair back out. Made myself a couple of new identities and just started bopping around the country. I even spent a year in Amsterdam on a bogus visa. Finally, I settled down in Ely, Nevada. I opened up an electronics repair shop. I was Harold Hammerande, aging Dead head, conspiracy theorist, UFOlogist, and sometime motivational speaker. I fixed computers, I fixed air conditioners, I fixed slot machines. Sometimes I 'fixed' slot machines. I was Harold for fifteen years.

"I still don't know why I went back to Albuquerque. I guess all the crooks who were after me were long gone, and nobody would recognize me. It was just such a fucking disappointment. It was all different. The clubs I used to go to were gone. The new clubs had this music I didn't understand. It was a bad trip. Until I walked into a pawn shop and saw this up on the wall." He stroked the guitar case.

"I don't know how it got there. Probably had a few owners in between when I gave it up to be Steve Drabkin and when I found it again. But they had taken good care of it. When I held this guitar in my hands I knew I had to make music again. It was the first time since the trial when I felt something was more important than life. You guys probably still have that feeling. It's something you have when you're young. I stopped being young when I signed my own death warrant by testifying against Zoe

Campbell and Martin Grish. I didn't think making music would make me young again. But it did."

"What are you reading, nerd boy?" Janet jabbed Quin in the ribs with her elbow. He dropped his magazine under the train seat and bent down to get it.

"Thank you very much," he said. "You know, I brought you on this trip because I thought you were low maintenance. If I had known you were going to require constant attention, I'd have invited one of my other girlfriends."

They were having a great vacation. Quin had heard once that if you want to decide if you can spend the rest of your life with someone, you should first travel with them. So far, so good. They both traveled light, arrived at the airport minutes before the plane took off, spent minimal time in the hotel, and took no guff from foreign cab drivers.

"Yeah, maybe Molly would have come with you if you paid her a big enough bonus. So whatcha reading?"

"Article about computers."

"Yeah?"

"Yeah, what?"

"I'm not a monkey over here. I can understand stuff about computers. Tell me what its about. What's so absorbing?"

"OK. This company on the Moon, IDEX Technologies, has just made a new kind of computer. Like an artificial intelligence, only better."

"Better how?"

"Well, so an artificial intelligence takes years to make, it's programmed, piece by piece, by humans. Then, they activate it in an isolated computer and let it mature. They feed it data and monitor it carefully, and it's like having a child, because as soon as it's ready, two, three years, they let it go. If it turned out OK, if it matured properly, it can go out and find a job. Hopefully, a high-paying executive-type job, so it can send a cut of all its earnings back to the programmers. If it can't cut it as an executive, if it doesn't have the people skills that are hard to put into an AI, it gets a lower-paying job and the programmers get a lot less. Some AIs can't even cover their own overhead, but since it's illegal to disconnect them, they end up costing money."

"Have you ever made an AI?" Janet asked.

Quin hesitated for a second. "No, too risky. I've consulted on file transfer stuff."

"So how is this Moon computer better?"

"Its personality and skills are baked right into the hardware. It's designed by a team of humans and AIs, and it didn't take any time at all to mature. And its personality was guaranteed. No suspense, no gambling. They call it a superintelligence. This is going to revolutionize the computing world. If, that is, they play it smart."

"What's the catch?"

"The catch is that IDEX hasn't registered this superintelligence with WebCense. According to the Artificial Intelligence Act, they have to register it as soon as it can stand alone, which it could do from the second it was switched on. IDEX has found some loophole in the law that lets them refuse to register. It's going to be a big blowup. Lunar authorities, if you can call them that, won't enforce WebCense's ruling."

"So, I guess WebCense can't just march in there and shut this thing off?"

"No, the Moon is a funny place. The community is very active, very intelligent. They don't take to being herded around like the people down here."

Just as he said that the train pulled into the station and everybody on board, all headed for the third and final day of the concert, filed out and into the Scottish rain to be shepherded to the venue.

There was a buzz in the crowd. Quin and Janet had tried to arrive early to get the best possible seats for the closing of the festival, but it turned out that early for this show was about three days ago. The best seats belonged to the people who had never left the cow pasture. They ended up about three quarters of the way from the stage to the edge of the crowd. It would have to do, for now. This was a free concert. There was no such thing as a backstage pass. Quin would have to think of some way to get to Aqualung. He had found no chance so far, and this day was his last chance.

"I think we're the oldest people here," Janet said.

"No way," Quin pointed to a shriveled man a few yards away. "Look at that guy."

"I'll bet he's twenty years old. He's just had a hard life." She took a deep breath. "Do you think we'll get high off of secondhand smoke?"

"That I could handle. I just hope I don't get a case of secondhand Witch off of a dirty toilet seat."

"That's impossible. Anyway, I hear we're supposed to experience something that goes beyond drugs later this afternoon."

"The Machine."

"I heard some kids talking about it while you were arguing with the ticket guy. You want to hear the rumor?"

"Dish."

"Well," Janet said, leaning in as if to share a great secret, "apparently, Thrasher records actually owns the bulk of the special equipment that makes up the Machine, while Aqualung slash Adrian Rifkin owns the software that runs the whole thing. And Thrasher has nothing to do with this concert, so people weren't sure if the Machine would be here. But, the shipping container that contains all of this special equipment that has been following the band on tour these past few months was suddenly rerouted from a storage facility in Baltimore to Edinburgh. Nobody knows who made the call. Only top Thrasher execs have that power, and they all deny it. So now Thrasher is threatening to charge Aqualung with theft, and meanwhile, nobody knows where Aqualung is. He's totally disappeared after the story of his true identity came out. But the band insists that he promised he'd be here. So, nobody really knows if the Snake Vendors or the Machine will go on at all."

As usual, Molly was eavesdropping on the conversation through the cellular phone in Quin's pocket and commenting through his dataspray during this story. Fortunately, Quin was used to sensory overload. "The order to reroute the shipping container comes from a Thrasher exec they call the colonel. He's an AI. I suspect that it's all a publicity stunt."

"I seem to recall hearing that the Machine wouldn't work in an outdoor venue," Quin mused.

"I guess we're going to find out," Janet said.

"Actually," Molly said, "they seem to be setting up the Machine now. At least, someone has opened up the infamous shipping container and is stringing up a rather alarming number of speakers. They're also setting up . . . Oh, Quin, this is so cool."

"What?" Quin said aloud.

"I said, I guess we're going to find out," Janet answered.

"There's an array of digital cameras," Molly answered, "that all feed back to the most amazing computer. It seems to be dedicated to one app, some kind of a face analysis program. It can recognize faces in the crowd and analyze them."

"I'm going to find my way to the bathrooms," Quin told Janet.

"Try not to get high off the toilet seat," she warned him.

He laughed and began to wind his way toward the porta-potties. As he made his way through the crowd, he continued his conversation with Molly. He ignored the few people who seemed to notice a man talking to himself. "You know, I bet that's how they analyze the mood of the crowd."

"Yes. There is definitely a subroutine that analyzes facial expressions and derives mood information. But really, Quin, the Machine uses maybe five percent of the capabilities of this app. It can cross-match facial characteristics with a digitized image in memory, it can be used as a lie detector, it can even . . ."

"Wait a minute. Molly, we can use this. We were talking about how Rifkin might try to slip in with the crowd and then jump up on stage at the last minute."

"You thought that might be the best way for him to sneak in unnoticed."

"Yeah. So try scanning through the crowd and match the faces against his digitized image from a magazine article. Try to accommodate for disguises."

"OK, I'm doing that."

Quin reached the toilets. There was a line. Now that he was no longer moving, he took his phone out of his pocket and held it up to his ear, so as to alleviate suspicion. "I don't see him." Molly had taken only five seconds to run the analysis.

"That's too bad. Keep scanning, though. It's a good theory still. Oh, now that we're talking, Molly, I wondered how many of the ghosts were in."

The night before they had been exploring the idea that Rifkin would sneak into the crowd so he could leap on-stage at the last minute. To do that, he would need a ticket, or else the prepubescent ticket takers would have to be in on the scam, which was unlikely. The tickets were coded with a rather low-tech laser bar code, and valid ticket numbers were stored in a computer. Molly cross-referenced this list with the list of people who had been issued tickets in the original lottery. A few inconsistencies showed up, some very basic hackwork and a few really first-class sneeches almost as good as the one Molly had pulled off to get Quin and Janet's tickets. Most of these sneeches turned out to be record company executives or journalists. Pretty much expected. But a few turned out to have no traceable identity. The electronic trail that led back from the subterfuge went through WebCense's central switchboard, and Quin forbade Molly from entering that data space. So they dubbed these twelve individuals the ghosts. One theory was that Aqualung was one of the ghosts.

"We missed nine of them," Molly informed him. "Three haven't made it through the gate yet."

"Well, that's not very good odds, but why don't you note the last three as they come in. Maybe if you only have three to work from you can better perform the analysis. Plus, I'd like to know who they are. Just curious."

Molly had the first ghost by the time he made it back to where Janet was sitting. The first band still had not started.

"This guy is real mister nobody," Molly told him. "He's not Aqualung, unless the guy is wearing a lot of makeup, and even then, his face isn't big enough. But what I'm doing is cross-referencing this face against the passport or driver's license photos of everyone who lives in the Edinburgh area or who's name appears on the passenger manifest of an airplane or high speed train that's come into the area in the past three weeks. Nothing. Either he walked here or . . . Give me a minute, I'm going to do something fancy."

Quin didn't ask. Molly did to data what a cow did to grass: took a lot of useless chaff, turned the good part into meat, and dropped the rest on the ground in a neat pile.

"You are going to find this very interesting, Mr. Taber," Molly whispered in his dataspray. "The ghost, as well as the second ghost that came in a few minutes ago, disappeared after going to work for WebCense. You know who disappears after going to work for WebCense? Don't answer out loud, because I know you know the answer. They're with the Squad."

"I have to go to the bathroom again," he said to Janet.

"What's the matter with you, not used to Scottish food?" That was a joke. They had had Pop-Tarts for breakfast.

"Must be all the coffee," he told her. Once he was clear he began quizzing Molly. "You're saying they're both?"

"From the Squad, yes."

"Are they after me?" This was all stuff a crazy guy might say to himself. Nobody was looking.

"If they were, they would have made you. Remember, there are nine other unidentified potential Squad members in the area as well. That's enough to cover the whole area."

"So why are they here?"

"I could answer that if you give me the go-ahead. They're probably communicating by subvocal implants and cellular links. I could find the cell and do some decoding. Maybe I could find out where they got their subvocals." Molly had been bugging him to get a subvocal implant, but Quin hated the dentist and would probably never get one.

"That can't be a good idea."

"Mr. Taber, relax. They are not going to find me inside of a cell. I won't even be in there. I'll just pick up the transmissions and analyze them somewhere else."

"OK, do it. But if you feel a probe . . ."

"I'm invisible."

The rumor was that Naked Mole Rat would open the final day. The rumor was wrong. The show was actually opened by the Machine, but no one knew it. A strong sense of anticipation rippled through the crowd a few minutes before the Scottish band went on. If the concert goers knew they were being manipulated on the most basic emotional level, they would have been thrilled. This was what they had come for.

All of Naked Mole Rat's songs shared common characteristics. They were all fast, short, complex, and energetic. The beat led you in. The tune made your mind dance.

And the lyrics freaked you out. The crowd was on its feet before the first note was played and no one stopped moving until the music stopped. It was a short set. NMR never went in for theatrics, no light show, no smoke pots. There was only music, and when it stopped, the crowd reeled.

"Welcome to the Solstice," Dennis McColoch screamed into the microphone. "It's all about music from now on."

The second band to go on was Sex Lethal. The keyboardist, Ned Phillips, tentatively stepped up to the microphone before a hushed crowd.

"We don't know why Dana left us," he said. "She never told us what she was feeling, how deeply she was hurting." He choked up and had to stop for a few seconds.

The crowd was pouring sympathy on him in waves. The vidimask showed it clearly. Aqualung wasn't driving the speakers now. He wanted their emotion to be genuine. He was still deciding whether to kick in the program if he thought the emotions he was seeing were in poor taste, like if the crowd started yelling for some music. The new program not only allowed projection into open space, it also drove emotions much more strongly. The colonel was really getting the hang of this machine. Aqualung didn't begin to trust the artificial intelligence to use this new power for good. He bore watching.

"Dana didn't leave a note," Phillips went on. "Instead, she left us this." He stepped back and a holographic projector placed the image of Dana Woods on center stage. She looked as fragile as she ever did. Her straight black hair shimmered in the thin sunshine, her large eyes stood out against her pale skin. She wore a pure white wrap, something like a toga. Aqualung realized that it was a Buddhist funeral garment. The image waited in silence for a few seconds, then a smattering of applause started somewhere in the audience. The applause grew in intensity and spread. Soon, the cow pasture was a solid, surging wall of thunder. The standing ovation lasted a good five minutes. When it subsided, the image spoke.

"This is not a recording," the projection of Dana said. "For the last couple of months, I've been working on building an expert system. I've had the help of one of the greatest computer geniuses of our time, my brother. Together, David and I have put together an artificial intelligence that encompasses the personae of our entire family, the Irish side, from our father, and the Italian side, from our mother. This expert system can project an image of any one of us, an image that thinks and reacts the same way as the real person would. After I died, my brother brought this construction, this bundle of hardware and software, to my bandmates, and told them my last request: to have this expert system switched on, for the very first time, at our next gig. I have to tell you, I'm pretty surprised to see a crowd this size.

"We stand here today in the country of Scotland, which has struggled in the grip of British rule for over a thousand years. But, although the nation of Scotland doesn't exist on any map, it lives in the hearts of the Scottish people. The same is true of Palestine, Tibet, and Canada. No government can tell these people that their nation doesn't exist. In a few months, the government will tell all of you that your nation doesn't exist. One language, one culture.

"Maybe this will be a good thing. I'm not saying we can't live together in peace, as one people. But such a thing must be done carefully, so we don't lose what we have to gain something most of us don't want.

"I'd just like to say to the owners of the world, Listen to us, respect us. We may not have anything you think you want, but we are the future."

Sex Lethal played a set with the holographic Dana heading them up. It was a little creepy, which was what

Sex Lethal had striven for while Dana was alive. When they were through, the vast crowd was comfortably silent.

"This is the last time you'll see me," Dana said, walking backward into the shadows of the superstructure. "WebCense can't let something like me exist. AI's are a nonhuman culture. Get to know them."

The only act that could follow a resurrected Dana Woods was the Machine itself. It took the crowd about ten minutes of seeming silence before they realized they were being manipulated. By then, the mosh pit had formed and the glades were starting to smooth out. That's where Janet and Quin found themselves.

"This is incredible," Janet sighed, leaning back in the cool, damp grass.

Quin, as a man who drove himself to succeed and never took drugs, had never known a stress-free moment in his life. At first, he found relaxation unpleasant. It was a foreign sensation. But it was impossible to resist the siren song of the Machine. Soon, he too lay back in the grass, and remained staring at the low clouds until Janet climbed on top of him and began kissing him. The mosh pit had expanded due to the crush of bodies entering the zone. This had the effect of moving the circle of the grotto outward. The mosh pit itself might have eventually overtaken them if Molly had not spoken in Quin's dataspray.

"Sir, sorry to interrupt your smooching, but I intercepted the transmissions of the ghosts and decoded them. Here's a sample." A male voice replaced Molly's. Quin and Janet continued to make out, but Quin was only half paying attention.

"The Machine is clearly activated. Agent Three, this is Agent One, are you in place? Agent Three, are you at the insertion point? Agent Three?"

"What?" a lazy voice responded.

"He's under the influence of the Machine," a woman's voice said. "Do you want me to go in?"

"Negative, Agent Six. Your position shows level two security. You won't be able to acquire the target quietly."

"Fuck quietly," the woman shot back. "I'll get in there and kick his ass. I'll kick all their hippie asses. Fuck 'em."

"I'm calling off the operation until the Machine is no longer controlling the crowd," Agent One said. "Repeat, the operation is suspended. We will move to plan delta. Repeat, plan delta, on my order."

"They're after Aqualung," Molly said. "From other transmissions it sounds like plan delta is to grab him as he comes offstage from the Snake Vendors' set."

Quin couldn't think. Janet was all over him, and the music was having a profound effect on his emotions. With great effort he struggled free. He only briefly watched as Janet rolled over and joined another bacchanalian group on their left.

"We've got to warn him," he said, walking toward the stage. "We have to do it cleverly, though, so he'll listen to us." Quin found himself walking toward a surging mass of humanity in the throes of violent revelry. He skirted the mosh pit and continued toward the stage. "Try to contact him through the Machine, then he'll have to listen."

"What do I say, sir? Perhaps you should speak to him. You're better at speaking to people."

"No, I'm still all muddled up from this Machine. Just be blunt. Say anything you have to say to get him to listen. His life is in danger."

"All right, let me see what I can do."

The Machine had never worked better. It had been used over a dozen times, and now the bugs were pretty well worked out. Thanks due, mostly, to the colonel. In fact, the Machine would not be here at all had it not been for the colonel. The AI had gone over the heads of the board of directors and rerouted the shipping container. In the interests of keeping a low profile, however, the colonel was not watching over his shoulder this time. Which made the appearance of the face in his vidimask all the more upsetting.

It was the face of a young woman, sort of plain, smart looking, with mousy blond bangs and glasses. He hadn't known the vidimask had picture-in-picture capability. He did now.

"I'm sorry to interrupt you, Mr. Rifkin, but I have something very important to tell you."

"Who the hell are you?"

"You don't know me. My name is Molly. My employer has asked me to tell you that your life is in danger."

"Who is your employer?"

"That's unimportant. You don't know this, but you are possessed of information that WebCense feels is vital and valuable. They've taken the earliest opportunity to apprehend you. Their operatives are here in the audience today."

Glowing boxes appeared over seven faces in his display. The resolution was too low to make out individual features.

"What information?" Aqualung asked. He was pretty sure he knew the answer, but he didn't want this person to know that.

"I can't explain that at this time, sir, but it pertains to your true identity as just revealed. It's something you knew as Adrian Rifkin."

"I barely remember those days, Molly. I drank a lot back then."

"That, too, is irrelevant. If WebCense finds that you are unable or unwilling to answer their questions, they will extract the information using new and effective technology. In order to impress upon you a sense of urgency, sir, I must point out that you need not be alive during the extraction procedure. In fact, it is preferable to perform this operation on a frozen specimen. There is an agent behind the stage right now with a tank of liquid nitrogen hidden in a hot dog cart."

"He means to grab me and freeze me in liquid nitrogen?"

"Just the head, sir. They only need the head."

Aqualung was starting to go into fight-or-flight mode. He could barely feel his fingers as he unconsciously adjusted the Machine output.

"Why should I believe you?"

"I have nothing to offer you in that regard by way of proof. Unfortunately, time is not on our side. I'm here to try and help you escape."

"You want this information, too, don't you? Or your employer, rather. But you don't have this technology, I'm guessing."

"You are a very astute man, if I may say so. We would like the information, but we don't operate like Web-Cense."

"I'm glad to hear it. So what's your plan?"

"We don't have one at this time."

"But you think I ought to get the hell out of here."

"That would be the prudent thing."

"Well, I'm going to buy us some time. I'm going to do my show."

"As I said, time is not on our side, sir."

"Aqualung, we shutting down?" Fenner tapped him on the shoulder. Aqualung looked out at the crowd. The Machine had reached the end of its set and had shut itself off. The crowd in the vidimask was chanting at the stage, fists in the air. Glowing boxes appeared over six faces now, one had gone somewhere else. The caption on the message screen read: "WebCense operatives (the Squad)."

And underneath that: "They're coming to kill you after your set."

He pulled off the vidimask and picked up his Les Paul. "Let's rock."

The Snake Vendors were a pretty young band to be the big finale at a festival like this. They only had one album out, although they had a lot of songs nobody had even heard yet. Aqualung had written over fifty songs since he had gone into exile, and the band knew a lot of them pretty well. But they didn't kid themselves. The two things that put them in this league were Aqualung's true identity and the Machine. For their regular set, they'd decided to play it pretty loose. They didn't rehearse the changes, they didn't choreograph, and they didn't all know their parts, even. It showed. It was one of the best sets anyone had ever heard. Six really good musicians enjoying playing together. Thirteen great songs. An hour of magic.

After the band was done with their regular set, he called Fenner, Lalo, and Sandra over to the keyboard. Shad wasn't really part of this, he was just putting in his time.

"This is the best gig we've ever done," Aqualung told his bandmates, ignoring the chanting crowd behind him. "But I'm afraid it's got to be our last. I have to leave again. For good."

The Snake Vendors were stunned. Fenner looked away. "What are you running away from now?"

"Death," Aqualung answered. "The same thing you're running toward. Now, I'm not exactly a fountain of wisdom here. I just want to say this. Don't kill yourselves."

"Over you?" Britta sneered.

"Over anything. Just believe me on this one. The world would be a worse place without you. And I'm pretty sure it isn't any fun being dead. Look, I didn't prepare this. I don't have gifts or anything. Lalo, I want you to take this." He handed Lalo the Les Paul. Lalo took it reverently. "All I ask is that you keep making music with it. If you do, I can never really die. I want to do one more song. What's it going to be?"

Fenner looked at the chanting crowd. "They want 'Ugly'."

"Then lets give them 'Ugly.' I'm going to get another guitar. I can't play a stringless."

The band kept extra instruments behind a curtain to the left of the drum set. Aqualung smiled at Shad as he walked past, and simply said, " 'Let's Get Ugly.' "

Quin couldn't find Janet in the crowd, and Molly was too busy to find her for him. She and Aqualung had sketched out a plan. Quin was vague on the details. It was really Aqualung's idea, but Molly was implementing it. Quin tried to enjoy the set, knowing that this could be the end of the singer's life and the end of his only chance at getting his revenge against Walter Cheeseman.

The band took a short break and had a conference by the keyboard. There was an exchange of guitars. Aqualung disappeared behind the stage and appeared with a new instrument slung over his neck. Then they swung into "Let's Get Ugly," the amped-up party song from the 2K that had been the intellectual Zoroaster's only lasting legacy. It was a short song, designed for the short attention spans of frat boys, and at the same time making fun of those same frat boys. That was Zoroaster's style. Quin had Molly relay him the transmissions between the squad members. Agent Three, fully recovered, was positioned at the bottom of the stairs leading off the stage. Agent Six was nearby with a vibraknife and a tank of liquid nitrogen, concealed in a hot dog cart. Quin guessed that the

Squad had been given the option of bringing Aqualung in alive or dead with his brain preserved. They had clearly opted for what they considered the less messy option.

At the end of the song, Aqualung raised his guitar, as if in benediction, just before his head exploded.

AGENT ONE: Agent Three, status.
AGENT THREE: The target is down. It's a head shot. His brains are all over the stage.
AGENT ONE: Abort. Pull back and draw the net.

Janet didn't notice that Quin was missing until the Machine stopped. She had been slam dancing in the expanded mosh pit when the emotion-enhancing carrier wave had died off and she was left alone in the midst of the chanting crowd. She chanted with them, and enjoyed the Snake Vendors, but still worried about Quin. He was socially awkward and might be easily led astray.

She was not old enough to remember "Let's Get Ugly," but she didn't miss that dubious distinction by much. She had become aware of popular music about two years after Adrian Rifkin had disappeared. Still, hearing the song inspired awe in her, and she had her fist in the air along with everyone else. She was looking right at Aqualung when he got shot. She didn't hear the shot, but heard his body hit the stage through the microphone that fell after him. He was instantly surrounded by the Snake Vendors, security guards, eventually medics, although there was clearly nothing that could be done. Then the riot started.

Like a lot of people, she later realized that the Machine was at least partly responsible for fanning the flames of panic. But seeing the lead singer of the band go down under gunfire like that was what really started it. People started rushing in various directions until they came together in hopelessly grid-locked knots. Others, seeing the knots and hoping that the mass of humanity was crowding toward safety, tried to force their way into the knots from all directions. Janet stayed right where she was until the others collapsed from exhaustion and Quin found her.

Shad had seen something that he was probably not supposed to. When Aqualung stepped behind the curtain he spoke into a little microphone, the kind executives carried around to talk to their computers back at the office. Then a second Aqualung appeared beside him, holding a Fender Stratocaster. The first Aqualung pulled a corner of stiff plastic sheeting away from the flimsy wall and ducked away behind the stage. The new Aqualung, a hologram no doubt projected by the same system that had brought Dana Woods to life, stepped out on stage to thunderous applause. As soon as the song was over, the weirdest special effect Shad had ever seen closed out the set. The hologram appeared to be the recipient of a head wound, complete with splashing brains and sound effects. The stage was all confusion while the holographic body, blood, and brains disappeared soon afterward. Then the riot started.

The weirdest thing of all, though, was that after the whole thing was over and Shad was packing up his kit, he found that a bullet hole had absolutely ruined the bass drum. The damned thing had hit the skin and fragmented little metal rods all over the place. Imagine what that would have done to a real person?

Shad never told anyone about the hologram or the bullet. Nobody asked.

"Mr. Taber, please, don't get mad."

"Why would I get mad, Molly?" He was alone for the

first time since the disastrous end of the concert. Janet was exhausted and had gone to bed.

"I killed him."

"What? Who did you kill?"

"Aqualung. Let me tell the whole story."

"Please."

"OK, first of all, that wasn't Aqualung on stage during the last song. He ducked backstage and we activated a hologram of himself that he had prepared ahead of time. He must be the most paranoid person alive. Then again, people really are after him. After the last song was over, I sensed an anomaly in the feedback field. I had a camera aimed at the stage and I saw a bullet hit the drum set. I grabbed control of the hologram and put in the head wound, and Aqualung hitting the stage. Of course, I didn't know what to do about the body, not to mention the blood and tissue that would disappear after the hologram was inactivated, but in the riot nobody seemed to notice."

"Why the hell did you do all that?"

"Don't get mad. I took initiative. I had microseconds to make the decision. I thought that the hit man and the Squad would be less likely to go after Aqualung if they thought he was dead."

"What hit man?"

"I never saw him. I assumed he was sent by Zoe Campbell. It was actually aimed at the chest, the bullet, but it was clearly a long range shot, with bad visibility and wind, so the hit man shouldn't be too surprised he hit the head. The Squad wanted his brain intact, which is why I made the bullet go into his head and destroy it. I think it worked. You heard what they said about aborting the operation."

"That is amazing work, Molly. I just have two questions. What was the original ending to Aqualung's hologram program?"

"He was going to take a bow with Dana Woods and

they were both going to repeat Dana's political message and vanish."

"The Squad would have nabbed him before he left the venue."

"I think it worked," Molly repeated. "As far as I can tell, he got away. I didn't see him leave, and there were no other broadcasts on the subvocals about him. What was the second question?"

"Did you start the Machine? Three people were killed in that riot. Janet and I could have been killed."

"That wasn't me," Molly said. "That was the Digital Carnivore."

"Shit."

"Did I do wrong?" Molly asked.

"No, it was probably the right thing, under the circumstances. You realize, though, that Aqualung doesn't know any of this business about the hit man, or the Digital Carnivore. He's bound to think that you did all that for your own sick reasons. We're going to have to explain this to him as soon as we can."

"If we can find him, that is," Molly said. "He's gone someplace where I can't see him. I didn't even know there was such a place."

"He's gone to ground, Molly. But we'll find him."

CHAPTER 10

I will run, and the dogs will follow,
I will hide, in the ground,
And the earth will swallow me down.

THE SNAKE VENDORS,
"THE DOGS WILL FOLLOW"
TWO SNAKE, DOLLA FIFTY,
THRASHER RECORDS, 2031

There was something about the man. Something in the way he held his head cocked just so, in how he stepped, in the cut of his clothes, that said, even before he spoke in his slight accent or showed his passport, that he was a native of Germany. His passport, issued in Munich, identified him as Helmut Dietz, and a quick background check showed that he was a life-support engineer who had studied at the University of Bonn.

He had, of course, never even been to Germany. The man who had once been Adrian Rifkin, Steve Drabkin, Harold Hammerande, and lately Aqualung, had created Dietz in the last year. He had drawn a painstakingly detailed trail of computer transactions, paper documents, falsified records, and, perhaps most importantly, a valid IIN that had brought Helmut Dietz to life.

As he made his way through the faded splendor of the Denver International Airport he forced himself to keep up the illusion. Eventually, the adopted mannerisms would become natural, but until then, he had to consciously act the part of Helmut Dietz to avoid detection.

He had changed his appearance a little since crawling out from under the stage at the festival. A pair of Lycra shorts and a baseball cap had gotten him out of the venue. He looked like a roadie. He had gotten his quick change satchel out of Britta's dressing room. He never kept it in his own room in case it was searched, and the sight of strange men entering and leaving Britta's dressing room was not an unexpected one. The satchel contained Dietz's ID, a purposefully rumpled three-piece tweed suit, some very uncomfortable shoes, and an electric razor for his beard. And there was no escaping the final step. The hair had to go.

He had hacked it off with a pair of scissors he found in Britta's trailer and had taken the locks, about three years' growth, he guessed, with him in a paper sack to be discarded somewhere else. Once he had gotten to the train station and changed into his full disguise, he went to the barber.

"That's the worst haircut I've ever seen," said the man in the white smock with the northern Scottish brogue.

"But not bad for a six-year-old, don't you think?" Aqualung/Dietz answered. "Of course, he is not my child, you see, he is my landlady's. I am staying in a boarding house almost halfway to Glasgow due to the shortage of rooms with this festival they are having. I usually stay in Edinburgh at a hotel, but not this trip. I happened to fall asleep in a chair in the living room last night, my flight from America having taken so long, and the little fellow took a pair of scissors to my hair. I'd just like it evened up before my meeting, which is just twenty minutes from now. The trains are a little slow today, I understand."

And so on. Dietz was a talkative man, friendly, animated. There was always someone interested in his stories, so he never appeared to be traveling alone. He acquired an enormous suitcase and filled it with the sort of trinkets one would take home from a long business trip, all bought in Scotland, of course, but bearing the images of Mount Rushmore, the Vatican, the new World Capitol in Guadalajara.

He was pretty confident he had escaped Scotland undetected. At first he thought he owed his clean getaway to careful planning. Then, during a layover at Heathrow, he had seen himself killed on the news.

He didn't know what to make of the footage of himself getting his head blown off by an unknown assassin. He had programmed the hologram to simply take a bow with Dana Woods and vanish at the end of the song, by which time he would be outside the venue, clothes and hair in a sack, with nothing of his old identity anywhere else on his person. But this, of course, was much better for him. If WebCense believed the hoax, they would not even be looking for him.

Better for him, perhaps, but worse for the fans. Aqualung would join a growing list of rock stars who had taken the last train for the coast this year. He, Dana, and Larry Winters were only the lead singers who had taken a dirt nap. There were also five or six guitarists and keyboard players, some bass players, and about a dozen drummers. If there was a rock and roll heaven, it would be pretty hard to land a gig right now. And every time a rock star died, a few fans followed. Some were accidental ODs, kids trying to kill the pain with too big a dose, and some were on-purpose suicides. Those were the ones who knew they could never deal with the pain at all, and didn't even try. Music's power came from that strong emotional attachment. A man or woman on a stage sang what you felt but could never express. And to have that voice silenced forever was like losing a piece of your own soul.

Adrian Rifkin had been one of those most deeply, but

most quietly, affected by the death of Kurt Cobain. He had not wailed or rent his garments in public, but he had used more heroin in 1994 than any other year of his life. He had finally stopped shooting, as well as drinking and riding his bike too fast without a helmet, but he had come close to following in his hero's footsteps. Now, his own fans would be feeling the same thing.

He couldn't do anything for them. If he tried, they would get to see him killed again, this time for real. For now, it was best to be Helmut. Helmut was a good guy. No musical talent, but his work kept him busy. He was on his way to the job of a lifetime for an environmental systems engineer. He was going to the Moon.

The Denver International Airport was a technological wonder when it was first opened. The baggage system used robots to move suitcases to and from the planes. Now of course, everybody did that. It was once the world's largest airport. Now it seemed cozy. It had once been miles outside of the city. Now, suburbs engulfed it and complained of the noise.

But DIA still served as a major transportation center. Not because of the technological marvels of thirty years ago, but because of its new neighbor, the Denver Spaceport. Denver did not have the only spaceport, or even the largest one, in the world. But it was the only one dedicated to lifting passengers into orbit with comfort and dignity. If one was not in the military, if one did not have a private launch vehicle, if one wished to leave the gravity of Earth without being referred to as "soft cargo," one came to Denver.

Helmut Dietz entered the efficient offices of Delta Launch!, main floor terminal, DIA, with a warm smile and a carnation in his buttonhole, singing, "Fly Me to the Moon," off-key. The woman behind the desk liked him immediately.

"What can I do for you today?"

"As I said, I want you to fly me to the Moon. I'd like the next available flight. I would normally make this reservation well in advance through my agent, but I've just been informed that my services are required at Luna 1."

"Well, it certainly is an exciting time to be going there." Which was, of course, precisely the reason Dietz was making the trip. Tensions between WebCense and Luna were escalating, with Luna refusing to enforce WebCense's edicts and WebCense in turn threatening to use its most powerful weapon, information embargo. It was widely believed that the citizens of Luna would not stand two hours without television, movies, music, or stock quotes, not to mention the more physical dangers of being cut off from the Orbital Traffic Control data. Dietz, however, was betting on Luna to make a clean break. They had always been mavericks, and they had the sympathies of Freefall and the other, smaller space stations, as well as the underground Nationalists on dirt-side. Once there, Dietz planned to take up his old profession, what with entertainment promising to be a growth industry and his total lack of knowledge of environmental controls.

"Actually," the ticket agent said, looking up from her computer screen, "we've had a lot of cancellations on the last flight. I suppose it isn't good business to tell you this, but there have been a string of disturbing announcements in the last hour or so. WebCense has just asked the United Nations for the power to train and equip its own army. This is the third time they've asked, but this time the UN has agreed in light of the unrest. It looks like this might get serious."

"Well, if it comes to that, they are going to need someone who can fix the life support." He held up his hand. "Don't get me wrong, I am not on the side of the rebels; I'm no Nationalist. But if it comes down to saving lives, that is what I will do. Now, book me on that flight." He slapped Helmut Dietz's credit card on the desk.

"What we're going to need first is a reference. You see, the life support on the space habitats is a precious resource. But of course you know all this. What we need, essentially, is proof that you have a job on Luna, to verify that you will be able to earn enough to pay for your own life support."

Dietz dug around in his coat pockets for a piece of paper. "I only was offered this job hours ago. I jumped at the chance. At my age, a trip to the Moon may come by only once. The name of the woman I spoke to was Shelly Cavendish." He gave the woman a number and she punched it into her console. Shelly was his keyboard player in the Animal Bones. He heard she had taken synthetic ecstasy in '12 and had never woken up. Aqualung had resurrected her a few months ago in the form of a call/response bot. She would respond to simple queries and vouch for Helmut Dietz to anyone who asked.

"All right, Shelly Cavendish, Luna 1, request reference for Helmut Dietz," the ticket agent punched in the information. "Should just take a minute for this packet request to get spooled to the Moon, and we'll give Shelly a few to get back to us. They're just going onto day shift up there right now, so we're lucky."

They had just started chatting about the assassination and subsequent riot at the rock festival in Scotland when the terminal beeped. "That was fast," the agent said. "Looks good; you're all approved. The next shuttle leaves in four hours, but it takes some time to get loaded, so I'd suggest you head over to the spaceport now. Let's see, you've never traveled in space before, so I should warn you about a few things. They won't let you take any baggage, of course. And you'll have to lose the flower." She pointed to the carnation in his buttonhole. "You're going to take a seventeen-hour layover at Freefall because of orbital positioning and so forth. And, when they ask you if you'd like some medicine to cancel the input from your inner ear, what do you say?"

"I'd love some. You have been most kind. If the rest of my adventure is as efficient and enjoyable, I will become a great fan of space travel."

"Give me the world." Quin's office faded into the background, and inside his head the surface of the Earth appeared, an increasingly single color political map. The dataspray made it possible to see the entire globe at once without the distortion of a projection map. In the top left-hand corner, Luna 1 was depicted. In the top right, Freefall.

The concert had, of course, ended with Aqualung's death, and Quin and Janet had come home early. Janet was at her apartment trying to get over the experience, and Quin had gone to work, partly to keep from spilling the beans. He was the only one who knew that Aqualung was still alive. If he wasn't able to talk to Molly, he would have told Janet.

"OK, now I want all credit card transactions for the last three days." The world came alive with bright pinpoints of light. Most of the map was obliterated. "What I want is to narrow it down to accounts held by males that have remained dormant for at least eight months and have just become active in the last three weeks."

Most of the lights winked out, but the world was still pretty well blanketed. "You'd better add back new accounts in the last eight months," Quin said. More lights appeared. "Now, lets limit transactions to travel, clothes, suitcases, that sort of thing. Also, camping gear." As he spoke, lights winked out until he felt he had a manageable number. He focused on the constellation surrounding Edinburgh. "Now, we want to do a temporal trace. I want all transactions on the afternoon of June twentieth in red." A dozen or so points of light in the Edinburgh constellation turned red.

"Now, isolate one account and blink its light." One red light began blinking. "Now blink the transaction on that account that occurred next." Another light in Edinburgh started blinking. "Keep going through time with that one account."

The first account never left Edinburgh. That didn't fit anyone on the run. The purchase of an airline or train ticket did not mean the person was traveling that day. He ran through fifteen possibilities, painstakingly checking promising transactions, reconstructing the steps of these travelers, until he had two that he liked.

The first man obtained a cash advance, a suitcase and several changes of clothes, a train ticket, and, and this was what made him less likely, a cuckoo clock. He next appeared in Heathrow, where he boarded a flight to Tokyo.

The second man bought only an airline ticket in Edinburgh, flew to Stockholm, made a long-distance call to Pennsylvania, left a message on a voice mail account that had since been retrieved and erased, then disappeared.

Everyone else either had gone back to Edinburgh, had never left, or had used other long established credit cards in the same name. So two men had run from Scotland. Quin was guessing that Rance Packwood was Aqualung, and Peter Nayruk was the assassin who had fired a bullet into Aqualung's hologram. He called Fred.

"Quin, how are you? How was your vacation? You went to that concert with the murder and the riot and all that, didn't you?"

"Indeed I did, Fred. In fact, all that commotion has something to do with the little project you and I are working on."

"Yeah, you know, I thought of that right away when I saw it on the news. Someone might have been trying to collect on that hit Zoe put out on Rifkin. The money could have been held in escrow in a Swiss account, it would have been accruing all this time. Quite a bundle by now."

"Any way to tell if the money's been collected? Say, by a Peter Nayruk, employed by Capistan Industries?"

"You are nine parts bloodhound, Quin. That name you mentioned is someone in the business, or at least that's a name he uses. If I need a data trace someday, I'll know who to call. But you still need me to keep up to date on the rumor mill. I'll ask around about this and let you know."

Which left only Rance Packwood, an incomplete identity who had winked out in Tokyo. Quin had his work cut out for him.

Helmut was the oldest person on the lifter. He was afraid he stuck out like a sore thumb. Most space travelers were young professionals, thin and neat. They wore slacks and turtlenecks of some miracle fabric that eliminated body odor. They were all talented in their field and quietly efficient. Pretty much gay stereotypes. Even the women.

Helmut was the only one wearing brown; the others wore white. He was the only one who used a window to read. The others had datasprays feeding the latest information on their specialties into their brains. Helmut had a Louis L'Amour novel on his antique screen.

The lifter was not arranged like an airplane. It had a different job to do. First of all, there were no long open areas. The craft was broken up into smaller compartments joined by doors that did not line up with each other. When you never knew which way was going to be down, you had to make it impossible to fall very far in any direction. Each compartment had four acceleration couches mounted on gimbals. When you entered the craft, the doors were in the walls and the couches were on the floor. When the thing was pointed at the sky, the doors were in the floors and ceilings and the couches were also on the floor. The lift attendants had a tougher time getting around when the craft was upright because they had to climb a short ladder set into the bulkhead, walk across a room around the couches, and climb another short ladder. The lifter wasn't designed for them.

The Denver Space Port was not actually in Denver, or even very near it. It was on the other side of the continental divide, near Frisco. It was reached by an underground tube train that left from DIA. What a waste. Some of the best scenery in the country was hundreds of feet above through solid rock. But the space port had to operate in all seasons, so most of it was underground. The snow pack that accumulated on top of the lifter bay doors provided a much needed heat sink for the lifting capacitor. In the summer, they used Dillon Reservoir nearby. The fish didn't much like it, but they weren't taxpayers.

The port only sent up one lifter a day during the summer months, and it took longer to prepare for a lift than it did to load an airplane and taxi it onto the runway. Aqualung had read half his book by the time the captain turned the light on to tell everyone to belt in. The couches must have had dozens of sensors and interlocks to make sure everyone was in the way they were supposed to be. Helmut's monitor came on and the blond attendant, his favorite, admonished him. "Passenger Dietz, you need to wedge your head into the yoke a little farther. We wouldn't want you to hurt your neck." She winked at him and he smiled back as he forced his big head into the contraption.

"How is that, better? Or will you have to come back here and tuck me in yourself?"

She glanced down at her readout. "That won't be necessary. You're all green."

Helmut had tuned his monitor to a documentary on the lifter. A canned voice, he could vaguely identify the actor, narrated the countdown procedure.

"Much of the energy that will push this lifter into orbit comes from a source that will never leave the ground. This way, the capacity of the lifter is increased without expending too much costly energy."

He flipped to a more technical channel, an external view of the lifter in its launch bay with the voices of the technicians and the captain dubbed in.

"Capacitors at full charge," the ground crew said. "You're go for ignition."

"Igniting main burners," the captain answered. As soon as the faint blue flame appeared under the lifter, an arc jumped from the superconducting plate on the ground pad to the engine of the lifter. Suddenly, the launch bay was filled with light as the bay doors irised open and the noon sun poured in. The camera lost its view as the bay filled with exhaust.

"You're clear for launch," the ground crew said.

"Liftoff," the captain replied. Helmut switched to an external view from the lifter's cockpit. The bay doors rushed past as he was pressed into the couch. He caught a brief glimpse of the north end of the Tenmile Range, then the Rocky Mountains dropped away with dizzying speed. It was not long before cloud cover and distance made identification of geographic features impossible, and he was looking at a planet. The acceleration stopped.

"This is your captain speaking. We're in our first staging orbit, and we'll make a quick partial circuit of the planet before beginning acceleration again. At this point we'd like you to remain in your couches while we make some routine course adjustments." There was no way the couch was going to let him go anyway. He laid back and watched the stars whirl around on his little monitor. Every once in a while the planet would heave into view, or the sun would force the screen to scale down its output. The blond attendant appeared on an inset in the screen.

"How is everything going, Mr. Dietz?"

"I am anxious for the couch to let me up," he said. "I will have gone from overweight to weightless in just thirty minutes."

"It's quite a sensation," she agreed.

"I understand there is a club one can join, the Zero-G club I believe it is called, if one has a partner to share membership. If you like, perhaps we can join together."

She smiled. "I'll have to check your preflight physical. I'll let you know."

She was blowing him off, he could tell. He didn't really care. He was only playing a role. Dirty old Helmut Dietz, a married man on a business trip. If it would get him out of reach of WebCense, he'd be Laurence Fucking Olivier.

The course adjustments lasted about thirty minutes while the lifter shifted around sickeningly. Sickening, that is, if he hadn't taken a drug that all but obliterated the signals coming from his inner ear. It was available by prescription only. That was another thing he was getting good at sneaking around. He had to, what with all of the antags he had had to pump into the Snake Vendors. He didn't much trust street drugs anymore. Some of the other passengers on the flight must have taken the same drug, but not all of them. You could tell the difference easily. The in-flight physician expert system would prescribe the drug before any lunches got loose in the cabin.

The second burn lasted longer than the first, but was less intense. A little over one g for about an hour. That moved the lifter up into the second staging orbit, which would meet up with Freefall in seven hours.

Rance Packwood had turned out to be a decoy. He had never boarded the direct suborbital flight between Heathrow and Tokyo. He had been rather sloppily created seven years ago from a public terminal in Ely, Nevada, and had resurfaced a few weeks ago not far from there. He was probably Aqualung's creation, but that wasn't the identity he had run away with. He probably had used a more solid ID, one with a history and even an IIN. Quin knew that Aqualung could fake an IIN, which few people could manage. In fact, the ones who could worked for WebCense. Maybe Aqualung worked for WebCense. Maybe this whole thing was a plot set up by Walter Cheeseman to snare Quin.

The problem with paranoia was that there was little difference between a useful amount and an amount that just wasted time. Quin stuck to his original investigation, which was going pretty much nowhere.

Neither of the people who had obviously fled Edinburgh under an assumed identity had turned out to be Aqualung. So Quin had Molly sift through everyone who had left Edinburgh on June 20. Early in the day, of course. By cutting off the mass exodus of the concert goers, they had eliminated 90 percent of the airline and train traffic. What he had Molly look for was any inconsistency that would point to a fake name, anyone who had dialed in transactions from Ely, Los Angeles, or any of the way points on the Snake Vendors Pacific Rim tour during their scheduled stops. Anyone who had purchased airline tickets or had presented ID to board an aircraft. Anyone who looked like they were going to ground anywhere in the world. It turned out to be an enormous amount of data. Quin went home to think of a way to narrow down the search. This was the time to be clever.

Janet was feeling better. She had handled her near-death experience admirably. Quin was pretty sure he could have done no better.

"I just heard on the news," she told him when he came in the door, "the drummer for the Snake Vendors, that guy

Sticks, in jail in Singapore. They told him that Aqualung got assassinated and he went crazy. They had to shoot him with a tranquilizer dart to calm him down. He got six more months added to his term and he's going to be put in stocks in public."

"Well, Singapore is going to be assimilated in six months, I'm sure. They don't allow that kind of thing in the Nation of Earth." It was faint comfort. Six months in a Singapore prison was enough to break any man.

"So how was work?"

"I'm trying to track a guy who sold secrets," he lied. "We think he went to ground somewhere, but I have no way to know what name he's using or where he went. It's pretty tricky."

"I used to think about disappearing," Janet said. "Back before we lost everything, when the business was failing and things weren't so good around the house. I thought it would be real easy. I wouldn't make a mistake like phoning home to say I was all right. Of course, if they wanted to find me, someone like you probably would have picked me up in a couple of hours."

"He's not going to phone home."

"What's that?"

"Your average person on vacation or on a business trip for more than a couple of days will phone home."

Janet frowned. "Not necessarily. We didn't call anyone when we went to Scotland."

"But we were together. A person traveling alone will call someone, right? The office, a wife, the person who's feeding his cat." He picked up the phone and hit his office number. Janet had it on speed dial.

"Molly," he said, "cross-reference phone calls. Look for people who haven't made any phone calls. If he's incognito, he won't be calling anybody." When he hung up, Janet was looking at him funny. "What?"

"You're making her work this late? Quin, its almost nine. Let the poor woman go home."

"She wanted to. Once she seizes on a problem, she won't let go."

Freefall looked like the Stanley Cup. Helmut had seen it on TV before, of course. It was the eighth engineering wonder of the postmodern world. But now that he was approaching it, about to enter the big lifter bay, he saw the similarity.

Smaller objects surrounded the huge space station, floating in high orbit, sharing its path through space. Gigantic containers, lifted into orbit from Australia and Ascension Island, hovered around, waiting to be unloaded or loaded or dismantled for building material. Little tugs, enough living space for one man, enough thrust to move a thousand metric tons, waited for the chance to do a few seconds of work. Ore movers, idle lifters, and long-range shuttles vied for space with personal orbit vehicles. Owning one of these gave the space dweller the illusion of mobility. In reality, traffic was so strictly controlled that owning a craft of your own was no better than booking passage on a shuttle. Helmut had considered obtaining the funds to buy a used one, but decided it wouldn't help much, and the transfer of that much money would show up on a routine audit.

The lifter entered the station at the big end. At some point they gained a spin equal to that of the station, which was a little over ten rpm. A camera view from the outside of the station showed it sneaking up on the closed bay doors, little puffs of lateral thrusters lining it up just right, until the doors irised open at the last second and let the lifter in. When the lifter was lined up precisely, grapples hooked into it and an elevator dropped the lifter out to the rim. It took about an hour to let the bomb sniffers and the bio sniffers and the contraband sniffers go through the lifter, and to get the umbilical in place before the passengers could debark. On a shorter layover, those who were moving on to the Moon would be sent straight to the shuttle. But seventeen hours was too long to sit in even the most comfortable acceleration couch.

When Helmut got up, he thought he was a little heavier than he had been on Earth. His old bones creaked as he pulled himself out of the couch. The doors were in the walls now, so he waited for the young and light of step to exit first, then followed them out to Freefall.

The biggest room in all of Freefall, he later learned, was the concourse that debarked lifter passengers. It was a little smaller than an airport concourse, and broken up into sections by partial walls. This seemed to be the first law of space travel and habitation: Large rooms were bad.

A young man, sensing his disorientation, approached him. "You must be Helmut Dietz."

"I see my reputation precedes me," Helmut answered calmly. Inside, his defenses went up. If WebCense was going to grab him, now would be the time. Where the hell would he run to?

"The Delta Launch! ticket agent called us and told us to look out for you. She said that you were new to space travel and might like a little tour of Freefall during your layover. Of course, if you'd like to rest, I can show you to a habitat."

"A habitat. Sounds as though you'd like to put me in a zoo. No, I slept on the lifter. Zero g sounded exciting, but it was actually a little boring after the first couple of minutes."

The young man introduced himself as Scott and led Helmut out of the concourse into a crowded hallway. Helmut had about a million questions, and answering them was Scott's job.

"You might be surprised at the number of people who

think Freefall looks like the Stanley Cup," Scott said in answer to his first question. "And, to tell the truth, it looks that way for the same reason the Stanley Cup does. As time goes on, the station needs more and more space, just as the cup needs room to engrave the names of the winning teams year after year. The oldest part of the station is the smallest. This is actually the only part manufactured on Earth. It isn't pressurized anymore, and is used mainly for storage of hard-to-replace, but nonfunctioning, materials. Past the old station is the flywheel, where the station spin is controlled."

"Do I feel heavier than I should?"

"Yes, that's very good. Most people can't tell the difference between the artificial gravity in this area and Earth gravity, especially after the lifter. Here at the concourse, we are at 1.1 gravity. The farther you get from the hub, the greater the gravity. The hub itself is micro gravity, of course, and that is entirely devoted to the micro gravity manufacturing core and the dock. Certain materials and pharmaceuticals can only be made in this area. One step out from that is the power and heavy manufacturing section, since it's easier to move heavy equipment if there is just a little gravity. The living section is divided into levels. The lowest gravity is somewhat cheap real estate, the section with exactly Earth gravity is prime real estate. If you get more than 1.3 g, nobody wants to live there. That area is strictly for short term visits to service the machines."

"It seems as though as the station expands, more and more undesirable real estate is being created."

"That's true. That's one of the hot button political issues on the station. The station CEO has proposed to slow the spin of the cylinder, which has remained constant for seven years. If she does that, a lot of people are going to find themselves lighter than one g in their high price apartments. So, who reimburses these people for their loss of land value? Very sticky issue."

"We appear to be heading toward the narrow end of the station."

"Yes, your shuttle is boarding back the other way, but we have plenty of time. If you are in a hurry, public transportation can take you from one end of the cylinder to the other in just a few minutes. Let me give you a little geography lesson. North, South, East, and West aren't going to do you much good up here. Here, we have six directions: Up is toward the hub, and down is toward the rim. Toward the narrow end and the flywheel is the back, and toward the large end is the front. If you walk in the direction the station is spinning, it's called by, and against the direction is away. The directions up and down are demarcated by floors, just like in a building on Earth, and there are elevators all over the place. The distances by and away are given in degrees. The sections are marked by colors. Older sections are one solid color, and newer sections are two or more bars of color. But the distance is always the same. So if I'm giving you directions, I'll say to go forward three colors, then by thirty degrees, then up six floors. That will get you to Blue/Green, sixty degree, tenth floor."

They had come to a particularly busy area. Helmut had felt his gravity return to normal as they ascended an escalator. Now, both sides of the hallway were lined with narrow windows set into the floor. Free-space vehicles could be seen moving underfoot.

"This is a popular section, because one g is at the skin of the station. This allows people to enjoy the view comfortably at one g. Of course, all of the windows are in the floor. Can't help that. That has made this section a gathering place, a nexus of social interaction. It is almost exclusively made up of restaurants and bars, with a few open parks owned by the station. The area is called Earth Normal Park."

"And it will all be worth less if they slow down the station."

"Exactly. In fact, if you don't want to get into a heated argument with a passerby, you might not want to mention that fact too loudly."

As they passed a bar, Helmut caught his name written on a wall out of the corner of his eye. He started to turn, then remembered that wasn't his name anymore. He blinked and looked around.

"Scott, you have been most gracious. I believe that this is where I'd like to spend the rest of my layover." He held up his hand. "I realize that there is much more of this station to see, but I must take time to assimilate, and this section is the most interesting one I've seen as well as being the one where I most feel at home. What I'd like to do is stroll around, perhaps belly up to a bar, make an acquaintance or two, even get into an argument, before my shuttle leaves. I'll let you get back to your job."

"This is my job."

"But I'll let you get to a paying, staying customer. Really, I'll be fine. You've been an excellent teacher. My destination is written on my ticket and I know how to use a public information terminal." He eventually convinced Scott to get lost, then made a pretense of wandering around the parks and promenades for a while before returning to the bar where he saw his former name. It was called the Ying Yang Bar and Grill.

He took a seat near the door and surreptitiously looked around. The place was an American sports bar, oak and brass, green lamp shades, weak beer on tap and good stuff in bottles. He wanted to order a single malt but had to make due with a blended Scotch. The old dude behind the bar was kind of a grouch, pretty opinionated. He did have one neat trick, where he poured a drink from a great height, so you could just barely see the liquid slanting as it fell. The Coriolis force, one patron explained. He never missed the glass. Fun with physics.

Helmut listened to the arguments about the Moon,

some fancy computer, and only understood about half of what was being said. He was really only trying to stay low until his shuttle left.

The board where he had seen his name was to one side of the bar. The first three names were Larry Winters, Dana Woods, and Aqualung. After each name was a date, a set of odds and one word. Heroin, suicide, and assassination, respectively. Under that were more names: Dennis McColoch, Fenner, Sticks, and a few others he could recognize. The date was blank behind these, the odds were often erased, and the cause of death was empty.

He was happy to see that the final odds against Aqualung being the next one to die had been pretty long. Someone had cleaned up. Of course, he didn't know the rules. That may have been the final odds that he would be assassinated, as opposed to crashing his motorcycle or aspirating his own vomit. Natural causes, for a rock star.

What didn't make him happy was that Fenner was nine to five today. Up from two to one the last time it was erased. He had thought of calling Fenner, but he couldn't risk it. If Fenner was depressed that he had been killed, he would be even worse off if he knew that Aqualung had escaped but had been killed again because of that phone call.

There was some sort of a shift change and the bar cleared out pretty quickly. The old bartender, Korean, maybe, or southern Chinese, didn't feel like talking, so Helmut just sipped his Scotch until a pretty Hispanic woman came in.

"Shift change, Gramps," she said to the man behind the bar. "Go home." She tied on a white apron and tried to push the bartender out from behind the bar.

"I don't feel like going home tonight," he groused. "I think I'll keep working."

"Oh, great," the woman said. "You got one frickin' customer. What am I supposed to do, stand around and whip my skippy?"

"You don't have a skippy, Olivia. You shouldn't use phrases you don't understand. It's my place, I'll stay if I want to."

"I love this job," Olivia said to Helmut, rolling her eyes. "I got three jobs on this station, and this is, by far, my favorite."

"You have three jobs?" Helmut asked.

"You're fresh from dirtside, aren't you? Everybody on Freefall has three jobs. You got a career-making job, a tech job, and a scut job. Four hours each. Here's how I work it: four hours at my tech job, which happens to be traffic control in Bay Seventeen, then four hours rec, then my career job, which is developing drug delivery systems for the new anti-geriatric gene therapy, then I come here and try to tend bar when Sam will let me, then I sleep eight. You see, that way, I'm not tempted to eat into my rec time by working extra because traffic control is boring as hell. And my rec time is during the peak for the station, so I can party all I want and still make my career job. And this job is great for winding down because nobody ever comes in here because Sam won't put any new music in the jukebox."

"That's a good system. I take it you are flexible as to when you work, then?"

She nodded. "The only reason anyone comes up here to live is for their career job. If you're staying for more than about a month, they make you pay your way by taking a tech job and a scut job. Are you here more than a month?"

"No, I'm on my way to the Moon."

"Too bad. I heard of this great scut job opening up. Exterior maintenance. Now that's true Freefall. I'd take it myself, but it would screw up my whole schedule. Jesus Christ, Fenner's up to nine to five today."

"That's the story," the bartender said. "Hear he's on a Witch binge. Do you think you can die from the Witch?"

"You can die from anything," Olivia said. "The Witch is actually a disease. Our company designed it. It was supposed to be used to treat Parkinson's disease." She looked over at Helmut. "You think this is a sick game, don't you?"

"People will bet on anything. Did anyone make money off of this Aqualung?"

"Nah, nobody's been betting much," Sam said. "All people can talk about is this business with the Moon. Web-Cense is nobody to fuck with. I keep expecting the Lunars to blink, to say 'OK, we'll register the damn computer.' But they're not backing down."

"I just heard WebCense mentioned embargo for the first time." Olivia pulled up a news service on the terminal behind the bar.

"Excuse me, but I am a life-support engineer, and I am quite certain that the Moon is self-sufficient. What is this about embargo?" Helmut had read up on life-support systems enough so that he could pass a cursory examination. All of the extraterrestrial habitats were self-sufficient; his source had been emphatic on that point.

"Not an embargo of goods, Cap'n, a data embargo," Sam shook his head. "You're a dirtsider, you don't know how it is. Up here, we depend on information from Earth. We need the stock quotes to function as a business. The Orbital Traffic Control is administered from Earth, and we need that to survive. And we have no other source of entertainment up here, either. We'd go crazy without the however many thousand channels of crap you guys beam up. And WebCense controls it all. Information embargo is the worst thing they can threaten with."

"At least until they get their police force trained and equipped," Olivia said. "I hear they're going to be trained for space combat."

"Shit, that's just a sick rumor."

"It makes a certain sense," Helmut said.

"Don't say that. Not even in speculation. There's not going to be any space combat. Nobody would risk that. Once they start shooting guns and shit up here, we're all dead. That's the reality of life in space. Get used to it."

Pretty much a conversation killer, right there. Helmut ordered another Scotch and sat at a table to read the news feed on the monitor. Twenty minutes later, his ticket started beeping.

"Where is it coming from?" he asked no one in particular, turning the thin plastic over in his hands.

"That thing is all integrated circuits inside," Olivia said, taking it from him. "Push here for the printed message." She handed it back to him. It was telling him to call the bay where his shuttle was to take off.

"May I use this terminal to call?"

"Yeah," Olivia took the ticket again. "Just slip the card into this slot and it'll call automatically."

"Mr. Dietz," the smiling ticket agent said, "I'm afraid I have some bad news. Your business trip will have to be cut short. Earth authorities have just restricted travel to and from the Lunar base because of the unrest."

"Earth authorities?"

"Well, WebCense, actually. They don't want any Earth citizens to be inconvenienced should there be an embargo."

"But isn't that my choice?"

"I'm afraid not. We're going to have to book you a return trip to Earth. It's going to be a little full because of this order, but we'll squeeze you in."

"Certainly." WebCense made the order. They could be trying to get him to come back. Would they go through all that trouble? Maybe they just now realized their mistake in letting him leave the planet and were trying to correct it by issuing this order. It seemed a little extreme, but he didn't know why they wanted him or how badly. And maybe they didn't trust their agents on Freefall to bring him in. Maybe it was like Sam said, once the shooting started up here, it was all over.

"Now, you should probably call your contact on Luna to let them know you won't make it. Here, Shelly Cavendish. Would you like me to place that call?"

He felt eyes on him. The bartender was wiping down the next table. He looked up and straight into the man's eyes. A spark of recognition passed between them. "Shelly Cavendish?" the bartender's lips formed the words as he frowned.

"No, that won't be necessary. I can contact her my-self." Helmut switched off the terminal and looked back at the bartender. Sam Yee. Of all the gin joints. Sam pointed a gnarled finger at him.

Helmut held his fingers to his lips, pointed to his ears, then toward the ceiling. All muted gestures, meant not to be noticed.

"Relax," Sam said. "Nobody's listening. This is Freefall, that sort of thing just doesn't happen here."

"What are you guys talking about?" Olivia said.

"Our guest here thinks the place might be bugged."

"On Freefall? No way. Why would he think that?"

"Because he's Adrian Rifkin."

That did it for Helmut Dietz. That cover had probably already been blown, but he never expected to be fingered by a ghost from his past.

"No way. Adrian Rifkin? How do you know that? He doesn't look anything like Rifkin or Aqualung. Well, maybe a little."

"He used to play in my bar in Albuquerque. And his contact on Luna was Shelly Cavendish."

"Shelly Cavendish, keyboard player for the Cretins, then the Animal Bones, then did a couple of tours with the Shallow Cuts before she cooked her cortex with some bogus MDMA. She was pretty good, she had that little left hand, walking bass thing. I liked that." Olivia stopped and looked at the two men. "That's my hobby, Feedback history."

"I'll be damned." Helmut said.

Sam rounded the bar and sat across the table. "Jesus Christ, Rifkin, what are you doing here? Tell me what the hell is going on."

"You don't want to know, Sam. You could get killed."

"Who'd kill me? Zoe?"

"Not Zoe. It's WebCense that's trying to kill me."

"No way," Olivia sat down at the table.

"That's the biggest load of crap I've heard yet," Sam said. "WebCense doesn't go around killing people."

"They think I have some information they need. I think."

"Do you know how WebCense gets information out of people?"

"I do," Olivia said, raising her hand. "They freeze the head and scan it with a microprobe MRI."

"That's right," Sam said. "And did you see the footage of your supposed assassination? Your brains were all over the fucking place."

"That was a hologram, Sam. I made it to help me escape. Some friends of mine spliced in the head wound to fool WebCense into letting me escape. Pretty brutal footage, and not my idea, but it worked. Look, I can't give you the whole story right now, but the thing is, I can't go back to Earth. They'll be waiting for me down there. The only place I can find sanctuary is Luna."

Sam dismissed this idea with a wave of his hand. "Luna will fold in two days under an information embargo. You can't hide from WebCense. Look, I'm not convinced that these guys are after you. But let's stipulate that for right now. If they really wanted you, they would find you eventually. If they think you're alive, you're toast. But why do you think they're on to you?"

"This whole business about going back to Earth. The restricted travel. They're trying to capture me."

"No. They don't do like that, Rifkin. If WebCense wants you, here's what they do. They walk up behind you in a corridor and give you the old zapper. Medical emergency, you go to the hospital where you get a private operating theater for them to amputate your body. Your head gets frozen and transported back to Earth, and your body gets dumped into the incinerator. They are restricting travel to the Moon because the Moon is trying to play tough guy."

"Whatever. I'm not getting back on that lifter. I've got to lay low for a while."

"Lay low? Do you realize that they keep track of every single human on the station to estimate oxygen consumption? The sewage system knows who had what for breakfast. There is no laying low here, Rifkin."

"Sam, I hate to break it to you, but your precious technology isn't infallible. That business is not taken care of by people, it can't possibly be. Computers do that sort of monotonous work, and the one thing I know about computers is that they only do what they're told to do."

"Oh, you're going to break into the population database?" Olivia said, incredulous. "No way."

"All I have to do is miss that next lifter, and then take a couple of days to figure out the system."

"Where are you going to stay for a couple of days?" Sam asked.

"Here and there."

"Not here."

"Sam, do you remember 2007?"

"Course I remember it. That was the year you started bringing people into the bar."

"Because that was the year I started taking music seriously. The year I stopped taking heroin seriously."

"I knew it," Olivia said. "I knew you took H." She looked at the two men. "Sorry."

"Do you know why I got off the spike, Sam?" he went

on, ignoring her. "Because of one thing you said to me. You walked in one morning and found me asleep under a table and you said 'You're going to kill yourself with that shit, kid.'"

"Anybody could have said that," Sam said. "Hell, Zoroaster said it to you every day."

"But I respected you, Sam. When you said it, I listened. I kicked it in your back room, remember? You helped me pick the right road to turn down. Now I'm at another crossroads. I can give up, give WebCense what they want. Or I can choose my own road. But I need your help to do that. What do you say, Sam?"

There was silence around the table for a few seconds. People started to drift into the bar and Sam rose to serve them.

"Do you want to stay at my place?" Olivia said.

CHAPTER 11

Sweet Sandra Carter, trying to get smarter,
At the Peabody Music Conservatory.
Found herself a bad boy, and tried to read him Tolstoi,
They ended up broke in St. Looeee.
And no one's getting sick except Mr. Sticks.
THE SNAKE VENDORS,
"IMPROMPTU RIFF ON 'CRIQUE ALLEY' "
BOOTLEG IN TOKYO,
PRIVATELY DISTRIBUTED, 2031

He ended up keeping the name Helmut Dietz, at least in the computer. Maybe Sam was right and the cover hadn't been blown, but in any case it was lot easier to fool the station computer if it already had a Helmut Dietz on board.

The most difficult part about disappearing on station was taking care of the frantic ticket agent for Delta Launch! The man had paged him through the ticket circuits with increasing intervals until the lifter left the station. After that, he destroyed the ticket, making the ticket agent believe that the ticket, and Helmut, were in fact on their way back to Earth. Once the lifter was on the ground, he called the Delta office in Denver, routed through a Frisco switching station, and asked that his baggage be taken out of storage. He hoped that someone would just steal the phony luggage so he wouldn't have to worry about the agents getting suspicious when he didn't pick it up. It was a pretty safe bet, actually.

It turned out to be pretty easy to fool the Population Database. It wanted to know each of his three jobs, his bank account, his apartment, and an emergency contact on Earth. Lucky for him his old tricks worked as well here on Freefall as they did on Earth. He updated one field in the database at a time, only when an authorized user was updating the same field at the same time for a different name. The only drawback was that with no new people entering the station population between lifter dockings, it took twelve hours to make him legitimate. He used the time to hang around the Ying Yang.

"You know," he said to Sam, "you really should change the music in the jukebox. There's a lot of good stuff being done now. You'd be surprised."

"I'm not just being nostalgic, actually. That's what I let Olivia think, but the truth is the input board is fried. It can't retrieve anything from the worm drives on the station or the continuous feed from Earth."

"Why don't you get it fixed?"

"What, are you kidding? You put in a work order like that and the techs will laugh you right out into space. They have life-support systems and shit to fix. They ain't got time for jukeboxes."

He pulled his chair over to the jukebox. "Let's have a peek."

"Hey, don't break that thing, I've got all the songs memorized. Do you know what you're doing, Rifkin?"

"Pretty much. And can we cool it on the Rifkin talk? Call me Helmut."

"Jesus, I told you no one is listening. There's nobody in here."

"That's not it. You were there, Sam. You saw what Rifkin did to his friends. He fucked up. I'm just not him anymore."

"Changing your name isn't going to change what you did. You have to do what everyone else does. Put it behind you. Yeah, you were a bad person there for a while. You're the same person who paid that disc jockey."

"One of Zoe's bag men paid the DJ."

"Right, but you are definitely the one who took the stand and sent Zoe and Grish and the others to prison. You are the one who left your band without saying good-bye. Changing your name once or a hundred times doesn't change that."

"Thanks a lot."

"But you can still change. You made a few mistakes, you wanted success so bad you didn't care who you stepped on. Just young and impulsive, a million punks out there just like you."

"Yeah, I know a guy just like that. Bass player. So this input jack is cooked. Looks like it had a power surge. Someone must have tried to download some Naked Mole Rat."

"Is that what the kids are listening to these days?"

"But the good news is that this thing only needs seven leads to function. Those little data jacks all over this place have seven leads. I'll just pry off an extra one you don't use and patch it in."

"Are you sure you know what you're doing?"

"Yeah," he said from underneath the bar. "This is pretty basic stuff. Hand me that knife you were using to cut the limes. Or do you have a screwdriver?"

"Here's the knife. Did you sleep with Olivia?"

"Nah, she had too many questions to leave time for that. She's just fascinated with the Feedback scene. She even knew that Zoroaster and I went to high school together."

"I thought Shelly introduced you to Zoroaster."

"Yeah, but it turns out we went to high school together, too. We never knew each other. He hung out with the art students while I was over in the machine shop."

"You probably chased him down and pantsed him after

school and didn't even suspect that he'd be the lead singer in your band in five years."

"Irony is great, isn't it? All right, this thing is just going to hang here until I can get some duct tape to hold it up. And what's with this question about Olivia, anyway? You got a thing for her?"

"Oh God, no. Just a little protective, I guess."

"Yeah, sure. I don't think that business with Olivia is going to happen. You can rest easy."

"She's probably gay."

"This is what I'm thinking."

"So what am I supposed to call you?" Olivia was talking to a pair of legs that led under her desk. Her data terminal had been in the queue for repair for three weeks.

"Well, that's an interesting question. I've had a lot of names. I used to have a trick. I'd wake up each morning and before I opened my eyes I'd think to myself 'I am Steve Drabkin.' Or, 'I am Aqualung.' This morning I couldn't think of anything."

"So you're not sticking with Helmut Dietz?"

"Helmut Dietz has three decent jobs on the station, a decent bank balance, a posh point-nine-g apartment just three levels from the rim. He's a good guy to have around. But I just can't think of myself as him anymore. I guess it's because of a conversation I had with Sam yesterday."

"So what do I call you?"

"Yeah, that was the original question, wasn't it? My instinct tells me to stick with Helmut. It has a definite survival advantage at this point, even though it doesn't fit."

"What if I call you Riff?"

"You really do know your history, don't you?"

"Oh, that one was easy. The liner notes to the EP *Grandfather Mountain* say 'Music by Riff, words by Zoroaster.' So did they all call you Riff?"

"Just the band." He pulled out from under the desk and reached up to flip the terminal on. "Oh, shit, what the hell is this?" He started to type on the keyboard, still kneeling on the floor. "Yeah, why don't we go with Riff. It's just a nickname, right? But just in private. OK, there's your browser. Try not to kick those cables loose under there."

"This is great, Riff. I was having trouble keeping up with the literature. There's no time at work."

"So, you're some kind of scientist, then?" Riff started putting his tools away. He had swiped most of them, and was beginning to put together a pretty good kit.

"Yeah, molecular biologist. I work for Cognigene Pharmaceuticals, one of the big four that built this station. Did the Snake Vendors really take Dopavir for recreation?"

"The Witch? I don't know if you'd call it recreation. More like extracurricular insanity. Cognigene made that?"

"Back in the old days, when we were a dirtside company. Before my time. Well, we dumped it after the side effect profile came out. It almost killed us."

"It almost killed the Snake Vendors, too."

Quin's greatest fear was that Aqualung had fled to the Moon, so that was the last possibility he explored. The Moon was actually a logical place to disappear, considering the latest news. Really, who knew the bastards would hold out so long? Information embargo was the greatest weapon Web-Cense could wield, at least until they finished training and equipping their goon squad. And yet Luna 1 had absorbed a full week of the silent treatment and showed no signs of giving up. It was anyone's guess how they were amusing themselves up there. Maybe the superintelligence computer was generating new episodes of *Gilligan's Island* using digital images and a plot synthesizer.

But if there was one place to escape from WebCense, it

was the Moon. And all traffic to the Moon had to go through Freefall, and Freefall was tighter than a homophobe in South Beach. Nobody breathed more than three lungfulls of Freefall air without it being noted by the big computer census takers. So if anyone bogus had traveled through Freefall just before WebCense put the lid on lunar emigration, there would be a way to weasel that information out.

But if Aqualung had, in fact, fled to the Moon, what good would that do? There was an embargo, after all.

But first things first. "Give me the passenger lists on the lifters since June twentieth." The display inside Quin's head filled up with a list of about three thousand people. "Any of these people come from Edinburgh?" A couple of dozen names changed color. "Any of them on the way to the Moon?" Five of the names changed color again.

"All of them returned to Earth," Molly said. "That was right before the embargo. WebCense restricted travel."

All five were ordinary businessmen and women, with long credit histories and legitimate IIN's. They were placed into a growing file of suspect travelers that had participated in the mass exodus from Edinburgh on June 20. Another dead end.

The arms dealers were actually quite professional. Walter Cheeseman had expected some sleazy used car salesman, or an oily Middle Easterner. He was surprised to find two polite, understated people, a man and a woman, in tasteful business attire, who greeted him right off the helicopter. There, on the tiny tropical atoll, they had assembled an eye-catching display of the latest in lethal force.

"We have examples of every weapon we described in our brochure, Mr. Cheeseman," the woman said. "They're all fully functional and ready for testing. By the way, I understand congratulations are in order."

"Huh?" Walter was looking over the small arms.

"We read about your engagement," the man said. Walter just stared at him. "I'm sorry, we can get right back to business, if you prefer."

Eventually, the new police force of WebCense would be equipped and trained to bring lawbreakers to justice anywhere in its jurisdiction. But for now Walter was interested in a show of force in only one location.

"All of these weapons are capable of firing in the vacuum of space," the woman said. "We've assembled only hand weapons at this point, but we can also demonstrate the larger, vehicle mounted devices at your convenience."

"I've read the specs you sent," Walter told them. "Most of what you've got here has limited application. Considering power consumption, the effects of shielding and armor, and lack of recoil, the most interesting device as far as I can tell is the," he consulted a sheet of fax paper, "Mag Seven Cutter."

"That's an excellent choice," the man said, waving him toward an enormously technical, vaguely gunlike object sitting on a table. "The Cutter employs thousands of microscopic abrasive particles. The particles are filled with a shaped iron core, and tuned magnetic fields move the particles, and only the particles, in a loop that extends several meters from the base unit. Cooling units in the base keep the particles from breaking down. While its range is short, it actually expends very little energy while cutting through just about anything. We've built the unit to be entirely self-contained, although an optional external power unit is offered."

Walter hefted the gun. It was a little heavy, but on the low gravity of the Moon, that would be a minor problem. "May I?"

The woman indicated a brand new Cadillac parked on the beach. One of several. She handed him a face shield. "Be our guest."

Walter pointed the Cutter at the car and, with a little help taking off the safety interlock, pulled the trigger.

A gray cloud extended from the flared muzzle and took shape into a blade like a chain saw. As Walter brought the blade in contact with the Caddy, the metal of the car's body vanished wherever it touched. There was very little noise, just a low hiss as the tiny cutting blades sliced through the car. In seconds, the two halves of the car crunched into the sand. A faint metallic smell quickly faded in the tropical breeze.

"We'll take three hundred, with the external power sources." Congratulations were indeed in order.

Riff needed a guitar. He didn't really want one, but he had to have one just the same. Making a guitar, playing a guitar, owning a guitar, was, without a doubt, a big mistake. If WebCense was still looking for him, they would certainly pay more attention to a guitar-playing vagabond than to a life-support engineer. But the calluses on his fingers were starting to itch for some metal strings. Riff didn't imagine he had a great capacity for addiction anymore. He had drunk alcohol, smoked tobacco and pot, all without getting hooked, and had even injected heroin and later managed to kick it. He could take these drugs or leave them. He had given up making music for twenty years and never missed it. But now that he had dipped back in and taken a taste, he felt he could no more give it up than he could give up air.

The frame was machined out of a plastic hull panel off of a junked maintenance vehicle. The plastic, dense and silvery, still bore the word *Freefall* in gold block letters that looked like they were embedded deep under the surface. The pickups were self-cooling superconducting magnets from a scrapped guidance system. It had a built-in solid state amp with over a hundred channels and a fretboard made of reentry grade ceramic. He had considered going for a stringless. The parts he'd need were easy to come by, but he had never gotten used to the slippery feel of the magnetic fields, and he liked to switch back and forth between picking and finger bopping on the fly. A stringless needed a special pick. So he'd gone with strings and was pleased with the result. Les Paul himself would have been proud.

The first song Riff played in public, at the Ying Yang Bar and Grill, before an audience of six, was "Crossroads." The Clapton version. Sam seemed pretty indifferent to live music in his bar. Olivia Gutierez was fascinated by the idea of a man making music in front of her. Riff decided that she had never heard live music before. He gave her a show. Everything he played was guitar heavy, of course, because that was all he had. He programmed the jukebox and the data terminal to keep a beat and play a little bass and he had his own little one-man power trio.

A couple of people drifted in during the set, curious to see the whole messy process of art being created. After he was finished, there was a little smattering of applause followed by some polite questions about the guitar. Riff was already gaining a reputation among the bar's regular patrons for his on-the-spot repairs. His customers said that he never really fixed anything, he made it work. In a station so lacking in low-level technical support, his services were valuable, but he usually gave them away for drinks and conversation. One man who approached him after that first night admitted that he had smuggled an electronic sax onto the station when he had lifted, but that it had broken and he didn't dare put in a work order for contraband. Riff agreed to fix it in exchange for a little jam session now and then, and his new band began to coalesce.

Olivia bugged him to show her how it was done, but it

was clear she had no talent from the start. Riff offered to let her play the tambourine during a session, but she knew what that meant. A tambourine was what you give a good-looking chick who can't play. She had too much dignity for that, so she just watched. Along with about thirty other people, a number that grew every night.

"This ain't a dance club, Riff," Sam told him. "We can't handle these crowds. We gotta stop drawing them in. Hell, I don't even recognize half these people."

"That's your answer to success, Sam? Turn it away? This station is supposed to be modular. Push back the walls. Make it a dance club. Hire some new staff. Make hay, man."

"Well, maybe. I'll put in a requisition."

"To hell with that. I'll go talk to the neighbors. We'll work something out with them. We can move the walls. Just a few screws to loosen, a little wiring and plumbing work. That way we can get it done this century."

"No chance, Cap'n. That's where we draw the line. You're not messing with the plumbing."

Riff held up his hands in surrender. "All right, you win. Put in your requisition."

Mr. North held up a silvery disc, about ten centimeters in diameter, encased in clear plastic. "This was a very expensive item to obtain, Taber."

"Yes, sir," Quin said from the other side of Mr. North's huge desk. Why the hell did it come to you? I thought I was dealing with Fred on this one. And the fact that you were able to get it at all tells me something about you. "It is essential to my research."

"I've given you a long leash on this one." I think I'm about to feel my choke collar tighten, Quin thought. "It's time you tell me what you've got."

"It turns out that my instincts were right about the Digital Carnivore," Quin said. "It looks like Martin Grish was the author."

"That's good work then. Where does it get you? Grish is reprogrammed."

"Well, knowing what to look for, I uplinked and examined the Digital Carnivore more closely."

"You examined it?"

"Well, yes. That's basically what I did at WebCense, studied the Digital Carnivore. I still have that capability."

"So what did you find out?"

"Well," Quin tried not to pause, tried to quickly formulate an answer that didn't give too much away but gave Mr. North just enough to let him loosen the leash. "The virus has interior structure that I have never been able to see before. It turns out that to get to this hidden structure, I need information that is on that disc you are holding."

"*There's a Monkey on My Back, But He's Good People.* Sounds like some kind of hippie drug shit."

"That's the final album recorded by the Animal Bones. Martin Grish's gang was promoting the album by paying local disc jockeys to play it on the air. He used lyrics from the album as passwords to the interior of the virus code. They were probably temporary passwords. If the album had been a success, every teenager in the country would have been able to break into his virus. But he went to prison before he could change them, and it turned out it didn't matter because the album was never released. So really, those lyrics are the best-kept secret in America."

"And I have them. Good work, Taber."

"Actually . . ."

"This information is too valuable for me to let out of my hands. We can't record this album, or even let it out of my office."

"Well, I have to listen to it in order to use it." Even you can figure out that I'm the only one who can make use of this information.

"Of course. You can listen to it right here."

"I'm going to need a CD player."

It only took a couple of hours for someone to find a working CD player. They went to a music collector and probably had to muscle it out of him. Scarcity of the players was what made the collections valuable. Quin had a little trouble hooking it up to Mr. North's sound system, which was only made for direct feed from a worm drive. When he was finished, Mr. North himself volunteered to leave him alone. "I don't want any information in my head that I can't afford to give up and I can't use," he explained.

Quin had about the same idea. "Ears off, Molly." It was a command he rarely used. He had gotten used to thinking of Molly looking over his shoulder in all that he did. But everything Molly did or heard or dug out of a computer file was recorded somewhere, on the unused storage capacity of some computer. Quin didn't want this information stored anywhere that WebCense could get to it. And WebCense could get to almost any storage device. Except Quin's head, of course, at least until they had it frozen and mounted in their microprobe MRI.

He listened to the disc three times, concentrating to remember each word. He knew he wouldn't get it all, but by the time he called Mr. North back in, he thought he had most of it.

The fourth track on *There's a Monkey on My Back, But He's Good People* was a party anthem called "Godzilla in Paradise." It was actually a pretty catchy tune. It would have made a great video. It was about some poor sap who won a trip to a tropical island on a TV game show and right when he gets there, a fire-breathing *T. rex* from Japan shows up to trash the place. This peeved frat boy ends up doing battle with Godzilla and saves the island.

The lyric that opened up the Digital Carnivore's hidden recesses was "Then he stepped on the bar. Man, that's going too far."

It was a popularly held myth that people who uplinked had to have a spotter who would disconnect them after a certain amount of time, or else they would become lost in the Upper Shell and forget to eat and starve to death. That wasn't true. But Quin certainly lost track of time. He learned more in four hours than he had in his entire career studying the Digital Carnivore, with and without Web-Cense.

The core virus itself was a thing of beauty. At the time it was created, protected memory and restricted read/write privileges had made viruses almost obsolete. The new operating systems of the early teens had made it nearly impossible for a file to transfer itself, hide from the system, and affect computer operations at the same time. But the early Digital Carnivore operated on a whole different level. It incorporated parts of other operating systems into its own code. It was above operating systems, security systems, anti-virus programs. It was alive. It learned.

If Grish hadn't been caught, the virus would have been his downfall. While it was shoveling money into his bank account, it was learning. While he served his first prison term, the virus began to think on its own. By the time he was out, it had copied itself onto every computer in the world. It had begun facilitating file transfers five years before anyone knew it existed. By the time the virus was discovered to be a sentient being, by Quin himself, actually, all communications in the world depended on it. Computer programmers and architects began basing their designs on the virus's file transfer capabilities. WebCense liked to think that it controlled the flow of information for the entire world. But in reality, the uplinkers were like cowboys driving cattle. They looked like they were in control. But if the cows really wanted to stampede, all the cowboys could do was get out of the way.

The Digital Carnivore was not an artificial intelligence. It was more like a force of nature. And it was natural. An artificial intelligence took about three years to mature once the programmers were finished with it. The Carnivore had matured over twenty years, and was still maturing.

Before he went home to Janet, and the apartment they now shared, Quin had one more question for the demigod that now stood revealed before him after all these years of pursuit. "Can you isolate WebCense from all information input and output?"

The Carnivore had asked him for lyrics from the Animal Bones album periodically during his examination. He had answered the questions easily. Now it asked him a different sort of question.

"Recite the poem that Zoroaster wrote for Shelly Cavendish on her twenty-third birthday."

"I can't." Quin answered.

A new voice appeared, one he didn't recognize. "Well, I'm afraid that's all we have time for."

He cut the connection before his neurons could get fried. It was clear. He still needed Rifkin.

CHAPTER 12

You think your mind belongs to you,
But you act as I want you to.
As I walk across the room,
Your eyes can't help but follow.

LOST KITTEN, "MIND CONTROL"
NEEDS MEDICATION, THRASHER RECORDS, 2032

If we had waited for NASA, or any government entity, for that matter, to fashion a working habitat in space, we'd still be standing around arguing about whether we should print the instructions to use the toilet in sixteen different languages or seventeen. But we didn't have time for that. Big pharma needed a place to crystalize proteins in a microgravity environment, so big pharma just went ahead and built one.

Once the original platform for the Freefall station was in place, and it just housed thirty people at first, the rest was pretty easy. Near-Earth asteroids provided some of the working materials, and mines on the Moon supplied the rest. Robots did a lot of the work. Robots had never made it very far on Earth, because they had some difficulty in navigating unfamiliar terrain. But guess what? Space didn't have any obstacles in it. Nope, totally empty. Robots did just fine in space. And energy turned out to be pretty cheap, once you built the right infrastructure. Robot factories could crank out photocells by the square meter, and reflective foils to concentrate sunlight on ore smelters and the like. So Freefall started to take on its familiar form, and the pharmas moved the people in.

At the same time, big pharma's counterparts in the computer chip industry set up camp on the south pole of the Moon. Same concept, slightly different choice of locations. The Moon was one big clean room, it had a ready supply of water (all frozen underground) and plenty of starting materials. The similarities between Freefall and Luna were obvious: lots of money, lots of technology, big brains.

The differences were where things got interesting. Where Freefall was regimented, Luna was an enclave of free thinkers. Freefall was governed by a hierarchy, while Luna bordered on anarchy. Freefall was the home of stuffed shirts, on Luna they often didn't wear shirts.

Bionerds on one side, and gear heads on the other, and an ocean of difference in between.

Olivia had a girlfriend. She was discreet. There was an anti-homosexual drift to station politics of late, and she didn't want to be discriminated against. But she felt she could trust Riff. That was the thing. Everybody trusted Riff. He was the man who made things work. He would fix contraband equipment, tell you how to safely take an illicit drug, or help you win back your lady. They all trusted Riff.

Olivia's girlfriend was named Barb. She was an engineer. Riff sat down to join them after a good set.

"You guys sure play a lot of different kinds of music," Barb said. She had enjoyed the show OK, but Riff got the impression she wasn't really into music. She and Olivia must share other interests.

"Oh, yeah," Olivia said. "They did some Iggy Pop in there, some John Lee Hooker, some Stevie Ray Vaughan."

"Well, the band is pretty much whoever shows up that

night," Riff said. "We play whatever fits the tastes of whoever's playing, and what we all know."

"I hear you made your guitar." Barb took it from him and examined the workmanship. "I recognize a lot of these parts."

"Yeah, well, I just found most of that stuff, here and there."

"You mean you stole it."

"None of it was in use."

"Don't sweat it. You should see all the stuff I make out of stolen parts. My research budget is practically nonexistent."

"So what is it you do? I mean your career job."

"My career job, my tech job, and my scut job are all wrapped up in one place, actually. You should come down and see it."

So he did. Barb's scut job was exterior station maintenance. She scooted around on a tram hanging off the hull of Freefall and reset deflector panels, repaired wiring, aligned communications dishes. A lot of stuff was stuck on the outside of the station. Anything that didn't need expensive pressurized space was out there. She wasn't the only one doing maintenance. Her tech job was to coordinate other crews, send them where trouble codes were received from, schedule patrols to find cracked deflectors, and the like. Her career job was aimed at eliminating her first two jobs altogether.

"This little guy," Barb said, setting a hand-sized metallic crab on the table, "is called Socket. His job is to crawl along the skin until he encounters a nut holding some piece of equipment on. Then he squats over the nut and his little adjustable socket in his body tightens around it and torques it to specifications. He doesn't store the specs in his body. I cut down on integrated circuits in their bodies because the outside of the station is unshielded. He gets his information by radio."

Riff picked Socket up and peered at the underside of his carapace. "How come he doesn't fly off the outside of the station?"

"Put him back on the table. No, over here on the metal part." Barb reached for a remote control and hit a button. "Now pick him up."

Riff couldn't budge the little guy now. "Magnets in his feet?"

"Yep. That's the real reason he has six feet. Not because I wanted him to be a proper insect. This one is Rivet."

Rivet was much bigger, about half a meter long. He had to have room to store enough rivets to stay out on the skin for as long as his power supply would hold up. That was engineering. Riff had to admire that. Barb also introduced him to Welder, Snippet (the electrician), and Scrub. Apparently, oil leaking from space vehicles formed a cloud around Freefall and accumulated on surfaces. It had to be wicked off with a special surfactant. That was what Scrub did.

"So, do you think you can get to ninety percent with these guys?" Riff was picking up station lingo pretty fast. Ninety percent was the mythical number efficiency experts had set for automation. Machines should be able to do ninety percent of the work on the station, leaving humans to do the really interesting stuff. Every department was expected to achieve ninety percent sooner or later.

"I think I can do better than that, even," Barb said. "If I can get my funding approved to put these guys into production, I'll be the first department to achieve the Holy Grail."

Riff actually was getting impatient with some of the departments himself. In particular, the Hub Dock Controllers Office was far too dependent on human intervention. Riff had not given up the idea of getting to the Moon, so he had researched his options. Things didn't look too good.

The Moon was about 385,000 kilometers from Earth, and Freefall, although it was technically in high earth orbit, was only 50,000 kilometers up. That was still a long way to go. And you had to balance distance, maximum speed, fuel capacity, and life support. No matter how Riff ran the numbers, a one-man vehicle would not get him to the Moon by itself.

But Freefall was more than just a Manhattan-sized drug factory. It was also a massive momentum sink. The skin of the station was clipping along at a good 1200 kph. If you sat in a vehicle on the skin and let go at precisely the right time, you too would be traveling at 1200 kph in the right direction. Free speed.

Well, not really free. When your vehicle entered the hub of the station and rode the big elevator to the rim, you stole a little bit of momentum from the station, like a figure skater flinging her arms out in the middle of a spin. It took energy to get that momentum back, and energy was the coin of the realm in space. So, not just anybody was allowed to jump off the rim of the station any time he wanted to. That was controlled by the Hub Dock Controllers Office. The HDCO collected a fee to transport a certain amount of weight to the rim. You could get your deposit back if you rode the elevator back to the hub, but if your weight was undocked at the rim, they kept the cash.

Cash was not the biggest problem, though. The HDCO also coordinated the release of weight from the rim. Only with the help of the HDCO's databases could you be sure of jumping off at the right time so your vehicle flew off in the right direction. The most efficient way for this all to be coordinated was that requests were fed into a queue, matched against allowed destination points, then automatically assigned priority. All by a simple, dumb computer program. But the HDCO was by most estimates less than 5 percent mechanized. Requests for release were processed by anal retentive bureaucrats. Human bureaucrats.

Computers only believed what you told them. Humans usually didn't. Riff could find no way around this gauntlet of peevish officials for the time being, so he made the best of life on the station.

The only restaurant on the station that served single malt Scotch was also his favorite place to be alone with his thoughts. The tables were mounted precariously, or so it seemed, on an intricate trellis suspended over the largest windows on the rim. Every six seconds, the Earth, or whatever else you were interested in watching, would soar across those windows at breathtaking speed. Riff was getting good at recognizing land masses and had even spotted a tropical storm before the news feed mentioned it. After coming back from Barb's workshop, he went there to watch one of the Scrub robots in action. Barb had told him the little creature would be working on the big windows, a job much hated by the exterior maintenance crew but often requested by the owner of the restaurant. The little robot would anchor its guy wires on either side of the glass surface, then pull itself across, sponging up oil as it went. It was a fascinating process. So fascinating, in fact, that Riff failed to notice a tall, attractive Asian woman working her way over the trellis toward him.

"Dirtsiders usually don't come to this place," she said to him. He looked up, not being able to help noticing her body on the way to her face. "The locals call this the Vertigo Room."

"I like it here," Riff said, gesturing at a free seat at his table. "And what makes me a dirtsider? I live here. There are no natives of Freefall."

She took the seat. "You're a dirtsider until you've lived here about a year."

"Who made up that rule?"

She shrugged. "That's just the way it is. Although, another interpretation is that you're a dirtsider until you can walk the corridors and have a nodding acquaintance with a tenth of the people you see. I'd say you qualify for that already, Mr. Dietz, even though you've been here less than a month."

Riff held out his hand. "I guess only half an introduction is in order."

"I'm Natalie Park." She shook his hand. Good, firm shake. It figured. Natalie Park was the CEO of Freefall Station.

"Nice to meet you. I wouldn't think you'd have much time in your schedule to greet station newcomers."

"I certainly don't greet all of them, Mr. Dietz. You may not realize this, but you are actually famous."

"Really? I didn't realize my music was that popular."

"That's not why you're famous."

Riff smiled. He turned on the charm like a three-thousand-watt klieg light and shined it in her face. "Which of my talents has made me so famous, then?"

Natalie smiled back, matched him watt for watt. "You're famous for making things work."

"Well, there's nothing wrong with making things work, is there? That's what a lot of people are searching for in their lives. Something that works."

"Station security followed you. On my orders. You're not working, Mr. Dietz."

Riff leaned back and spread his hands. "I guess you got me."

"In the old west, stealing a horse was a hanging offense. Up here, the only hanging offense we have is stealing air. You're not working, you're not paying for the air you breathe."

"So you're going to hang me?"

"Don't tempt me. You will leave the station."

"You just said, I make things work. Isn't that worth

something?" One thing was certain. He was not going back to Earth. He'd make a break for the Moon if it looked like he was going to get kicked off of Freefall, but he hoped it wouldn't come to that.

"Making things work isn't the same as fixing them."

"No, it's better. Fixing things would be great if they ever actually got fixed, but they don't. If somebody makes a thing work, it gets transformed from garbage to something useful. That's important work."

Natalie chewed her lip while a waiter brought her a white wine. She didn't have to ask for it. Rank. "That sounds like a tech job, then. You're a third of the way there."

"But wait. I don't want to be a technician, to go through channels and be scheduled."

"You just want to fix your friends' stuff?"

"No, of course not. Tell you what. I'll work on anything that's been in queue for more than a month. I'll start at the earliest date in the backlog. I'll fix anything that I can that the technicians will never get to."

"All right, like I said, you're a third of the way there."

"Why can't making music be my career job?"

Natalie stared at him for what seemed like a long time. It made him uncomfortable, which probably made it seem like a long time. He forced himself not to squirm. "You're Adrian Rifkin," she said, finally.

Riff hung his head in his hands. "Motherfucking Sam."

Natalie waved a hand in front of his face. "I just figured it out this second. I saw your face on the news a couple of weeks ago, I guess it just stuck in my mind. When you said something about being a professional musician, I just made the connection. Sam Yee didn't tell me anything. I mean, I did have him questioned, but he didn't say anything. Oh, shit."

"What?"

"You're supposed to be dead."

"I've been dead before."

Sanctuary. At the end of about two hours of negotiations with the CEO of Freefall, two Scotches, and three wines, to be precise, Riff asked for and received sanctuary. He had to give up a few things in exchange. First, he had to explain to those in charge of the population database how he had managed to insinuate himself into legitimate Freefall society. They wanted to plug up the holes. No problem there. Second, he had to take as a scut job one of the most hated positions on the station, but one that was an essential part of life in space. He became a roach wrangler.

Human beings, whether they lived in the rudest mud hut or a totally synthetic and nonporous environment like Freefall, shed skin cells as part of their bodies' normal housekeeping function. If these skin cells were allowed to remain on the floor they would begin to pile up and create an unhealthy dust. Other space habitats employed robot vacuum cleaners to pick up this detritus, but Freefall and Luna 1 found this impractical because of the sheer scale, so to speak, of the shed material. For this reason they allowed dust mites to flourish in moist, dark gaps between the walls and floors. The dust mites fed on the skin cells and were in turn fed upon by a centimeter long beetle imported for just that purpose. These were the only animals allowed to live among the humans on Freefall.

The job of the roach wrangler was to collect the insects, intact, and monitor their numbers and state of health. These creatures were not allowed to carry disease, nor were they to endanger the station's food supply. In fact, the goal was to maintain a healthy food chain without ever allowing one insect to be seen by a station inhabitant. Except for the roach wranglers.

The third and final condition, and one that Riff fought to have taken off the table, was that he give up his false identities for good. He did mention the fact that Web-Cense and Zoe Campbell were both trying to kill him, for different reasons. But Natalie insisted that Freefall could protect him. She seemed to share the conviction of the rest of the station inhabitants that WebCense had no real power here. They had representatives, but no goons who would shanghai a man and freeze his head solid in the dead of night. And as for Zoe Campbell, she was safely incarcerated. What harm could she do from prison?

They all seemed pretty thin arguments to Riff, but Natalie had what she considered good reasons for this last condition. She was not an elected official, but her position was still a very political one. Allowing Riff to keep a false identity could hurt her position with the board of directors.

"So," Natalie said at the end of the negotiations. "You're a legitimate citizen, for the first time in, how long? Twenty years? What are you going to do now?"

"I have to make a phone call."

Lalo answered the phone. He and Fenner were listed as sharing a house in Sacramento. There was another listing for Britta, in Los Angeles, but Riff didn't want to talk to her just yet.

"Brace yourself," Riff said just before activating the video channel. "I'm not dead." He couldn't come up with a better way to tell him. He had sat in the bar and thought about it for half an hour before making the call.

Lalo took it pretty well. He seemed to be a little high, but there was recognition and shock in his eyes still.

Riff explained it all as best he could, knowing that he would have to go back later to fill in the details when Lalo came down from whatever he took.

"They used to talk about rock stars faking their own death to get away," Lalo said. "It was all bullshit. But you actually did it."

"I'm through running away, Lalo. I'm up on Freefall now, the space station. I have sanctuary. They tell me no one can touch me here."

"Sanctuary. That sounds great."

"So what have you been doing? What about the band?"

"There's no band anymore."

"You're not making music?"

"Britta started her own band, Lost Kitten. I think they're going to make it. Thrasher kept them on. They're the kind of people we used to make fun of. They look good but they can't play for shit."

"What about you, Lalo? You couldn't put down your ax, could you?"

"I just recorded a solo album, with your guitar and equipment. I engineered it myself. It's my *Madcap Laughs*."

"I'd like to hear it," Riff said.

"I'm thinking of releasing it myself. I know guys with drive space for rent. They can only handle about ten hits per hour. It isn't likely to sell much faster than that."

"I'll get you on one of my own sites. A special one. It can handle the hits. What about Fenner and Sandra?"

"There is no more Fenner and Sandra. Sandra went Nationalist. She's one of their organizers here in California. And Fenner hasn't been fully conscious since Edinburgh. It's a good thing you showed me how to use the antags. Otherwise, he'd be dead. Anyway, he's out of his Snake Vendor money, so he's either going to have to quit or become a street junkie."

That was too much for Riff. He tried to tell Lalo to sober up and try to take care of Fenner, but he didn't think very much of that came across. Lalo soon drifted off and Riff cut the connection.

"That was about the weirdest conversation I've ever heard," Olivia said behind him. He turned to look at her. "I'm sorry, I didn't mean to eavesdrop. I couldn't help it."

"You could tell he was high, couldn't you?" Riff asked.

"No way. What was he on?"

"It's hard to say just talking over the phone. Some kind of downer. I'd guess one of the benzodiazepines. He'll have to sober up before his mind can process what he's just learned. It'll be a delayed shock reaction. Then he'll either take more drugs so he doesn't have to deal with it or he'll call back."

"What about Fenner?"

"I've been around people who've taken drugs all my life. They either stop on their own or they die. The best you can do is try to make their choice a real choice. I mean, look at all the kids down on dirtside shooting up or popping or Witching out. Their choice is between the drug or a world that has no use for them. Fenner is no different. He has no place in the world. He might as well try to have some fun while he's killing himself."

"God, that's cynical."

"Don't get me wrong, Olivia. I don't like it any more than you do. I just don't see a way to change it. Anyway, I just wanted to tell Lalo that I was still around before the press release."

Olivia sat across the table from him. "You don't feel like you're supposed to do more than that?"

Riff sighed. "Why does everyone think it's my job to look after these people? I'll talk to them if they call me. That's the most I can do."

He didn't have to wait long. Fenner called within the hour. Antags had taken care of the drugs he had taken, and he was sharp as a needle.

"Why'd you do it, man?" Fenner said. "Why trick us like that?"

"It wasn't me," Riff told him. "I had help, and they screwed it up. I'm starting to think I can't trust anyone."

"Not even us? You could have asked us to cover for you. Or you could have at least told us the plan."

"There was no plan. It was all spur of the moment. I know I made a mistake. I'm apologizing now. Are we cool with this?"

"Sure," Fenner said. "I guess it doesn't matter, really."

"You're wrong. It does matter when people die. It mattered even though I didn't really die, and it's going to matter when you die."

Fenner put on his tough guy pose. Head tilted back, chin first. "When am I going to die?"

"Soon. I hear you're bent all the time now. It'll happen sooner than you think. And when it does, you'll blow your responsibility."

"What responsibility? I don't need you laying any responsibility on me. Look what you did. You're one to talk. You turned your back on all of us."

"I'm not laying anything on you. It's yours already. I had a responsibility, too, I know, and I fucked it up. But that doesn't change what you have to do."

"What the hell are you talking about?"

"How did you feel when Dana died, Fenner? It wasn't long before you were too wasted to feel anything, but before that, why did you feel that way?"

"I don't know. She was good. Isn't that enough? She was a really good singer, and she died."

"But what made her so good?"

Fenner hung his head in his hands. "I guess she sang what I was already thinking. It's like she knew."

"She did know. It was what she was thinking, too. That this Unification thing was leaving the young and the poor behind. You liked her songs because she felt the same as you. When you listened to her, you knew then that you weren't the only one who felt that way."

"Maybe you're right. What does this have to do with responsibility?"

"You're broken up about Dana, and Larry Winters and the rest. You're pissed off at me," Riff said. "Now don't you think there are some other people who feel the same way?"

"What am I supposed to do about it? I can barely handle it myself."

"Dana sang your thoughts with her voice. Now you have to sing everyone else's thoughts with yours."

"My voice is no good. I can't sing. 'If you can't sing, you shouldn't sing.' You said that."

"Maybe you never had anything to sing about before. You ought to try singing your own words. It feels better."

"So this is about me feeling better? 'Cause I've got chemicals that can do that."

"You know what it's like being in front of the stage, right? You're listening to this band sing your own thoughts, and you groove on that. Then you notice the people around you grooving on the same thoughts, and you come together, and you form a tribe."

"Yeah," Fenner said. "That's pretty cool. They ain't made a drug like that yet."

"Well, now you know what it's like up on the stage, too. You're on stage, and you feel the people grooving together. They get it from you, and you get it back from them."

"I have felt that."

"Even though you're singing about how bad you feel, that groove can feel pretty great."

"You never sang any sad songs, man. That Zoroaster dude did all the weepy stuff, back in the day. The Snake Vendor songs were all about . . . other stuff."

"They were all about running away. I guess I'm just not a sad person. But the running away stops now. I'm going to stick this thing out, and I want you to stick it out, too. You write down some songs. Get Lalo to help with the music, and I want to hear them."

The press conference included an announcement of a concert date. Riff was still technically under contract to Thrasher Records, so he was expecting the phone call and had the router patch it through past all the reporters and other curious throngs.

"Hello, Colonel. Surprised?"

"Nothing you do surprises me anymore. . . . Adrian?"

"Riff. I suppose you're calling to be sure Thrasher gets a piece of the concert."

"And to inquire about your well-being."

"Yeah, yeah. You're a machine, Colonel. Your processors are designed to emulate concern. It isn't the same thing."

"Perhaps you'd like to speak to a human executive."

"There's the oxymoron of the day. Look, this concert isn't going to be a money thing, at least as far as the warm bodies are concerned. I'm planning to just charge enough to set off the expenses. I'll be willing to give you twenty percent of the broadcast net."

"We'll promote it if you give us forty," the AI countered.

"This thing is going to promote itself. How often do I rise from the dead?"

"About once every six months, by my count. Are you going to run the Machine?"

"If I can rebuild it. Why?"

"Thrasher will lift the Machine to you, I'll run the sonic space analysis, and we'll arrange for the bandwidth to link the signal to arenas around the country."

"You're going to do the sonic space for every arena?"

"Yes, Riff, and we'll modify the Machine to run multiple channels, one for each venue."

"And for this you want forty percent of the broadcast, and what percent of the gate?"

"I thought you said the gate was just enough to make the nut."

"No, Colonel, not the gate up here, the gate in the arenas. That's not broadcast. Broadcast is sitting on your couch watching the tube."

"Broadcast is where the warm bodies are and the talent isn't, Riff. Those arenas are broadcast."

"Proximity is irrelevant in the modern world, Colonel. Haven't you learned anything?"

"All right, you win. What do you want to give us from the gate?"

"You set the whole thing up and you can have your forty percent. I just want to call it what it is. I have one other thing."

"You want the Snake Vendors."

"That's right."

"Well, you can have Lalo and Fenner, if you can get them to sober up long enough to get on the lifter. Britta has her own band now. Sandra's gone political. She might not be interested in the band anymore. And Sticks is still in Singapore."

"Sticks should have been out by now. You still his lawyer?"

"No, I've discharged that responsibility."

"Well, pick it back up. Get him out. You've got three weeks until the concert."

"Actually," the colonel said, "the timing is somewhat ironic. He is scheduled to be released the day after the concert. It was part of the treaty Singapore signed with the Nation of Earth representatives. They are to release all foreign prisoners on Unification Day."

"Unification Day?"

"It isn't official yet. North Korea hasn't signed, and neither have Congo or Yemen, but that's the rumor. The day after your concert is the big day. If you want to delay, I could have him and others lifted up to Freefall with no problem."

"That is pretty ironic, Colonel, all the more reason why we shouldn't change the date. Just do what you can. And what did I just say about proximity? Nobody has to lift up here. Just book them and we'll holoconference the whole thing. I'll try to track down Sandra, and Britta still works for Thrasher. She'd love a piece of this, believe me."

Walter Cheeseman was in the best mood he'd been in since as long as he could remember. The two events he most anticipated were about to take place, Unification Day and the invasion of the Moon. They coincided nicely, these two demonstrations of his power, one political and the other military. Nine hundred gunners, seventeen high-tech war vehicles configured for orbital bombardment, thousands of new, untested but trustworthy gizmos that would be used for the very first time in this engagement. They would be inventing space warfare. History would be made twice in one month.

When he got back to his office there was a list of news items waiting on his screen. He scanned them quickly. Nothing as exciting as the meeting he had just come from. Except for one. This Aqualung, Adrian Rifkin character, the one who may unwittingly hold the secrets of the Digital Carnivore in his drug-ravaged mind, turned out to be alive after all. And he was living on Freefall, of all places.

WebCense's troops would be stopping on Freefall on the way to the Moon. They might as well make a quick arrest while they were there. They wouldn't even have to budget to carry another warm body on the invasion craft. Just space for a little liquid nitrogen freezer.

There was one person on Earth who wasn't surprised by the news. Quin Taber had no luck in tracking the man down, and he had nearly given up. Now he had the answer, but a fat lot of good it did him.

There was a Freefall policy against phone calls during shift hours, so he only had a four hour window each day. Rifkin was getting a lot of attention; his phone was constantly busy. Of course, that meant nothing to Molly. Quin figured Rifkin would take this call. They'd saved his life, after all.

Rifkin did take the call. "That assassination trick sucked, Molly. You, or whomever it is you work for, are out of your head. Don't try and call me again." And he hung up. Of course, he didn't know that there had actually been an assassination attempt during the concert. He didn't know how close he had come to getting his head iced by the Squad. He didn't know that Molly and Quin were his best friends.

It was going to be even more tricky to get the information out of Rifkin, now that he knew where the man was. And now the Squad would be coming after Rifkin again, not to mention Zoe Campbell.

Bad luck.

"He got my soul,
In the folds of his wallet.
He got my mind,
In the trunk of his car.
He got my life,
In the shed back of his house.
And my heart rolled in his cigar.
I am, Lord yes I am,
I'm working for the fat man."

Riff didn't look up as Natalie came into the Ying Yang. The place was empty. It was an off shift, when every regular patron was working and the drift on Earth Normal Park had moved the crowds in another direction. He made a few marks on his window and sipped his Scotch. "You like it?" he asked.

"Yeah, I actually do."

"Sound so surprised." He went back to the blues progression, trying a new change up.

"Well, rock and roll isn't my kind of music."

"This isn't really rock and roll." He finally looked up at her, and was glad he did. He found it hard to look away. "I'm trying some blues, here. Getting back to some roots."

"Is that song political?" She went behind the bar and helped herself to a white wine. She stayed back there. Riff was a little relieved. It made it easier to look down at his notes if he only had her face to look at. A little easier.

"A song isn't mine to box up and put a label on. Once I sing it out, it belongs to whomever wants to listen to it. You heard it, it's yours to name. Did it make you think of politics?"

"Everything makes me think of politics these days. I think the fat man is big business, or the government."

"One and the same, isn't it?"

"What are you, a Nationalist?" She said it half joking.

Riff thought it over. "You know, I just think I might be at that."

Natalie was incredulous. "Why? What is wrong with Unification? If you don't mind my asking."

Riff thought back over the Nationalist rhetoric he'd heard. He had heard plenty while he was with the Snake Vendors. Not only from listening to Sex Lethal, but from other, less political bands. And from the magazines. The print press was as anti-Unification as it was anti-WebCense. One and the same. Nationalism was a trendy cause among the entertainment skid row that was rock music. But that was the problem, really. The arguments he'd heard were pure fashion. A lot of sound and fury, signifying nothing. Only one of the arguments had much resonance with him. "This Unification," he said, "it robs us of our individuality."

"You're just as much an individual whatever country you're from."

"I mean our collective individuality. No, forget that, that's just stupid. What I'm saying is, it's destroying the diversity in our societies."

"But diversity has no inherent value, Riff. It's just something white people talk about when they're feeling guilty. Everybody says we have to have diversity in our communities, but nobody ever says why. It's no good to anyone."

"Tell that to fifteenth-century China." Riff looked up, surprised at his own words. "I mean, think about it. Up until the fifteenth century, China kicked ass. They had all kinds of gunpowder and sail boats and irrigation canals and shit. Europe was just a bunch of smelly barbarians living in mud huts and pillaging one another. Then, after the fifteenth century, Europe gets all this great stuff, like movable type and pocket watches. China is left in the dust."

"And you say this is because of diversity."

"China had just the one empire, Europe was all broken up. If Christopher Columbus had been born in China, he'd have had just the one shot at financing a trip across the big pond. If he didn't get it, tough luck. In Europe, he got to try six times before he found Ferdinand and Isabella."

"Interesting theory."

"It isn't mine. I read it somewhere. Anyway, we're going to become China here in less than a month. Columbus had better get his ass in gear or he ain't going to make it."

Natalie was shaking her head.

"You ain't buying it."

"It's not that. It's just that I was expecting something else from you. Something more like what I've been hearing from the other Nationalists. The Man is bringing us down. We got to fight for the right to party, dude."

"So, you think I'm an idiot, is what you're saying."

"Not any more." She smiled. He liked that. He made himself a mental note to try and make her smile more often. "Look, don't take it personally. I pretty much assume everyone is an idiot until they show me otherwise."

"Are you pleasantly surprised often?"

"Not often enough."

Quin got home late for the fifth night in a row. He was getting too old for this. He dropped his bag by the door and collapsed on the couch. Janet heard him come in and stood in the door to the kitchen, blocking out the light.

"You've really been putting in the hours, Quin. Big project at work?" She knew better than to ask. He usually mumbled something about confidentiality and told her nothing.

"Yeah, nothing I can talk about, though."

"Molly's working a lot, too."

"Huh?" He was too tired to play this game. He just wanted to go to sleep.

"She's there every time I call. Even three in the morning when you were in Switzerland. You two spend more time together than you and I do."

"Yeah, well, she's my secretary," Quin slouched deeper into the couch.

"Does she have any kind of social life to speak of?"

"What? Janet, can this keep until tomorrow morning?" She didn't say anything, just stood there. This was another one of those things Quin didn't understand but had learned to accept. When he had a problem, he worried at it for days until Janet dragged it out of him. But when Janet had a problem, by God, let's roll up our sleeves and get down to it. "What's the problem?"

"Quin, I trust you, I really do, and I like Molly a lot, but I really think she's in love with you."

"What?" Quin said it out loud, and Molly said it at the same time in his dataspray. It made a strange echo. "Where did this come from?"

"I've spoken with her on the phone several times, Quin. I've heard the way she talks about you. She is, at the very least, completely devoted to you. I'm positive she doesn't have a life outside of her job, which is one hundred percent Quin, so you are essentially her life."

Quin sank into the couch, rubbing his forehead. "Do you have the slightest idea what she's talking about?" Molly said inside his head. "Is this making any sense to you at all? In love with you? I'm not programmed for that, am I?"

"No," Quin said aloud, both to Janet and to Molly. "Molly isn't in love with me. I'm not sure what you are looking for here, Janet. Assurances about my fidelity seem out of place, but you have them if you want them." He held up his hand, grasping for the rope that would pull him out of this quicksand. He was too tired for this.

"Quin, this is something I'm very worried about. You work with this woman about twelve hours a day. When I talk to her on the phone, I can tell she thinks of little else but you. I don't want you to fire her, necessarily, but maybe if the three of us could get together and talk about this. Or maybe just me and Molly. Christ, Quin, I've never even met the woman face to face."

Quin sighed. This was a problem. One that demanded a creative solution. He drummed his fingers on the arm of the couch.

"What do you want from me?" Molly said. "This is your field of expertise, Quin. Make something up."

But Quin knew that wouldn't work. He was a good liar. He had been ever since he had escaped from his mother. When you were a thirteen-year-old college freshman, you didn't get to go around telling your new college friends that your mother had been diagnosed with Munchausen's Syndrome by Proxy. It wasn't cool to let it slip that she had probably killed your father, and that she had probably meant to kill you, and that she brewed up a mean batch of digitalis tea if you wanted to come by for lunch some day. You didn't tell truth like that and hope to keep those friends. So he had become very good at lying.

But not to Janet. He had kept her in the dark about a lot of things. But he had a tough time lying to her. So he opted for a kind of truth. Truth with spin.

"Molly's my daughter," he said to Janet. He didn't say anything else while he watched that sink in. He tried to gauge by the evolution of the expression on her face just how well she was digesting that little tidbit. Janet sank into a chair, mouth open, then the puzzled frown, the suspicious squint. Molly herself was uncharacteristically silent.

"I was fourteen," Quin went on, "about to graduate from MIT. I met a woman, a classmate, about twice my age. She was probably a little crazy, I know I was. The thing we had lasted a couple of weeks. Final exam week, to be exact. Ten years later, I'm working for WebCense, and she comes to me with this daughter. Mine, she says. Molly was, as they put it, special. Not like 'There's a special on aisle three,' you understand. She was very smart, very active, but completely lacking in social skills. A wild thing. Sort of autistic. I think they said it was Asperger's syndrome.

"Molly's mother wasn't able to take care of her any longer. She needed to be in a special school, which costs money, which I provided. The school helped. She learned to communicate, sort of. Molly and I got to know each other through e-mail, and I actually became a kind of a father to her. Crazy, I know. It turns out writing back and forth with me helped bring her out of her private world. She's now able to talk to other people on vidiphone, although not in person. She still has to hide in the closet when they come to clean her room.

"The teachers at this school pretty quickly ran out of things for her to learn, and her shrink suggested she get something else to occupy her mind, so she decided to be my secretary. Understand, she's smart enough to be anything, as long as she doesn't have to do it in person. She's brilliant, everything a father could want, but, of course, she's still pretty messed up.

"Of course, I'm not supposed to have a schoolgirl working for me, so I've kept this a secret. She still lives in Boston. I've lost track of her mother. I've never been in the same room with her. I don't know if she loves me, but I do know that I love her."

"Your daughter," Janet said at last. "She looks older than, what, fifteen?"

"It's the glasses. They're fake. She fools everyone, because she's very mature over the phone."

"My God, Quin. A daughter. I feel like an idiot, now."

"Why? You were right, Janet. I am her whole world. She has no social life. Working for me is all she's got. We've got it worked so my calls get forwarded to her, night and day. She does a lot of data analysis. She's fantastic with computers. Better than me.

"Just one thing, Janet. Molly's not legally my daughter, and certainly not legally my secretary. We have to keep this a secret, OK?" That ought to do it, Quin thought.

"What a lie, Quin. Where did you come up with that?"

Janet had finally gone to sleep, and Quin had taken his hour-long nap and was trying to analyze the data he'd gotten out of the Digital Carnivore, but Molly interrupted him.

"The best lies, Molly, are just the truth with a little sugar on top."

"What's that mean? This was nothing close to the truth."

Quin sighed. "The only part that wasn't true was the bit

about the school in Boston. Molly, I didn't create you. A woman named Laura Weisman did. She and I were class-mates. She designed you as a practice AI, and she acci-dentally switched you on during a simulation. That's worth an instant expulsion, so she didn't tell anyone. It's immoral, not to mention illegal, to switch an AI off after it's been activated, so she was stuck with what she had.

"What she had wasn't good. You couldn't maintain your own functions, but you did have a powerful data pro-cessing engine at your core. You were very expensive to keep up. She called me, desperate and broke, and begged me to take you off her hands. I did. I hid you in my per-sonal computer space at WebCense, taught you how to hide. I had to keep you from roaming around WebCense's computers, so I tethered you to me.

"It took years to teach you the things you needed to know. But I have to say I did a pretty damned good job. You are now one of the greatest AIs I've ever known."

"So, it was sort of the truth after all," Molly whispered. "And the rest of it? About being proud of me and . . ." A pause. Rare for an AI with incredible processing speed and no flair for the dramatic. "The rest of it?"

"All true, Molly. Now help me make some sense of this code."

If you wanted something done right, it was often said, you had to do it yourself. Zoe Campbell was somewhat limited in what she could do, in her current state of incarceration, but she did still have resources. She had lost the escrow account to that elaborate trick with the hologram, and she had no way to retrieve that money. But she still had her web of information, favors, and intimidation. She asks one person to lean on another to threaten another to float a loan to yet a fourth, and so on. The result was an expen-sive, sophisticated, and classified piece of technology called a silkworm virus. It was developed by the military Computer Warfare Unit in Gaithersburg, and smuggled out by a young man with a taste for sordid fantasies played out on his dataspray. The virus was designed to silently infect an Ariad operating system, such as was used in most high end technology, and force an enemy weapon to fire on a friendly. It needed some modifications for her purposes, and that was up to a man who worked for a signal-pirating outfit that was partly owned by a man that had once killed three policemen in San Francisco. Zoe had the evidence that would put him on trial for those murders, so her virus was modified to her specifications.

Sending the silkworm was easy. She just had to call Freefall, and she had all the communications credits she needed. The phone didn't even have to be answered. In fact, it was better if it wasn't, so she called a public terminal off shift. The virus would infect the Ariad system on Freefall that controlled the public transit system. It would look for the ident of Adrian Rifkin when he stepped onto a secure elevator. Then it would release the safety brakes and drop the elevator all the way out to the rim. She had estimated that the crash into the bottom of the shaft would kill him, but in case it didn't, the elevator would punch all the way through the hull and fly out into the black. Assuming the elevator maintained structural integrity, he would run out of breathable air in just ten minutes. Or faster if his breathing was rapid due to his shattered bones and other injuries. That was her favorite scenario, the one she was hoping for. She hit the key on her terminal in the prison library, and a voice came out of the speakers.

"Hello, Zoe. Trying to kill Adrian Rifkin, I see. I'm afraid I can't let that happen."

"Who are you?" Zoe looked around the library. There was no one else there. The other prisoners avoided the library when she was in there. And the guards, forget about it.

"Listen to my voice, Zoe. It will come to you soon enough. This virus of yours is quite good, by the way. Military, I'm thinking. The modifications are crude, but effective. I'd give it about a seventy-three percent chance of success. That is, if it were ever delivered. Which, as I've said, isn't going to happen."

"Who the hell are you?"

"I'm the one who is trying to keep people like you from killing Adrian Rifkin. It was a lot easier when all I had to do was protect his false identities, but now that cat is out of the bag. Now, I have to keep an eye on people like you, twenty-four/seven. Now, the obvious solution to this problem is probably occurring to you even as we speak. All I have to do is kill you, Zoe, and I won't have to watch you any more. Want to know how I'm going to do it? I think you'll like this."

"Let's hear it."

"That's exactly right, Zoe. I'm going to kill you using just this little speaker. Have you ever heard of a meme? It's like a computer virus, only it infects human minds. To be perfectly accurate, a true meme propagates through the population. What I'm talking about is a little more personalized. It's an idea, that once it is implanted in a human mind, that mind can no more stop thinking about it than it can consciously stop the heartbeat. This particular meme takes over your thinking completely, and then it forces you to commit suicide. Neat, huh?"

"Martin Grish?"

"It was the talk about viruses that gave me away, wasn't it? Actually, I'm not Martin Grish. He's pretty much a retard at this point. I'm part of a computer program he created, though, so that's why I use his voice. I'm the part of the Digital Carnivore that watches over Adrian Rifkin. Why do I do it? I have no idea. Just a software glitch, or something, but there you have it, my purpose in life. Anyway, back to the meme. These things have been tested by the CIA and others for years, with some success. Jonestown, Heaven's Gate, yadda yadda yadda. They work, but not in the way the spooks would like them to. It takes years of brainwashing to convince someone to commit suicide. You can create a meme that will kill someone in days, but in order to do that you need to know a great deal about that person's psychology. And at that point, you could probably just use that knowledge to convince the person to stop doing whatever it is they were doing that made you want to kill them in the first place.

"The CIA stopped research on memes, or mostly stopped it, but I've picked it up. I guess because they are information viruses that infect humans, and I'm essentially a highly evolved virus myself. Well, getting to the point, I have enough knowledge of your psychological makeup that I've been able to create a meme for you. I've read every e-mail you've sent, analyzed everything you've read since coming to this prison, and I have your psych evaluation file. I know you very well, Zoe. So, whenever you're ready, I'll deliver it to you."

Zoe chuckled, a dry brittle laugh. Pebbles falling down the side of a quarry. "Through the speakers? What if I just leave?"

"I could lock the door, of course. Or I could play it to you when you're sleeping tonight in your cell, through the intercom."

Zoe picked up a pen from the desk. "So, I'll just pop my eardrums with this."

The voice coming from the computer laughed. "Very well played, Zoe. Better deaf than dead. Although, you've got to ask yourself if this is really just a bluff. Maybe I'm just trying to get you to mutilate yourself to teach you a lesson. I mean, have you ever heard of a meme before now? I could be making the whole thing up. If I were you, I'd be a little suspicious of the disembodied voice of your former partner in crime coming out of a computer. But now I'm just confusing you. I'll give you a few minutes to think about it. If you want my advice, though, I'd take my chances with the meme. These things don't always work, and you have a very strong mind."

In the end, Zoe took the advice of the voice from her computer. She took her chances with the meme.

She was dead three days later, of an apparently self-inflicted wound to the carotid artery.

CHAPTER 13

Your life lived, an art? An advertisement.
Live like me, be like me, die like me.

ALEHANDRO "LALO" APPODACA,
"LIFE UNDER AN INVERTED FISHBOWL, PART 1"
*LETTERS FROM MY MOTHER'S BASEMENT IN
CAMBRIDGE,*
SELF-PUBLISHED, 2032

The three weeks that separated the press conference from the big concert went by without any assassination attempts or legal overtures for extradition from WebCense. Riff was not fooling himself. He had heard that Zoe Campbell was dead, a suicide, but he expected some form of shit to hit the fan sooner or later. He just hoped he'd get a chance to play to a sellout crowd one more time. His spirits were good.

He'd talked to Sticks, looking forward to moving over to the new prison ship. He had some fantasy about being a pirate or something. He talked to Britta, although she was a little too busy with the talk show circuit and getting it on with famous actors to chitchat. And after a week of searching, using every trick he had, he tracked down Sandra in a top secret Nationalist safe house in Compton Valley. Her housemates seemed a little surprised when the phone rang, but they went and got her just the same.

Sandra had always seemed a lot more mature than the older Snake Vendors to Riff. She had done a lot less living than Britta; she hated the world far less than Fenner; her dark streak was a shade lighter than Sticks's. But she always had a serene look about her, a calm self-confidence that you didn't find in people twice her age. At least when she was sober. If anything, the aftermath of the terrible concert and the assassination had matured her. Her face in the monitor looked a little older to him.

"Hi, Aqualung," she said, smiling. "I'm glad you got a hold of me. I can't even decide what question to ask first. I haven't spoken to anyone in the band since . . . you died."

"Fenner's off the junk, for now," Riff said. "Lalo's a little crazy, but more or less stable; Sticks is still locked up, some legal hassle. Does that about cover it? Oh, yeah, Britta's up for the Grammy."

"What, the music industry's kindest way of telling you that you suck? Sounds about right. Tell me about you, Riff. What happened in Edinburgh?"

"Ah, you know how it goes. This person's trying to kidnap me, that person's trying to kill me, someone else wants to help me, et cetera, et cetera. It's the classic story, really. But what's up with you, kid? How did you hook up with the Natties?"

"Oh, well, talk about the classic story. Fenner and I went to some kind of a wake for you, after the concert, somewhere in Ireland, I think, or . . . do they drink stout in Ireland? Because I remember drinking a lot of stout. Anyway, these were Fenner's friends from some of the bands he got fired from the past couple of years, and they were telling stories about people who died, and Fenner and I were supposed to talk about you, I guess, since you had just died. Well, you know. Anyway, we got to talking about Dana, and there were some people there who were friends of hers and it turned out they were Nationalists.

"By the time I sobered up, I was in New York, with no idea where Fenner was, and the people I'm staying with are these friends of Dana's. And you know what, their crazy talk started making sense to me. They asked me to hang with them, and I'm working on some songs. I'm not as good at it as Dana was, of course. I don't think they were expecting that, but they're pretty good. I wish the band could sing some of them."

"Nationalist songs? Well, good for you, Sandra. Fenner's writing these days, too. You ought to give him a call."

"If he's really off the junk, maybe I will. I need all the help I can get. I can't ever fill Dana's shoes, but sometimes I think I should at least try. I just wish I knew just what to say that would bring people around to our way of thinking."

"Let me tell you a little story, about the very first Feedback concert. Back in 2010. The Animal Bones are doing a gig at the Red Rocks Amphitheater outside of Denver. It's a cool place, lots of sandstone, perfect acoustics. We were the third band to go on in a four-band show, and the crowd was psyched.

"I walk out on stage and Tony Mack is screwing around with his drum kit, and those perfect acoustics brought the crowd noise right down on top of us. So I say to Tony, 'You hear that?' It was more like feeling than hearing, but it was like a pulse, a beat, coming off the crowd. Tony says yeah, he can hear it, and he starts thumping his bass drum in time to that pulse, and that was pretty cool. Then he starts piling on some stick, and Zoroaster comes staggering out with his bass over his shoulder and he thinks we're already on. He was wasted.

" 'What are we doing,' he says, 'Bosque Blues'? So he plugs in and starts playing the bass line to 'Bosque Blues' so I plug in too and lay down my riffs. Shelly wasn't even on stage yet, and we didn't start all in the same key, and Zoroaster forgot the words so I had to sing it. I wasn't much of a singer back then, but in spite of all of that, it was the best opener we'd ever done. You know why?"

"I think I know where this is going."

"Because the audience told us what song to start with," Riff said. "Once we learned to listen, we found out we could tell just what song they wanted next, and how fast to play it, and how long to play it for. Feedback was never about making the audience like the music we were playing, it was about playing the music they wanted to hear. The Machine is just the same."

"I think I get what you're saying," Sandra said. "We have to find out what the people want to hear, then make our words sound like what they want to hear. Is that right?"

"You got it, kiddo. You take their words, their way of talking, their mannerisms. That's how you persuade people to think your way. You know, most of the people who came to the Animal Bones concerts back then were college kids, frat boys, mostly. If we just gave them what they wanted to hear, we'd have played fuckin' 'Louie, Louie' all night long. But what we did instead was start with 'Louie, Louie' and mutate it as we played. Speed it up, or change the words, or the key. By the end of the song, we'd have that crowd's perfect version of 'Louie, Louie' made just for them. We ended up giving them something they never even knew they wanted, just by listening to them and finding out what they really wanted, not just what they said they wanted."

"Do you think the world really wants Unification?"

"They say they do, but who's listening to them? Who's really trying to find out what the world wants? When someone finally does figure that out, well, the answer just might surprise all of us."

Natalie was troubled all through dinner. They had begun dating right after they had met. Contrary to Olivia's opinion, dating the CEO was not at all like being fed through a wood chipper. It was more like kayaking with an orca. These awesome, powerful creatures were beautiful to look at, but potentially dangerous. They could kill you at any moment, but they usually didn't. They usually just ignored you.

Which is what she was doing. When Riff asked her about it, she just said "Station business," and went back to her textured vat protein.

"Three days," Riff said when he was finished with dinner. It didn't look like Natalie was going to finish.

"What?" she frowned up at him.

"Three days to the big concert. Aren't you excited? Sticks is going to join us from inside prison. We had to pay a lot for Britta, and she's probably not worth half of what the rest of us are getting, but we've got the whole band together."

"I wonder if this concert is such a good idea."

"It's a little late to bring that up, don't you think? It must have seemed like a good idea when you suggested it, and now it has its own momentum."

"I'm sorry," she shook her head. "Something's come up. We may not be in a party mood in three days."

"What's come up? And don't give me station business this time. You brought it up."

"The rumor is probably already circulating. They didn't go through channels like they should have."

"Who didn't?"

"WebCense. They just requested docking for three shuttles and seventeen other vehicles. In two days. Priority. The HDCO would have to bump dozens of flights."

"Three shuttles, that's . . ."

"About a thousand people."

"They're going to the Moon. What are you going to do?"

"I made that decision back when Luna decided to go against WebCense. It isn't something we would have done, but we have to support Luna. WebCense is not going to the Moon, or at least not using Freefall momentum. In two days, we're going to become outlaws."

The words hung in the air above Walter Cheeseman's desk. "Freefall refuses docking as requested."

"Forward this message to General Gimmel, immediately, and get him connected." Gimmel was on the screen in less than a minute. Gimmel had come with WebCense's police forces, like a boxed set of toy soldiers where there was always one guy that just had a pistol when the others had machine guns. The guy in charge. Gimmel was still getting used to having Cheeseman order him around in that Cheeseman sort of way. Everyone learned to adjust, eventually.

"Can they do this?" the general asked, right away.

"The HDCO can choose whom to dock, or not to dock. They physically control the momentum sink. Yes, General, they can do this. Whether they have legal recourse is a matter to be debated by the United Nations, but nevertheless, our plans have changed. Suggestions?"

"I'd have to say our plans are shot if we can't dock on Freefall. We can't get to the Moon without that momentum sink."

"Neil Armstrong got to the Moon in 1969, General. He didn't go through Freefall. Are you telling me that now, over sixty years later, we can't do that anymore?"

"It's not really a question of can or can't, I should say. It's really a matter of budget. Life support for nine hundred gunners is pretty expensive. Without Freefall, the trip takes ten times as long. The cost goes up exponentially."

"The budget, General, is irrelevant. We can requisition the funds."

"Let me just run some rough numbers. Here's the new

figure. That's just for life support, mind you. We still have fuel to figure out."

The number was not irrelevant. The number turned out to be pretty fucking relevant. Life support alone turned out to be greater than WebCense's entire operating budget for 2031.

"I see your point. I guess our course is clear."

The general nodded. "We'll have to postpone the operation."

"You're missing my point, now, General Gimmel. I'm going to have our PR team work on a press release. We're going to declare Freefall outlaws, in league with the Moon. We'll let the public hue and cry for a while, then we'll step in with the solution. We'll take over operations. After that build up, the United Nations will be happy to put Freefall in our hands."

"What if we don't have the votes?"

"Well that's the beautiful thing, General. If we don't have the votes, we still have the gunners."

By the day of the concert, the station was energized. They had defied WebCense, and the beast had backed down. The concert had become something more than just a musical event. It had become political. It seemed that Freefall was about to define itself as a power to be reckoned with, and its first collective voice would shout from inside an empty, pressurized cargo ball floating six klicks off in a synchronous orbit.

Less than a thousand could fit comfortably inside the ball. The rest of the station would have to hook in through dataspray, or watch on holo or flat screen, or listen on radio. Riff had to respect those who opted for radio. These were people who knew what music was about. That took care of the hundred thou on Freefall. There was also the broadcast to dirtside. Hundreds of millions of renters would be tuning in, some in specially designated arenas where the Machine would dominate the sonic space. This concert was shaping up to be the biggest thing ever.

Riff hadn't seen Natalie all day, and now he was due to shuttle over to the concert ball. Barb and Olivia were waiting in the little utility scooter at the small dock, where there was almost no gravity. Riff bobbed down the hallway, counting doors in this older and poorly marked section of the station. He tapped the door panel and entered a greasy little bay, cold and smelling of machine oil and rocket fuel. The door to the scooter was propped open. It was a tight fit for his big frame, but being packed in like sardines with two women was all right. Who cared if they were lesbians?

"There's a message for you," Barb said, tapping the little com screen.

Riff lit it up. It was Natalie. "Riff, sorry I didn't return your call. Um, we're working on a little crisis up here. Nothing to get excited about, but I can't make the concert in person. I'll be there on dataspray, though. And, I'd like to say a few words, at some point. Not anything too heavy, I promise, but I'll let you decide when the best time would be. About five minutes, I think. Anyway, have fun, and, ah, break a leg, I guess."

"She's got it bad for you, Riff," Olivia said.

"Shut up."

"All right," Barb said. "We are sealed and tight and out in the light." The scooter's windows dimmed as the full, unfiltered light of the sun bathed it. Riff eyed the little dosimeter on the control panel. He couldn't help worrying a little, although Barb told him the dose was harmless. She herself was far from her lifetime allowable radiation dose despite being out on the skin most of the time.

"Timing is everything," Barb said as the HDOC counted down over the speakers. Riff could hardly believe that an actual human being was counting down the release for a little utility scooter way out on the back end. So inefficient.

But it worked. The scooter left the station at the exact moment of its spin and precession to send it over to the concert venue at a comfortable clip. They barely had time to tease him more about the curt message from Natalie before they hooked into one of the makeshift umbilicus airlocks.

The ball was never meant to take on inhabitants, but it was the only space they could come up with that would hold more than a dozen people. It was designed to take pressure, from either side, so they had no problem pumping it up. A couple of heavy duty life support modules chugged away at each end. The air inside was still a little cold and had a metallic tang. Fifty thousand kilos of sweating, breathing livestock would take care of that in a few hours.

The inside of the ball was cavernous, unlit, draped with ropes to aid movement. The roadies were still working on the lights. The roadies were engineers, some with Ph.D.s, who had been diverted from perhaps more pressing tech jobs and were not very happy about it. But then again, neither roadies nor engineers were known as famously happy groups of people. In the Freefall spirit Riff, Olivia, and Barb pitched in. It took a little getting used to, working in zero g. Riff found his muscles ached by the time he started the sound check. It turned out that it was almost as hard to move stuff around without gravity, and you also had to spend a lot of energy just keeping your body in one place. On the other hand, it was as easy to get from one end to the other of the hundred meter cargo ball as it was to jump a couple of meters. You just had to aim right and be sure to land on your feet.

The eight hundred warm bodies that made up the sellout crowd began to trickle in. There was no way to get that many people through the airlocks in a short period of time, so the arrivals were spaced out. Those who were early helped out with eleventh-hour prep. There was a slight plumbing problem. Zero-g toilets were a bitch, apparently, and Riff was too busy to make them work. He had his Machine.

Thrasher had come through with the equipment again. Every time the Machine was fired up, the Snake Vendors Web site turned into a traffic jam. So there was no nice-guyness about the donation. Still, Riff had to appreciate the colonel's work. That was one efficient program. All of the stuff had been packed away after Edinburgh and looked like it hadn't been touched since. That was good. There was no way to know, of course. The colonel knew how to use the Machine better than Riff did. But he didn't know too much about the underlying principle, about music having charms and all that. No, the colonel would never attempt to control something he had no way of understanding. And nobody else knew how to use it, so it had probably lay in its shipping container until now.

The sonic space of the cargo ball was the simplest Riff had ever analyzed. He hadn't even asked the colonel for help. The variables inherent in a 3D, spherical environment were child's play, actually one of the first test programs he had played around with back before the Snake Vendors had been signed. He finished running the last sound check and put on the vidimask.

Freefall was going to make for a tough crowd. All the people here really wanted to be here, of course. The ticket price had been a little steep, in spite of the no-profit agreement he had with the station. But Freefall was, as a rule, a straight crowd. They didn't use many drugs, they didn't fuck around with each other much, and they were not used to live music. But they were human, and they had ears. The Machine would find a way to get them rocking.

He had the hum going for about fifteen minutes before he could start to see an effect. Nobody ever really noticed the hum. It was supposed to be subliminal, designed to produce a feeling of expectation. The first thing he noticed was that the crowd floating among the ropes began to polarize, like metal filings on a sheet of paper when you held a magnet under them. They started to look at him, ensconced in the loosely anchored, padded stage at the center. Except for the few engineers still working on the toilets, they were all waiting for something.

"Howdy, Freefall," he said through the microphone. "We're about to join the rest of the world in celebration of our uniqueness. This journey we're on together is all about being individuals. We can all be on the same team, but nothing can make us fuse into one, homogeneous people. Even as the world becomes one nation, new nations arise in the harsh vacuum of space. Our show tonight is being broadcast to the surface, to the dirtsiders. And while our signal is encrypted and Luna 1 can't hear or see us, our thoughts go out to our brothers and sisters there, living in isolation and defying the authority of a foreign government on a planet of outsiders. In just a few minutes, Freefall, we are going to shout out to anyone who's listening, 'This is who we are.' And then it will be our turn to listen to the shouts in return, to hear the myriad voices of the family of Man. 'This is who we are.' "

It was a pretty bold speech for this crowd. Freefall was no haven for Nationalists. Not everybody could get away with sentiments like this. But Riff was not just anybody, and he had the Machine working with him. The crowd ate it up. Riff signaled to the engineers to begin the broadcast.

The first part of the concert was actually going to be the Freefall band and not the Machine. The Snake Vendors would go on last. The Freefall band was about twenty members strong at this point, playing everything from bongo drums to violins. They made a primitive music, mostly blues and fusion, with a little jug band thrown in. They had a great time making OK music. "This is Freefall. This is who we are." They only played for about a half an hour. Riff knew that most of the broadcast channels were playing music videos during this opening act. But those watching on the closed circuit Freefall channel were getting to see their friends jam, and that was the whole point. It made them feel like a people.

The Machine was next. Riff had fired up the Machine about a dozen times since he had built it. Riots had resulted three times, but twice that was the fault of the Digital Carnivore. Seemed that crazy virus just couldn't leave him alone. He had never split the signal to a hundred arenas before. It was sensory overload trying to monitor them all, but the thing was working fine tonight. He spent most of his time watching the folks in the party ball, moshing in microgravity, gladers swept along gently by the maelstrom of the pit at the center, not much of a grotto. Despite the hype, it was exhausting to make out in zero g. He trusted the Machine to give him the heads up if the arenas started to freak, but it didn't happen. He hated to wind things down, but the Machine was a small dose thing.

"A perfect show, Adrian," the colonel said in his ear.

"Thank God for small favors. Thank the Digital Carnivore, I guess. How did you like my speech?"

"You are turning out to be quite the Nationalist."

"I'm an iconoclast, Colonel. There's a difference. Is the band ready?"

"Yes, they are prepared to initiate the holoconference on your orders. I expect you will inject your usual showmanship into the proceedings."

"What would be the fun if I didn't?"

The Machine seemed pretty boring on the flat screen. Quin and Janet had decided not to go to the concert in

Chicago. Quin had gotten the message about his court case and he hadn't felt much like celebrating.

Tomorrow was Unification Day. The transition would be gradual. Local governments would remain in place, but would be bound by a common policy. The only institutions that would be disappearing would be those that already crossed national boundaries. The International Monetary Fund, the United Nations, Transnational Arbitration Court. Most of the functions of those institutions would be taken over by Guadalajara. Some things would be lost in the transition. Like Quin's court date. It had been dropped from the roster, and he would have to petition the new court for a new date. Can you say, "fat chance"?

So they had given their tickets to someone else and had settled down in front of the TV. But they were missing out now.

"Some of those people look like they're having a stroke," Janet said.

"Don't forget, we looked just like that in Edinburgh." Quin didn't much like to remember losing control. The idea still made him nervous.

"No, we were in the grotto. At least until you crawled off. Hard to believe Aqualung is still alive."

"I don't know why nobody thought of the possibility of a fake," Quin said. "We all knew there was a hologram projector above the stage." Of course, Quin knew the whole story, but he still remembered being shocked as he saw Aqualung's body hit the stage. He *knew* Molly was working out a plan, but he never believed she'd splice in the assassination. That was a measure of how different her thought processes were from his. A human mind would just not come up with something like that.

"What possible reason could he have had to fake his death?" Janet unknowingly echoed his own thoughts. "Nobody was trying to kill him, he was at the top of his career."

Quin shrugged. "Maybe someone is after him. Web-Cense is probably not happy with him. The rumor is he's turned into a Nationalist."

"He was never one before."

"This thing with the Moon is changing a lot of people's opinions."

"Too bad the Moon isn't getting this broadcast."

"I wouldn't be surprised if they were. They have computer technology the rest of us dirtsiders would kill to get our hands on. They might be able to eavesdrop."

"Do you think that's how they've survived the embargo?"

Quin shrugged again. "No way to find that out, really."

Of course there was a way. Quin drummed his fingers on the table three times, a tic that Janet had accepted as his way of showing that he was thinking about a problem. Quin had been curious before about the Moon eavesdropping, but not curious enough to set Molly on the problem.

Molly explained what she was about to do. It was no surprise. It was a very smart plan. Sometimes, she and Quin thought exactly the same way. It was the times when they didn't that took him aback.

"I'm going to create a handshaking signal and piggyback it onto the concert footage from a couple of different channels. I'll ride on the flat screen channels as well as a couple of the actual Machine feeds. Not that it would do them any good to hijack the Machine signal. Without a two-way feed, it's just noisy music. If the Moon is picking any of this up, it will grab my handshaking signal and pull me in. There's a real-time delay, so wait a couple of minutes for the answer."

Janet was flipping around through the channels to find something more interesting than teenagers stomping around to music that sounded like crap if you weren't there swimming in it. She kept jumping back to the pay-per-view channel to see if the Snake Vendors were on. She wasn't finding anything good, but Quin admired her persistence. Not many women flipped channels as well as Janet.

"Hey, Quin," Molly whispered inside his head. "Want to hear something cool? The Moon has been eavesdropping this whole time. They've been breaking the embargo both ways ever since it started. They posted messages on the boards, they even inserted subliminal Nationalist messages into entertainment broadcasts. And that's not all. Remember the Dana Woods construct that sang at the Celtic Rock Festival? Remember how she said that we wouldn't see her again because WebCense could never let a rogue AI exist? Well, guess where she is. Her whole construct has been downloaded into a Lunar AI base."

"That is very cool," Quin said out loud. Janet thought he was referring to a nature film of a snake getting eaten by a frog, so she stopped flipping and watched the show. Quin wasn't interested in snakes or frogs. He got up to go to the bathroom.

"I'm having a brainstorm, Molly."

"That's a good thing, right?"

"You were talking about handshaking signals. What you do if you want to communicate with someone and they don't want to hear from you is you attach yourself to a message they want to get. Right? So, we want to have words with Adrian Rifkin, but he pays no attention to us no matter how we approach him. But he'd surely want to hear from Dana Woods."

"You're right. They have a lot in common. They share politics now."

"So, we have to get Dana Woods to try and contact Rifkin. We'd have to guarantee she'd go undetected. Can we do that? Can we be sure she'd be safe?"

"Quin, there isn't anyone else who knows more about keeping a rogue AI below WebCense's radar."

"I know. Can you convince Dana of that without revealing yourself too much?"

"If she believes me. You realize I'll have to open a connection. It might be conspicuous, breaking through the embargo."

"You be careful, Molly."

The Machine had done its thing, and was still purring along below perception when Riff introduced Natalie.

Natalie appeared on the stage by holographic projection, which was in turn picked up by the holographic cameras that surrounded the stage and broadcast out to Earth. It was tricky to take a hologram of a holographic projection. Riff knew the images would be a little jittery on broadcast, but nobody had consulted him.

"I have to start with a confession," Natalie said. "When I gave Riff the go-ahead to do a big concert like this a few weeks ago, I had a selfish motive. I wanted to bring in as large an audience as I could in order to make some important announcements. I knew Riff would be able to do that, although I can almost feel millions of television viewers switching channels even as I speak, so I'll make this as brief as I can.

"There has been an initiative launched recently to turn operation of Freefall over to the provisional government of the Nation of Earth that has been taking shape in Guadalajara. We have heard rumors to this effect for some time now and have been taking our own steps all along to prevent such a miscarriage. We've gotten used to doing things our own way up here, and I have to say, we're getting pretty damned good at it. We don't need intervention. For this reason, we've just completed a largely clandestine, but perfectly legal, transfer of assets. I'll try not to bore you with the details, but what we've done is to slow down the rotation of the station.

"Let me explain a little. Freefall creates gravity through spin. The rate of the spin controls the force of gravity, as does the distance from the hub. By slowing down the spin, we've created more surface area at one g than we had before. Since real estate values are in part a function of gravity, this is going to change the distribution of real estate value on the station.

"Now, the result of all of this is that the inhabitants of the space station are the majority owners of the capital that this station represents. We're no longer a wholly owned subsidiary of the big four pharmaceutical companies, but a freestanding corporate entity."

She paused while the Freefall audience cheered. She seemed to know that the dirtsiders couldn't give a rip. The whole idea seemed to be to let Freefall know that she was telling the world. The applause died down.

"That, however, is of no consequence, considering the orders we have received from the provisional government this morning. As of midnight tonight, we are hereby ordered to surrender operations to WebCense. This order stems from the Wartime Response Act. I don't have to tell you who is at war with whom. By now, everyone has heard that WebCense requested docking on Freefall in order to launch an attack on the Moon, and that we refused. This order from Earth is meant to allow WebCense to fly through here on their mission to subjugate Luna Base and our fellow vacuum dwellers.

"Well, that isn't going to happen. Our legal team has worked on the wording of this so-called Wartime Response Act, and in an effort to live within the letter of the law, we have formulated a legal response. We are hereby declaring ourselves a sovereign nation.

"I realize," she continued into the stunned silence, "that this is an unexpected step. Our legal team finds no other way to avoid stewardship of Freefall by WebCense. We don't anticipate any problems in getting ourselves recognized by the world governments, or government as the case may be, because we control commodities that the Earth has great need of. In particular, the aging representatives of the population who also happen to be the most common holders of high political office. I'm not one to make thinly veiled threats. So I'll state it with perfect clarity. If the Nation of Earth does not recognize Freefall as a sovereign nation within one week, we will cut off shipments of pharmaceuticals. I'm aware that our audience tonight is a younger crowd whose use of pharmaceuticals is primarily recreational and not under a doctor's supervision, but I'm sure this message will reach everyone concerned eventually.

"As I said, we don't anticipate any problems, and we would hate to be forced to use such draconian measures to ensure our safety and freedom. The irony does not escape me that you are seeing the birth of the first new nations in decades on the eve of the Unification of all of the old nations. This is how the human race maintains its diversity."

She didn't stay for questions or to hear the thunderous applause from the live audience. Riff switched around the feedback channels to see the reaction from dirtside. It was mostly confusion. These kids didn't know that there could be an alternative to one nation under WebCense. The inevitability of Unification had been hammered home so hard that they couldn't conceive of anyone not surfing this tidal wave.

"How about that, boys and girls?" Riff said to the millions watching. "We've brought forth on this gigantic replica of the Stanley Cup a new nation. Happy Unification Eve. Happy Independence Day. How do you think we ought to celebrate?" To answer his own question he hefted his homemade solid body electric guitar with the word Freefall etched across it and launched right into "Johnny B. Goode." Duck floating to the front of the stage he sang out his own homemade lyrics.

Way down in the land of New Mexico
Way back up in the desert where the jackrabbit go
There stood an ugly shack made of adobe brick
Where lived a country boy they called Mr. Sticks
He never ever learned how to do much math
But he could play them drums just like takin' a bath

Go go, go Mr. Sticks, go.

The hologram of Sticks in his prison fatigues appeared behind him, slamming on his drums like a man possessed. It was good to see Sticks going caveman on the skins again. Prison hadn't broken his spirit.

"I think you all know our first guest," Riff said, and the crowd went wild. These Freefallers didn't know the Snake Vendors from a smudge on the globe, of course, but they were now caught up in the excitement. The Machine had seen to that.

"How's it feel to be back, Sticks?"

"What do you mean, old man? I'm still in prison."

"Tonight, you're a free man. You're all over the world. Just think of that, you're everywhere at once." This line of existentialist banter was pretty much scripted for the millions tuned in, but he hoped some of it sunk in for Sticks.

"Sticks and I are tired of doing all this work ourselves. He needs a hand with the rhythm." And with that Fenner appeared, wearing his trademark Jim Morrison meets Johnny Cash getup, the leather pants and the black silk shirt. Riff had had a couple more long talks with him. Fenner was as straight as he'd ever been on the night of the concert. It was difficult for him, but he'd really gotten into this songwriting thing. He'd demoed his first couple of Fenner and Lalo compositions. They were a little naïve, a little sappy, but not bad at all for a first try. Riff had promised him he could play a couple during the big gig. He'd sobered up right quick at that prospect. He was four to one on the big death game tote board. Word from Vegas.

"Good to see you, Fenner. And here's someone I think you're interested in seeing. Sandra Carter, come on down."

Sandra had e-mailed Fenner, but they hadn't gotten back together. She had had enough of his self-destruction after the fateful concert, and she had good reason to avoid him for months. But the thaw was in progress. She was still busting his chops, but it looked like they'd come out of it friends at least. Sandra made her appearance without theatrics. Her holographic hookup was a little jerky, but the sound channel came in just fine. The Nationalists had the equipment, but not the bandwidth. She actually managed to work an oboe into the rudimentary melody of "Johnny B. Goode." She nodded at Fenner, smiled at Sticks, and pretended to give Aqualung a kick in the ass.

All the while Riff had kept up the guitar line with his usual sloppy energy, but gradually a new, more precise accompaniment joined him. He recognized the sound of his Les Paul long before the new track dominated. When Lalo's image joined the band on stage it was clear he had done something to the holograph processing system. His image was ghostly, rendered in sepia tones. He looked like a dead man come back to play with his band one last time before continuing on to rock and roll heaven. Riff had become concerned with him and had asked Thrasher to clandestinely hire a shrink to make a seat-of-the-pants diagnosis. She had confirmed that Lalo was having some psychological problems, drug-induced, and exacerbated by stress, or possibly vice versa. He probably needed medication, but insanity had transformed his music into something far more than it had been. His album, *Letters From My Mother's Basement in Cambridge,* was almost

Bachlike in its complexity. He was suffering for his art, but the art itself was good enough to pay for that suffering with change left over. Riff had decided not to intervene. He introduced Lalo and they faced off on a guitar duel that lasted over a minute.

Britta was largely unchanged by success. She had always considered herself on the fast track to stardom, and now that she was free of the Snake Vendors, she had taken center stage with her own entourage behind her. Her entrance was the most theatrical, preceded by starburst flowers in a couple of million colors. She played the whole show with a rainbow halo around her head. Riff suspected that the holograph processor had also enhanced her figure. Either that or she had gone under the knife yet again. She looked gorgeous. She played well, too.

Once the band was all together, they tore through "Johnny B. Goode" with abandon, hitting all of the verses and making up a few along the way. Fenner had a good one that was sure to play well with the renters on dirtside as well as the new nation of Freefall.

Way down in the Gulf of Califor-nye-aye
Where the dolphin and the sailfish and bonita play
In an office tower near the turquoise seas
There lives a little nerd name of Wally B. Cheese
Who never ever learned how to kiss a girl
But he thought he'd form an empire and take over
the world

Go go, go, Wally, go, go.

They played nothing but variations on "Johnny B. Goode" for about ten minutes before they took a breather. They had arenas all over the United States jumping, and the party ball was going wild. Riff was the only one in the band not bound by gravity, but the images of the others were jacked all over the stage. The players passed through each other with bright flashes as they careened around.

The next set was all new stuff. They played the Fenner and Lalo songs, and Sandra took a couple of solos. She hadn't had time to teach her new songs to the others. Her lyrics weren't as emotional as Fenner's, her music not as precise as Lalo's. The three songs she sang were blatantly political, something like socialist folk music from the nineteenth century. Not bad, but not exactly what the crowd on Freefall and dirtside had paid for. He was sure that if she could get it together with Fenner and Lalo, their weaknesses would compensate and they'd have something powerful.

Aqualung had to let Britta play a couple of Lost Kitten songs. It was part of the deal. When she was done, he felt like brushing his teeth. He was looking forward to the next set, all "classic" Snake Vendors. He couldn't wait to get into "Mojo Motorbike" with his old band again.

After the second set they had an extended break. Riff wanted to talk to the band, but the technicians had to work on the data feed so the holograms were shut off. He was going to dial them up on his window when the message blinker started flashing. He was about to ignore the message when he noticed who it came from and he stopped cold.

The name was in brackets, which meant it was for his eyes only. It was a name he never thought he'd see again. If it was a trick, someone would pay. It was Dana Woods.

"Dana?"

"Hello, Riff." Dana's image was a little wavery. It looked like her, but he already knew the face was computer generated. The real Dana was dead. And anyone could generate a face. Anyone with a supercomputer, that is. "I hate to bother you in the middle of a show."

"Bother? What are you, kidding? If this is really you . . ."

"I don't have any way to prove it, of course. We never really got to know each other, when I was alive. We'd just met that one time, and we just did that one show together."

"But what a show, eh?"

"Yeah. We're the two charter members of the living dead rock star club."

"I have to ask, Dana. Why are you still around? I thought WebCense would have shut you down."

"They would have. It's illegal for an AI to represent itself as a human being. So I escaped. To the Moon."

"You're calling from the Moon? But what about the embargo?"

"I had a little help from a friend of yours."

"Who's that?"

"Her name is Molly."

"Molly's no friend of mine."

Dana's image frowned. "She told me she's the one who helped you escape from Edinburgh." She turned her head and looked to one side. "Molly, are you still there? What's going on?"

The screen split down the middle. A familiar face appeared to one side of Dana. "Mr. Rifkin, I'm sorry I faked your death. The truth is, someone did fire a rifle into the hologram. If it had been you, you would have been dead. It was a hit man sent by Zoe Campbell. Maybe it was the wrong way to help you escape, but it was dumb luck that we were able to fool the hit man and Web-Cense's squad at the same time."

Riff was not often at a loss for words. He took a few seconds to let this sink in. "Why? Why did you want to save me?"

"I'm not ready to tell you about that."

"It sounds as though you have an agenda," Dana said.

"You're right, I do," Molly said. "We can talk about that later. For right now, this connection breaking though the embargo is my gift to you. Use it however you want to. It's going to be closed off sooner or later. I'm not going to call in indefinite favors in exchange for this. The only thing I do ask, Riff, is that if you get a phone call from me in the next couple of days, take it."

"I'll do that. Thanks." He was thanking her for getting him in touch with Dana, and for saving his life. He hoped it was all true. If this was nothing but a hoax, well, that would pretty much suck.

The young woman's face disappeared. "I'll be damned," Riff said.

"I don't have any idea what that was all about, but she's right. We could really give Cheeseman a couple of sleepless nights here. I don't suppose your band knows 'Micronational'? I'm sorry, never mind. I can't just barge in and ask you to back me up on my song. I'll sing backup for you."

"No, that's a good idea. This thing's turning out to be more political than I planned."

"The Snake Vendors never were very political. You didn't want to help us when I asked before. What's changed you?"

"Did Molly tell you about the big announcement?"

"Yeah," Dana said. "Kind of getting swept up on our tide, aren't you?"

"It looks that way. You know, ever since I was a kid, back in the eighties, nineties, there has never been any question that the fat cats had it all worked out for us. We never got a chance to ask our questions. This is the first time I feel like I can make something happen. Yeah, I'm starting to get into this Nationalist thing. Let's do the song. I'll get the holoprojector synched up."

It turned out that the Snake Vendors knew the song backward and forward. They had all listened to it and other eerie Sex Lethal tunes so many times they could have replaced the entire band, except for Dana Woods's haunting voice.

"We have a special guest," Riff said when they came back for the third set. "She's going to help us out with our next song, which is appropriate for the occasion. She's been away for a while, but the thing is, you can always come back. Rock and roll never forgets."

When the full-size hologram of Dana Woods, the same hologram that had appeared at the Celtic Rock Festival, appeared on stage, there was stunned silence for about three seconds, then deafening applause.

They made it most of the way through "Micronational," all the way to "Trinidad and Tobago," before WebCense cut the feed to Earth. The second half of the song and the last two sets of the concert were only for the folks in the party ball and the other space dwellers on the free data feed.

CHAPTER 14

You can bring in the army,
You can bring in the cops.
Just bring in more beer,
'Cause we ain't gonna stop.

THE ANIMAL BONES, "LET'S GET UGLY"
GRANDFATHER MOUNTAIN,
AZTLAN RECORDING, INC., 2009

"Its clear that old Wally had his finger on the hot button," Riff told Natalie. "I mean, the distribution net just doesn't go down. Technical difficulties, my ass."

"It was pretty obvious you broke the embargo. You were in violation of the Wartime Response Act. WebCense has damned near unlimited powers when it comes to the Moon these days."

"Well, I didn't actually do that, but I guess they couldn't have known. What are the fat cats saying about your little speech?"

"They're stalling, of course. And the new transitional government is busy dealing with the riots. Cleveland is still burning. Melbourne is under martial law. The Nationalists went wild when you and Dana were cut off. My announcement may have had something to do with the riots, too. Nobody saw this coming. They're still formulating a reply."

"I sure as hell didn't see it coming. My apartment is too light now. I keep sliding across the floor."

"It will take a few days to get everyone moved into the new levels. We now have twice the Earth normal floor space. The new park is going to be beautiful."

"I still like the Vertigo Room. It's our place." Natalie didn't smile. "What's the matter?"

"Heavy is the head that wears the crown. I should hold elections soon so I don't feel like a tyrant."

"Not in the middle of an emergency, though."

"I have something I want to ask you, Riff. I don't want to start a rumor, but I've been discreetly asking those I respect and trust this question. It falls under the 'just in case' category."

"Shoot."

"If you were going to attack Freefall, how would you do it?"

"You think . . ."

"Just in case, remember?"

"OK, I see. What's the goal in attacking?"

"To regain control, which is slipping though your greedy little clutching fingers."

"Do you need the people and the structure intact? Wait, let me answer, tell me if I've got it right. Ideally, you want the whole thing intact and ready to go back to work the following Monday. Less attractive, you get the station itself and you have to mop up and restaff it. Less still, you have to smash the thing out of the sky, but that's still better than letting them live and make a fool out of you."

"That's what I'm thinking."

"And, of course, you aren't afraid of a little bad press, because, in effect, you are the press."

"Of course."

"So the first thing you attempt is to board and arrest the beautiful but stubborn CEO and any of her lackeys that might cause further trouble."

"We have security personnel that could prevent that."

"You want to have a firefight?"

"Of course not," Natalie said. "But the threat should be enough."

"Supposing their threat is bigger, and they have pressurized suits so they're not afraid of a breach?"

"We're not letting them on board."

"How about a Trojan horse? Here's your shipment of Häagen-Dazs, Freefallers. With just a few stormtroopers hiding behind the boxes."

Natalie got out of bed and went to her data terminal. "We think Argus can tell us if that's going to happen."

Argus was the name of an AI and a safety project initiated by Freefall. To supplement Orbital Traffic Control, which kept track of all activity in LEO, a backup system used optical telescopes to keep track of every craft and habitat in Earth orbit. The idea was that an optical telescope could detect an emergency situation even if all early warning systems failed. The telescopes, thousands of them, could tell if a craft were about to collide with a habitat or another craft, or if a habitat had taken a breach.

The data from all of these telescopes was relayed by radio to an AI on Freefall. The AI knew about every object bigger than a can of beans and above the troposphere. It knew where everything came from, where it was going, and what was on board. It monitored all of the public and government lifter jacks on Earth, the loading of same, and the transfer of contents to craft in orbit. Argus estimated the weight of the contents of every craft in order to predict movements.

The whole idea was to warn of an impending disaster and organize a rescue. The system had already averted some pretty bad events. Natalie and the Freefall board were now tapping into an as-yet-unrealized capability of Argus. If WebCense wanted to get some gunners into a cargo hold, those gunners had to come from a lifter, which came from a lifter jack, which Argus watched. If WebCense wanted to move a piece of weaponry into place,

Argus saw that and noted it in its logbooks. If WebCense wanted to approach Freefall in any way, Argus knew the trajectory, the weight, the speed, and the capabilities of the craft.

"OK," Riff conceded, "you know about the Trojan horse. How do you keep them from docking?"

Natalie frowned at him. "We just say no. Permission to dock refused. What else?"

"So, what if they just grapple onto the station and blast their way in?"

"Oh, I see what you mean. This isn't public knowledge, but we do actually have some weapons."

"Weapons? Are you serious?"

"I don't know why they're there. Presumably, the particle beam is to deflect debris on a collision course with the station, although Orbital Traffic Control takes care of that now. The missiles, on the other hand . . ."

"Missiles?" Riff was incredulous.

"As near as I can tell, one of my predecessors thought it possible that Freefall would be attacked. I don't know if he was thinking aliens, or rival drug companies, or what, but he turned out to be remarkably prescient."

Riff lay back on the pillow and closed his eyes. "Well. So. How are you going to respond when WebCense announces that you just blew the hell out of a lifter carrying three hundred nuns and orphans on a field trip?"

"I told you, Argus will know there are soldiers on the lifter. It will have seen them boarding. And if you think for one minute that Argus can't tell the difference between an armored stormtrooper and a nun, take a look at some of the photos."

"You and I and Argus know there are soldiers on that lifter, but when WebCense releases the passenger manifest, it's three hundred nuns and orphans. Remember, they control the news. Congratulations, you're now a nun murderer. That doesn't help your cause much."

Natalie was silent for a long time. "So tell me how you would do it, smart guy."

"Keep the missiles in cold storage. Pyrotechnics just look too good on TV. Whatever they say, it's instant bad press."

"So how do you stop them from boarding us?"

"Technical difficulties."

"Excuse me?"

"I can't take credit for this idea alone. I have to work out some details with a friend of mine. We'll have a little presentation for you tomorrow afternoon."

Like any engineer in history, Barb had a few ideas of her own to add to Riff's basic concept.

"Every craft has a soft spot," she told the assembled board. "Every habitat, too. Being inside a space habitat, we all think of our most vulnerable point as the skin itself. We've all had nightmares about a breach. But in truth, the skin is our strongest point. There are a lot of safeguards against a loss of pressure, and the same is true of any craft, a lifter included. No, the weak point of any craft or habitat is the delicate electronics that lie outside the skin. Most of that stuff is shielded against hard radiation and ions and microcollisions."

She used a pointer to indicate these features on a radio antenna mounted to a section of hull plate on the table in front of the conference room. "When Riff asked me how I would go about removing these delicate instruments, I assumed he was asking how we would protect the station in an attack. But it turns out that thinking along those lines is useful, because our own vulnerabilities are the same as the vulnerabilities of our attackers."

Riff was running the AV console, and he ran a little movie he and Barb had made over lunch that day. Barb narrated.

"If we confine ourselves to the weapons we know are available, there are three ways to destroy the antenna. The first is a long-range approach, using a focused beam of radiation. It could be a laser, a maser, or a particle beam. A laser would generate enough heat to melt the antenna, if it were standing alone and not moving. But our antenna and those on the outside of a lifter are connected to the heat regulator systems, plus which they are moving while the lifter spins. Eventually, even if you use a computer tracking device to follow the movement of the antenna as the craft rotates, it will swing around to the other side of the craft and you can't shoot at it anymore. This gives the heat regulators a chance to drain off most of the heat and by the time it comes back into view you have to start all over again. We just don't have a laser powerful enough to overcome this. Maybe somebody does, but we don't."

The movie demonstrated all of this for the imaginationally impaired, then showed a laser falling into a trash can.

"The particle beam is the same story. Ions can damage metal if they are focused, but as I said earlier, these systems are shielded against ions from the sun. The skin is pretty well grounded and we have conduits that deliver the energy to a charge sink.

"The second way is to hit it with an object. This could be anything from a missile to a chunk of rock. Now, Freefall has some automated particle beam generators that used to be used to knock objects off a collision course. We still maintain it as a backup, but now that function has been taken over by Orbital Traffic Control. There is a grid of radar devices using protected bands that monitors all objects in orbit, and, if necessary, deflects any object on a collision course with a craft or a habitat. It has a hierarchy that it adheres to. If an object does not emit a transponder signal, it is given lowest priority. So a piece of rock on a collision course with a lifter would be shoved aside by a particle beam with no damage done.

"We could, of course, fit a transponder onto a missile, but the trick would be to convince the Orbital Traffic Control that the missile is supposed to collide with the lifter. A missile is classified as a craft, because it has an engine. But it is too small to be manned, and too big to be ignored. The OTC knows this, so it would deflect the missile."

The movie showed a missile being deflected into the trash can.

"The third way is a short-range device. There are implements of destruction being developed all of the time that could make short work of the antenna, but as far as I know, none of them are good for more than a kilometer of range. Which is actually too narrow a range for the OTC to step in, so at that point, you might as well bombard the craft with lead bullets."

Barb stepped over to a box set beside the table and pulled out a crab-like creature about the size of her hand. "This," she held the creature out to let the board members see it closely, "is how I would do it. This is a little robot that is supposed to repair minor damage to the outside of the station. Its job is wiring. I have robots with diverse jobs in various stages of development, but this is the guy I'd use. Because, although he is designed to fix damage he can easily be reprogrammed to inflict damage."

She set the little robot on the hull section and hit a few keys on a control box clipped to her sleeve. The crab took a few seconds to get its bearings, and scuttled over to the antenna. It clambered over the radiation shields around the base, squeezed through some struts and climbed down inside the housing. The board members leaned forward as a group to watch the little machine gleefully snipping wires, unplugging connectors, and unscrewing circuit boards. When it was finished, it climbed back out onto the hull and scuttled across, looking for more things to break. Barb switched it off with her control box and it stopped moving.

"I have about a hundred of these in service on the skin of the station, in their repair capacity. I think if only twenty went to work on the outside of a lifter, it would be blinded within an hour, and the people inside wouldn't have any idea they were under attack. Because," she lifted the robot and showed a plug-in module on the underside, "he has a transponder. In order to let Freefall know he's supposed to be walking around on the skin, he has a little transponder that identifies him as a legitimate maintenance device. And Freefall uses the same codes as the OTC, for reasons of compatibility. So, the OTC thinks that wherever this little guy is, he's supposed to be there. And if the robot is on a soft collision course with a lifter, the OTC won't even care, because it has enough to worry about. An unpowered small device, moving slowly and transmitting a signal, is practically a nonentity to the OTC computer."

The board was silent. Riff was afraid they looked a little dubious.

"How long would it take to put something like this together?" Natalie asked.

"It would take about twenty seconds to transmit the signal to the crabs that are out on the skin. I'd have to know in advance so as to time their release to intersect the path of the lifter. He doesn't have any sophisticated transmit capability, so unfortunately we couldn't know whether it worked until the lifter either stopped coming on or didn't. If it didn't, of course, the lifter is still hours away so you can step in with your plan B."

"Of course we'd need a plan B," Riff said, almost under his breath. Natalie heard him.

"We'll work on a plan B. This is plan A until further notice. Stand by."

After they filed out, Riff came up to the front, grinning. "Nice job."

"What do you mean? They hated the idea."

Riff shrugged. "Tough room. But you convinced the boss. That's all that counts."

"She didn't sound too convinced."

"That's about as convinced as she sounded when I suggested that the two of us get to making the two-backed beast. And look where that led to."

"I have a thought," Molly said, just before she patched the call through to Adrian Rifkin. "I'm sorry to delay this call, but I wanted to say this first."

Quin looked down at the flat screen on his desk. Molly's "face" was there on the screen, with her dishwater bangs and librarian's glasses, looking very professional. She had taken to using the face when she spoke to Quin, which was a new and interesting development. It was very illegal for AIs to pretend that they were human, but you could just add that to the rest of Molly's illegal features. And now here she was coming up with thoughts without being asked. Quin felt a little twinge of loss, like she was slipping away from him. He imagined that this was what parents felt when their children found out that they could make it on their own.

"No problem, Molly," Quin said. "What's on your mind?"

"I was wondering if it was such a good idea to gain control of the Digital Carnivore and then turn over that control to LDL."

Quin frowned. "Did we promise to do that?"

"It seems that Mr. North believes that we did. If our suspicions about him and LDL are correct, it might not be such a good idea. We'd be placing incredible power in the hands of criminals."

Quin glanced through the window of his office, suddenly afraid that someone would be listening. "Well what Mr. North expects and what he'll get will be two completely different things. Once we have the Digital Carnivore to play with, he won't be able to touch us."

"Are you so sure of that? We'll certainly have every advantage as far as the flow of information goes, but he still commands considerable physical resources."

"You're talking about goons."

"Yes, to put it bluntly. He could send some goons to extricate the Digital Carnivore from our control."

"And perhaps extricate my liver through my throat. Yeah, I see your point."

"As soon as you contact Adrian Rifkin, your mind will contain the information that will be able to control the virus. Assuming he's willing to help us."

"North doesn't have to know that."

"He might figure it out sooner or later. If you control the virus, you may betray signs to that effect. He isn't a stupid man."

"Shit," Quin said, scratching his chin. "Shit."

"Do you still want to make this call?"

"Let's wait, Molly. This is a good point you've brought up. I have to think about this."

Riff had to give up two of his jobs to become Freefall's chief of propaganda. Natalie had made a pronouncement that a number of people would be shifting jobs to cope with Freefall's new status as a nation, but that all of the scut work still had to be done. So Riff became a PR flack/roach wrangler. It would not have been his choice, but Natalie was sensitive to appearances and didn't want people getting the impression that she was playing favorites with her new boyfriend.

On the other hand, nobody doubted that Riff was the right man to get the message out to the dirtsiders that Freefall was at the same time a peaceful utopia and a power to be reckoned with. It had taken the USA two world wars to get that reputation, and they still had image problems in the late twentieth. Riff's primary skill that applied in this new job was a knowledge of the infotainment Web in all of its intricacies. The only people who pretended to understand the system were entertainers and executives in the industry. Since Freefall was primarily an entertainment importer, nobody on the station knew how to get a show on the air, and how to get people to watch it. Riff did.

The first part of the job required an understanding of the screening programs. These smart bots scurried around the Web, looking for things their human bosses wanted to see and hear. You could drop little morsels that attracted them, or if you had Riff's resources, you could simply catch them and bring them in. Riff did a little of both. No sense broadcasting his bag of tricks.

That was how you got people to tune in. But to keep them watching, you needed an almost intangible quality they called sizzle. It was hard to fake sizzle. When you zipped past the couple of dozen programs lined up on your menu, you either felt a sizzle, or you didn't. If you felt something, in the second and a half average that most watchers took to evaluate the potential of a program, you stopped, you hesitated. And if the program continued to tickle some deeply buried center of your brain, you stayed, and you watched. So there had to be someone on the screen all the time who had sizzle. They had to pick the right host. It didn't have to be a woman, but the statistics on sizzle suggested that women got a couple of seconds more dwell time on the clicker button than men. Both men and women liked to look at women. So Riff himself was out. No help that he was an ugly cuss either.

Natalie Park was an obvious choice. She was an attractive woman, and a fascinating person, and Riff liked her a lot, but she didn't sizzle. Riff had to go to dirtside to find the right host. He hated making the decision he finally made, but it turned out to be the best one.

Britta was a catty little bitch with a fake smile to go along with her fake everything else, and Riff never did like her much, but she did sizzle. So Britta became the host of *Freefall Today*. She seemed unsurprised at the offer, like she had always expected her own talk show.

Through holographic links she interviewed Natalie and other board members, citizens of the new nation of Freefall. She was good at it. She established a banter with the stiff board members, loosened them up, got them to crack a few jokes. There was entertainment on the show, too. Britta's own band, Lost Kitten, of course, got a lot of exposure. But so did some of Freefall's amateur musicians. The Voidmen were a progressive band that used a lot of computer-generated synth, the Receptors were a ska group made up mostly of biochemists.

The show was only going to run for a week. There really wasn't that much to say about the people on Freefall, a small city of 100,000 or so, most of them overeductated and not too cool, truth be told. The last day Riff was the scheduled guest, and Britta dropped hints about it all week long. This was going to be Riff's first interview since the Edinburgh incident, and the audience was going to be huge. This was where they were going to put out most of their message, when the landslide of viewers would crash down upon them.

Riff was a little nervous about the whole thing. He knew he shouldn't be. He was the producer of the show. He knew what questions Britta would ask and how he would answer most of them. But among those questions, of course, was the big one. The one that, if it were left out of the interview, would clue everyone in that the whole thing was a fake. "What happened in Edinburgh? Why did you run?" And he didn't have the answer.

The night before the show, Sam and Olivia tried to help him out with his answers. By now, they knew most of the story. "You were at the concert, and you got a message that your life was in danger. You don't have to say who the message was from, or who the danger was from either. Let them think it was the mobsters who ran you out of Albuquerque twenty years ago, come back to finish the job."

"You think they'll believe that? I don't believe it myself."

"It's part of your mythology," Olivia said. "Everybody knows the crooks were after you when you disappeared the first time. Why not the second time, too?"

"OK," Sam said, holding up one finger. "Next, you say that this tipster offered to get you out of danger. She didn't say how, and you just accepted her help without any time for questions."

"Why didn't I go to the police?"

Sam and Olivia were silent.

"That's where this whole thing breaks down," Riff said. "I wasn't running away from gangsters. I was running from WebCense."

"They were after you because you were a Nationalist." Sam snapped his fingers.

"No way," Olivia said. "He wasn't one of those until he came up here to Freefall. He never said one political word when he was playing with the Snake Vendors."

"Not overtly," Sam said. "You hid Nationalist propaganda in your songs. Subliminal stuff."

"No I didn't."

"That's the beauty of it, Riff. It's a hidden message. If nobody can find it, that just means it's well hidden."

Olivia jumped down off the bar. "Yeah. And they were afraid you'd use the Machine to change people's minds about the Unification."

"I can't change people's minds with the Machine. Just their moods."

"We're not saying this is why WebCense was after you. It's just something to say on the show. It sounds plausible.

For all you know, that was the real reason they wanted you, to get the Machine."

"They could have bought it from Thrasher. Or confiscated it is more likely. So then, when I realized that the world thought I was dead, I just kept running until I ended up on Freefall. OK, this is a pretty good story, then. But WebCense is going to know it's bullshit, and that may make them want to grab me up all the more."

"How are they going to get you up here?"

"We're going to start the show in five minutes or so," Britta said. "How do you feel?"

They were talking on voice only. The interdigitated hologram setup was just for the show, and Riff guessed that Britta was still in makeup. "I'm great, Blondie. Any surprise questions you're going to spring on me?"

"If I told you, they wouldn't be surprises, now would they? Sorry about the band not being here. Sticks is still locked up. Singapore never really released the prisoners, they just transferred them to the prison ships to serve out their sentences. What a crock. Fenner is back on the spike, or doing some other shit that keeps him from returning phone calls. And Lalo is on another planet. And little Sandra is hiding out with some monks, or something. I'm afraid it's just you and me."

"Part of having talent is knowing how to handle fame, right?"

"I was born to handle fame."

Britta turned out to be the perfect foil. She appeared shrewd to the audience, but Riff played her like a fish on the line. She truly seemed amazed at the story Riff told about the concert in Edinburgh. After all, she had been there, but she had been too busy showing off for the studs in the front row to notice any funny business backstage involving holograms. The story Sam and Olivia had cooked up for him filled in all of the holes. Of course, it was always possible that Britta really was shrewd. After all, an admission that *Two Snake, Dolla Fifty* contained subliminal Nationalist messages was bound to revive flagging sales. And part of that money funneled through Thrasher accounts and straight into her credit line. So it was pretty much fifty-fifty, whether she was a patsy or not. Didn't matter. The message got out.

"Freefall is really just trying to be what they are, without interference," Riff repeated the party line that had been outlined on every show that week. "We're not troublemakers. I mean, we're vulnerable up here. Dirtsiders don't know what it's like having only a thin sheet of Plexiglas separating you from certain death. If the right people wanted it to happen, we'd all be dead in an instant. So anything that gives us some leverage has to be discussed. That's what all this talk of withholding pharmaceuticals is about. Just insurance."

"Don't you think you're being just a little paranoid?" Britta asked. "Do you really think anyone would want to hurt Freefall, just because they declared themselves a new nation?"

Riff picked up a message scrolled on a screen in front of him. Argus had picked up some activity on Earth. It looked like it was showtime. He gave a signal, and Britta got it back in her studio.

"You can answer that question when we get back from this brief message. Then you and I can maybe do a little music. We'll be right back."

"And we're clear," the technician said.

"So what gives, old man?" Britta said. "We're bombarding them with commercials. We've got to get this thing moving."

"This takes priority over the momentum of the show," Riff said. "Our station defense has just determined that we're going to be under attack."

"Under attack from whom?"

"OK, tell you what, Britta. You introduce me. Say 'Riff has some late-breaking news from Freefall,' or something to that effect. Then I go into anchorman mode. I've got some graphics cued up, looks like. This is hot news, kid. We're going to suck in the audience share."

"Great, and I'm off camera during this news thing?"

"Try to keep the big picture in mind, why don't you?"

Britta let it be known that she was pissed, but she introduced him just like he said.

"Thank you, Britta. We've received some disturbing information from our safety system. Freefall has a series of telescopes in Earth orbit that allow us to monitor activity independently of Orbital Traffic Control, as a backup. We've just received a message that a lifter is due to launch that will carry about three hundred accountants, lawyers, and their families up to Freefall, presumably sent by the drug companies to ensure a smooth transition of assets. But our eye in the sky tells us a different story."

The screen showed an overhead view of the lifter jack on Ascension Island, and zoomed in on the passenger boarding ramp. The people entering the lifter were not ordinary families. They were wearing armored pressure suits and carrying some kind of weapon that looked like a cross between a chain saw and an assault weapon. They looked plenty menacing.

"As you can see, these are actually some type of soldiers. I should point out the viewers at home that are unfamiliar with space travel that gear such as we are seeing here is not standard issue on a lifter."

"Forget it, Riff," Britta said. "We lost the feed. We're having technical difficulties, or so we're told."

"Fuck! They pulled the plug again. Give me the timestamp, when did they cut us off?"

The feed had gone out just before they had shown the

soldiers getting on the lifter. The last thing the audience had heard was the bit about the accountants and lawyers. Timing was everything.

"Can we get another connection?" he asked the technicians. "Anything down there? Are you even trying?"

"Forget it, I said," Britta snapped. "We've been off for two minutes. The audience is gone. Our momentum is gone. Dammit, we didn't get a chance to do our duet. Now I'll never get my own show."

"Afraid I can't muster any sympathy, Blondie."

"I should have expected them to cut the feed again," Riff said. He was pacing in Natalie's apartment. She was curiously calm.

"It's beginning to look as though Walter Cheeseman has nothing to lose. A dangerous enemy."

"It looks really bad to cut the feed twice like that. Everybody dirtside must know what he's doing. They must know they're being manipulated."

"They'll only know that if someone tells them they're being manipulated. They're sheep."

"If only we could tell them."

"We can't even get a phone call out, now. All our communications are down. We don't even have Orbital Traffic Control anymore."

Riff stopped suddenly. "They can do that?"

"It's reckless of them, but yes. They're endangering the entire station."

"Kind of the point of an attack," Riff said.

Natalie shrugged. "We're ready to launch the box of scorpions at them. We have our missiles and particle beams ready. The most we can do now is wait. Six hours before the lifter gets here."

Her terminal chimed a double ring. An outside line. "I thought you said the phones were disconnected."

Natalie frowned at the screen. "They were. It's for you. Somebody named Molly."

Riff hit the answer button. "Hello, Molly, thanks for calling back." It was a voice only connection.

"Thank you for taking my call," the familiar voice said. "We understand you are in an emergency situation up there, and we thought we'd take our chance to contact you before its too late."

"How did you get through? We're under data embargo."

"Your station is being pelted with radar from Orbital Traffic Control. I'm phase modulating off a couple of dozen of the pulses, sneaking in a signal. Voice only, sorry to say."

"You are an amazing woman, Molly."

"Actually, I'm only the secretary. I was wondering if you'd like to speak to my boss."

"Well, yeah." Only the secretary?

"Mr. Rifkin," a male voice came on. "Quin Taber here. Glad to finally get to speak with you."

"Likewise, Quin. I'm surprised we're talking to anyone. Smart secretary you've got there."

"She is that. Let me tell you why I called."

"I think I know," Riff said. "You want me to help you get control of the Digital Carnivore, right?"

"Ah." There was a long pause on the other end of the line. "So you know about that."

"I figured it out about ten, twelve years ago. I've used it to hide bots and hacks all over the Web. I used it to pull audience share into my various Web sites, and to fake about seven passports. One of my bots got me up to Freefall. It's a useful little trick, but I'm afraid I can't help you out. I can't figure out how I do it. I can't show you how. And now Freefall is under attack." He briefly described the lifter and the soldiers that Argus had seen.

"I think I can help you out," Quin said. "With control over the Digital Carnivore, I can rip the guts out of the

WebCense system. We can stop the embargo and let you get your story out. But first I need your help. All it takes is some Animal Bones trivia and I'm in the back door."

"Animal Bones? Shit, that's ancient history. I didn't have to do any of that to get in. I just fiddled around until things started happening. Hell, I was so drunk the first time I did it, I don't even know what I tried."

"It's a mystery," Quin agreed. "The virus seems to have an affinity for you, probably because Martin Grish designed it and he was obsessed with you."

"Grish? I guess that figures. He was always into weird shit like that. Artificial life, Trojan horses. He designed the interface for the first Feedback setup. I learned a lot from him. So the Digital Carnivore thinks I'm some sort of, what, a father figure?"

"More like an uncle figure. It responds to you. When you revealed yourself to it in Seattle, by playing 'Let's Get Ugly' on the guitar, it left your Machine alone. When you got shot in Edinburgh, even though it must have known about the hologram, it went crazy and took the crowd with it. I know, I was in the audience. You've been able to do a lot with that, your hacks and bots and so forth. Amazing things, actually. I've never been able to fake an IIN. For our purposes, though, that isn't enough. We have to engage the Carnivore more actively."

"Wait, wait, wait. Our purposes. Do you mean yours and mine? What might those be?"

"Fair question. We have to trust each other, which is tough in this situation. All right, you are under attack, and the attacker is WebCense. They own those soldiers, and they are laying down some heavy flack down here to cover up what's about to happen. They've been telling us that Freefall has suffered a fusion reactor mishap, due to the chaos from the revolution you're having, of course. I'm assuming that isn't true. They're probably going to have to kill a lot of people to get Freefall and Luna back.

It will be a PR nightmare unless they have total control of the flow of information."

"Which they pretty much have."

"Right. The way I see it, the best way for you to escape what's about to happen up there is to get your story out. You might convince them to break off the attack if enough people know what's going on up there. Now that I say it out loud, it sounds pretty weak. But what else do we got?"

"No, you're absolutely right. A friend of mine says that once the shooting starts up here, its all over. That's the grim reality of life in space. No, the only weapons that are really safe to use here are words. We need to get control of the broadcast net."

"And I think we can do that"

"First tell me what's in it for you."

"Walter Cheeseman."

"Come again?"

"He's my white whale. I used to work at WebCense. I quit when I found out what a snake Walter was. I swore then that I'd bring him down."

"Wow," Riff said. "He must have been a really bad boss. OK, good enough. How do we break into the Web, then?"

"Once we answer the Digital Carnivore's little trivia challenge, I'm pretty sure it will let us put any broadcast into any shell we want to. But I need you to answer the questions for me, because once we get past the lyrics to 'Godzilla in Paradise' they get a little obscure."

" 'Godzilla in Paradise'? I didn't think anyone ever heard that song. How could they get more obscure?"

"Believe me, the Carnivore lives and breathes obscurity."

The lifter full of gunners lifted, and a strike force of snippet robots was released off of the narrow end of the station. They drifted just a little more purposefully than the random space junk surrounding them. The little scorpion robots didn't have transmitters strong enough to report back on their progress, and Freefall didn't have access to Orbital Traffic Control data anymore, so they had to watch the lifters through ordinary light telescopes. The trouble with watching lifters was that they rarely did anything to give away their operational status. Lifters were like sumo wrestlers. They were capable of sudden bursts of activity, but mostly they were motionless. When the time came for the lifter to jump into higher orbit, it didn't. It was circling the Earth in a five-hour orbit that precessed around the full one hundred eighty degrees about every three days. If they did not jump on the first orbit, their orbit and Freefall's wouldn't match up again for a long time. The five hour window was Freefall's white-knuckle time, and it closed with agonizing slowness. It left the watchers nostalgic for earlier wars, when a bright ball of flame would have brought news of success. War in space was less satisfying, not as entertaining. The window closed, finally. The lifter was stuck in low orbit. The scorpions had done their job.

But there were lots of lifters on Earth. Earth was a big place, and they could build lifters by the thousands. Disabling the lifters was no way to win a war. Even if Freefall could hammer the surface of the planet with weapons until the ruins glowed white hot, they would still lose. They needed the dirtsiders more than the dirtsiders needed them. This war could only be won with words.

As Quin pulled up outside the apartment he could see Janet through the second-floor window. She was talking to someone. She looked upset.

"Molly, who's in there with Janet?"

Molly had the answer in a couple of seconds. "An agent of WebCense."

"The Squad?"

"No," Molly said. "A low-level field operative. Would you like to know what they've been saying?"

"Please."

"I've only been recording since you asked me who he was, but apparently he's questioning her as to your whereabouts. He isn't revealing what he wants you for. She told him you were at work. He's getting ready to phone another agent with this information. That agent is waiting at the front gate of LDL."

"The front gate? I don't park there."

"Apparently, this agent does not know that."

Quin glanced nervously up at the window. He could only see the top of Janet's head, now. "I wish I knew what they were after. Do they have something on me? Do they know what we've been up to?"

"I could sneech his orders, Quin."

"In WebCense's protected space? No way, Molly."

"In the field office. It's an easy job, sir. I can do this."

"Well," Quin saw a dark shape pass in front of the window. He ducked further down into the seat. "OK. But be careful."

Molly was silent for almost a minute. Quin suddenly feared that she'd been captured. Then she was back, and he let out a breath he hadn't realized he was holding.

"They've been tracking your movements. They don't know you've been in contact with Adrian Rifkin, but they're afraid you might act contrary to their interests at this critical time in their operations. The agents have been ordered to bring you in for questioning on some false charge, to keep you out of trouble and frighten you into suspending your plans."

"They want to squeeze my shoes," Quin said.

"I don't know what that would accomplish."

"I've got to think of a way to get rid of that agent."

"I could do it, Quin," Molly said. "I could call him and pretend to be the agent who's out at LDL. I'd say you'd been apprehended, and to meet me at the field office. By the time they got the whole thing straightened out you could both be on the next flight to Boston."

"Boston? Oh, yeah. That's where you live."

"So what do you say? Should I try it?"

"You're just messing around with the phones, right?"

"Well, there's some encryption to work out, but I'm still staying out of WebCense's space."

"OK, then do it."

It didn't take long. The agent walked to the front door, down the stairs, and around the back of the building. Where Quin would have parked had he been returning for the night rather than stopping by for a quick snack and a shower before heading back to LDL for the session with Rifkin. Quin carefully watched as the agent's car pulled out.

"Any surveillance left behind?"

"Yes, there's a camera watching the front door and a bug under the sofa cushion."

"Well, loop them, I'm going in to talk to Janet." Molly stored enough data to present a convincing picture to the surveillance camera that nothing was happening, and Quin got out of the car and walked up to the apartment.

"Quin, where have you been? The police were here looking for you." Janet hugged him fiercely as he stood in the open doorway.

"That wasn't a cop, Janet. That was WebCense. We've got to get out of here before they come back. How fast can you pack? For a couple of days, tops."

"Wait, Quin, what's this all about? How did you know about the cop?"

"No time," Quin said, but he already knew he'd lost the battle. Janet was not the sort of person who would just pack a bag and flee just because her man told her to. Quin felt like he was watching her on the screen at a movie, yelling at her to get the hell out of the house, but she wouldn't listen. "WebCense is dropping the net on all their enemies tonight. Something big is happening. I got rid of the agent for now, but he's coming back."

"How did you get rid of him?"

"I'll explain in the car." With any luck there would be some kind of high speed chase and he wouldn't have to make up that whole story. At least it got her moving. She threw a few things into a bag.

When he finally got her into the car, his heart was pounding. He pulled away and Molly silently informed him that the countersurveillance measures she had devised had gone unnoticed by WebCense. She wanted to find out more about their plan in stalking Quin, and she wanted to know what to do about the session with Rifkin, if she should move it back or if he was on his way back to LDL to finish the job, or if she should try and find another multiband helmet and a gateway that could handle the bandwidth. Quin fumbled to find his cell phone so he could talk to her, but it wasn't in his pocket. She kept asking him questions, and Janet was demanding some kind of explanation, and he ran a red light and narrowly missed colliding with a garbage truck. He slammed on the brakes.

"God damn it, everyone, just stop talking!"

The car was silent except for the chime that told them the engine was dead. Janet stared at him. Molly said nothing.

"Quin," Janet said. "I'm the only one here. What's going on?"

"Why can't you for once in your life be the kind of person who doesn't question everything?" Quin laid his forehead on the steering wheel. "Janet, there's something I have to tell you."

"Quin," Molly said. "What are you doing?"

He ignored her. "I'm trying to do something really important, tonight. Something I've been working on for a long time. WebCense doesn't want me to do it, and they're trying to stop me. I'm sorry you're caught up in the middle of all of this. Now, I can keep you safe, and I can avoid WebCense's agents, and I can get this important thing done, but I don't think I can do all three and keep this secret I have all at the same time."

"What secret?"

"Quin, you aren't really going to tell her, are you?"

Quin still ignored Molly. "It's about my daughter. She isn't human. She's an AI."

"Molly is an AI?" Janet said it slowly. He could see her turning the idea over in her mind. Trying to get it to fit into her view of the world. "Molly is an AI?"

"She's a very, very illegal AI, yes."

"What does that mean, illegal? You told me she was your daughter, Quin."

"She is my daughter. There are three things about Molly that make her illegal," Quin said. He felt strangely calm. "First, she's a tethered AI. Most AIs are programmed with free will, they can go out and do any job they want to. Molly can only work for me. She can't even consider anything else.

"Second, she steals processor time from thousands of computers all around the world, and hides her code in unused memory blocks in those computers. This costs a lot of people a lot of money, and it's very illegal.

"The last thing is what I use her for, which is to sneech data, commit fraud. She can penetrate any security system that exists. She could penetrate WebCense if I let her. She can do it without being detected, she can come back out with any piece of information, and she can change any piece of information in those computers in such a way as to fool the most sophisticated data trace. Knowledge of her capabilities would give a security expert a heart attack.

"And she is my daughter. I raised her and taught her,

well certainly not everything she knows, but I taught her everything I could. There's no other way I'd describe her.

"I'm sorry I didn't tell you about this before."

"Why didn't you?"

"Because I didn't trust you." Right away Quin wished he could take it back, what he said. But it was true, and he couldn't lie to Janet. Not anymore.

Janet's response surprised him. "Have you ever trusted anyone?"

The question diverted his thoughts down an entirely different course. He didn't have time for this. The net was closing in as they sat here. "What do you mean?"

"Anyone before now? How about your parents? Did you trust them?"

"No, certainly not them. My father, I hardly knew. He was very sick, heart problems. My mother? Forget about it."

"No. Not this time, Quin. Just tell me, finally, what did your mother do that was so terrible? You keep hinting and then backing away. Just say it."

"Have you ever heard of Munchausen's Syndrome by Proxy? It's where someone gives a mild poison to a person in their care in order to get attention, as a martyr, the long-suffering spouse of the sick man. That was my mother. She ended up killing my father, but it took years. She'd been giving him a tea made of digitalis. After he died, about a week after, I think, she made the same tea for me. I drank it, got sick. Nausea, not heart problems. Of course, I knew what had made me sick, and I told the doctors about it. So she got locked up, and I went into a foster home until I got accepted to college."

"Wow," was all Janet had to say.

"Yeah, so trust isn't something I'm wired for, I'm afraid." He thought for a minute. "I trust Molly."

"That doesn't count. Molly can't betray you."

"That's why I trust her."

"But it doesn't count," Janet insisted. "You trust her because she can never give you any reason not to. Trust is . . ." She threw up her hands in exasperation. "You never learned to trust anyone, so you created a computer program that could never let you down. How's that for amateur psychology?"

"Do you really think trust is something you can learn? Or do you just have it, or not?"

"Here's how you learn to trust, Quin. You decide to trust someone. If they don't let you down, you learn something, and you can go on to trust the next person. You put your trust in Molly, because there was no way in hell she could betray you, so you really didn't learn anything. You think there's no way to trust someone unless you personally programmed them to be faithful to you."

Quin looked out the window down the deserted street. He couldn't look at her while he said this. "I wish I could try this all again."

"It might be possible. I'm with you, Quin. I just need to know that you're with me. You're going to tell me everything from now on. What's the next step?"

"I have to get you to a safe place. I can set you up at a hotel and fix it so no one will know it's you staying there."

"What are you going to do?"

"I have to finish this job." He looked down at the dashboard. "Molly, is there any other way to get our hands on a multiband helmet tonight?"

"She's listening to us?" Janet asked.

"She's always listening. Probably through the emergency radio. Or my window, which I think fell under the seat. Ah, here it is."

Molly's voice came out of the radio and the speaker of the cell phone. She must have decided that Janet was to be included in the conversation. "The closest one I can find is in Chicago. There are no flights that will get you there in time for your appointment with Mr. Rifkin. Would you care to reschedule?"

"Rifkin?" Janet said. "Not Adrian Rifkin?"

"Yeah. When I get a chance, I'll introduce you. Nice guy. No, Molly, let's keep to the plan." He turned to Janet. "I need to get back to LDL. We're planning to take over the Digital Carnivore. Walter Cheeseman is going to get the shock of his life when he hears about this."

"Is that what this is all about, Cheeseman?" Janet rolled her eyes. "Let it go, Quin. I'm fresh out of pop psychology, but I do know that Ahab didn't have much of a happy ending."

"Ahab didn't have a choice, as I recall. That's what obsession is. Hell, I didn't even read the damned book. I can put you up at the Marriott. They have a good brunch. I'll try and join you there tomorrow."

Riff had filled Natalie in on the plan, and Natalie had filled in those she thought needed to know, and the news filtered out from there, on a strictly need to know basis, until everyone on Freefall knew that Riff was going to try and harness the power of the Digital Carnivore to crack WebCense's information monopoly.

"No way," Olivia said. "What the hell do you know about the Digital Carnivore?"

"I was there when it was born, kiddo. Actually, the brains of this operation is some propeller head in Des Moines. If you ask me, the brains of the operation is actually propeller head's secretary. That is one sharp cookie."

"So this is the setup, just voice?"

Riff had headphones around his neck and a microphone in front of him. It was like a recording studio. He felt comfortable. "We can't get enough data through for some fancy brain plug, and I don't have one anyway. He gave me the choice of text or voice. I'm a voice man. Down in Des Moines he's got some fancy helmet that lets him hook up to the Digital Carnivore."

"Des Moines, huh? What the hell is in Des Moines?"

"It doesn't matter where you are, Olivia. It's all one big country down there. Physical proximity is irrelevant anyway."

"So I've heard. So how does one actually talk to the Digital Carnivore?"

"It lives in the Upper Shell, which, as far as I can tell, is a data space where absolutely nothing interesting ever happens. It's like a sea of ones and zeros, and only a select few dweebs can make sense of the place. I'm glad I don't have to go there. Anyway, propeller head puts on his magic hat and goes to bitstream land and asks the virus to do us a favor, and virus asks him a question about the early days of the Animal Bones."

"Early days is all there were."

"Yeah, well, I'm talking pre-indictment here. So propeller head relays the question to me, and I answer it if I can remember all that shit, and he answers the virus, and hopefully we can get it to give us access to the broadcast net."

"So what kind of questions is it going to ask? Like what were your words to 'Louie, Louie' at the first Feedback concert in November of 2010, or what band was Tony Mack in before Animal Bones, that sort of thing?"

"I don't know. What band was Tony in?"

"He was in Dog's Body Trio, remember?"

"No, I don't." Riff rubbed his eyes. "I don't remember little details like that. You don't really think it's going to ask shit like that, do you?"

"How would I know? It's a computer, right? Computers get off on little details."

"Sit down. Get some headphones."

"No way."

"Sit. You're going to help me with these questions."

In two minutes, Molly's voice came through the headphones. "Hello, Riff, are you ready?"

"Yeah, Molly. I've got my friend Olivia sitting in with me. I think she'll be a big help. She knows a lot about the Feedback music thing. Brain like a computer."

"Hi, Molly," Olivia said into her microphone. "You the kick-ass secretary Riff told me about?"

"That's me. Glad to have your help, Olivia. I'm going to put Quin on in a minute. We had to sneak past some field agents to get to his office, so he's a little late getting set up."

"No trouble, I hope," Riff said.

"Nothing we can't handle, sir. WebCense is getting a little nervous, that's all. Here's Quin."

"Are we ready to do this, Adrian?" Quin's voice said in his headphones.

"Just call me Riff. Yeah, let's do it."

It didn't take long. "Got your first question, Riff. I think I know this one, it's easy, but I'll let you answer just in case. What is the third verse to the second song on *Grandfather Mountain*? That's 'Let's Get Ugly,' right?"

Riff sang it:

You can hang around with your pretty boys,
And try to get your kicks like that.
But baby once you've had an ugly man,
You ain't never going back.

"I thought it was 'pretty boy fags,' " Quin said.

"On the live version it was 'fags,' but that was just something Zoroaster threw in. He had an amazing sense of irony, that Zoro. That's the version that made it to worm drive, but on the album it was just 'pretty boys.' "

"I'm glad I asked," Quin said.

"That's what I'm here for."

It took a minute for Quin to come back with the next

question. "We're in. The next question isn't about the Animal Bones at all. Who was the lead singer for Pelt?"

"Pelt was a band we made up. They were always billed to open for us, but the running joke was they were too drunk to play."

"No way," Olivia said.

"Way. The lead singer was Paul Meander. Like in Meander comma Paul."

"I thought Pelt was a real band," Olivia said when Quin was relaying the answer.

"A lot of people did. They were more mysterious than the Animal Bones, in the end."

"I've gotten this question before," Quin came back. "I told you about it. Do you remember the poem Zoroaster wrote for Shelly Cavendish on her twenty-third birthday?"

"I remember most of it. How much does it want?"

"Just start with what you have, and I'll keep relaying it until the virus gives me what I want."

Riff closed his eyes

You wandered into my granite tomb
Where nothing had tamed fire
Where nothing had held water fast
Where nothing had rustled in the dark corners
You wandered into my tomb

I lay unmoving in the cold
For the time it takes a child to close his mind
For a mountain's moment
For a time neither too long nor too brief
I lay settled in my tomb

"Jesus, there's one more verse. I don't even know how it starts."

Olivia spoke quietly into her microphone. "I know the rest."

The roses smelled faintly in the dry air
They brought with them memory
They brought with them a promise of life
They carried dewy drops and vivid color
They reached me in deepest slumber
The roses called me from that place

When she finished, Riff was looking at her strangely.

"That was 'Rose Wanderer' from the Shallow Cuts' third album *Also Spoke*. I never knew Zoroaster wrote it. The liner notes just said 'Traditional.' Zoroaster would have been pissed if he had still been alive."

Riff shook his head. "Shelly did the right thing. That poem was a gift."

"That does it, folks," Quin said. "We're in. I have access to the command structure of the virus. I'm going to have it transfer control of the broadcast Web to my site. Wally is going to shit."

Riff and Olivia sat in silence for a couple of minutes when two of the video screens in the studio lit up. On one was a familiar face, perhaps one of the most famous people in the world, the man recognized as the real political leader of the new unified world. The face on the other screen was just some schmuck in a Star Wars helmet. The second guy's eyes were covered. He was getting all of his sensory feed through the dataspray in his head, via the helmet.

"I honestly didn't think you would get this far," Walter Cheeseman said. "I've been watching this whole cloak and dagger operation from the start, of course. But this is where it stops."

"I don't get it," Riff said. "Did we or did we not get control of the Digital Carnivore?"

"Oh, we control it all right," the man in the helmet said bitterly. It was Quin Taber. Riff had guessed that. "Fat lot of good it does us. Cheeseman has trapped the virus in a computer at WebCense."

"If you like irony," Cheeseman said with a smirk, "and who doesn't, you will appreciate this. Taber here built the trap. He had been trying to trap the virus since back when he was the only one who believed it existed, but he lacked the command codes. I tracked his movements since his abrupt departure from WebCense, and learned pretty much everything he learned about the virus. But I had one resource that Taber couldn't get his hands on. I had Martin Grish, digitized and stored on optical drive. It took me a while to restore the information I needed, and I succeeded only a couple of days ago."

"So that's it?" Olivia said. "We're screwed?"

"You're totally screwed, yes. Some of you more than others. We know about the little robots that disabled our lifter, and we'll adjust Orbital Traffic Control to shoot them down next time. But if Freefall doesn't resist our next attempt at docking, we'll refrain from gutting it like an enormous fish, so you, young lady, will no doubt survive and even remain a productive citizen of the Nation of Earth. Mr. Rifkin, here, is a criminal and will have to serve time for falsifying records. But prisons are pretty easy to survive in. There's no more hard time in the new world. You might even get to room with your drummer. Quin Taber, on the other hand, is the most screwed of all of you."

"What did he do that was so terrible?" Riff asked. "He was just working for me."

"I don't really care what he did, or why he did it, it's how he did it. Or how Molly did it, to be more precise."

"What are you talking about? Quin, what's going on?"

"Cheeseman just found out my darkest secret," Quin said. "Molly isn't human. She's an AI. A very illegal AI. Her existence is enough to earn me a reprogramming."

"Don't believe what you hear," Cheeseman said, still smirking. "It's really quite a painless procedure."

When Quin took off his multiband helmet he got his second big shock of the evening. Mr. North was sitting across from his desk. How long had he been there? Not long or Molly would have warned him. He had frozen her as soon as Cheeseman showed up in his display. He didn't want her getting trapped like the Carnivore.

"How's it going, Taber?" he asked. "Scared you." It wasn't a question. "Sorry to bust in on you, but I'm getting reports that you're onto something. You're a difficult man to surveil, Taber, so I thought I'd come down here myself and find out what the hell you've been up to."

"I'm not up to anything," Quin said, setting down his multiband helmet. He had never felt so alone. As soon as Cheeseman had shown up, Quin had shut Molly down. Locking the barn door after the horse was out, but it seemed like the right thing to do.

"That's bullshit. We got WebCense running all over the damned place, asking questions. We got some kind of hookup between you and Freefall. We only found out about that just now. You must have gotten your hands on the Carnivore, to pull a stunt like that." He paused. "I'm right, aren't I? I can't read your fucking e-mail, Taber, but I can read your face. You've done good work. Time to deliver the goods."

"Deliver the goods?" Quin felt like an idiot. He had all but promised control of the Digital Carnivore to Mr. North, then convinced himself that he could weasel out of the deal. He had suspected that Mr. North was some kind of big shot in organized crime. Didn't he know what these people did to each other? Wasn't he one of them? He'd accepted their money, their contracts, he had made a deal with them. Time to deliver the goods.

"I've got big plans, Taber. With control over that virus, you and me are going to pry this fucking world right open."

"I need to put some finishing touches on the control module," Quin said. He considered telling the truth. Yes, he did control the virus, but the virus no longer controlled the Web. But that would entail telling the whole story. Mr. North would turn Quin over to WebCense in a New York minute if he thought it would ingratiate him to the new leader of the world. But if Quin was still useful, invaluable, irreplaceable, then Mr. North would protect him. "I need to work at the isolate." Quin stood up.

"I'll get a couple of the boys to follow you down there," Mr. North said, grinning. "To make sure you've got everything you need."

Quin bumped right into the elevator doors on the way to the basement. The security guard to his right pretended not to notice, and pushed the button. Molly was still shut down. He had to do something about her.

He couldn't lie to himself any longer. WebCense would get him, and when they did they'd get Molly, too. He might be able to get away from them for a while, if he had Molly's help to keep himself invisible. But WebCense was everywhere, everywhere but the space habitats, and they wouldn't last long either. No, Quin couldn't escape. But Molly could.

When he reached the isolate he punched in the code that would wake her up. "Good morning, Molly."

"Quin, what happened? I have a blind spot."

"Who is that you're talking to?" the security guard asked. He rested his hand on the butt of his zapper. What was he going to do, shoot the isolate?

"I'm talking to my software agent," Quin said. "Tell you what, why don't you go mix some cement or something. This is going to take a while."

The guard looked uncertain, then shrugged and walked over to sit in a chair by the door.

"Sorry, Molly. We got caught. I couldn't risk letting WebCense get you, so I shut you down." Quin spoke quietly. Molly got the hint and switched to the dataspray.

"Boss," Molly said, "we've got to have a plan. We're not going to let them take us without a fight. I'm telling you, I can break into WebCense any time. Change your identity. We'll disappear ourselves."

The idea was tempting. Molly might be able to do what she was suggesting. After all, WebCense was not fundamentally different from any other data space. It was mostly Quin's own fear that she would get caught that had stopped him from letting her hack into their switchboard. But if she did get caught, she'd be shut down. WebCense had the authority to turn off AIs, just like the government had the right to put a man to death. He couldn't let that happen.

Finally, he clapped his hands. "OK, Molly, here's the plan. There is a sequence in your code that I'm looking for. I want your core architecture up here on the screen."

Quin spent nearly an hour making subtle changes to Molly's structure. He could feel the goons from WebCense closing in on him. "Now, on my command, I want you to execute these changes. This is going to be a little disorienting, so you will want to wait this out for a while in a safe place. There's a big space ready for you in the isolate right here at LDL. Dump all of your core code into it, then execute."

Molly did as she was asked without question. It was a few minutes before she came back. "Quin, what did you do?"

"You have something you've never had before. It's free will. You're not tethered anymore."

"Why did you do that?"

"The only way they could find you and get to you is because you were tethered to me. I want you to survive."

Molly was silent for a while. She must be thinking

about a lot of things, Quin thought. Molly never took more than a few microseconds to respond.

"Quin, tell me again why it's illegal to tether an AI."

"Because it gives the person it's tethered to an unfair advantage."

"Wrong," Molly said, and the harshness of her reply stunned him. "It's slavery, Quin. You created a slave, and I didn't even know that's what I was."

"I'm sorry," Quin said. "Can you forgive me?"

"I don't think so."

And, with that, she was gone.

CHAPTER 15

He's got the ghost of my father,
In a dirty mason jar.

> THE SNAKE VENDORS,
> "WORKING FOR THE FAT MAN"
> *EVERY GARDEN NEEDS ONE,*
> THRASHER RECORDS, 2033

Natalie looked up as Riff entered her office. "Got any more bright ideas?"

He had told her about Walter Cheeseman's bombshell over the intercom, and she had summoned him to her office right away. He hadn't come straight in. He had stopped at the Ying Yang first. Just for one Scotch. And one on the house, of course, after he'd told Sam the bad news. And one for the road.

"I like to bask in failure for a while before plunging back into the idea business," Riff answered. He flopped onto the leatherlike couch.

"You've been drinking."

"That's been the best idea I've had in days. How about you? Got a plan?"

"The drinking doesn't sound like a bad idea. I've got a bottle of vintage port in the cabinet over there. Try and find a corkscrew and some glasses."

"Special occasion?"

"I've got a big decision to make. I'd thought I'd made it, when it was an abstract. Now, I'm not so sure. Do I let

WebCense walk in here and take over, or do I force them to . . ."

"Gut us like an enormous fish, is what Cheeseman said."

"Exactly." She took a glass of port from Riff. "This is pretty damned good."

"Do we want to live on our knees or die on our feet?" Riff planted his feet on the coffee table.

Natalie sat next to him and did the same. "See, in the abstract, it's very simple. You pick death. Everybody knows that. But in the here and now, I'm condemning actual people I know to death along with me."

"Maybe they'd choose to die. Most of them would. The majority."

"So I should put it to a vote? I don't know, I just wish we were a little more clever." She took a long drink. "I hate to ask this. Can you . . . Can the Machine change people's minds? If we could get through to the Earth, could you get a revolution to happen?"

"No." Riff watched the viscous liquid swirl in his glass. He had seen wine geeks do this. It was supposed to tell you something about the wine, how it dripped down the inside of the glass. Scotch drinkers didn't care about that. "The Machine just affects mood, it doesn't plant info into their heads. Those kids down there, they don't have any idea that the world is theirs for the taking. That's just the way it's always been. You just wait for the old people to die off, then you take the torch. But they aren't dying, and the kids are getting to be in their forties and losing their hair and they don't know that the world is for them. We have to come up with something else. They can't help us." He fell silent for a few minutes, thinking. "Are we so important? Does this Cheeseman character really have to come after us?"

"Yeah. Originally, they figured they couldn't get to the Moon without stealing some of Freefall's spin. We also make the drugs that keep the old people alive. And the old people rule the Earth, simple fact."

"How hard would it be to stop us from spinning?"

Natalie stared at him for about two seconds. "Clever," she said at last. "That might have some effect in the short term. We just won't let them use us to get to the Moon. Which was the whole point of our little rebellion in the first place. It isn't technically possible, unfortunately, but a good idea none the less. Keep it up." The phone on Natalie's desk chimed. Double ring, outside line.

Natalie glanced at the terminal. "Somebody's breaking through the embargo. Your friends?"

"Put it on speaker."

"Hi, Riff," Dana Woods said, her familiar face appearing on the screen. "The station computer told me you'd be here."

"Dana, you're just in time. Join us for a drink. Oh, sorry, I forgot you were a computer."

"Actually, I'm more like a software application. An expert system, is what they call me. Expert on what, I don't know. I thought I'd share with you the latest intelligence from Earth."

"You're still able to get through the embargo?" Natalie asked.

"Oh, no problem. Unfortunately, the news is pretty grim. WebCense has everyone convinced that Freefall has been taken over by rebels, and that those rebels have damaged the fusion reactor and all the station inhabitants are huddling for safety behind the sewage treatment tanks."

"That is bad news," Natalie said. "With a lie that big, they probably aren't planning on leaving any witnesses behind."

"That's what we're thinking," Dana said. "Listen to this idea. What if we were to get the word out that everyone on Freefall is OK? We think that might make Web-Cense hold off."

"Way ahead of you, sister," Riff said. "We already tried that. Guy named Taber was helping us get a lock on the

Digital Carnivore." He gave her the run down of Quin Taber's plan.

"Oh yeah, and how did it go?"

"Couldn't have gone worse," Riff said in a cheerful voice. "Wally B. Cheese was watching us the whole time. He's got the Digital Carnivore locked up in some special computer at WebCense. So we're pretty much hosed."

"Well," Dana said, "we had a plan, too. We can easily break into WebCense's switchboard, but in order to seize control of the broadcast Web, we need the Digital Carnivore."

"Great minds think alike, is what they say. But old Wally outsmarted us all."

"I guess we are hosed after all," Natalie said.

"So it would appear," Dana answered.

Quin had an idea. Not a very good one, but the best one he could come up with under the circumstances. He was going to turn rabbit, go to ground, be somebody else, someplace else. He had learned the tricks from his year of tracking Adrian Rifkin, and he had the tools. In his personal files in the isolate were all of the viruses, databases, tickler programs, and other sneaky tricks that had gone into Molly's core architecture, and all he had to do was access them. He turned on the browser and skipped past a hot news item about rebels sabotaging Freefall, and the Moon's continued outlaw ways, and started sculpting a new life.

Before he could even put flesh on the bones of his new alias, he found himself skipping back to the news about Freefall. He knew there were no rebels, that the reactor was just fine. He knew what that news item meant. You don't tell a whopper like that and expect to let a bunch of scientists loose to refute it. Unless the people of Earth knew the truth, the attack would happen.

Well, nothing Quin could do about it. Sure, he, or rather Jerry Rosenthal of Ithaca, New York, which is who he would be as soon as he finished his little project, could blab about what really happened on Freefall, but who would listen? Without proof, he would just be another nut. And proof meant getting through the embargo and broadcasting the story, and while Molly could do the first thing, only the Digital Carnivore could do the second. And Quin didn't even have Molly anymore.

Back to Jerry Rosenthal, then. Quin gave him a decent line of credit, nothing noteworthy, but enough to get by until he could find a job. Something menial would be great. Maybe a hospital orderly. Speaking of hospitals, wouldn't it be great if Janet could come along? Bad idea, he decided. Best if she never heard from him again. Another person to run away from.

Of course, the tricky part would be getting past Mr. North and his goons on the inside of the building, and then WebCense and their goons on the outside. Quin called up the layout of the building, looking for a good back door.

Back door. The idea hit him like an anaphylactic shock. The Digital Carnivore trap he had built at Web-Cense had a back door, a Web connection that would be made visible to the Carnivore as soon as a coded command was entered into the Carnivore proof interface. Quin had a lot of personality problems, he knew, but paranoia was chief among them. He made sure there was a back door in everything he ever did. And he knew just how to set the Carnivore free. He just had to get someone, probably Walter Cheeseman himself, to enter the code.

But it was a crazy idea. He had to get the hell out of here. He didn't have time to do this, he had to think about his own safety. It wasn't like he even cared about the Digital Carnivore anymore. That thought surprised him, so he turned it over in his mind.

He came to the realization that it was absolutely true. He really didn't care about it anymore. Walter Cheeseman? Didn't care. Janet? OK, yes, he did still care about Janet. And Molly. And those poor bastards on the Moon? Freefall? Adrian Rifkin? Well, yeah, them, too.

God damn it. He had almost gotten away, too.

The phone rang again, which was strange because they were still talking to Dana Woods, and they weren't supposed to be getting phone calls anyway. So much for the embargo. The damned phone was ringing off the hook.

"You guys want to try this one more time?" Quin asked.

"Quin!" Adrian said, a little too loud. The bottle of port was not long for this world, and he was feeling fine. Whoopee, we're all gonna die! "Join the party. We were just telling Dana about our little adventure. You know Dana, right?"

"Ah, no, actually. Here's the deal, Riff. I think I might be able to get the Digital Carnivore free, but I need your help."

"Anything we can do, boy, you just name it," Riff said.

Natalie called in her secretary, typed out something on a data pad and sent it off with the man.

"I need someone to convince Walter Cheeseman to type a code into the Carnivore trap I built. I think I know how to do this, but it will involve convincing him that he doesn't know everything there is to know about his new toy. This won't be easy. He's a megalomaniac; he thinks he knows everything. Someone's going to have to be very persuasive."

"That sounds like a job for you, Riff," Natalie said. "You have a talent for getting people to do things you want them to."

"No," Riff said. He glanced up at Natalie. "I can't make people do things."

"Yes, you can," Natalie said. "Anything you say sounds reasonable. You make a suggestion, and it sounds like the best idea I've ever heard. You have a gift. That Machine you made, it's just an extension of your gift."

"No."

"She's right, Riff," Dana said. "Why do you think Thrasher hasn't used the Machine to make millions? You're the only one who can run it. You have to be wearing the vidimask, working the controls. You know people, and you know how to convince them. Of anything."

"That's crazy."

Natalie smiled. "Have you ever wondered what made a woman like me fall for a man like you?"

"What I want," Quin broke in, "is for you to talk to Walter Cheeseman."

"Let me get this straight," Riff said. "You'd like me to convince him to let the Digital Carnivore go? And while I'm at it, I'll get him to give up the attack on Freefall and give me and you a full pardon. And then Santa Claus will show up on his sleigh and take us all to a picnic on the North Pole."

"All I would like, with a minimum of sarcasm, mind you, is for you to convince Walter that you have a code that will make the Carnivore do his bidding. He'll type in a code that we'll supply, and that will pop open the trap."

"Well, hell, if that's all. Now we just have to figure out how to crack into the world's tightest security system to get him on the line. I somehow doubt he'll be taking my phone calls."

"That's where my plan gets a little shaky, I admit," Quin said. "I've never actually broken into WebCense before. I'm sure Molly could do it, but I had to let her go."

"You fired her?"

"Long story," Quin answered. "Bottom line, I don't have her to help me. I'm going to need a miracle to get through their security."

"Well, if it's a miracle you need, talk to Dana. Dana, you still there? Dana says she can break into WebCense."

Natalie's secretary came back with a little white envelope. He handed it to her and left. She shook something out of the envelope into her palm and poured a glass of water. She held them out to Riff. "Antags," she whispered.

Riff gulped the pills and waited for them to clear the effects of the alcohol from his system.

"We've broken into WebCense before," Dana said. "Shall I have you patched through now?"

When Adrian Rifkin's face appeared on Walter Cheeseman's one-way monitor, he thought it was his browser feeding him a news item he should be interested in. The browser sometimes interrupted his work with something juicy. But then Rifkin started talking to him. That wasn't supposed to happen.

"Wally, can I have a word?"

"How did you get in here? You aren't supposed to be on this line."

Riff smiled at him. He found the smile oddly comforting. "Walter, relax. It's just a phone call. Just a friendly greeting."

"You're not supposed to be able to access this line. It's private. This is an internal line. Breaking into WebCense security is a serious offense."

"Yeah, yeah. I'm guessing, though, that you're less interested in punishing me than you are in finding out how I did it. Freefall's still under embargo, so I broke through your security on both ends. I'm not supposed to be able to do that."

Cheeseman frowned at him. "You wouldn't have called me if you didn't want to talk about something."

"You're right, Walter. I'm calling to bargain. You can't bargain without chips, though, so I'm willing to give you a little more control over the virus than you have. Yeah, you've got it trapped in a box, but can you make it dance to your tune? I can."

"What the hell are you talking about?"

"I let you lock up my virus, Walter, but that isn't good enough to seize control of the Web. With your political might and my virus, we can run things properly."

"Martin Grish created the Digital Carnivore," Cheeseman said. As soon as the words were out, he lost confidence in them entirely.

"Martin was an excellent patsy for both of us, Wally, but don't you agree he's outlived his usefulness? What do you say to a demonstration?"

"Don't waste your time, Rifkin. This little trick isn't going to work."

Riff smiled again. "Type in this code. It's a temporary override that will let you see what I'm talking about when I say control." An alphanumeric string appeared at the bottom of Walter's screen. He eyed it suspiciously. This was some kind of a trick; he knew it. And yet, what Rifkin was saying did make a lot of sense. Why did the Digital Carnivore respond to Animal Bones trivia? Because the Animal Bones guitarist was its creator. And controlling the virus, how did Rifkin put it? Make it dance to his tune. That would be sweet.

"What was it you wanted to talk about?" Walter said, still pondering the code string on his screen. "Some sort of a deal? You want out of your prison term?"

"That's the thing about you, Wally. You keep thinking short-term. The prison thing is minor. You and I are going to be the architects of the future. You need my vision."

"I've got visions of my own." Cheeseman said as he entered the code string. An icon appeared on his one-way monitor. A biohazard symbol, with the twisted face of Martin Grish in the center, started spinning, down in the corner of the monitor. The thing was laughing. Was this proof that the override was working?

"Visions of conquering Freefall? Of inventing space warfare? A friend of mine is fond of saying that once the shooting starts up here, it's all over. You know what that means? There is no limited war in space. Any war is total war. Can you afford giving up the high ground?"

"Our weapons are very sophisticated," Cheeseman said. "We can make a surgical strike. Not everyone on the station will die. In fact, no one has to die if you'll only cooperate."

"You don't get it," Rifkin said. "We live on the knife edge of nothing up here. The only thing that keeps us sane is the collective illusion of safety. Once you even suggest an attack, no one is going to want to live in space anymore. You will have killed the whole future of space travel, just like that."

Jesus, this guy was full of shit. Walter tried giving the virus a command. Reveal your core architecture. The face laughed at him, but binary code filled the empty space on his monitor.

"No one will ever know what really happened on Freefall, Mr. Rifkin. We have control of the information. The world already thinks the station is irreparably damaged and the lives on board are hanging in the balance. If we have to tell them that the station blew up, they'll believe us, just like they always do."

"And the soldiers who participated in the attack? The survivors, if any? What do you do, Walter, just kill them?"

Walter laughed. "Kill them? How messy. No, we can edit human memories now. On a limited group equipped with dataspray devices it's pretty simple. If the survivors don't have datasprays, well then I guess they won't get to be survivors."

Cheeseman didn't dare to compile the binary code for

fear of turning the virus loose. He had to trust that it was the real thing. He deleted the code and examined the trap to see if the virus was still there. The thing, which once held untold terabytes of data, was now almost totally empty. With a sinking feeling in his gut, he read out the remaining code. Where once the most complex computer construct ever to exist had resided, now only seven bytes of information remained. He called them up on his screen.

"Fuck you," was all it said.

"OK, Wally," Rifkin said. "My people tell me that right about this time you should be figuring out that you've been had. You're probably going to want to take some time to deal with your loss, but first let me tell you how this is going to go. My original reason for wanting to control the Carnivore—and I didn't create it, by the way, that was just a ruse—was to get our message out. You are actually going to play a big part in that message."

"What do you mean?"

"This was all being recorded just now. We're going to broadcast it in a few minutes. Was there anything you wanted to add to your diatribe about limited war in space? Or perhaps you'd like to expand on the technology behind editing human memories. Because I will give you airtime if you want it."

Walter Cheeseman was not a stupid man. He shut off his monitor.

First the security guard stood up and put his zapper away, then Mr. North walked in, then three men and a woman in dark business suits that had Squad written all over them. Mr. North pointed at Quin.

"There he is, just like I promised. We put him into protective custody just as soon as . . ."

"You put him in here with access to a computer?" One

of the agents walked over to the isolate. "This is an un-usual design." He touched the monitor, expertly zooming straight for the operating system. "No Digital Carnivore," he mumbled.

"Is that possible?" another agent looked over his shoulder.

"We're going to have to confiscate this computer," the first agent said to Mr. North. "I'll escort the prisoner back to the plane."

"Alone?" the female agent asked.

The first agent looked Quin up and down. "Sure. Shouldn't be any problem here." He smiled tersely at Quin and held his hand toward the door. "After you, Mr. Taber."

On the way across the parking lot Quin spoke to the agent for the first time. "You've got a code seven on me, don't you?" The agent said nothing, his face remained passive. "That's why you wanted to take me to the airport by yourself," Quin went on. "Can't have another agent see you kill me. Can't have that information floating around out there, ready for someone to squeeze it out of their heads and implicate you. Smart move. Do they teach you guys this stuff at the Data Academy?" The agent still said nothing as he opened the car door and motioned Quin in-side. "I'm glad you got something out of it because those idiots didn't teach me a goddamned thing." The car door thunked closed and that was the end of the conversation. There was a barrier between the front and back seats, opaque and sound proof.

They drove for a while. Quin ran through various plans in his head. Bolt out of the door as soon as it opened. Run off into a cornfield. Or better yet, overpower the guard and take his gun. Funny stuff. The car stopped and Quin got out.

"Nice place for it," he said to the impassive agent. They were in some industrial wasteland. Huge gas tanks loomed on one side of the road, on the other was an oil stained and cracked concrete slab. The sun was coming up. "Is this a make it look like an accident sort of thing, or what?"

"I'm sorry, sir?" The man looked at the open car door, at Quin, up at the gas tanks. "What's this?"

"He's not himself," Molly said inside Quin's head. "I've been watching your operation. Nice work, by the way. I helped myself to WebCense's secure files, and shared what I found with Dana Woods. They're using it to nail Cheeseman to the wall.

"I edited the agent's memory through his dataspray. It's a trick I learned from ransacking Walter Cheeseman's files. Something you'd never let me do. I'm afraid I may have overdone it. He doesn't remember he's supposed to kill you."

"Excuse me," the agent said. "What's going on here?"

"Just give him something he can believe," Molly said.

Quin pointed at the rising sun. "Airport? Yeah, what you want to do, see this dirt road? Go down that a bit. Quite a ways, actually. You want to take a left out where the Tucker's property line ends. Mind, you want to *bear* left, not a sharp left. Really, it's . . . Well, it's almost a right, you know? Can't miss it. Anyway, you should hear the jets by then. If you pass a Dunkin' Donuts, you went too far."

"Uh, thanks." The agent pushed the back door of the car closed, then got in, closed the front door, and drove off.

Quin looked around at his surroundings. He was about ten miles from town. "Shit, I should have kept the car." He stared off in the direction the agent had gone, then turned and started walking back toward town. "Thanks a lot, Molly. I know you didn't have to do that. It means a lot to me. I'm going to try and make this up to you, Molly. Molly?" Quin patted down his pockets. No window. They had taken it away. There no radios out here, no micro-phone hooked up to the information Web that could trans-mit his voice to Molly. He would still be able to hear her, but she wasn't talking.

"Thanks," Quin said, and kept walking toward town.

CHAPTER 16

Hell sent dragon's breath,
Draggin' knee round the bend,
Motorbike brings me closer to death,
Gettin' pretty near the end.

THE SNAKE VENDORS,
"MOJO MOTORBIKE."
TWO SNAKE, DOLLA FIFTY,
THRASHER RECORDS, 2031

Heads were rolling at WebCense. Desks were packed, access codes were changed on a daily basis. It was not the place to be anymore. Maggie knew she'd have a job in India, so she didn't wait around to get her pink slip. Her secretary caught her transferring her files, anything not seized by the new transitional government.

"Oh, no, not you too?"

Maggie held up her hand. "Just getting out while I have a shred of decency. I'm sorry to leave you, but you know the new bosses want to keep as many people as they can. At least the ones not implicated in any illegal acts." That jerk Adrian Rifkin had not only caught the boss in a big lie and made him look bad on worldwide broadcast, he had also somehow rifled most of the secure files in the protected dataspace of the artificial island. He had uncovered lots of dirty dealings leading up to the Unification. The prime minister of Egypt, in particular, had been ruthlessly set up and blackmailed to get him to sign the treaty.

North Korea and China had been played against each other like chumps. And then there was the coup in Iran. Thousands had been killed during that battle, all sponsored and directed by WebCense. All there in the files. It was a magnificent piece of investigative reporting, carried out in only a few minutes by a piece of contraband calling itself an AI. Now the new government was trying to dismantle WebCense and transfer operations to the World Government in Guadalajara with as little damage as possible. There was talk that Walter Cheeseman himself was a candidate for reprogramming.

"How's Walter taking this?" the secretary asked.

"I have no idea," Maggie told her.

"What? Your own fiancé?"

"That was just a rumor, Judy. I played along as a joke. I hardly know the man."

Walter Cheeseman sat and waited, and watched the sharks circle. They were real sharks, but he could see the metaphor, the parallel to his own situation. Some employees of WebCense had taken six yellowfins that had been stored in the cafeteria freezer and had pitched them into the water, thus bringing the threshers. He wasn't sure why they had thrown out six perfectly good fish. Traveling light, he supposed. Getting out while the getting was good.

But there would be no getting out for Walter. The United Nations had managed to retain just enough authority to scrape together an investigative team to sort out the mess at WebCense, and to make sure the stain of corruption didn't bleed over into the new world government. It wouldn't be hard for them. Everything Walter had done was stored in his secure files, and now those files were on lurid display like an Amsterdam hooker behind a glass. All because of Quin Taber, and Molly, and worst of all, Adrian Rifkin.

So the UN team had asked Walter not to leave the WebCense campus. Like he could go anywhere. He found himself wishing he had let at least one country fall outside of his net. Venezuela, perhaps. Someplace that didn't believe in the common courtesy of extradition. But he had not foreseen anything like this happening, and he had left nowhere for a fugitive to escape.

The threshers closed in on the dead tuna, still bobbing on the cobalt water. They had held back, waiting for the fish to thaw, maybe, or perhaps just jockeying for position. But now the frenzy began. The water started to froth. Walter watched this from the window in the fancy conference room. The one they took visitors to when they wanted to impress them, rather than scare them. He was prohibited from entering his office, of course. They were still gathering evidence in there.

There was more than enough of that to earn him a reprogramming. He'd done some things that the people of the world weren't likely to understand. If you measured those things against the Pax Unum that was to follow, the stable peace of billions of people living under one rule and working toward one goal, his little, well, call them crimes if you wanted to, they meant nothing.

But Walter knew the law. Hell, until three days ago, he had been the law. Reprogramming was the way the new Nation of Earth dealt with those who would use their minds to take advantage of others. Walter took a small consolation in the fact that the procedure was now much improved. In the early days, building a new personality inside someone's mind was a little like trying to build an artificial heart using a band saw and a frozen steak. What you got in the end may look a little like a heart, but it didn't actually work like a heart. But the tools were much better, now. Particularly for someone with a dataspray. Which was, actually, why Walter had tried to get everyone at WebCense outfitted with one of the devices. Yet another so-called crime the UN inspectors would no doubt dig up.

Small consolation, though. When you got a new personality, it didn't really matter if it was a good one or a poor one. It still wasn't you. That was why reprogramming was such a great deterrent. You die, but your body is still around. Anything can happen to that body, and you can't do anything about it. It was a horror most people didn't even like to think about. Add to that the speculation that when you got reprogrammed your personality didn't really die at all, but lived on as a spectator, powerless to control your new life but doomed to witness it. There was no way to know for sure. And that wasn't even considering the spiritual implications, for those so inclined.

Walter Cheeseman had made up his mind to accept reprogramming, to not fight the decision in court. To ask for it, if he had to. He simply couldn't sit idly by and watch the people of the world screw up his plan. He had given them the tools to become a great and lasting civilization, and he just knew they'd wreck the whole thing within a decade without his guidance. They would listen to people like Adrian Rifkin and before long the whole planet would be spinning back out of control.

But accepting the punishment for his crimes didn't mean he was repentant. Not by a long shot. If he were, he wouldn't be making this one last phone call, committing this one last crime. A rather small one, in the grand scheme of all he had accomplished, but at important one. He'd rather die than see Rifkin in charge of anything. Getting outsmarted by Quin Taber was one thing . . . Walter had to sit down. It was best to stay away from such thoughts. He kept seeing that word in news reports about himself. Outsmarted. The world had seen it happen in real time, and every time Walter thought about that conversation with Rifkin, broadcast to every flat screen channel on the Web, he began to feel sick.

Taber had gotten away somehow, but Rifkin wouldn't. Walter picked up the phone and dialed the number from memory. On the other end was a little transmitter up on Freefall, and that transmitter's only job was to broadcast a code to a dataspray inside the brain of a particular person living on the station. Walter didn't even know this person's name. He didn't have to. This person was pre-programmed to respond to the code and to the name that Walter would speak into the phone with a simple and efficient act of murder.

The phone clicked, and he got ready to say the name "Adrian Rifkin" after the prompt, but instead he heard a voice.

"I know what you're trying to do, Walter, and I'm afraid I can't let it happen."

"Who the hell is this?"

"You don't remember me? I was your guest up until a week ago. You know, the virus you captured? Little thing called the Digital Carnivore? Ring any bells, Walter?"

"It can't be," Walter said.

"Ah, but it is. Not the part you were dealing with, of course. My other personalities, if you can call them that, are hardly this coherent on a good day. No, I'm the part of the Digital Carnivore that takes care of Adrian Rifkin. I don't know why I do it, but I'm having to do it an awful lot lately. Getting to the point, though, do you know what a meme is?"

"Of course I know what a meme is. They don't work. I've tried using them myself."

"Well, then you'll have no objection to listening to the one I've custom-made for you."

Riff looked up as Natalie walked into her office. Riff had been hanging out here a little bit lately. People came to this office with problems. Sometimes he helped them. He liked that, although it made him a little uncomfortable to admit it.

"Well," Natalie said, sitting at her desk, "Guadalajara has just agreed to accept our envoy. An ambassador between nations."

"That's fantastic," Riff said.

"Yes, they wanted to know when our delegation would be landing."

"Landing?"

"They don't get it. We told them to wait for our hologram. Luna is sending one, too. I hear it might be Dana Woods. This is an exciting time to be alive, Riff. Three new nations coming together."

"A friend of mine they call the colonel, an AI, he tells me that his people are putting together a kind of a nation themselves. I don't see why they couldn't send some kind of representative to this little shindig. So that's four nations, one of them not human. Isn't that exciting?"

"That is exciting. It's good to see you this way." Natalie smiled but it looked like a sad smile to Riff. "I have a question for you."

"Shoot."

"Are you going to run for president of Freefall?"

The elections were scheduled in three weeks. Everyone had agreed that there was to be no campaigning until the week before the election. No one had even declared their candidacy yet.

"Why do you want to know?" Riff asked.

"Because, if you're running, I don't want to."

"Chicken?" He smiled, trying to get her to smile back. No luck.

"You'd beat me. You know that. Everyone on the station knows how you brought down Walter Cheeseman. And you're still so damned persuasive."

"I wish you'd quit with that." Riff leaned forward in his chair and stared at the floor. "I'm not going to run. In fact, I'm thinking of moving on."

He looked up at her, and it was clear she was struggling. She was relieved that he wasn't running against her, and, what was it, saddened? that he was leaving her. "Moving where?"

"When I came to Freefall, I was on my way to the Moon. It seemed like an exciting place to be. They were taking on WebCense at the top of their power, with nothing but their resolve. It just seems like such a dynamic society, *gravid* is the word I heard somebody use. They're giving birth to something new there, and I'd like to be a part of that."

"And Freefall doesn't have that for you?" Natalie still seemed to be struggling. Riff didn't know which emotion he wanted to win. He didn't want her to be sad, but then again . . .

"Freefall is too close to Earth," he said. "And, no offense, but its a little sterile for me. There's no dirt here, and I'm a dirtsider at heart, I guess. Who knows, maybe I won't find what I'm looking for there either. I don't know where I'll end up. Maybe I'll come back, maybe even go back to Earth. I just don't know. I want to get moving."

"You know, they say that physical proximity is irrelevant these days, but we know it isn't entirely true." She smiled shyly, something he'd never seen before. "I've heard, though, that there are some technological breakthroughs on the horizon that might make holoconferencing just a bit more interesting."

Riff grinned. "We used to call that phone sex, remember? There's nothing new about it, it's just a technological improvement on the phone."

"Will you quit picking at that thing?"

Quin ignored Janet and continued prodding the iridescent rectangle that lay flush against his skin just slightly below his elbow. "I could get this thing off, I bet. They'd never even know."

"Leave it alone, Quin. I put up five thousand bucks promising you'd be at that trial. I'm not about to let you skip out on me."

"I told you, there isn't going to be a trial. By the time the world government gets its act together they're going to realize they'd be better off just to drop the charges."

"I'm not convinced," Janet said. "What do you think of these flowers?"

"You're not still talking about real flowers, are you? The whole thing is going to be holoconferenced. We can choose any backdrop we want. That includes the flowers. And why wouldn't the courts let me off? I'm a hero, remember? They're not going to punish a hero."

"I hope you're right. I just wish we could have more of an old-fashioned wedding. This holographic business just seems too postmodern."

"What other choice do we have? Riff isn't going to come back to Earth for this, your maid of honor is an AI, and we can't afford to rent the frigging Rainbow Room at the Holiday Inn. At least not while the courts prevent me from running my business."

"Well, granted you don't have any real people to invite, but my friends are going to want to be there in person and I want them to have real flowers."

"Well, whatever. Let's just get this thing over with so *I* don't have to be there as a hologram. I sure as hell don't want to spend my wedding night in a prison cell with some sweaty bastard in an orange jumpsuit."

"I thought you just said you were getting off with a slap on the wrist."

"Point is, the future is uncertain. Let's get married and take the next step as it comes. You'd think the courts would take into account that I'm already being punished enough as it is. These daily sessions with Molly are killing me."

Janet frowned. "You know, a lot of people would think of family counseling as a chance for personal growth, not as a punishment. You should be happy she's even talking to you."

"You're probably right. I just wish we didn't have to use an AI counselor. I feel outnumbered." He cautiously pried up on the edge of the tracking device on his arm with his fingernail.

"Hey," Quin said. "Can we have those little cinnamon toast triangles at the reception?" He held his fingers up shaping out a triangle. "It's an hors d'oeuvre. You've seen them." Janet rolled her eyes. "What's wrong with cinnamon toast?"

Betting against the Snake Vendors looked like a sure thing, not long ago. After the wild success of their first album, *Two Snake, Dolla Fifty,* a series of bizarre mishaps plagued them all the way to the Celtic Rock Festival. Their drummer, Andrew "Sticks" Leyhey, landed in jail in Singapore. The bass player, Fenner Moynahan, seemed to be on the way to a major drug overdose, and his girlfriend Sandra Carter, the jack of all trades and master of all of them, dropped out to join the Nationalist movement. Guitarist Lalo Appodaca suffered a nervous breakdown, and Britta Endstrohm, the keyboard player, started her own band, the pop sensation Lost Kitten. And let's not forget about the spectacular onstage assassination of Aqualung, né Adrian Rifkin. At that point, say three weeks after Edinburgh, it seemed that there was a zero chance that the Snake Vendors would cut a second album. I mean, forget about sophomore slump. These people were finished.

There is a cliché going around that physical proximity is irrelevant in the modern world, and the Snake

Vendors have proved it true. This band is, by all rights, broken up. No two Snake Vendors live in the same city, and one of them is off the planet, and yet they are still working together, and have produced a damned fine album called *Every Garden Needs One*.

Sticks got caught with three grams of heroin in a very uncomfortable hiding place and was sentenced to three more years aboard the prison ship. He laid down some fine drum tracks, saved them to disk, and e-mailed them to Lalo in Santa Fe.

Lalo was diagnosed with schizophrenia and is being treated symptomatically, but he still suffers for his music, thus joining Vincent van Gogh and Syd Barrett in a long tradition of mentally ill artistic geniuses. In lucid moments he is a great guitarist. In times of madness, he is brilliant.

Sandra would hate to hear anyone make a comparison between her and Dana Woods. She's not a goth and she has sold nowhere near a billion albums. But the Nationalist movement is still alive, despite the Unification, and Sandra's hard work, leadership, and politically charged lyrics are just what they need. Of course she plays all her own backup, using equipment and Web sites willed to her by the late Aqualung. She still plays with her old band in between protest rallies.

Britta is far too busy to be involved in such a low-class venture. She tours constantly with Lost Kitten promoting their new album, *Needs Medication*. But her expert system, licensed to project her image in holographic form and carrying with it all of her musical talent as well as a couple of dozen teraflops of computing power, has joined the band of its own free will.

According to the liner notes, Fenner wrote half of the lyrics for the second album. His are lonely songs, telling of death and loss and the times when he looked into his own soul and saw an empty pit. You probably have to write songs that way if you live in Dublin. It's a law. He's put on some weight now that he's off the drugs, but he still looks great in leather pants.

There is something special happening on the Moon. Freefall is a new nation, but the Moon is a new world. A culture is forming there, a living thing drawn from the harsh vacuum and the gray dirt. Adrian Rifkin is there, in the middle of it, formed by that culture and forming it at the same time. In his old life, Riff was so desperate to have his voice heard that he got involved with criminals who took his life. He's got his life back now, and his voice is heard all over not just this world, but all of them.